FOLLY AT THE FAIR

An Annie Oakley Mystery

KARI BOVEE

BOSQUE
PUBLISHING

A NOTE FROM THE AUTHOR

Like most of us, I'd heard the name Annie Oakley before, but she didn't interest me until several years ago when my father encouraged me to watch a PBS American Experience biographical special featuring Annie Oakley and her rise to fame.

I watched the show and became enchanted with this pint-sized wonder woman who was incredibly empowered at a time in history when most women weren't allowed to be empowered. She had talent, spunk, determination, modesty, and the courage to be herself—an expert markswoman and sharpshooter. She bested most men in the sport, including her husband, Frank Butler, and her boss, Buffalo Bill Cody—two of her most ardent supporters.

As a fan of historical fiction and historical mysteries, I thought it would be entertaining to put this feisty young woman in the role of an amateur detective. Based on everything I'd read about her, she certainly had the smarts, the compassion, and the desire to see justice served and order reign in the world. I've tried to maintain historical accuracy for the most part, but in this series, I have played with some facts: I've altered time-lines, added fictional characters, embellished historical characters, and put Annie into situations she never faced in real life—and I've had so much fun doing it.

The prequel novella, *Shoot like a Girl,* is the story of Annie before she joins the Wild West Show. Although she doesn't play the role of amateur detective in this book, we learn what drives her to seek order and justice for herself and others through her relationship with Buck, a horse who becomes her lifeline during a difficult period in her life. From this experience, Annie becomes impassioned to seek justice for those who cannot seek it for themselves, and we see her spring into action in *Girl with a Gun.* This sets her on a course to make order out of chaos, and try to set things right in a world that can go oh so wrong.

In *Peccadillo at the Palace,* we see Annie and the Wild West Show venture across the pond to England to perform for Queen Victoria's Golden Jubilee. It was such a pleasure to delve into the research for this novel. A long time Anglophile and also a lover of American History, I had always wanted to combine both my interests into one novel, and Violá! this was the perfect opportunity.

Folly at the Fair is a brand-new adventure for Annie when the Wild West Show takes part in the Columbian World's Exhibition in Chicago in 1893. It was exhilarating to immerse myself in what it might have been like to witness the spectacle of the famed White City while researching this novel.

I have delighted in imagining what was in the heart, mind, and soul of this young woman who faced many obstacles in her life, only to become one of the most famous women of all time. It's been gratifying to put her in difficult situations and see her come out of a shroud of mystery, shooting her way to the truth. I hope you, too, enjoy these and future adventures I've created for this amazing woman of history—Little Miss Sure Shot, Annie Oakley.

PROLOGUE

MAY 27, 1893
Chicago, Illinois

He wondered how she would react when she realized he intended to kill her. Would she scream? Cry? Curse him? Would she beg for her life? It was all too delicious to contemplate.

She isn't particularly beautiful, he thought, as she stared up at him with the adoring look he'd often seen in women's eyes when they regarded him. Her face was round, plump at the cheeks, which were tinted pink with infatuation. Her yellow-brown eyes were rimmed with long, straight lashes and were turned down at the corners. Her plump lips concealed a slight overbite, the edges of the teeth protruding unevenly. Better if she kept her mouth closed. Her face was average, but it was the curve of her breasts and rounded hips that had kept him intrigued these past few months. And, of course, her adoration of him.

But he wasn't very interested in her looks, or her mind, or anything of her person in general. She would serve as a means to an end.

"So you will meet her?" she asked, her voice breathy. "My

aunt?"

He ran the back of his hand down her throat. "Of course, my dear Mary."

"I've written to her and told her I would be home for a visit in a few weeks. She's so ill, I haven't told her you proposed yet. I thought we could surprise her. It might restore her to health." She leaned into him, wrapping her arms around his neck.

They stood, pressed together in his office, the day's work done. From the small window above the bookshelves, he could see the veil of dusk turn the sky a violent shade of orange. It would be dark soon. His heartbeat quickened. He always did his best work in the quiet and blackness of night.

"Do you think she will approve?" he asked, pulling her closer, his hands resting on her hips.

"How could she not? You've been so kind to me."

Yes, indeed, he had. She'd come to his place of business looking for work. Another girl from another faraway town hoping to meet the man of her dreams as droves of people came to the Columbian World's Exhibition. He hadn't hesitated to hire her. He had known that as a former clerk at her family's general store she'd make an excellent secretary. She'd been a quick study. Her skills as a typist grew with each day, and she was adept at notetaking and bookkeeping. She'd been a first-rate hire. And he had been able to tell from the way she had looked at him that first day that she could be his with very little effort.

He kissed her and crushed her body to his chest. "If only we could marry sooner," he said. "I'm not sure I can control myself much longer."

"You devil," she said, looking up at him, her eyes sparkling with mischief.

"Marry me tomorrow."

"Tomorrow? But my aunt. She should at least meet you first." She pulled back, rested her hands on his chest. "I'd hoped to marry when we visited. It would make her so glad to see me in my mother's wedding dress."

"If she doesn't approve of me, would it change your mind?" he asked, his eyes imploring her with well-rehearsed injury.

"Of course not. I had just hoped for a church wedding with my aunt in attendance. It would have meant so much to my parents to see me wed to such a fine gentleman. I wish they could have met you." Her brows rose, making her look younger and even more innocent than her twenty years portrayed.

"They wouldn't find it disagreeable that I am fifteen years your senior?"

She smiled up at him. "Papa was twenty years older than Mama."

"I see."

It hadn't taken her long to confide in him that she had been orphaned and raised by her aunt. Or that she'd just inherited her deceased parents' thriving store in Ames, Iowa, on her twentieth birthday. She had told him she'd come to Chicago determined to be an independent woman. She had no interest in the store, aside from the sizable financial benefit she would receive once she sold it, but she was in no hurry. He was certain that marrying a successful man like himself was the security she truly craved. The aged aunt would be no problem for him. The woman practically lay on her death bed. The aunt had no authority over the girl now, other than her apparent love for her. But love only accounted for so much.

He really wasn't in a hurry to marry her, but he wanted to devour her and he wouldn't be put off anymore. He had plans—and other women waiting for him. So many more women.

He gave her an indulgent smile. "You know I don't put much stock in church . . . or in God."

"Yes, I know. " She laid her head on his chest.

This wasn't going as he had planned. He had to change his strategy.

"I'm afraid I won't be able to accompany you home, my dear. If it is a church wedding you want, and in your hometown, we will have to wait until the Exhibition ends. I cannot be away from work with the city so full and business booming. It would be negligent and irresponsible."

"Oh." She pulled away again, panic in her eyes. "The Exhibition doesn't end for five more months. I don't know if she will live that long."

"I'm sorry, darling," he said.

She turned her back to him, and he could tell by the shaking of her shoulders that she had started to cry, bitterly disappointed.

"Don't cry, my love. I hate to see you so distressed." He gently set his hands on her shoulders and turned her so she was facing him again. He cupped her face and caressed her cheek bones with his thumbs. "Dear Mary . . . I cannot deny you anything. Marry me tomorrow, and we will go to Ames in the next week or so. I can only spare a couple of days. We will go and tell your aunt that you are wed. Would that please you? For your aunt to see that you've married? We would have to return immediately, you do understand, don't you?"

She nodded and closed her eyes, droplets seeping from beneath her dark lashes. He kissed her forehead, and his lips trailed to her eyes, kissing the sadness away. She raised her chin, and he opened his mouth over hers, tasting the salt from her tears as they seeped down her face.

"Tomorrow, you will be my wife," he whispered. "We are as good as married, my love."

She melted in his arms at his words. It had been so easy. She smiled beneath his lips, and he knew he had her. He lifted her into his arms and carried her out of his office and up the flight of stairs to the bedroom.

Sometime later, finally satiated, he slid out of bed as quietly as he could so as not to wake her. He dressed carefully, mechanically, all the while watching her sleep. A shaft of moonlight fell across her features, her skin luminous in the filtered light. Her ample bosom gently rose and fell with the deep breath of slumber.

He picked up a pillow and pressed it to her face. She awoke and struggled against him. He pressed harder. Her hands gripped his, her fingers like claws tearing at his flesh. Her legs kicked, flinging the covers off her plump, naked body. She let go of his hands and her arms flailed about wildly as she tried to reach for his face. But she was weakening. It wouldn't be long now. Her movements slowed, and her arms flapped flaccidly against his shoulders until they dropped to the bed. Her body convulsed in spasms, and then she was still. The deed was done.

Gently, he placed the pillow next to her and studied her face. Her mouth was frozen in a rictus of terror, her lips turning a faint hue of blue. The whites of her doe-like hazel eyes were red rimmed, and spidery veins bled into them, giving her the appearance of some kind of monster. He left them open.

He wrapped her in the bedsheet and lifted her from the bed, then laid her on the floor. He grabbed both feet and pulled her through the doorway and down the long hallway, the sheet trailing behind her head like a wilted bridal veil.

He dropped her feet unceremoniously when he came to the door at the end of the hall. Taking a keyring from his pocket, he fished through the keys until he found the right one. With some effort, he pulled open the door and, picking up her feet once again, dragged her inside the small six-by-eight-foot room. Once he got her settled with the sheet neatly wrapped around her body, he exited the room, locked the door, and walked back to his office, whistling a tune he'd heard earlier that day. What was the name of the song?

Ah, yes. It was called "Oh, Promise Me." It was a popular wedding song, in fact . . .

He tossed the keys on his desk and sat down, a satisfied sigh escaping his lips. Tomorrow, he would catch a train to Ames and visit Mary's poor, dying aunt, playing the grieving husband to bear the sad news.

And to take possession of the general store for imminent sale.

CHAPTER 1

BUFFALO BILL AND HIS CONGRESS OF ROUGH RIDERS
SHAKE UP COLUMBIAN WORLD'S FAIR!
– *The Chicago Herald,* Monday, June 5, 1893

ANNIE AND HER PRIZED HORSE, BUCK, CANTERED INTO THE stadium to roaring applause and the crowd shouting, "Annie! Annie! Annie!"

The masses looked like a giant wall of color circling the oval arena. Swags, banners, and flower boxes decorated the VIP boxes in the front while crowds above squeezed in upon bench seats. Men, women, and children were all dressed in their finery, the women in silk dresses and hats trimmed with flowers and jewel-toned ribbons, the men in gabardine suits with satin waist-coats, and slouch hats. They all waved brightly colored pennants in the air with the word *Oakley* or *Cody* sewn onto them. Some held up banners that read, LITTLE MISS SURE SHOT, BUCK THE WONDER HORSE OF THE WEST, and SURE SHOT ANNIE.

Annie put on her best show smile while she and Buck sped around the arena for their two customary welcoming laps. At the end of the second lap, she sat deep in her saddle, cueing Buck to a sliding stop. She tapped his shoulders with her toes, and he rose up on his hind legs, pawing at the air with his front hooves as Annie rode the upward momentum. A thrill ran through her at their synchronicity and their mental and emotional connection, as it always did in this part of the act. When Buck touched down, she squeezed with her left leg and turned her shoulders, and Buck pivoted onto the course.

Annie dropped the reins on Buck's neck, pulled her 1887 Winchester lever-action shotgun out of the scabbard on her saddle, and weaved through the course, shattering colored-glass bulbs off their tripods. Using her seat again, she brought Buck to a halt. She stroked his neck and let him rest a moment while she waited for the live pigeons to be released. Ten of the birds took wing, soaring into the sky. With expert precision and skill, Annie hit all of them in succession within fifteen seconds and then slid her shotgun back in its scabbard. She urged Buck to a canter again and then to an all-out run as she laid the reins down on his neck, pulled her pistols from the holster around her waist, and raced down the center of the arena, shooting the remaining glass bulbs into a rainbow of crystal chards. After she holstered her pistols again, she raced around the arena, waving to the crowd who had now risen to their feet, their shouts a cacophony of music to her ears. She brought Buck to another sliding stop right in front of Mr. Post, Buck's caretaker, who had ambled out to retrieve him.

Pulling her shotgun out of the scabbard again, she dismounted, reloaded her weapon, and then ran to her mark, twirling and waving to the crowd. She stopped and settled while one of the crew threw translucent blue, green, and yellow glass balls thirty feet into the air. She proceeded to shatter them all within seconds.

Frank, her husband, manager, and one-time sharp-shooting sensation, came trotting into the arena on a golden palomino quarter horse. Jep, the couple's yellow Labrador retriever, followed behind. Annie mustered a smile, still hurt and annoyed from an argument she and Frank had gotten into earlier. She was exhausted from the grueling performance schedule, and he kept adding speaking engagements, which she struggled with due to her shyness. And yes, at her core, she was shy and introverted; she just had mastered the art of show business.

Frank pulled off his hat and waved it to the crowd, who thundered their applause. The palomino came to a stop, and Frank threw his leg over the horn of the saddle and jumped to the ground where he joined Annie for a flourishing bow to the crowd. He, on the other hand, was a master entertainer and had always been able to enchant both men and women, personally and also onstage—or rather, in the arena.

After the applause died down, Frank jogged away from her, Jep on his heels. He grabbed a stool standing next to the Deadwood Stagecoach, and together, he and Jep walked to the north end of the arena, opposite the large gates. Frank set the stool against the wall, and when he whistled, the dog jumped up and sat on top of the stool. Frank gave Jep a hearty tousle on the head and then held out a treat. The dog sat stock-still, focused on Frank, then gobbled down the treat. To maintain the dog's focus, Frank took another treat from his pocket. From his other pocket, he pulled an apple and set it atop the dog's head.

Because Annie needed to shoot with absolute accuracy for this little feat, she used her rifle. Using shotgun shells for the mounted portion of her act provided a near guarantee that she could hit her mark, and it was less dangerous for the crowd as the shot spread, as no single bullet could accidentally and fatally harm someone. For further safety, they positioned the dog against the wall at the far end of the stadium where no spectators were allowed to sit. One of the crew raced out to bring Annie her rifle.

Holding the treat out in front of him to keep the dog's eyes trained on him, Frank slowly stepped away. Annie raised her rifle, found the sight, aimed just a hair above the apple, and shot.

The apple exploded into a pulpy mess, and the crowd roared with audible relief and thunderous applause. Jep jumped down from the stool, ran to Frank to get his treat, and then ran to Annie, lifting himself on his hind legs to put his paws on her shoulders and lick her face with great enthusiasm. Annie chuckled.

One of the crew whistled, and Jep ran out of the arena. Frank pulled a cigar from his pocket and made a big show about lighting it and placing it into his mouth. He tipped his hat to Annie and strode fifty paces away from her. The crowd loudly counted each one of his steps until he reached the wall. Taking off his hat, he turned to give Annie his profile. She raised her rifle, aimed, and the crowd hushed again. After what seemed like an interminable ten seconds, she fired, blowing the cigar to smithereens and out of Frank's mouth.

Triumphant, Frank pumped his fists in the air, ran toward Annie, threw his arms around her, and lifted her off her feet. He twirled her in a circle—another part of the act that usually thrilled her, but today she stiffened at his embrace. Happily oblivious to the tension between the two, the crowd stomped their feet on the bleachers, their joyous shouts filling the air.

Annie and Frank took three dramatic bows, and their horses were brought in to them. Annie handed her weapon to Mr. Post and mounted up. Once Frank was in his saddle, too, they cantered their horses around the arena, the horses moving in perfect rhythm and unison while Frank and Annie held hands. They exited the stadium to a standing ovation.

"What a crowd!" Frank said as they brought their horses to a stop. "You performed flawlessly, my dear. As usual." He pulled his horse closer to her and bent over to give her a kiss. Annie gave him a tight-lipped smile, as well as her cheek.

"What's this, Annie?" Frank asked, concern in his voice. Or was it that she'd hurt his feelings? "Are you still sore at me for arranging your upcoming appearance at the Woman's Building?"

Annie finally met his gaze. "It's not just that one appearance.

There are too many, Frank. You know I'm uncomfortable speaking in front of people. I don't mind shooting or performing. In fact, I love it. I—"

"Do you, though?" Frank asked pointedly. "You don't seem to enjoy it lately. I'm concerned about you, darling."

She hesitated. "I do, really. I'm just exhausted, Frank. Something needs to give. I don't know if I can continue to perform well this way—and we have several months left here in Chicago. I just want to go home." She hated hearing herself say the words. She hated that she felt this way. She'd always taken pride in her work, given her all whether she wanted to or not, whether she enjoyed it or not. She had been steadfast in her responsibility to the show and to all the people who depended on her, like her family, Buffalo Bill—whom they called "the Colonel"—Frank, and her fans.

"I'm sorry, darling. But we signed a contract to perform for the duration of the fair. I know you are feeling stretched, but you always perform to perfection. The crowds adore you. I apologize for upsetting you," he said, laying his hand on her shoulder. He gave it a reassuring squeeze.

Relieved at his apology, Annie smiled. "I know you are getting pressure from the Colonel and Mr. Salisbury about my appearances." Maybe this was the cause of his moodiness over the past several months? She knew the Colonel and the show's manager, Nate Salisbury, could be rather unrelenting. "Perhaps we can make some kind of compromise? I will speak with the Colonel. I can usually get through to him, make him understand."

"No," Frank said. "I'm your manager. It's my job to negotiate on your behalf."

Annie studied his face. His words told her he had heard her and acquiesced, but the slouch of his shoulders and the way he wouldn't meet her gaze discomfited her. She wished she knew what was bothering him. She'd asked on many occasions, but he would simply smile or pat her hand and say he was fine. She supposed that he, too, was feeling the pressure from their lives existing in a constant state of movement and impermanence. Aside from having very little respite from the last European tour, the months prior to their arrival in Chicago had been full of planning, packing, organizing, arranging appearances, and choosing costumes. Then, after they had arrived, they had helped set up the grounds by erecting tents, tepees, barns, pens, and so forth. It didn't compare to the difficulty they'd had getting prepared to voyage across the Atlantic—twice now to tour Europe—but this was the largest and one of the most important shows they had to prepare for in the United States.

Yes, Frank was probably weary, as well. Tired from the countless hours he spent managing her show business life, their finances, and the schedule, not to mention coaching her. She didn't do half as much as he did, and she seemed to be exhausted all the time. Her heart wrenched at the slowly eroding gulf between them. They had always been so close—better together than apart, best friends, two halves of one whole.

"Can we make amends, Frank? Please. I can't stand this. I'm sorry if I upset you, too."

Frank's face softened. "Say no more, dear. I will work something out to schedule fewer public speaking appearances and more shooting exhibitions for you."

"Thank you, darling." She offered a loving smile.

Jep the dog ran toward them and took a flying leap, landing in front of Frank's saddle. He laughed, hugging the dog to his chest. Annie's heart warmed to hear Frank's hearty chuckle again.

"Nice work, you two." The Colonel approached them riding his favorite mount, Duke, a liver chestnut with two white hind socks. "You handled the course well, Annie." He took off his hat, revealing a sweaty band of hair pressed to his head.

A flash of blue caught Annie's eye, and she turned her head to see a woman, attired in a fine blue dress and carrying a matching parasol, staring at her. The woman quickly turned away and walked off. Something about her seemed familiar, but Annie couldn't reconcile it. She saw so many people on any given day, this woman could have reminded her of anyone. She did find it unusual that the woman did not stay to talk. Most fans clamored to speak with Annie after a performance.

Other spectators began to mill about them, congratulating them on a fine show. Frank dismounted and joined the Colonel to converse and answer questions while Annie stayed atop Buck and did the same. When Frank reached up to lay a hand on Buck's neck, Annie noticed it was bleeding.

"Frank," she whispered. He turned to look at her, and she pointed to his hand.

He quickly lowered it. "I must have cut it on something."

"You should probably see Dr. Gordon. We heard he's around here somewhere," Annie said. Dr. Gordon was a local physician the Colonel had contracted to tend to his players on occasions such as this. He worked from his infirmary in Englewood but made daily visits to the grounds.

"Right, you are," Frank said. "I'll see you back at our tent."

"Miss Oakley, pose for a picture?" A photographer approached Buck from the side, carrying his tripod and a large leather case. Annie waved Frank on and waited patiently for the photographer to set up his camera.

She hoped the fatigue she felt down to her bones wouldn't show up in the photograph.

❧

An hour later, she entered their living-quarters tent, only to find that Frank wasn't there. Instead, a little girl who looked to be six or seven years old, with large, luminescent, caramel-colored eyes and equally glowing russet hair, sat primly at Annie's vanity stool, her hands in her lap. Her dress was finely made but was too small. Her hair was a mass of curls and hung to her shoulders, tied away from her face with a silk ribbon.

"Hello?" Annie said. "Are you lost?"

The girl shook her head.

"Are you sure?"

"Annnnieeee! Yoo-hoo!" a voice Annie recognized rang out.

Annie stepped outside the tent to see her dear friend Emma, dressed to the nines, as usual, in a burgundy dress with ivory-and-pink trim. An immense hat of the same colors graced her golden head.

"Emma!" The two women embraced, and Annie was immediately suffused with the invisible cloud of Emma's favorite lavender perfume. "I've missed you so much."

"And I you, dear friend. Let me look at you." Emma released Annie's shoulders and took hold of her hands, stepping back to assess her. "Oh, just look at you! Your costume! It's absolutely elegant. Just finished with a performance?"

"Yes." Annie squeezed her hands, delighted to be reunited with her friend.

"You look so mature! A woman of the world at twenty-four, well, I never!" A look of concern swept over Emma's face. "Though, I must say, you do look a bit thin, darling."

Annie swiped a hand in the air, laughing at Emma's assessment of her. "It's nothing." Even though Emma got her hands dirty investigating some of Chicago's grittiest crimes as a reporter for *The Chicago Herald*, she never could shake her blue-blooded background, complete with unfettered opinions and fashion acumen.

"The Colonel running you ragged, is he?" Emma raised an eyebrow.

"No more than usual," Annie said, keeping her voice cheerful.

"I've been told by my colleagues at the *Herald* that the show is raking in money. I bet the Expo commission wished they had agreed to the Colonel's terms to set up his show at Jackson Park instead of being so greedy. Touché!"

Annie laughed again, and then her eyes drifted to the little girl, who appeared at the opening of the tent and looked at her expectantly.

"Who is this?" Emma asked, the dimples in her creamy cheeks deepening.

"I don't know," Annie said. "I came back to my tent to find her sitting at my vanity."

"Maybe a young fan?"

Annie beckoned for the girl to come stand near her. When she did, Annie bent at the waist to meet the girl at eye level. "What is your name?"

"Liza." She pulled a folded piece of paper out of her pocket and handed it to Annie. "This is for you."

Annie took the paper and examined the seal. She broke it, unfolded the note, and read. Her stomach plummeted. "Oh, my goodness."

"What is it?" asked Emma.

"It is a letter from my old friend Alison from the infirmary, the poorhouse where I spent some time before I was farmed out to the McCrimmons. I never thought I would hear from her again . . ." Annie looked up from the paper and gazed past Emma to that time in her childhood. A tumult of memories arose, none of them pleasant. In her youth, she had temporarily resided at the Darke County Infirmary in her home state of Ohio, to learn to keep house and sew, in the hopes she could help make money for her impoverished family. With her new skills, she'd been sent to work for the McCrimmons, a couple in a nearby county, at fifty cents a week. Little did her mother, or Mrs. Edington of the infirmary, know that McCrimmon and his wife had not only withheld Annie's wages but they had neglected and abused her repeatedly.

Annie snapped back to the present and met Emma's gaze. "I don't think I ever knew Alison's last name, but she was newly orphaned and we became fast friends."

"But what does the letter say, dear?" Emma asked, never one

to be kept waiting for information of any kind—and never one to mind her own business.

"She says Liza is her daughter and has asked me to care for her." The sinking feeling in Annie's stomach grew heavier while, at the same time, the swimming in her head made her feel faint. Her heart went out to this beautiful child who had obviously been abandoned by her mother, who might well be in trouble, but this was absolutely the last thing Annie needed.

Emma took the note from Annie. "Care for her? For how long? An hour? A day?"

"Forever," Liza said in a small voice, turning her face up to Emma.

"Oh," Annie gasped, her heart wrenching. Alison had left this child in Annie's care? It didn't make any sense. The poor thing, left in the hands of strangers. Much like Annie and Alison had been when they were young.

Annie hadn't seen Alison since before she went to the McCrimmons. Alison had promised to write when Annie went away, but no letters had come. Annie later found out that the McCrimmons had burned any letters Annie received, isolating her from any outside communication. She had been twelve years old at the time. It had been well over a decade since she'd last seen Alison. And now this? Annie was dumbstruck.

"Did your mother bring you here, to Miss Oakley's tent?" Emma asked.

Liza shook her head. "She brought me to the gate, under the big sign."

"She just left you there." The words came out of Annie's mouth as an indignant statement, not a question born of curiosity. She and Alison had only been children when they'd known each other, but it seemed very uncharacteristic of Alison's sweet nature to drop her child off in a strange place full of strange people. What kind of mother would *abandon* her own daughter?

Pain twisted Annie's heart. She herself would never have the opportunity to have her own child. She'd been so devastated when she'd miscarried while on their first tour in England. She'd railed against the reality that she was pregnant at first, terrified of losing her freedom—and possibly her job—but she had grown used to the idea of having a baby and even looked forward to raising Frank's child. And then she had miscarried. Further pain burrowed into her heart when she had learned she would never bear children due to a weak cervix. It took her a long time to get over the guilt of not wanting such a precious gift from God. When she lost the baby, it felt like a punishment. But she knew in her heart God was not vengeful, no matter what the Bible said. God was love. And so was an innocent child.

Annie softened her voice. "How did you get to my tent?"

"Mama told me to ask people. A brown lady with a bright skirt and blanket on her shoulders told me."

Laughter diverted Annie's attention. She turned to see Frank walking toward them with a beautiful woman dressed in the type of clothing the Russian Cossack performers wore—the long, dark coat dress, belted at the waist, but unlike the males of the troupe, the woman's skirt twinkled with beads. Dark hair tumbled over her shoulder in a loose braid. A young boy walked at her side, holding on to her skirt. Annie had heard a woman would be joining the Cossacks troupe, but she never expected one so beautiful, or that she would have a child with her. Frank, handsome as ever in his leather vest and rakish Stetson hat, seemed completely absorbed with the woman. And she gazed at Frank with an intensity that made Annie's spine stiffen and her stomach flip with a pang of jealousy.

"Hello, dear," Frank said casually. His hand was wrapped in white gauze.

"Hello. How is your hand? Did you see Dr. Gordon?" She gave the woman a sideways glance.

"No. But this fine lady helped me clean it and wrap it. It's just a scratch." His face glowed as he smiled at the woman. Annie's stomach curdled.

"Oh, I see. And you are?" She hoped she sounded polite.

"This is Frida Mgloblishvili and her son, Ivan." Frank gestured toward the two of them. "Remember the Colonel asked me to collect them at the train station yesterday?"

Annie recalled he had mentioned something about going to the train station, but she had been preoccupied with writing a speech for one of her appearances and had forgotten.

Frank continued. "They've just arrived in the United States from the country of Georgia. She's one of the Cossack trick riders. I happened to be strolling by the Colonel's tent as he was going to give her the two-cent tour, but he was called away on other business so I offered to do it. Mrs. Mgloblishvili, this is my wife, Annie Oakley, and her friend Emma Wilson, a journalist who works here in Chicago and often travels with the show."

The woman approached Annie and took her hand. Her palm was warm but as rough as Annie's own, from working with horses and living the life of an outdoor traveling performer. She regarded Annie with a soft, brown gaze and a disarming smile, her velvety-looking olive skin stretching taut over her finely defined cheekbones.

"Your husband has told me many wonderful things about you, and of your beautiful horse, Buck. I, too, have a horse that is special to me. He is called Shiva. We have much in common, Miss Oakley." The woman spoke with a heavy accent, her words coming out slow and deliberate.

"How lovely. Thank you. Welcome to America." Annie's gaze landed on the little boy, who peeked at her from behind his mother's skirt.

The woman shook Emma's hand.

"Mgloblish— Mgloblishvili," Emma said, struggling with the word. "That's a mouthful."

"You pronounced it well." Frida acknowledged the statement with a nod and a sweep of her long, dark lashes. She then turned to Frank. "Thank you for showing me around. I have enjoyed your company."

Frank tipped his hat. "Thank you for doctoring my hand. Shall I escort you back to your comrades?"

"It is not necessary. I will find my way. Ivan and I will finish touring the camp on our own." She touched Frank's sleeve, her hand lingering almost like a caress. Annie's teeth tugged at her lower lip, surprised at the woman's forwardness.

As she and the boy walked away, Frank's eyes trailed her. Annie had never seen Frank look at a woman that way before. Aside from herself, that was. Of course, women were attracted to him, and many often openly flirted with him, but this Frida had a calmness and reserve that oozed a certain kind of sensuality that warned of a threat.

Annie tried to shake off the feeling, rationalizing that it was their earlier argument—and others that had plagued them of late —that made the feeling of impending danger arise. She usually never even paid attention to other women flirting with Frank. When he was the Colonel's main headliner, before he had to stop shooting, women following Frank around had been a matter of course.

And Annie certainly had her share of men flocking to get a word with her, or sending love letters, some with marriage proposals. And then there was the whole business of Peter Farnham, a fan who turned up everywhere—even on their tours in Europe—which made Frank on edge. But this kind of adulation came with being in the limelight. In the public's eyes, she belonged to them, like a commodity, an invention of their imagination, an artifact. It was the most poignant downside of fame.

"Miss Wilson," Frank greeted Emma. "It's been awhile."

"Almost two years," she said, planting air kisses on each side of Frank's face. "How are you?"

"You know. Same old, same old. Following this beauty around," he said, wrapping his arm around Annie's shoulders. "I suppose now that you are here, my wife will get into no end of trouble."

"Frank, ever the protective husband," Emma said with a tinkling laugh.

Frank released Annie's shoulders and took her hand, squeezing it. "Oh, I try. But you know Annie. Woman has a strong will and her own opinions. I'm sure it won't be long before you two find some kind of project to sink your teeth into. Just don't keep her from her purpose, Miss Wilson. We need her fit for her performances."

Annie forced a smile. Frank had been her manager for seven years and her husband for nine. While she loved the time their jobs allowed them to be together, the role of husband and the job of manager weaved in and out of each other, often creating a tangle. At times, Annie felt as if they were merely business partners. Frank had even taken to sometimes sleeping in their other tent if he had been out late or if Annie had been exhausted from performing. It never used to be that way. They had always preferred each other's company to that of anyone else's or to being alone.

"Who's this little mite?" Frank asked, pointing to Liza. "Friend of yours, Miss Wilson?"

"No, I've just met her." Emma chucked the girl under the chin with lace-gloved fingers. She glanced at Annie and then took Liza by the hand. "How would you like some ice cream?"

Liza grinned, nodding vigorously.

"Very well. I will take you to get a treat and then return you directly to Miss Oakley. Would that be all right?"

Liza nodded again, and Emma led her away.

"Who is that, Annie? What's going on?" Frank's voice raised in suspicion.

Annie took his hand and led him to the tent. "Frank, we need to talk."

CHAPTER 2

WILD WEST DARLING ANNIE OAKLEY STUNS CROWD
WITH EXPERT MARKSMANSHIP!
—Chicago Star Free Press, Monday, June 5, 1893

EMMA AND LIZA LEFT THE WILD WEST encampment at the 62nd Street gate to hail a coach. They didn't have to wait long. As they exited the gates, two dapple grays pulling a shiny black coach rounded the corner. When Emma raised her hand, the driver pulled the horses to a halt, hopped down from his perch, tipped his hat to Emma, and then helped them into the cab.

"Please take us to the French bakery near the South Pond," Emma said as he closed the coach door.

"I thought we were getting ice cream," Liza said.

"Oh, but we are, dear. They serve *the best* ice cream there."

Liza didn't respond but looked out the coach window. *Poor child,* Emma thought. To be abandoned by one's own mother. But then again, hadn't Emma herself been abandoned by her mother in a manner of speaking?

She hadn't spoken to her mother in years. But it hadn't always been that way. As an only child, Emma had been the jewel in her mother's crown and the apple of her father's eye. Privileged with inherited wealth from the early mining industry, Emma's father, Harold Wilson, had moved from the West and settled in New York's high society where he met Josephine Hodges, a second-generation American, upper-crust beauty whose family originally hailed from England. When Emma was just a baby, her parents had purchased a second home in Chicago, and the family split their time between the two cities.

Emma had an idyllic childhood until Emma's teens, when her mother set out to find wealthy eligible bachelors for her beautiful daughter. Strong-minded and strong-willed, Emma wanted to marry someone who shared her interests, someone she loved. She had retaliated by becoming engaged to a "lowly" police officer in Chicago named Carlton Chisolm. A scandal had ensued, and Emma had been cut off from the family fortune. Thus, her foray into journalism. In time, her father had relented and brought her back into the fold—at least financially. He provided Emma with a hefty allowance in the hopes she would leave her "uncouth" and "unladylike" profession, but she found she rather enjoyed her life as a journalist—and her generous allowance.

She wondered what sort of financial circumstances Liza had come from. She studied the little girl sitting across from her. The dress she wore had been finely made, if a bit too snug in the bodice and a tad short at the hem and the sleeves. Her straw boater sat primly on her head and looked to fit well, but the blue ribbon decorating the crown had faded.

"Do you and your mother live here in Chicago, or did you come for the Exhibition?" Emma asked, pulling the girl's attention away from the window.

She looked up at Emma with sad eyes. "We took the train."

"The train! That sounds exciting! Where did you take the train from?"

Liza shrugged her shoulders and then looked out the window again. The coach came to a stop, and the driver came around to the door to help them out. Emma handed him some coins, then took Liza's hand to cross the street to go to the bakery, but her attention was diverted by a small group of people, some of them wearing the uniform of the Exhibition Guard, the security force for Jackson Park that had been hired for the fair. The crowd gathered near the windmill at the south end of the South Pond. It appeared as if some sort of crime had been committed. Never one to miss out on an opportunity for a story, Emma simply *had* to know what was going on.

"Liza, do you mind if we go see what those people are doing over there before we get your ice cream?"

Liza pulled her finger out of her nose and shook her head.

As they approached the small group, a little towheaded boy about Liza's age kicked a leather ball toward her. It landed right in front of them.

"Well, it looks like someone wants to play ball with you," Emma said to Liza. "Hello!" she greeted the little boy. "What's your name?"

"Joshua," he said, not looking at her. His eyes were on Liza. "Want to kick the ball with me?"

"Josh!" an equally towheaded man from the crowd called out. "Don't bother the ladies."

"Not to worry, he is not bothering us!" Emma replied and then leaned down to talk to Liza. "Do you want to kick the ball with Joshua for a few minutes?"

Liza nodded and then kicked the ball to the boy.

"I'll be right over here," Emma said. She watched them play for a few minutes to make sure all was going well before she approached one of the men in uniform. He couldn't have been older than twenty. He had a small face and slender shoulders, making his Adam's apple appear much too large for his neck. Two other older guards were questioning some of the people gathered in small groups.

She reached into her handbag and pulled out a card. "Hello. I'm Emma Wilson, reporter for the *Herald*. What's happened here?"

The young guard looked at her card and then met her eyes. He smiled as if pleased with her looks. Most men were. "A body was found by one of the fairgoers—buried in a shallow grave." He pointed to a mound of earth. "The ambulance just hauled it off to the morgue."

"My goodness," Emma said. "How horrible! Was it a man? A—"

"Woman," the young man offered. "Second one since the Exhibition opened."

"The second dead body?" How had she not heard about this? "And the police? Have they been out to investigate?"

"We've alerted them. We've been instructed to get the bodies to the morgue. But I don't expect any investigating's been done. The police can hardly keep up with all the crime in the city, let alone the fair and Jackson Park. We in the Exhibition Guard handle the petty crimes, but not murder."

"I see." She had heard that the Chicago police force was already understaffed, and now with the addition of tens of thousands of people coming into the city for the Exhibition on a daily basis, they were surely inundated and overworked. The thought of these poor women, and their families or loved ones who might be searching for them, left a sour taste in her mouth.

"Thank you," she said to the young man.

Liza appeared at her elbow. "Can we get ice cream now?"

The towheaded man and his son waved to them from a distance. Emma waved back.

"Of course," she said. She took the girl's hand, and they headed toward the bakery. But she couldn't rid herself of the thought of those women, killed and then buried on the grounds of one of the most populated events in the history of the city, the state, even the whole country. Why bury them in such a well-trafficked and populated place?

Oh, how she would love to find out who did this and bring them to justice!

⚜

Annie motioned for Frank to step inside the tent with her. He followed and sat in the oak rocker he'd bought her for Christmas last year. He stretched out his long legs, crossing them at the ankles, and settled deep in the seat. Annie sat on the bed.

"Seems serious," he said.

Annie took in a deep breath. She hoped he would take the news well, but their emotions had been right at the surface for quite some time now. She hoped their resolution earlier that day about her publicity appearances was the beginning of a new understanding.

"Do you remember me telling you about Alison? My friend at the Darke County Infirmary?"

"Yes. Orphaned girl, right?" Frank hinged forward with his elbows atop his knees, holding his hat in his hands.

"The girl with Emma is called Liza. She is Alison's daughter. She arrived with this note." Annie got up from the bed and handed it to Frank.

He read it and then lifted his eyes to hers. "She wants you to care for the girl? For how long?"

Annie shrugged. "From what Liza said, forever."

Frank's eyes widened, and his brows shot up nearly to his hairline. "You mean *raise* the girl?"

Annie swallowed hard. "Yes. As you can see from the note, she doesn't feel she can provide for her or give her a good life. She says I am the only person she can trust with her daughter, but Frank—"

He held the note in the air. "This is impossible, you realize."

"I know," she acquiesced. "We can barely keep up with our own lives as it is. This is not optimal, but we can't turn the girl out. She has no one right now." Annie took the note back, studying it. Why would Alison do such a thing? She had to be in some kind of distress, or possibly even trouble.

"Well, what do you propose to do?" Frank leaned back in the rocker again, appraising her.

Irritation pricked at Annie's nerves.

What do you *propose to do?*

She was hoping to illicit his help. "I don't know, Frank. Find Alison?"

He stood up and rested his hands on his gun belt. "The mother can't be far. How long has the girl been here?"

"I can't say. We were gone for a few hours."

"Maybe we can find a local orphanage, take the girl there," Frank suggested.

She winced at his words but had to admit the idea had crossed her mind. She didn't know the first thing about raising a child, much less one who was not her own. She'd helped her mother with her younger siblings Hulda and John Henry, but that had been different. The ultimate responsibility had lain with their mother. And now, because she could not have her own children, Annie had devoted her life to Frank and her work. There was no room in her life for a child. But she remembered what Miss Nancy had told her. She had said Alison had been inconsolable since arriving at the Infirmary, until Annie showed up. Their friendship had snapped Alison out of her despondency. She couldn't let this little girl feel the same loneliness her mother had as a child.

"I won't abandon her, Frank. I have to find Alison."

He shook his head at her. "You don't have time for this, Annie. The Colonel and Nate have you and the rest of the performers on a punishing schedule. You have the rest of today off, but you've got practice tomorrow and then performances and appearances for the rest of the week."

"We get Sundays off, and the afternoon performance usually ends at four o'clock. That gives me time after to search for

Alison." She ginned up her enthusiasm. "I'll get Emma to help me. She loves a mystery, and she is very good at tracking people down." She wasn't exactly sure if the latter was true or not, but she thought it sounded convincing. Emma was a journalist, after all.

"Good Lord, Annie. I'm going to have to step in and say no." Frank elicited his manager's voice, towering over her.

Annie sucked in a breath through her nose, her jaw tight. "She is staying with us until I find her mother."

Frank slapped his hat down on top of his head. "You are the most stubborn woman I've ever met." His words sliced through her as deep as if he'd used a meat cleaver.

"Don't be a bully, Frank Butler. You might be able to tell me what to do when it comes to the show, but you can't tell me what to do when it comes to matters of the heart."

"I can't tell you a damned thing." He swiped at a tin cup and plate sitting on the table, knocking them across the room. They crashed into her wooden trunk with a loud bang.

Annie bit back tears, dismayed at the display of his temper and the ugly venom that had spewed from his words. She rose from the bed and picked up the strewn articles.

So much for making amends.

◈

Annie was about to go see Buck, something she always did when upset—his unconditional love and acceptance of her was a most soothing respite from toils and troubles—when she saw Emma and Liza walking toward her tent.

Emma looked as if she had a gun to her head, and Liza had tears streaming down her face.

"What's happened?" Annie asked, rushing to meet them.

"She won't stop crying," Emma whispered, exasperation in her voice. "She was fine until we got the ice cream. Then she started asking all kinds of questions about her mother—when she was coming back, why she didn't want her . . . I didn't know what to do." Still holding Liza's hand, Emma took it in both of hers in a gesture of affection. "Dear Liza, please don't cry. Miss Annie and I are going to figure this out."

Annie knelt down in front of the girl and placed her hands around her middle. "Yes, sweetheart. You are safe here with me, Emma, and Mr. Frank. We are going to take good care of you."

Liza scrunched up her face, which had turned a blotchy red. "I want my mama!"

Annie stood up and hugged the girl to her. She looked at Emma in desperation, who mouthed the words, *What do we do?*

"'Lo Annie."

Annie turned to see Bobby Bradley, her good friend and one of her fellow performers of the show, and Chief Red Shirt, one of the Indian performers, standing there watching them.

"Hi, Bobby. Chief."

Liza stopped crying and pulled herself away from Annie. Her mouth hung open as she stared at the tall, regal-looking Indian man, dressed in a bright-red shirt, and a beaded and boned vest. His hair hung to his waist in two ebony braids adorned with feathers and beads. The girl sniffled loudly.

"Aŋpétu wašté." The chief smiled down at the girl, revealing white teeth, greeting her good day in his native Lakota tongue. He nodded at Emma, who gave him a dazzling smile, her dimples deepening into a pleasing pink blush. Annie shook her head. Emma never could resist flirting with handsome men, and they all seemed to be helpless against her charms.

Liza looked at Annie for assurance. "Chief Red Shirt has said, 'Hello,'" Annie explained.

"Hello," Liza said between hiccups, curiosity in her voice.

"Chief, Bobby, this is Liza. She is going to be staying with me for— Well, staying with me. Liza, these are my two very good friends."

Bobby knelt down and held out his hand for her to shake. Unsure, Liza pressed herself against Annie's hip. "I'm one of the cowboys in the show. Wanna see something?" Bobby, who was a few years younger than Annie, had boyish looks and an equally Peter Pan–like demeanor that endeared him to everyone. With his shock of thick hair, and a face peppered with freckles, he had the perpetual bearing of rambunctious teenager.

Liza nodded.

"Lookee here," he said, pulling a coin from his pocket. "This here is a nickel." He held it up with his thumb and forefinger. Then he swiped his other hand in front of the nickel, and it disappeared.

Liza's mouth fell open.

"Where did it go?" Bobby asked.

Liza lifted her shoulders.

Bobby reached his hand behind her ear and revealed the coin. "Ah, there it is! I'm going to have to keep my eye on you, sister!"

Liza giggled, and Annie and Emma exchanged a relieved glance.

"Hey, Annie," Bobby said, standing up. "Me and the Chief are headed over to the Midway to see the Ferris wheel and maybe take a ride. You ladies want to come?"

"I've heard it's all the rage," Emma said, smiling again at the Chief.

"They say it holds over two thousand people at one time," said the Chief.

"What do you say, Liza?" Annie asked. "Do you want to go for a ride in the sky?"

Liza vigorously nodded.

"Perhaps we should ask Frank?" Annie said to the others. "We haven't had time to see anything yet. He might enjoy it."

"Well, I saw him workin' with one of the new horses just a minute ago. Looked like he had his hands full," said Bobby.

"Oh. All right." Annie was glad he had something to keep him occupied. It might improve his mood.

"Well, gentlemen," Emma said, "lead the way."

The chief held his arm out for Emma, and she took it, giving Annie a wink. Annie rolled her eyes at her friend, took Liza by the hand, and followed them to the Midway.

CHAPTER 3

FERRIS WHEEL, ENGINEERING MARVEL OF THE WORLD!
CARRIES OVER 2,000 PEOPLE AT ONE TIME!
– *Chicago Daily Journal*, Monday, June 5, 1893

ANNIE SUCKED IN HER BREATH AS SHE PEERED THROUGH THE iron-grated window. They stood in the forty-person Ferris wheel car, looking down at the splendor of what people were calling "the White City," a composite of sparkling, Beaux Arts–style white buildings that took up fourteen acres of the thousand-acre Exposition grounds at Jackson Park. The large machine gradually made its first rotation upward above the ground. Annie had never been up so high, and the feeling took her breath away.

As the car climbed into the sky at a slow, steady pace, Jackson Park was spread out beneath them in all its glory. Annie had toured some of the monolithic white buildings in the White City, which was the pride of the fair, but she had yet to visit them all. Here in the clouds, she felt as if they were all within her grasp. She held up her hand. If she closed one eye, she was able to surround the outline of the buildings below with her index finger and thumb. It was as if she could pinch each one, pluck them from the ground, and set them in her palm.

A faint smile crossed her lips as her eyes found the magnificent Columbian Fountain positioned in front of the grand Administration Building. Columbia, the female personification of the United States, sat atop her Barge of State, holding her torch aloft. Fame was positioned at the prow, Father Time at the helm. The craft was drawn by the Sea Horses of Commerce. Figures depicting the arts of Music, Architecture, and Sculpture and Painting rowed in unison with the industries of Agriculture, Science, Industry, and Commerce.

The other people in the car, about thirty of them in total, gasped and oohed in amazement as they viewed the many and massive buildings spread far and wide upon the landscape. Annie could feel their energy and enthusiasm wash over her like a wave.

"It's exhilarating being up this high." Annie said to Bobby, who was seated behind her on one of the benches in the middle of the car, his hands clutching the sides, his face white with fear. "You really should see it."

The Chief had picked up Liza and held her so that she could see.

"Yeah, Mr. Bobby. It's zilerating!" Liza said.

"I don't know what that word means," said Bobby, "but if it has anything to do with scared, that's already what I'm feeling," he said, frozen in place.

Annie tousled his hair. "It's one of Emma's words. Right, Emma? It means exciting." She looked over at Emma, who was pointing something out to Liza. Chief Red Shirt's lips turned up in amusement at Bobby's trepidation.

She was happy the chief seemed to be enjoying himself. He was often uncomfortable in a crowd and preferred to spend his time only in the company of the performers or his people. His experience in the Indian Wars made him skeptical of strangers—particularly white strangers—but he didn't have a problem performing for them. He'd once told Annie that he felt the reenactments of the battles fought between her people and his served to educate the masses and help the cause of the Lakota Sioux, who had been placed on reservations far from their homes. Red Shirt believed that knowledge was power, and Annie couldn't agree more.

"They built all of this for the Columbian Exhibition?" the Chief asked. "To celebrate Christopher Columbus's conquering of our lands?"

"Yes," Annie said. When he phrased the question that way, she could tell the concept disturbed him. She decided to change tack and focus the conversation on the impressive architecture. "It took the Exhibition team only two years to build it all. Quite a feat, actually." She turned to Bobby again. "Come to the window, Bobby. It really is beautiful."

"You can hold my hand," Liza said, still in the arms of the Chief.

Bobby carefully stood up, moving as if the floor of the car was going to slide out from under him. Once erect, he held on to Annie's arm and let her guide him to the window. Liza reached out her hand, and he took it. A soft, warm, June breeze blew into the car, and Annie felt the muscles in Bobby's arm relax as he viewed the spectacle below.

"Oh my. This must be what it feels like to be a bird." Bobby exhaled the words.

"Yes. It's the most incredible thing I've ever seen," said Annie. "See, it's not that frightening, Bobby."

Bobby let out a sigh of amazement and let go of Annie's arm and Liza's hand. He adjusted his gun belt and hooked his fingers into the small squares of the grated window. "No, ma'am. A sight to behold."

Annie and the Chief exchanged a smile. Many of the other passengers stared at the tall, stoic Chief with his long braids strewn with beads and feathers. Several people recognized Annie and smiled or said hello. Some of the gentlemen tipped their hats to her. She was glad they were polite enough not to bombard her with questions or autograph requests. She often didn't mind, but she wanted to enjoy this experience without her celebrity getting in the way.

She only wished Frank had come, too. He would love this. They would have to come back another time.

The wheel continued its ascent, and their car was almost at the peak of its rotation. The man who had let them into the car, a Mr. Davis, who was an employee of the Ferris wheel and operator of the car, told them about the construction of the buildings and gave them an aerial tour of Jackson Park.

Annie suddenly became aware of ragged breathing behind her. She turned to see a man pacing in a small area in the center of the car. His chest was heaving, and he had taken off his hat and was raking his fingers through his hair. His face was contorted with concern, and sweat glistened on his forehead. The other passengers stared at him as he moaned softly.

Annie looked up at the Chief. "You stay here with Liza. I'm going to see if that man is all right."

She slowly approached him. When they made brief eye contact, Annie smiled. "Sir, are you feeling ill?" she asked.

The man vigorously shook his head and turned away from her. He continued pacing like a caged animal. Annie reached out to touch his sleeve. He turned abruptly and flung her arm away, his eyes wild with accusation. The Chief, seeing this encounter, started to put Liza down and move toward them, but Annie shook her head, discouraging him. She wasn't sure how the man would react to the imposing figure of an Indian chief. Red Shirt stayed put but lowered Liza to the floor of the car. She stood on her tiptoes while Emma kept her occupied with the sights below.

"I'm sorry," Annie said, surprised at the agitated man's reaction. Though, in her experience with Buck and other animals, she knew that when frightened, they often acted out, sometimes violently. It wasn't any different with humans. "Please, sir, maybe you should sit down."

"Don't touch me," he snarled.

"I won't touch you. But you should sit down. You don't look well."

"We're going to die," he muttered.

"But we aren't," said Annie. "We are perfectly safe in here. The view is beautiful, and we aren't moving fast at all."

"We are going to *die*," the man said more loudly, raising the attention of the other passengers.

Men pulled their wives closer, and two mothers gathered their children to their skirts. Annie looked over and saw Liza's eyes wide with fear. Emma guided the girl to another window. Mr. Davis was still standing at the door—Annie assumed for the safety of the passengers—but he stopped the narrative of his aerial tour.

"You okay over there?" he said.

Just as he asked the question, a woman fainted, and he left his post at the door and went to her aid. Several others rushed over to help the woman, and together, they got her to one of the benches.

"Give 'er some room," he said to the others. He held smelling salts under her nose, and the woman started to come to.

Annie sensed the anxiety of the frightened man standing next to her. The rate of his breathing had increased, and sweat was now pouring from his hairline. He was transfixed on the fainting woman.

"Look at me, please," Annie said to him. She took hold of his elbow, and this time, he did not shake her off. His wild eyes met hers. "We are going to be fine." She took a hold of his other elbow. "Just look at me, and I will talk to you the whole time. Soon you will see that we will land safely and walk off out of this car perfectly intact. I promise." She sidestepped with him to the bench, their eyes locked.

The man's face had grown paler, and sweat trickled down his temples into his closely trimmed beard. Without the look of abject terror on his face, Annie considered that he might be quite handsome. His facial features were perfectly symmetrical with wide-set, large, dark eyes, a straight, thin nose well-proportioned to his face, and a well-defined square jaw beneath his manicured beard. His dress was modest, but he was clean and smelled of pine.

"There," Annie said. "See. Now, tell me, Mr. . . . ?

"Barnes," the man said, his voice a raspy whisper.

"Mr. Barnes. Do you live in Chicago, or have you traveled to see this wonderful World's Fair?"

"Live here."

"Have you always lived here?"

"Yes."

Annie snuck a glance at Emma and Liza, who were busily chatting away, much to her relief. She turned her attention back to Mr. Barnes.

"Do you have a wife, a family?" she asked.

Mr. Barnes looked down at his hands, which were clenched in his lap. His knuckles were splotched red and white from the pressure. "No family. Widowed."

"Oh dear. I am sorry. Do you have children?"

He shook his head. As if at the mention of the word *children*, a little girl much younger than Liza screamed her discontent with being set down by her mother, now unable to see the view below. Mr. Barnes jumped, his eyes wild again.

Annie squeezed his arm. "Mr. Barnes, look at me."

His eyes drifted toward hers, panic making the pupils as small as a pinprick. He clutched his hands together more tightly and began to twist them as if wringing out a wet dishtowel. The child wailed again, and the mother scolded her. Annie heard Emma telling Liza a make-believe story about a princess in the White City, obviously trying to distract her from the increasingly unstable situation in the car.

"You must stop squirming in my arms if you want to see below," the woman said to her little girl. "You've tired me out."

The little girl whined again, flailing her fists into her mother's skirt, wanting to be lifted up again, well on her way to a tantrum if her mother did not acquiesce. The child's cries grew louder and more persistent. The other passengers in the car, while occasionally looking over at the child, tried to ignore her. Mr. Barnes's body tensed, and he pulled himself out of Annie's grasp and stood up.

"Stop it! Stop the screaming!" he shouted at the little girl, who instantly became silent. She then cried even louder, frightened of the strange man yelling at her. The mother picked up the child and moved toward the other end of the car, terror on her face. All eyes were on Mr. Barnes and Annie. Emma pulled Liza closer to her. The Chief once more looked ready to pounce, but Annie implored him with her eyes to stay put. Bobby's hand rested on the handle of one of his pistols.

"I say, Mister," Mr. Davis said. "Keep your voice down. You've scared the child and this fine lady."

"It's all right," Annie said to Mr. Davis, raising her hand in assurance. "I've got him."

"Is he with you?" Mr. Davis asked.

"No."

"Is he bothering you?"

"No. I think he's just a little panicked at being up so high."

"Well, I can't have him shouting at the other passengers." Mr. Davis turned his attention again to the woman who had fainted.

"Mr. Barnes," Annie said, trying to get his attention. He had started his frantic pacing again. "Mr. Barnes, you are frightening the other passengers." She glanced out the window and realized that they were near the ground again.

"Look," she said, trying to sound enthused. "Look, Mr. Barnes. We are almost down to the ground. You will soon be out and able to set your feet on terra firma once again. See? You'll be fine. We are almost there."

As soon as the words were out of Annie's mouth, the car passed the landing and started to rise again. She cringed, remembering that the wheel would make two full rotations. Mr. Barnes looked toward the window, and recognition of what was happening registered on his face.

"No, no, no, no, no," he said, flinging himself at the door. "Let me out!"

"Someone restrain that man!" Mr. Davis said.

The Chief and Bobby started toward him, but he raced to the other side of the car, pulled a gun from somewhere under his coat, and pointed it at the crowd. Several women screamed. Mr. Davis stood up, leaving the prostrate woman in the hands of one of the other passengers.

"Sir, put down the gun," he said, walking toward Mr. Barnes slowly, his hands in the air.

"Let me out!" Mr. Barnes yelled.

"We're doing another rotation." Mr. Davis's voice remained calm. "It'll be about twenty minutes. You need to calm down and relax."

"Mr. Barnes," Annie said, "please listen to him. We are all going to be just fine." She nodded to the crowd and smiled at Liza, who had turned white as a sheet. Annie inched forward toward Mr. Barnes, confident she could get him to lower the gun.

Mr. Barnes growled at her and pointed the gun directly at Annie's face. Before she realized what was happening, a shot rang out, and Mr. Barnes dropped to the floor of the car. Amid the screaming of the other passengers, Annie turned to see black smoke swirling out of Bobby's Remington revolver, which he held trained on Mr. Barnes's inert body.

"He was about to pull the trigger, Annie. I couldn't let him shoot you." Bobby said, lowering his pistol.

Annie spun around to see Mr. Barnes lying on the floor, unconscious, blood oozing from his chest. She felt her own blood drain from her face.

"Bobby, what have you done?"

CHAPTER 4

BUFFALO BILL CODY PURCHASES 40 ADDITIONAL
HEAD OF HORSES FOR WILD WEST SHOW.
– *Chicago Record*, Monday, June 5, 1893

FRANK STOOD AT THE FENCE OF THE PEN WATCHING THE BAY horse. Pacing, the horse raised his head in the air and whinnied frantically for the rest of his small herd. He'd been doing this for the past several days, driving everyone mad with the constant screaming.

The Colonel and Nate Salisbury had purchased the herd for the show from a dealer in Chicago a few weeks ago. Although the horses had been visually vetted by the Colonel, who had a good eye for determining a horse's disposition, sometimes a wild one slipped in under his notice.

Casey Everett, the show's veterinarian, had said that often horse traders would sedate a problem animal, and this particular horse might have been drugged by the seller in an effort to be rid of him. Furious, the Colonel wanted to return the horse, but feeling an immediate kinship with the troubled horse, Frank offered to take him on. He had named him Diablo, the Spanish word for "devil," as he thought it appropriate. Frank, too, found himself at odds with the world.

It had been years since the doctors had told him he suffered from myopia, a nearsightedness that would get worse with age, and he thought he had reconciled the fact that his shooting career had ended. But with Annie's meteoric rise to fame, now worldwide, their life had been consumed by her own career and his sense of importance had diminished. Yes, he was important to Annie personally and professionally. She loved him as he never thought he would be loved. Not in the googly-eyed way that so many women he'd known before had loved him, like a dime novel hero, but for who he was underneath his once dashing-and-fearsome-shootist persona.

And yet, she had grown increasingly unhappy, battle-fatigued from performing. He couldn't help but feel responsible. But they had both agreed to Annie participating in the Columbian Exhibition and had signed iron-clad contracts. That's why they couldn't afford the distraction of the young girl. Annie was stretched to the limit as it was. He hoped the mother would have a change of heart and come to take the girl back. He couldn't imagine a mother up and leaving a child. His own relationship with his mother was nothing to crow about, but she would never have abandoned him.

Diablo dashed past him again at breakneck speed and then came to a sliding stop before striking at the air as if he had a giant bee in his bonnet. The Colonel wanted Diablo separated from his herd because he proved to be a distraction for the other horses. When Frank had volunteered to take Diablo and put him in a separate pen, he hadn't been able to even get a halter on him. They had to move the herd of six into the pen and then separate them out, which displeased Diablo to no end. Thus, the temper tantrum. Frank had to calm the horse quickly before the Colonel ordered him removed altogether—and there had been no time like the present. He decided to start working with the horse while he waited for Annie to come out to practice.

"You stay here," Frank said to Jep the dog, who stood next to him. While in Europe, Annie and Frank had found the dog in an alleyway. He'd been badly beaten up, either by a human or a stray pack of dogs—it was difficult to tell. Unable to find anyone to claim the dog, they decided to keep him. And, as dogs do, Jep had chosen Frank as his person.

Frank hopped over the fence and walked toward the horse, but Diablo took off at a run once again. Frank stopped in his tracks and stood still while the horse ran in panicked circles around in the pen.

After a few minutes, the horse stopped, his nostrils flaring and his sides heaving. His neck was patched with sweat. Frank took a few more steps forward, and the horse took off again.

Standing his ground, Frank waited. Diablo halted again, and having run off some of his adrenaline, blew out and lowered his head. Frank wondered if Annie had ever encountered such extreme behavior from Buck.

Buck had been abused by his former owner, Vernon McCrimmon, which would stand to make a horse skeptical of people. Perhaps someone had mistreated this animal. Either that or Diablo had been taken right off the prairie and hadn't had much human interaction.

Frank took another few steps toward the horse again, and the horse took off, but slower this time, at a trot. Now with foam coating his neck and shoulders, the horse was wearing down. Frank stayed put, waiting once again for the horse to stop. This time, it didn't take as long. Frank walked slowly toward Diablo, and instead of running, the horse pinned his ears and swung his hind end toward Frank. Diablo started to back up, preparing to kick, and Frank jumped away and waited, considering if he should continue. A kick to the face or chest would not be pleasant.

To his relief, the horse moved forward at a walk and then

resumed pacing. Frank approached, and Diablo swung around and charged at Frank with his teeth bared. Surprised and taken off guard, Frank moved away so quickly that he fell. The horse spooked and ran off as pain seared along Frank's tailbone, up into his spine and down through his legs.

The horse came at him again. Frank scuttled backward on his hands and feet, crab-like. He flipped over, stood, and ran to the fence, Diablo still in pursuit. Clambering over the railing, he landed with a thud on his left hip. He lay on the ground groaning, his hip and back in a vise of agony. After several minutes, the pain lessened ever so slightly and he rolled onto his hands and knees. Gradually, every movement like the stab of a knife into his flesh, he righted himself, only to see a group of the show's cowboys sitting atop their horses watching him.

"You all right?" one of them asked.

Frank prodded his hip and his lower back. Nothing was broken, it seemed, and the pain was slowly receding. He raised a hand in a silent gesture to indicate his body was fine. Known as an expert horseman, his pride was another thing altogether.

۞

Finished with its final rotation, the Ferris wheel made intermittent stops to let people out of the sixty-odd cars and load them again. Annie sat with the bleeding Mr. Barnes's head cradled in her lap. The Chief had torn a sleeve off his tunic and handed it to Annie to help staunch the blood flow oozing from the man's chest. She could see that the bullet had missed his heart and hit between his shoulder and collarbone. The Chief remained busy with Bobby, who'd become violently sick after shooting Mr. Barnes, while Mr. Davis was occupied with the fainting woman who had lost consciousness again after the incident.

What had started out as a beautiful and peaceful flight with the birds had turned out to be a thing of nightmarish events.

Like Mr. Barnes, a frantic need to get out of the car and get her feet on the ground pulsed through Annie's body.

Finally, the car approached the ground, and it was their turn to exit from the great wheel. Mr. Davis went back to his post at the door and waited for the all clear to unlock and open it. The passengers flooded out like water breaking from a dam. Mr. Davis escorted his weak and exasperated charge out the door and deposited her with a group who walked her over to one of the park's wrought iron benches. Mr. Davis then helped the Chief and Bobby, who had rallied from his emotional breakdown once the car touched down, to carry the bleeding Mr. Barnes out of the car. They laid him on a grassy patch of ground near some newly planted shrubs.

"Someone fetch a doctor," Mr. Davis ordered.

"I'll get Dr. Gordon," said Bobby, a tremor in his voice. Annie's heart went out to him. She knew he felt terrible about shooting Mr. Barnes. He took off running to the encampment.

Annie ripped the hem of her dress and pressed the fabric to the wound, the Chief's torn sleeve now soaked through. Mr. Barnes had fallen unconscious—probably from shock. She looked up to see that Emma had taken Liza to a park bench some distance away.

Good, she thought. *The poor child must be traumatized.*

Twenty minutes later, a dark coach drawn by two chestnut horses pulled up on the Midway across from them. A well-dressed man with a closely cropped beard hopped out of the cab, followed by Bobby. The driver, too, clambered down from his perch.

"I'm Dr. Gordon," the finely attired man said, concern sweeping across his classically handsome, square-shaped face.

"This man has been shot," Annie said, looking up at him. When their eyes met, she was struck at the intensity of his gaze. It was as if he could see right through her. The man knelt down next to her and examined Mr. Barnes' shoulder.

The man's eyelids fluttered open. "What happened?" he asked, wincing with pain.

"You panicked while on the Ferris wheel, Mr. Barnes," said Annie. "You pulled out a gun and—"

"You were going to shoot her," Bobby cut in. "I couldn't let you do that. I'm real sorry about it, sir, but you could have killed the world-famous Annie Oakley!"

The crowd that had gathered around them gasped.

"Annie Oakley, well, I'll be," the doctor said, his eyes dancing when they met hers. "Lee Gordon. I was hoping to make your acquaintance."

"Thank you, sir. Will Mr. Barnes be all right?" she asked, eager to divert the attention from herself.

"Let's see here. Mr. Barnes, do you mind if I raise you up? I'd like to examine the wound."

Mr. Barnes nodded in agreement but sucked air through his teeth and then groaned as Dr. Gordon helped him to sit up. With deft fingers, the doctor probed the wound, and Mr. Barnes howled in agony. Dr. Gordon leaned Barnes forward and examined the back of his shoulder, causing another torrent of hollering.

"Bear with me, Mr. Barnes." He gently laid Mr. Barnes back on the ground. "It's not as serious as it seems. The bullet went all the way through. Though unpleasant, that is a good thing. If I could get some help taking him to my infirmary, I can get him fixed up."

"I'm real sorry, Mr. Barnes," Bobby said again, his chin quivering.

Annie went to him and wrapped her arms around his shoulders. "It's going to be just fine, Bobby. You were just trying to protect me."

"It was careless," said one of the ladies comforting the woman who'd fainted. "That boy could have killed him—or one of us!"

"I saw his finger start to pull back on the trigger, Annie. I swear it," Bobby said, his voice cracking with emotion.

"Ma'am." Annie turned to the woman. "In my estimation, Bobby diffused what could have been a dangerous situation for all of us. This young man has perfect eyesight and is a crack shot, I can assure you. He knew exactly where the bullet would hit, and if he said he saw Mr. Barnes start to pull the trigger, then that is what happened." She fixed her gaze on the scowling woman, whose cheeks were turning crimson at being scolded by the famous Annie Oakley. She turned her attention back to the woman who had fainted.

"Is she all right?" Annie softened her tone as she asked Mr. Davis about the prostrate woman.

"I'm fine," said the woman, answering for Mr. Davis. "Practically restored. I would like to go home, please. Put my feet up, have some sherry. Should be right as rain after that." As if to prove her heartiness, she stood up, straightened her skirts, and tucked a loose strand of hair back into her bun. Even the color had come back into her cheeks, and she looked quite well.

The scowling woman took her by the elbow. "Lead the way, ma'am. I will see you to a hansom cab." The two women walked away arm in arm.

"Right," said the doctor. "If you please, young man, I didn't get your name?" He turned to Bobby. Annie made the introductions. "And your Indian friend?"

"This is Chief Red Shirt of the Lakota tribe, " Annie said.

"Pleased to make your acquaintance," said Dr. Gordon. "As I said, I'd like to take this man to my infirmary to attend to his wound."

"I'd like to go with you," Annie said to Dr. Gordon, "to make sure he is going to be okay. He said he doesn't have any family, and he's widowed."

"How very kind of you." The doctor met her gaze again. Annie silently sucked in a breath, surprised at the flutter of her heart when their eyes locked. She'd met men from all over the world—dignitaries, royalty, celebrities—but none of them had ever taken her breath away with merely a glance. Aside from Frank, of course. Surprised at her own reaction, she diverted her gaze, and the doctor turned his attention back to Mr. Barnes.

"We'll come too," said the Chief. Bobby nodded in agreement.

"Very well. I might need help getting him into the house," said the doctor. He turned his attention back to Mr. Barnes. "Don't worry, sir. We'll take good care of you," he said to him.

Mr. Barnes nodded through gritted teeth.

Annie walked over to the bench where Emma and Liza were sitting. Emma had her arm around the girl's shoulders. Liza had picked a flower and was pulling at the petals.

"Are you okay, Liza?" Annie asked. What a day for the girl: left by her mother that morning and then witnessing a man get shot in the afternoon.

Liza nodded. "Did that man die?"

"No, he didn't, sweetie. The doctor said he'd be fine, don't you worry." Her gaze met Emma's. "Could I have a word?"

"Sure. Liza, dear, we will be right over there." Emma pointed to a nearby tree. "We will be back in a tick."

The two walked out of earshot of the girl.

"Dr. Gordon wants to take Mr. Barnes to his infirmary," Annie explained. "I'd like to go with them, just to see Mr. Barnes settled in. Would you mind taking Liza back to my tent and staying with her until I get back?" She held up the pendant watch she wore on a chain around her neck. "It's four o'clock. I imagine I will be back in time for practice."

"Of course, dear. I do have a dinner engagement, but it isn't until eight o'clock."

"That should not be a problem. Thank you, Emma."

They returned to Liza, who had turned herself around on the bench, her upper body twisted to watch the people and carriages pass by on the Midway Plaisance. She righted herself when they approached and then rubbed her eyes with pudgy fists. The child must be exhausted.

"Liza, how would you like to go back to my tent with Miss Emma?"

The girl stared at them, as if unsure.

Emma smiled at her. "I will tell you another wonderful story about a princess in a faraway land. Would you like that?"

"Does the princess live in a castle this time? Does she have a golden pony?" Liza asked excitedly, suddenly not looking so tired anymore.

"Well, you'll just have to wait and see. What do you say? Shall we go back to the camp?"

Liza nodded and stood, grasping hold of Emma's hand.

Annie breathed a sigh of relief that the girl would have no objections. She squeezed Emma's arm in thanks. She watched them walk away and was struck with the amazing resilience of children.

CHAPTER 5

COSSACKS RIDERS FROM COUNTRY OF GEORGIA
FASCINATE AT WILD WEST SHOW!
– *The Chicago Evening Post*, Monday, June 5, 1893

"WE AREN'T FAR NOW," DR. GORDON SAID TO ANNIE, leaning over Mr. Barnes to look out the coach window. Bobby and the Chief had opted to ride standing in the boot. The carriage turned off the main road and made its way down a street lined with elm trees and large, three- and four-story graystones. The neighborhood was upscale, pristine, and looked almost too good to be real—certainly above a humble doctor's pay grade. Perhaps the man came from money?

The carriage pulled up to a three-story house nestled behind tall, wrought iron gates. It was tasteful and charming.

"Here we are," Dr. Gordon said. "Mr. Barnes, we'll have you fixed up in no time."

The driver appeared at the door to let them out and then scurried over to the gates and opened one of them. The Chief held Mr. Barnes under the arms while Bobby and Dr. Gordon each took hold of one of Mr. Barnes's legs. Annie trotted down the long walkway and up the stone steps to the front door. She rang the bell.

A young woman with a dark dress, white apron, and white lace cap on the crown of her blond head opened the door.

"Step aside, Nettie," the doctor said.

The girl gasped, holding the door wide as the men carried the patient inside, Annie following behind.

They entered the house into a vast but modestly appointed foyer. Another pretty young woman, this one with flaming red hair, sat behind a desk near the foot of the stairs, bent over some paperwork. At their entering, she looked up, her eyes widening in alarm at seeing the men carrying poor Mr. Barnes, who intermittently moaned with pain.

"Dr. Gordon, what's happened?" she asked.

"This man was shot. I must get him upstairs to a bed immediately."

Annie looked to the stairs to see a clean-shaven, young, blond Adonis of a man with steely eyes and a granite expression descending from them. "What's this?" he asked, blocking the stairway.

"Man's been shot," Dr. Gordon said. "I need to get him upstairs. Prepare the room, would you, David?"

The young man turned and bounded up the stairs, leading the way for Dr. Gordon, Bobby, and the Chief.

The red head from behind the desk came to stand next to Annie, her mouth hanging open and her eyes welling with tears. The blond girl had disappeared.

"Dr. Gordon said he'll be fine," Annie said, surprised by the girl's reaction. She worked at an infirmary, after all. Hadn't she seen all kinds of injury and illness? "The wound is superficial. He's just weak from blood loss."

"I see," said the girl, letting out her breath.

"I'm Annie." She held out her hand in introduction, hoping to put the girl more at ease.

She grasped it, her palm moist with nervous perspiration. "Elizabeth, but call me Beth. I'm new here—from Colorado. I haven't seen many of the doctor's patients, yet. I've never seen anyone who's been shot before. Did you see it happen?"

"Yes." Annie explained what had occurred at the Ferris wheel and Bobby's part in it.

"Was that the nice-looking man with freckles who helped to carry the patient upstairs to the doctor's infirmary?" Beth asked with a breathy quality in her voice.

"Yes," Annie smiled, amused. She'd never considered Bobby to be nice looking; she had always considered him to be a rambunctious little brother. "He's quite a sensitive soul, and I fear he is reprimanding himself severely. He feels terrible."

"My goodness. Are you quite well? I'm sure you are in shock. I think I'd faint dead away if I'd seen someone get shot."

How could she tell her that Annie herself had actually shot three people, one of them a woman no less, all in defense of herself and others?

Once, while a very drunk Mr. McCrimmon had severely whipped Buck for not being able to carry the oversized load in the wagon, Annie had decided she could no longer abide the sinful and unjust behavior of her employer. After confronting him about his conduct, McCrimmon had attacked her. Annie had shot him in the ankle and escaped for home upon Buck's back.

Mr. LeFleur, the previous manager of the show, had proved himself a rogue and Civil War spy who'd stolen Confederate gold. When he'd been found out by Annie and Bobby, he had taken Bobby by the throat and threatened to kill him. To save Bobby's life, Annie had shot LeFleur. Much as Bobby had done for her today.

As for the woman, when the show had traveled to England for Queen Victoria's Jubilee Celebration, Annie had employed the woman only to be assaulted and nearly killed by her.

The girl standing before her might never believe such stories anyway, so Annie didn't feel the need to divulge them. "I'm fine, really," was all Annie said.

Beth intently studied her face. "I don't mean to be presumptuous, but you look familiar. Have we met before?"

Annie indulged her with a smile. "I don't think so. But you may have seen one of my performances."

Beth's eyes widened. "Performances? Are you a stage actress?"

Annie told her who she was and about the Wild West Show.

"Annie Oakley? Well, my stars, I've read all about you, and I've seen your picture on posters. Why, you can outshoot any of those men in the show. And you can shoot a playing card in half!"

"Yes, I can." Annie knew it was sinful to take pride in such things. She had been taught to always remain humble, but hearing such enthusiasm from fans always made her heart want to burst.

"I so admire you," Beth said.

"Thank you." Heat crawled up Annie's neck and into her cheeks. Would she ever feel comfortable with people's admiration of her? She glanced out the window and then looked at her watch. She hoped the Chief and Bobby would come downstairs soon. She was anxious to get back to Liza, and she had a late-afternoon practice. Frank would be waiting for her.

"Oh, well, listen to me go on," Beth said, swatting the air. "Forgive me, but I must check to see if Dr. Gordon needs me to fetch any medicine or supplies for the patient."

"Forgiven," Annie said, offering her hand to Beth. "It was a pleasure to meet you."

"Oh, the pleasure is all mine!" She grasped Annie's hand. "My friends in Colorado will be green with envy when I write to them that I've met you." She giggled and then left down a hallway.

Annie waited patiently, looking around the sparsely appointed foyer. The space was not unwelcoming. The wooden floors, though well-trodden, glowed amber with the light from the two-pronged gas sconces glowing along the paneled walls. She didn't know much about decorating, aside from making Frank's and her tent as cozy as possible, but she thought the foyer could use the appeal and sound-dampening qualities of a nice plush rug. Perhaps a vase of flowers on the desk where Beth sat? She walked over to the desk to look at a large leather-bound book sitting on the corner of it. In gold letters, it read, REGISTER – DR. H. LEE GORDON.

The tinkling of glass sounded from down a hallway. Curious, Annie followed the sound and stopped outside a room seemingly being used as an apothecary. A young woman holding a large leather ledger in one hand, studied and moved bottles on a shelf with the other. She paused periodically to jot notes in the book. Another woman sat at a desk, measuring and pouring potions and powders into small bottles.

How wonderful that Dr. Gordon employed so many young women. She'd never seen a woman, much less two women, work in an apothecary. What a progressive man of the world this Dr. Gordon must be, much like the Colonel who, despite finding his marital fidelity a challenge, believed in the equality of women in the workforce. Annie and her other female cohorts employed by the show made every bit as much money as the male performers. Emma, with her suffragette agenda, would love to see this place and talk to these young women. Perhaps she could feature a story on them.

"Watanya Cecilia," the Chief's voice called from the foyer. He'd used the name lovingly bestowed upon her by the late Chief Sitting Bull. He'd christened her with the Lakota name, which translated to "Little Miss Sure Shot," when they had first met years earlier.

Annie made her way back to the foyer.

"Get him all settled, then?" she asked the Chief.

"Yes. The doctor and his apprentice have dressed his wound and given him a tonic. He seems much improved. Dr. Gordon said he would provide a room for him here at the house."

"Wonderful. How is Bobby? Is he still upset?"

The Chief pointed to the stairs, the corner of his mouth turning up in a wry smile.

Bobby and Beth slowly came down the stairs, engrossed in conversation. Bobby grinned from ear to ear. He followed the girl to the reception desk where she took out a piece of paper and wrote something on it, then handed it to Bobby. The expression on his face looked as if she'd given him a handful of gold coins.

"I'll meet you tomorrow, then?" Bobby asked, the smile on his face showing all his teeth.

"At the Cliff Dwellers exhibits, just outside the Anthropological Village," Beth told him. "The exhibits are inspired by the art of the Cliff Dwellers in Battle Rock, Colorado. It reminds me of home."

"Right then. Tomorrow, Beth." A pink flush darkened Bobby's cheeks.

Beth lowered her eyes for a moment and then gazed up at him behind a flutter of her sweeping dark lashes. "I look forward to it, Bobby."

Annie had the distinct impression that Bobby had forgotten she and Chief Red Shirt were in the room, or even existed at all. She and the Chief exchanged a glance. Bobby couldn't seem to tear his eyes away from the girl.

"The coachman is waiting for us." Annie grabbed him by the elbow and led him out the front door, the Chief following behind. Once in the coach, Bobby, still grinning, stared out the window, his thoughts obviously still with the lovely Beth.

"You are feeling better, Bobby?" Annie asked.

He met her gaze, smiling. "I suppose." He turned to look out the window, his smile vanishing, replaced with an anguished grim line. "I feel terrible about shooting that man, Mr. Barnes. But I couldn't let—"

"Thank you, Bobby. I appreciate what you did for me."

"Fear breeds evil, and people do evil things when they are

afraid. You stopped that man from the evil that lies within him," said the Chief.

"He's going to be fine, though," said Bobby, as if to assure himself. "The doctor said he'll be fine."

"Yes. Thank goodness." Annie patted his knee. "That girl in there? Beth? Seems like you two had a lot to talk about," she teased.

"She likes poems," he said, "by Walt Whitman."

"Really? Bobby, I had no idea you knew anything about poetry."

A grin split his face again. "Well, I don't. But I aim to."

CHAPTER 6

Bodies of Two Women Found on Expo Grounds!
Investigation Underway!
– *The Chicago Herald*, Tuesday, June 6, 1893

THE FOLLOWING MORNING, EMMA WOKE FROM A DELICIOUS dream. She did not open her eyes, wanting to remain in the warmth of the sun at Saint-Tropez, sitting upon the blanket, soaking up the heat of the sand, watching the waves tumble in on the shore—even though she was only at the Palmer House Hotel in Chicago, Illinois.

After Annie had returned from Dr. Gordon's infirmary, Emma left to meet Mitchell, her latest conquest of the past few months, for dinner at the hotel where she had taken up residence over the last year. A faint smile turned up her lips as she mused at their passion throughout the night. She rolled over onto her side, opening her eyes, and watched the rise and fall of Mitchell's chest, the sunlight polishing the delicate curls of his chest hair to gleaming gold. Her gaze traveled to his profile, lingering on the strong, straight nose, prominent cheekbones, and full lips that had kissed her so tenderly.

He must have sensed her staring at him because he awakened and immediately rolled his head on the pillow to face her. "Good morning. Sorry I overslept," he murmured. He reached out to push a stray curl from her forehead and tucked it behind her ear.

"No apology necessary. You quite exerted yourself last night," she teased.

"Was it too much? I mean—too many times? I didn't hurt you, did I?"

"Of course not," she assured him.

He reached out and placed his hand on her hip. "Marry me." His hazel-eyed gaze penetrated right through her, piercing her heart.

"You are already married, my darling." She said the words with resignation, but somehow the truth of them gave her a sense of relief. She rather liked their arrangement. She had no intention of being a wife. She wanted her independence, her freedom.

"You know the fact that my wife and I are both Catholic makes things much more difficult, but I *will* file for divorce." Mitchell had married his childhood sweetheart, and their affection had not lasted beyond the first year. The two had lived apart for nearly a decade—he in a small townhouse in the city, she in a large estate in Englewood. It had to be miserable, Emma thought, but the fact that his wife was from one of the wealthiest families in the state, and of high social standing and staunchly Catholic, didn't help matters. At least they didn't have any children.

"I don't think we should rush into anything," she said. "The scandal would hurt your business, not to mention your family." She ran her hand over his chest.

She'd met Mitchell's father before she'd met Mitchell. The editor of the *Herald* had assigned her to an ongoing story involving his father's insurance company, Hargrove Insurance, where Mitchell was a junior partner. She'd been tasked with investigating a rash of insurance fraud cases that had plagued the insurance industry in the city since the expansion of the population due to the fair.

"You deserve more than an occasional tryst in a hotel room," he said. "I want to give you more. I want to make a home for you, give you children, a family."

Emma raised herself on an elbow. "I have my work. What about that?" She thought about the two women who'd been buried on the Expo grounds. She'd love to sink her teeth into the story, and she couldn't be distracted with thoughts of marriage and domesticity. It would never compare to the thrill she got from being immersed in solving a crime. "What about my traveling? My causes? Are you really willing to marry someone who will not, under any circumstances, play the role of domesticated female?"

Annie had been one of the first women she'd known who'd successfully escaped that role. She'd gone out into the world on her own terms as the breadwinner of her family and had become a tremendous success in her own right. Emma admired that about her friend and wanted to create a life for herself *by* herself, by *being* herself, as Annie had.

Mitchell was clearly much more progressive than his family, but would his family abide by his marrying a woman who wanted to be completely independent? Who wanted to travel the world in search of a good story, as opposed to a nice Catholic girl who wanted to nestle into hearth and home, providing many children to carry on the family name?

It was difficult enough with her own family. Her mother had disowned her, and her father had never given up on the idea that she'd come around to embrace his blue-blooded ideals of a successful marriage for her with high standing in the community.

Mitchell remained silent and turned to stare at the ceiling. She could almost see the wheels spinning in his head as he tried to come up with a favorable answer. She knew he wouldn't. His father had shown her the utmost respect as a journalist, which was refreshing indeed, but his family would never accept into their fold a woman who worked in a man's world and made her living by traveling. Not to mention they would blame her for the divorce.

"I am happy with the way things are, Mitchell. I don't see why they need to change."

He turned to face her again. "But if someone should find out about our liaisons—"

"You are concerned about my reputation?" It almost sounded as if he were concerned about his own.

"I am concerned about *you*," he said. "I love you."

She looked into his eyes, not sure what to say. While she enjoyed his companionship, his intelligence, his business acumen, and their recent foray into true intimacy, she didn't know if she returned his feelings. *Love* was a word that carried a certain commitment with it, one she wasn't ready to make.

She reached up, placed her hand on his cheek, and kissed him, hoping it would suffice for the words he longed to hear. It reignited the flame of his passion, and he kissed her back with such ardor, she knew she'd been successful. For now.

❧

Annie was awakened by a warm sensation on her cheek. She opened her eyes to see a shaft of light penetrating through a hole in her tent and landing on her face. She'd have to have it mended. She reached over to touch Frank and remembered he'd opted to spend the night in the other tent. He'd been upset at her for showing up too late to practice, and besides, Liza had needed a place to sleep.

She sat up, looking at Liza on the cot at the end of her bed. The girl slept deeply, buried under the blankets, her reddish-brown hair tumbling over the pillow, her face covered. The folds of the blanket rose and fell with her breathing.

Annie got out of bed and knelt down next to the cot. She gently pulled the covers from Liza's face. She looked so much like Alison had as a child. Had Alison's appearance changed much in adulthood? She wondered what she might look like now.

"Hello, sleepyhead," Annie said softly. "Time to get up."

Liza blinked her eyes open and then rolled over. Annie decided to give her a few more minutes of rest. She walked to the bureau and poured water from the pitcher into the ewer, and washed her face.

"Miss Annie?" Liza asked, her voice small. She lay on her stomach, her head propped in her hands, watching Annie.

"Good morning, Liza. Did you sleep well?"

"I miss Mama." The girl's bottom lip protruded.

"I know you do. And we will find her."

"Why doesn't she want me anymore? Did I do something bad?"

Annie's heart flooded with pity for the girl, at her feeling as if she had done something to cause her mother to give her away. She left the bureau and knelt down in front of the cot to look straight into the girl's caramel colored eyes.

"Of course you didn't. You are a sweet little girl. I'm not sure why your mother brought you to me, but I am sure it came from a place of love. And I am happy to have you here. We will find your mother and sort all of this out, but until then, how would you like to meet my friend Ska and her little boy, Chayton, and then go to see my horse? We can go to their tent to say hello and then go to the corrals and watch Mr. Post and the others get the horses ready for the performance."

Liza grinned, revealing pink gums where her two front teeth had once been.

"I will ask Ska if you could watch my performance this morning with her and Chayton. Would you like that?"

"What kind of performance?" Liza pushed a stray curl from her forehead.

"Well, I ride my horse and shoot at targets with my gun. Sometimes Mr. Frank, my husband, and also Mr. Bobby—you remember him—perform with me. We have lots of fun. Would you like to see it?"

"Yes, please."

Annie smiled at the girl's politeness. "We all need to have a little fun sometimes." She tapped her index finger on the girl's nose. "Let's get dressed and be on our way, then."

෴

Annie led Liza through the maze of Western-style tents and into the Indian encampment. The air was filled with the good smells of pemmican—a mixture of buffalo meat, berries, and animal fat. Ska was standing next to the firepit in front of her tepee, stirring something in a pot. She was a small woman, fine boned and delicate looking, but hearty as a mule. Ska had been an adept tracker and scout before her husband, Ohitekah, a skilled horseman and expert archer, joined the Wild West Show. Chayton, their six-year-old son, lay on the ground in a grassy area off to the side of the tepee, immersed in imaginative play.

"Good morning!" Annie said, greeting her friend.

"Hiŋhaŋni láȟčiŋ," Ska said in Lakota, returning the sentiment. "Who do you have there?"

Annie introduced her to Liza, who shyly waved at Ska. Ohitekah came out of the tent. When Annie introduced him to Liza, she ducked behind Annie, obviously intimidated by him. Annie couldn't really blame her. Although he was one of the most sincere and kindest men she had ever met, Ohitekah was an imposing figure with his strong, bony facial features and a large mouth that naturally turned down into a frown. He said a few words to Ska in Lakota and then bade Annie goodbye and left.

"Chayton," Ska called over to him. He got up and came over to his mother. He was a sweet-looking boy with a broad face, chubby cheeks, and wild hair that swept over his forehead above wide, dark eyes and a brow that, much like his father's, always registered concern. "This is Miss Annie's friend, Liza." Ska reached out and brushed his hair from his eyes. He pulled away as if affronted.

"Want to see my marbles?" he said to Liza.

She looked up at Annie, seeking approval. "Go ahead," Annie said. "I'll just be a minute with Ska, and then we will go meet Buck."

The children went over to the grassy area and commenced playing as if they'd known each other for years.

"That smells wonderful," Annie said. "Wohanpi?"

Ska was an expert cook and had taught Annie to prepare wohanpi, a fine bison, turnip, and potato soup.

"Yes, would you like some?" Ska asked. "I know Frank likes it."

The dish had become a favorite of Frank's, and Annie loved cooking it for him, but she hadn't had time to do any cooking for Frank for months. She didn't cook often when they were on the road, but sometimes preparing a meal took her mind off things and helped her relax.

"Oh, no, thank you. We'll get something at the mess tent." Annie sat on a chair next to the fire.

"Where is Frank?" Ska asked, as if reading her mind. She had those kind of eyes, the kind that could see right into one's soul.

Not wanting Ska to read too much into her thoughts and emotions, Annie stared into the fire. "I don't know. We've quarreled again." She told Ska about how Liza had come to be with her. "I thought I would see Frank this morning, but he must have gone on to breakfast. He is sleeping in our other tent for the time being. He's none too happy about this situation with Liza. He feels she will be a distraction."

Ska stopped stirring and put her fists on her hips. "He's not wrong. She will be a distraction. But you must follow your heart, Annie. The child needs you. You will decide what is right."

Annie looked over at Liza, making sure she wouldn't be able to hear her. "Taking care of a child is the last thing I need right now—or want right now. The tension between Frank and me is already at the snapping point, and now this has happened."

"You and Frank are having trouble?"

Annie sighed sadly. "Yes. I don't know what is wrong with him. He's moody, silent, irritable. When we returned from Europe the first time and went back to my family's farm in North Star, Ohio, for a few months, everything was wonderful. We relaxed and spent time together, taking long walks and visiting with my family. I worked in the garden and cooked, and Frank worked the fields. But then we had to go overseas again with the show, and he became more and more sullen. I thought purchasing the house in New Jersey earlier this year would settle us, but then we had to come here. It bothers me that sometimes I cannot reach him."

"He loves you very much. It is hard to understand the mind of a man, and they do not talk about their feelings. You must be patient."

Annie nodded. "You're right, of course. We are just going through a rough patch."

"It will get better." Ska plopped a few more small pieces of potato into the soup.

Annie wanted to believe her friend, but until she found Alison, or found out what had happened to Alison, she didn't hold out much hope. For now, she had to just take things one day at a time.

"I told Liza she could meet Buck and then possibly watch my performance this morning. Would you mind sitting with her?"

Ska set down the wooden spoon. "Not at all. I believe Ohitekah goes on some time after you. Chayton always loves to watch."

Annie looked over at the children playing. "They seem to be getting along well. Thank you, Ska."

"It is nothing," Ska said, her full lips turning up in a warm smile.

Annie smiled back, grateful to have such a good friend in Ska and hopeful that she would soon be able to patch things up with Frank.

CHAPTER 7

BUFFALO BILL PERFORMS ENACTMENT OF
CUSTER'S LAST STAND AT WILD WEST SHOW TODAY!
– *Chicago Daily Journal*, Tuesday, June 6, 1893

ANNIE AND LIZA ARRIVED AT THE BARN TO FIND FRANK leaning against the wooden railing of the Cossacks' horse pens talking to Frida. Frank was in the process of lighting a cigarette for the exotic beauty, holding it against the cigar resting between his lips. Annie gritted her teeth. Of all the people in the entire show, why did she have to find Frank in conversation with the beautiful Georgian?

The Cossacks were always scheduled to perform before Annie and Bobby, and Annie wondered if Frida would be performing today. She also wondered what Frida and Frank were talking about.

Annie and Liza approached Buck's pen. The horse had his nose shoved into a bucket of molasses and oats, his favorite pre-performance treat. Mr. Post stood next to him, his ever increasingly stooped posture making it more and more difficult to run brushes —one in each hand—over Buck's golden coat. But he persisted despite aching bones and fingers. She had tried to encourage him to get one of the younger stable hands to do Buck's grooming, but Mr. Post insisted on grooming Buck and the Colonel's horses himself.

She released Liza's hand and leaned her elbows on the railing of the fence.

"'Lo, Annie." Mr. Post looked up from his grooming. "Who've you got there?"

"This is my friend Liza. She will be staying with me for a while. She wanted to meet Buck."

"Hello, little miss." Mr. Post held one of the brushes up in greeting.

Liza lifted her hand, waving at him.

"Would you like to pet Buck?" Annie asked her.

The girl's eyes widened, and she shook her head.

"There's nothing to be afraid of. Buck wouldn't hurt a ladybug like you." Annie took the girl's hand again and led her to the gate. Annie lifted the chain from the post and ushered the girl into the pen. Liza scooted closer to Annie, and her hand tightened around Annie's fingers.

"It's okay," Annie assured her. They approached Buck, his head still in the bucket. Annie knelt down, and Liza knelt with her. "Just stick your palm out to him so he can smell you." The girl obeyed, and Buck raised his head, setting his muzzle in the girl's hand. She giggled with delight.

Annie smiled. "See? He likes you."

Buck raised his head higher and sniffed at the girl's ear. She giggled again as his warm breath made her hair dance. Liza slowly placed her hand between his eyes and stroked the star on his forehead with gentle, short pats. Buck closed his eyes.

"Want to brush 'im?" Mr. Post asked, looking down at the girl with a watery gaze. He handed her a brush and then stroked his long, gray beard, his rheumy eyes twinkling with amusement.

Liza gently ran the brush over Buck's face. The horse resumed eating.

It made Annie smile to see the little girl so tenderly ministering to her horse and Buck so relaxed with her. Buck had always been a bit high-strung and skeptical of people, especially those he was unfamiliar with, but he didn't seem to mind Liza in the least. She wondered what it would be like to teach Liza to ride, to teach her to care for a horse. What would it be like to bring this child into her life and raise her? She couldn't deny the warmth she felt in her heart when she actually thought about it. But as a performer, her life was not her own. She had a job to do, responsibilities. When she had her miscarriage and was informed that children were highly unlikely, she'd accepted that reality.

With the girl thusly occupied, Annie stood up and motioned for Mr. Post to join her at the fence. She told him about Liza's situation and asked if he'd seen the girl before. He hadn't. Frank joined them, but Annie refused to look at him, angry and, well, hurt that he hadn't come to the tent to wish her good morning.

"Morning," he said finally.

She didn't respond.

"It's a fine day, Mr. Butler," Mr. Post said. "If you all will excuse me, I've work to do." He tipped his hat to Annie and walked away.

"Ready for today?" Frank took a puff from his cigar and then exhaled, studying it, refusing to look at her, too.

Was that really all he had to say? How about, *Hello, darling. How was your night? Sleep well?*

"Yes," she said, her voice clipped. "I think I'll use the Remingtons. The Colts need to be oiled. I haven't had time to oil them since Liza arrived."

"The course and your act has been changed. With all of these performances, the Colonel and Salisbury are worried about tiring the animals. They want to keep everyone fresh. I think we should go over it together. Bobby's run through the course, but you ought to do the same before they open the grandstand."

"Fine, Frank." Annie couldn't stand the stiffness between them. "Do we need to talk? Are you still upset with me about Liza?"

He dropped his cigar to the ground and tamped it into the dirt with the toe of his boot to put out the burning ash.

"It's not the girl I object to. It is your insistence on caring for her. You are overextended as it is. I'm concerned about—"

"The show? My performance?"

He finally met her gaze. "I'm concerned about *you*, Annie. That is always my first concern. Not as your manager, but as your husband. You take on too much."

She hated to admit it, but he did have a point. In the past several years, she'd taken on solving the murder of Kimi, her Indian assistant and costume designer of the show, and also the murder of Dick Carver, the Colonel's former partner and archnemesis. She and Emma had gotten involved in another murder in England and had helped to thwart an assassination attempt on Queen Victoria. She had also been responsible for the care of her sister Hulda while on the first tour in Europe and providing for her family financially since the age of twelve. She couldn't seem to get away from it. Helping others and seeking justice had become a part of her ever since her father died when she was a youngster.

"I'm sorry, Frank. I know you have my best interest at heart. But you do understand the position I am in. Alison trusts no one but me."

He shook his head. "It is a lot to ask of a person. Any person, but especially you with all of your responsibilities."

"I agree. And the sooner I find Alison, the sooner I will be free of this responsibility." She had said the words and thought she meant it, so why the sudden pang of sadness? Did she really want to be rid of Liza?

Annie climbed through the fence railing and wrapped her

arms around Frank's middle, laying her head on his chest. He returned the hug, holding her tight.

"We will talk about this later," he said, releasing her, his voice soft. He looped a stray curl behind her ear. "Right now, we need to get you out on this course."

It wasn't the response she'd hoped for, but she would take it for now.

⚬⚬⚬

After she'd practiced running through the changes of the course with Frank coaching her, Annie and Liza made a quick trip to Annie's tent so that she could change into her costume, and then they headed to the mess tent where she was to meet Ska and Chayton. Annie grabbed two bowls of oatmeal from the show's cook, Hal, and gave one to Liza. They sat down to eat, but Annie suddenly wasn't very hungry.

Liza had eaten half of her breakfast when Ska and Chayton entered through the doorway. The boy came running up to them. "Hi, Liza," he said. "My mother says you are going to come with us to watch my father fight the great battle."

Liza grinned at him, the oatmeal forgotten.

"We will see you later," Ska said and led the children away.

Annie went back to swirling her spoon in the gruel. She forced down a couple of bites and then returned the bowl to Hal. As she was leaving the tent, she ran into Emma.

"There you are," Emma said. "Red Shirt said I would find you here."

"Hello, Emma. Walk with me. I go on in a few minutes." Annie started walking in the direction of the stadium. The aroma of wood fires filled the air as the wives and children of many of the performers gathered around them, preparing for the noonday meal. Hal's food wasn't to the liking of everyone. Many of the Native people liked to eat their traditional food, and at times, the cowboys got rowdy in the mess tent, which also served as their local saloon, even in the morning. "I was just heading over to the arena to see the Cossacks perform before my act."

"Haven't you seen them perform a million times before?"

"I want to see what is so special about Frida. Frank is quite taken with her." Annie tried to keep the bitterness out of her voice and the pettiness out of her heart.

"Oh, really? Well, then we must go see her perform." Emma looped her arm through Annie's. "I wanted to speak with you about something. I made an interesting discovery yesterday, a potential banger of a story, and it hasn't been covered yet."

"Oh?" Annie said absently, still distracted by her thoughts of Frank and Frida.

"Two bodies have been found buried on the Expo grounds—women, buried in shallow graves."

Violently pulled out of her reverie, Annie stopped in her tracks. "Oh my goodness. How horrible!"

"Indeed," Emma said. "Obviously murdered. I aim to investigate and find out what happened and who killed them. We make such a good team. What do you say, Sherlock? Want to put on your deerstalker hat, and pull out your magnifying glass to help? You have such great instincts."

Annie bit her lip. Solving crimes did happen to be one of her hidden talents, and they did make a great team, she had to admit. Annie had successfully discovered who'd murdered Kimi and had also uncovered the truth about Mr. LeFleur's secret stash of Confederate gold.

Together, they were even better. In 1887, Annie and Emma were successful in solving the murder of Queen Victoria's esteemed servant, Amal Bhakta, and had also discovered who had formed a plot to kill the Queen herself. It was then that Emma had christened Annie "Sherlock" and herself "Watson," from the popular Sir Arthur Conan Doyle mystery series featuring the detective Sherlock Holmes.

"As tempting as that sounds, and as much as I would love to

help you, Emma, I have my hands full with Liza and finding Alison, among other things."

"Of course you do, darling. I understand. I shall have to carry on without you," Emma said with a sigh, and they resumed walking. "But *after* I see these intriguing Cossacks."

"Hello, Miss Oakley!" a man shouted. He stood with a group of people who all stared at her, the women smiling and talking behind gloved hands as she passed. The Colonel made the encampment of the Wild West Show a welcome place for everyone and encouraged people to tour the grounds.

Annie waved but didn't slow her pace. She never minded greeting fans, but she tried to make it a practice to not speak with them until after her performance. She liked to stay focused. And today, she had enough on her mind without having to make polite small talk with strangers.

When they reached the stadium, Annie led Emma to a gate near where the players entered the grand arena. A man guarding it waved them through. The Colonel had reserved a special box for friends and family of the performers. It was cordoned off from the other boxes to provide them some privacy. Annie and Emma walked to the front row of the box and sat down in the wooden chairs.

The Colonel, and several of the other cowboys and Indians were just finishing the Battle of Little Bighorn. The Colonel, as Custer, was "impaled" by a snub-tipped lance and dragged off his sixteen-hand chestnut horse, Duke, by some of the Sioux warriors. The sound of blanks firing through the air and the Indians whooping and hollering added to the cacophony of sound blaring throughout the arena.

Bobby, driving the Deadwood Stagecoach, circled the battle, firing at some of the Indians, but the Indian warriors were victorious. Bobby feigned injury and fell to the ground, leaving the horse to run with the stagecoach, unchecked, throughout the arena. The crowd whistled and applauded.

The act over, the slain rose from the dead and bowed for the audience who cheered with wild abandon. As the crew came out and cleared the battlefield, Bobby stopped the fleeing horses, climbed back on board the coach, and circled the arena once more. The murmuring crowd took their time getting settled back into their seats to await the next act.

Emma, still on her feet clapping, turned to Annie. "It is always exhilarating to see the Colonel play war!" She sat down, rearranging her skirt, her cheeks glowing pink with excitement. "I've not seen that one before. Is it new?"

Annie nodded. "The crowd loves it, as you can see."

The bloodlust of people always amazed Annie. The crowds clamored to see violence, war, and death. Raised to believe that violence and war were sins, she sometimes struggled with the notion of glorifying them for entertainment. Her father had fought in the Civil War and had suffered nightmares and a nervous disposition until the day he died. She often wondered what he would think of her working with this outfit and hoped that if he was looking down on her now, he'd understand.

The audience hushed as the Cossacks entered the arena, marching on foot in their knee-length white tunics belted at the waist and sporting militaristic, striped high collars and epaulets, their tall, white fur hats gleaming in the sun. Frida was positioned in the middle of the seven, her diminutive frame standing out among them. They brandished long, curved swords and sang, their voices surprisingly strong as they rang out throughout the stadium. They approached a wooden stage that had been quickly erected in the middle of the arena and climbed the stairs one at a time in perfect rhythm. They lined up onstage, abruptly stopped singing, sheathed their swords, and began to dance while starting up another song as their horses were brought to them.

Frida stepped from the stage onto the back of her horse, her feet positioned on each side of the horse's spine, while her counterparts continued their dancing and singing. She looked so confident and graceful, like a consummate performer. Another horse was led over to her, and she took its reins. Then the same happened with yet another horse. She shouted something in her native language, and the horses began to walk. She shouted something else, and they all picked up a canter. Annie was amazed at Frida's balance, how her knees flexed and moved with the horse's motion. It was pure harmony.

Standing astride the middle horse, Frida guided all three at a canter around the arena. She hopped from the middle horse's back to the back of the horse to her left, and then stepped across the horse in the middle to the horse on her right, the horses never breaking stride. She was like a stone skipping across the water. Her elegance was mesmerizing. Annie's skill in the saddle paled in comparison. While quite the horsewoman herself, she'd never ever think of standing atop Buck and shooting at targets, but maybe she *should* consider it.

Frida lowered herself to sit atop the blanket strapped to the horse's back, and then holding on to a strap at the horse's withers, she swung herself to the side of the horse and spun herself upside down. She dipped backward, her feet touching the ground, and then swung herself upside down again.

"Oh my goodness!" Emma gasped. "She is amazing!"

"Yes," said Annie, just as breathless. "Quite talented. And beautiful." She thought about Frank and Frida talking earlier, Frank completely immersed in the conversation. After nine years of marriage, she still sometimes had trouble believing that Frank had chosen her above all other women of the world. She also still hoped he didn't regret that decision. Watching Frida outride all the men of her troupe caused Annie to have conflicting emotions, one of which, she hated to admit, was envy. She saw Frank standing near the box, his arms casually crossed at his chest, watching the spectacle unfold before him and grinning like a schoolboy.

Soon, Frida's counterparts joined her, managing two or three horses at a time, all doing risky tricks. One rider removed his saddle and then dismounted while riding at a full gallop. When the horse sped close to him again, he swung himself back on board, saddle in hand, and proceeded to secure it to the horse's back.

"I need to get ready," Annie said.

Emma looked over at her. "You are already in costume, which, by the way, is beautiful. Hulda make it?"

"Yes." Annie had chosen the light-tan suede coat her sister had designed. It was strewn with intricate beading in a classic American Indian motif. She also wore the matching skirt with fringe that dusted the knees of her dark-brown gators. The coat was a little heavy for Chicago in June, but she like the way the color matched Buck's coat and contrasted with the deep-brown leather of her saddle. Her name was branded on the saddle's skirt in sterling silver, polished to gleaming by Mr. Post.

"I'm going to stay here and take some notes," Emma said. "I'd love to do a story on these Cossacks. It might make a good entertainment piece."

"But aren't you going to investigate the story of the two bodies? Don't you like to write about crime, scandal, and mystery?" Annie asked. Had Frida's brilliance gotten to Emma, too?

"Well, yes, of course. That's my bailiwick, but I need to be well-rounded, show my range as a writer. I need to be writing as many pieces as possible. I can write this one in my sleep." Emma, clearly satisfied with herself, took her notepad and pencil from her oversized reticule and began scribbling.

Annie made her way out of the arena and the stadium to where Mr. Post and Buck waited for her. She tried her best not to think poorly of Frida. After all, she barely knew the woman.

Once outside the stadium, Annie was quickly besieged by a group of people who immediately recognized her. "Miss Oakley," one of the women said. "I can't believe it's you. My husband and I have come to see your act three times now. You are simply astounding!"

"Thank you, ma'am. I'm glad you are enjoying the show." She

smiled and tried to walk around the woman, hoping to head through the group and get to Buck.

The woman stepped in front of her. "When did you learn to shoot like that? I heard you've been a crack shot since you were a little girl. Is that true?"

Annie bit her lip, anxious to get away but not able to do so gracefully without appearing rude. "Yes. I learned quite young. It's taken years of practice to get where I am today. Thank you for your kind words, but I must get ready. I go on in a few minutes." She pushed past the woman, and as she did so, she made eye contact with another woman in a handsome dark-blue dress with matching parasol. The woman's eyes widened in surprise.

Had this been the woman she'd seen before? Annie was about to say something to her when the woman turned her head abruptly and walked away. Astonished by the woman's hasty departure, it took a moment for Annie to snap to and address the rest of her fans, thanking them for their compliments and kind words.

She finally broke through the mob of spectators and approached Mr. Post, who held Buck, saddled and ready to go, by the reins.

"You get caught in that crush?" he asked.

"Yes. I understand that the Colonel wants to be welcoming to the spectators by letting them visit the camp and all, but sometimes—"

"It's inconvenient and annoying," Mr. Post finished for her, spitting a stream of brown chaw and saliva to the ground.

"Agreed." She took the reins from him. "Where is Frank? He usually likes to give me some words of encouragement before a performance." She flipped the reins over Buck's neck and then bent her leg at the knee in a silent request for Mr. Post to give her a boost in the saddle.

"He's getting ready to join you. Getting his horse saddled, I think. He probably spent too much time watching the Cossacks and is now scrambling," Mr. Post said. "They sure do some good trick riding." He grunted as he helped heft her onto the saddle. He then checked the girth and back cinch for appropriate snugness.

Annie's lips pressed together and her jaw clenched. "I see," she said, not even bothering to try to hide her irritation. "Of course."

"You are good to go, girl." He slapped her on the knee.

"Thank you, Mr. Post." She pulled herself straight in the saddle, determined not to let her annoyance at Frank affect her resolve to go out there and give it her all. Although, she'd be lying to herself if she didn't admit that her stomach curdled at the thought of having to perform after the amazing Georgian horsemen and their beautiful centerpiece.

CHAPTER 8

Bobby Bradley of Wild West Show Shoots Man in
Ferris Wheel!
Is Cody's Show a Danger to the Public?
– *The Chicago Morning Herald*, Wednesday, June 7, 1893

The next morning, Annie awoke to the sound of
sniffling coming from Liza's cot. She looked over to Frank's side
of the bed and sighed, missing him even though they had been at
odds. She hoped she would be able to find Alison soon so that
she and Frank could get back to their normal lives.

Annie planned to solicit the use of a conveyance from the
Colonel to visit the police station that afternoon after her
performance. She had asked Frank if he wanted to come along,
but he said he would be working with the Cossacks to advise
them on the purchase of a few more horses. According to Frida,
several in their act were suffering from fatigue, and two had
come up lame. Frank had an expert eye when it came to a horse's
confirmation and soundness, and he had seemed more than
happy to comply with Frida's request. Annie decided it best if

she reserved her opinion on the matter. She had to find Alison or her life would simply crumble right in front of her.

She dragged herself out of bed and pulled on a dressing gown. More sniffling came from the cot.

"What is it Liza?" she asked, stroking the girl's head. "Missing your mother?"

Liza looked up at her with bloodshot eyes. It appeared she'd been crying for some time. She wiped her hand across her pink nose, then clutched at the blankets.

"We are going to get some help today to find your mother," Annie said. "Let's get dressed and get some breakfast."

Liza sniffled loudly and nodded at Annie. They got dressed and checked in on the other tent where Frank had been sleeping. He wasn't there, as Annie had predicted, so they headed over to the mess tent. When they entered, they were met with the delicious aroma of freshly baked biscuits, flapjacks, bacon, and coffee. Annie had Hal scoop up some oatmeal for Liza while she poured herself some steaming coffee from the tin coffee pot resting on the grate of the camp range. Hal brought them some biscuits slathered in fresh butter, and the two joined several of the other players seated at one of the long tables.

When their bellies were full, Annie took hold of Liza's hand. They walked over to the double-sized tent that served as the Colonel and Mr. Salisbury's office. The shared tent not only served as their base of operations, replete with a large filing cabinet, two massive desks, gun cases, a safe, and trunks of various shapes and sizes, but it was also where the two held meetings with the players and crew to discuss all matter of show business.

Reaching the tent flap, Annie sang out, "Colonel, it's me, Annie. May I come in?"

No answer.

"Colonel?" Annie stepped inside to find Colonel Cody sitting in a fine wingback chair in front of his walnut desk with an attractive woman with deep-auburn hair on his lap. The woman jumped up, smoothing her skirts, her face the color of a cherry.

The Colonel, equally distressed, stood up as well, feigning that nothing inappropriate was going on.

"Oh. I am so sorry," Annie said, "When you didn't answer—" She wished she hadn't just witnessed what she had witnessed. Why had she barged in like that? Sometimes she became so intent on her mission, whatever that mission might be, that all common sense went out the window.

She'd only met the Colonel's wife, Louise, once, but she was a lovely woman and not deserving of the Colonel's running around on her. Annie had hoped that after his affair with Twila, his long-term mistress, he'd mended his ways, but apparently not. The Colonel had always treated Annie with the utmost respect, as a person, a woman, and an employee, but sometimes she found it hard to respect him for falling so easily into weakness.

Annie met this most recent conquest's surprised gaze with a hard glare.

"Um, hello, Annie," the Colonel stammered. "Miss Chelton was just leaving." The woman rushed out of the tent, anxiety trailing in her wake.

"What can I do for you?" the Colonel asked, then cleared his throat, trying to cover his embarrassment. He briefly eyed Liza and then indicated for Annie to sit in the offending chair while he walked around to the other side of his desk and sat down.

Annie, still holding Liza's hand, politely declined, trying to regain her own composure. She bit her tongue to prevent herself from scolding the Colonel for his continued provocative behavior. He was her employer, after all, and what she had just seen, and his relationship with his wife, was none of her business. Saying something would only get her into trouble. But oh, how she wanted to say something!

"Colonel, this is Liza, the daughter of one of my friends from long ago," she said, sticking to the task at hand. She placed her hands on the girl's shoulders. The Colonel nodded a greeting to the girl and looked at Annie expectantly. Annie explained the situation and asked to borrow one of the show's coaches.

"Can't you take the girl to one of the orphanages in town?" the Colonel said, sounding infuriatingly like Frank. "Maybe a church or something?"

"No, I cannot. I'd like to visit the police station to see if they can help me locate her mother. I can't abandon the girl, Colonel, for various reasons of my own, and I am asking you to understand."

"What does Frank say about all this?"

Annie bit the inside of her cheek to stop herself from blurting out that she was her own woman and that while Frank was indeed her manager and her beloved husband, she could do as her conscience dictated without getting his approval. "He is on board with my decision."

"It won't affect your performances? We have a heavy schedule."

"No." Annie stood taller, straightened her back. "It will not. You have my word."

Have I ever given you reason to doubt my integrity? Has my personal life ever affected my performance?

She was a little hurt at his lack of faith in her.

The Colonel sighed. "Can't you leave her with the police?"

"Colonel—" Annie started, her voice raising an octave. She cast a quick glance at Liza, who looked up at her with doleful eyes.

"All right, all right." His tone softened. "I don't like it, but I suppose you can't leave the little mite with just anyone. *But* your first responsibility is to the show." The Colonel leaned back in his chair, shaking his head.

"You have a funny beard," Liza said.

The Colonel finally looked at the girl in earnest, his eyebrows pressing together. Liza giggled again, and his face relaxed. He stroked the aforementioned beard that culminated into a fine point three inches below his chin. He looked from the girl to Annie, then back to the girl again, and his lips turned up in the faintest smile.

"Funny, huh?" he said. "What was your name again, little girl?"

"Liza," she said.

"Well, Liza, you be good for Miss Annie here. She'll find your mama. By the way, you've given me a spectacular idea, little Liza." He took the pen from the inkwell and scribbled something on a piece of paper. "I'll have to run it by Nate, but, by God, I think it's brilliant."

As if on cue, Nate Salisbury stepped inside the tent, carrying a folded newspaper. Striking as usual in a chocolate-brown suit, gold satin vest, and a gold watch fob gleaming at his waist, he strode past Annie and went directly to the Colonel, shoving the paper at him. "Sir, we have a problem."

The Colonel picked up the paper and read. "Dear God, what in the blazes?" He read a few more seconds and then tossed the paper onto the desk. Annie reached down, picked it up, and read the headline: BOBBY BRADLEY OF WILD WEST SHOW SHOOTS MAN IN FERRIS WHEEL! IS CODY'S SHOW A DANGER TO THE PUBLIC?

Annie fumed. There was no mention of her and *why* he'd done it. The story was not accurate. Why couldn't all reporters be as transparent and ethical as Emma? Why did these journalists always want to cause a stir? To sell more papers, she guessed.

"I had hoped it wouldn't come to this," she said under her breath.

"You knew about this?" the Colonel asked.

"Yes. I was with him. So was Chief Red Shirt. The man panicked and pulled a gun—there were about thirty people in the car. He aimed the gun at me, and Bobby said he saw the man start to pull the trigger, so he shot him between the clavicle bone and the shoulder."

"And you didn't think to tell me or Nate?" The Colonel's face clouded over with renewed anger. Before Annie could answer, he turned to his show manager. "Get Bobby in here on the double. We need to figure out how to turn this story. I didn't work my tail off to take part in the fair for nothing. Those highbrows in charge of the Expo denied us the opportunity to present at Jackson Park on my terms, so Nate and I had to lease this plot of land, and it isn't cheap, I can assure you. Even though we have been showing up those Expo officials to the tune of five thousand dollars a day, I don't want anything ruining that. This could cause big problems for us."

Annie set the paper down, disappointed for Bobby.

Mr. Salisbury left without another word. The Colonel glared at Annie. Liza slipped behind her, hiding from the Colonel's anger. Annie reached behind her and patted Liza on the arm.

"I'm so sorry, Colonel. I know where the doctor took the man. I'll take Emma there, and maybe she can speak with Mr. Barnes and Dr. Gordon to turn the story. She was with us at the Ferris wheel, too, so she knows what happened. And she can get a quote from me. She is such a good journalist, and a well-respected one. I'm sure she can help, as she has helped us before," Annie reminded him, alluding to the time a slanderous article was printed about her and Emma was able to get the offending paper to retract their story.

"I'm sure Mr. Barnes is reasonable now, and that he will feel terrible about this," Annie continued in an attempt to reassure the Colonel. "He meant no harm. He was just frightened. And the doctor told us he would be fine. I can fix this, sir."

Mr. Salisbury came back into the tent with Bobby trailing behind him.

"Mr. Salisbury said you wanted to see me?" Bobby said, twisting his hat in his hands.

The Colonel just held out the paper to him and Bobby read.

"Hell's bells," he said, looking up at the Colonel. "I didn't mean no harm, sir. He was going to shoot Annie here in the face."

"Bobby, I've explained what happened," said Annie. "And I have an idea how we can fix this. Sir, I'll take the coach to the *Herald* to find Emma, and then we will go to the infirmary to speak with Mr. Barnes and Dr. Gordon. Bobby can even come with me. Then we can go to the police station to elicit help in finding Liza's mother."

The Colonel sighed, then nodded.

"What's this about?" asked Mr. Salisbury, hands on hips and scowling.

"Colonel, would you mind filling him in?" Annie implored. "We must go if I am to be back for this afternoon's performance."

"See that you are not late," he ordered. "Bobby, we are going to have to suspend you for the time being. We can't have you performing until we get this thing cleared up."

Bobby's face fell. A natural-born thespian and expert shot, Bobby loved performing. He often got the crowd roaring with laughter with his comedic antics. He'd perfected the trick of shooting all his targets while standing on his head, Annie and Frank holding him upright from the ankles. He often rode into the arena seated backward in his saddle, looking lost and confused while the other cowboys battled the Natives.

"Don't worry, Bobby," Annie said. "Emma will help get this straightened out right away." Annie bent down to meet Liza at eye level. "I've got to help Mr. Bobby with something. Do you mind playing with Chayton for a while?"

Liza shook her head. "He's funny."

"Yes, he is," Annie said. "Let's go find him and Ska. I shan't be long." She led Liza out of the tent, Bobby following. She turned to say something to him when she saw the flash of a dark-blue skirt duck behind a tent. Several other people strolled past smiling at her. Annie smiled back but averted her gaze, in too much of a hurry to engage with fans and wondering if she was being followed and why.

CHAPTER 9

WILD WEST SHOW'S BOBBY BRADLEY SUSPENDED FROM
PERFORMING!
– *Chicago Record*, Wednesday, June 7, 1893

"THIS IS AN INFIRMARY?" EMMA ASKED AS THE COACH PULLED
up to the gates in front of the large graystone.

To her, it looked more like one of her parents' country
estates. She'd never known a doctor who could afford to reside in
such an extravagant abode. She'd once been courted by a doctor
after her liaison with Carlton had ended, but the relationship
hadn't worked out. He had wanted to marry, and Emma had
wanted her freedom.

"Yes, it is also Dr. Gordon's home," Annie said.

"My goodness." Emma stepped out of the coach after the
driver opened the door for her. She stood in front of the
wrought iron gates, admiring the house and the grounds.

"These are exquisite," she said, her attention drawn to the
two golden lion heads adorning the gates. Each head was encircled by intricately fashioned laurel wreaths. The house sat

squarely in the middle of the two-acre lot. A nurse catered to a patient in a wheelchair under one of the elm trees that populated the grounds. Benches sat atop a blanket of verdant grass. A peaceful place to convalesce, indeed.

Annie and Bobby climbed out of the coach after her.

"Of all the doctors I've ever known, none of them live like this. Must be family money," Emma mused.

"I really have no idea, Emma. I didn't think it polite to ask." Annie's voice rose a prickly octave. Emma knew she often offended Annie's democratic sensibilities with her opinionated comments. As a journalist, she always strove to keep her opinions to herself, but personally, she just couldn't seem to help herself. She'd been raised in a society family, and her blue-blooded contemporaries made it a way of life to be critical and judgmental. They were particularly hard on themselves as a group.

Her friend always espoused that everyone was equal in God's eyes, and even though she'd been exposed to some of the wealthiest people at home and abroad, including royalty, Annie still had trouble reconciling the higher class's snobbery. Emma admired that about Annie but also thought it naive.

Bobby opened the gates for them, and they walked down the long path to the front door. The same golden lion heads in the form of door knockers stared at them from the front double doors. Bobby lifted one of the rings hanging from the lion's mouth and rapped three times.

A girl with pale-yellow hair opened the door. Her large blue eyes were rimmed in crimson, and the areas below her lower lashes were puffy and pink. She looked as if she'd been crying.

She greeted them with a forced smile. Annie asked if Dr. Gordon was in, and the girl shook her head.

"Who's at the door, Nettie?" Another young woman pulled the door open farther. Her face lit up as her eyes darted from Annie to Emma and then to Bobby.

"Hello," she said. "Welcome back."

"'Lo," Bobby said, yanking his hat off his head.

"It's nice to see you again. What can we do for you?" She said the words to Annie, but her eyes kept flicking over to Bobby, who twisted his hat in his hands and stared at his boots. He didn't seem to share the girl's enthusiasm in the encounter, probably worried about Mr. Barnes and the story that had been printed.

"Hello, Beth," Annie said. "We've come to see Dr. Gordon. When will he return?"

"Should be back anytime. Left a couple of hours ago."

"What about his assistant? Mr.—?"

"David?" Beth's lip curled in what could be interpreted as disdain. "I'm not sure where he is. Maybe out back in the green-house? He can't get enough of those plants."

"We came to inquire after Mr. Barnes," Emma said to the girl. "I'm Emma Wilson, reporter for the *Herald*. How is the patient doing?"

Beth shrugged a shoulder. "Fine as far as I know. Nurse Bonnie and Dr. Gordon have been tending to him."

"May we speak with Mr. Barnes?" Emma asked.

"We are under strict instructions not to bother him," Beth said. "Dr. Gordon says he needs his rest."

Annie nodded. "We understand. Could we wait for Dr. Gordon, then?"

"Yes. That would be fine." Beth's face lit up again. "I am on my break and was just about to have some lunch. Would you care to join me?"

"Oh, but we don't want to intrude," said Annie.

"I insist. Mrs. Harper loves to feed people. She is Dr. Gordon's cook. He really should be back anytime now."

"Excellent!" Emma said, stepping into the foyer, followed by Annie.

Bobby, who still seemed to find his shoes to be the subject of some fascination, hesitated. He must be agonizing over the Colonel's forbidding him to perform. The sooner they could speak with Mr. Barnes and the doctor, the sooner she could write her story vindicating the poor boy. That is, if they were all in agreement with what happened. Bobby always seemed to take things so hard. She wanted to tell him to buck up and stop sniveling, but she knew she'd get a reprimand from Annie.

They all removed their hats and handed them to Nettie, the teary-eyed housemaid. She took them, sniffling loudly, and walked away with slumped shoulders.

"Is she quite well?" Emma asked. "The girl looks like she just lost her best friend."

Beth shook her head. "Not her best friend, but her sister, Deborah. Deborah used to live here with us. She helped in the infirmary. Two weeks ago, she just up and left. There was a note on Nettie's dresser that their mother was ill, and had fallen and broken her leg, and Deborah needed to go home to Kansas City, Missouri, to take care of her. She's heard nothing from her sister or her mother since. Been moping around for days. Please, this way."

Beth led them through the foyer down a long, dark hallway. Gas lamps flickered on the walls, which were lined with a ghastly floral wallpaper. Emma blinked as her eyes adjusted to the dimness. Beth led them into the dining room, and despite the summer heat of June, it felt damp and cool—a veritable cavern.

"Oh dear. The fire's gone out. I'll fetch some wood," Beth said.

"I'll get it, Miss Beth. Just show me the way," Bobby finally spoke up, his voice cracking with nervousness.

Beth blushed up to her eyebrows. "How kind of you."

The two stood gawking at each other for several uncomfortable seconds before Beth cleared her throat and led Bobby out of the room.

"I'd say he's smitten," said Emma.

"He said she loves poetry," Annie whispered behind her hand. "Apparently, he does now, too, though I have never once heard him mention it."

"The things we'll do for love," Emma said on a sigh. Usually never one to put much stock in romantic relationships, she felt quite sentimental of late. Could she be in love with Mitchell? It certainly felt like it. She wondered if she should tell Annie. They never kept things from each other, and Annie seemed so distracted and out of sorts. She'd hardly said a word in the carriage on the way over.

"Love? Are you all right, Emma?" Annie asked, sounding surprised.

"Hmm? Yes, perfectly. Why do you ask?" she said in an attempt to tease. Her gaze drifted to the ceiling patterned with decorative square molding.

"You rarely, if ever, speak of love."

Emma chuckled, suddenly bursting to tell her the news, unable to keep the smile from her face. Annie's brows furrowed as if she were confused, as if Emma's behavior was strange indeed.

"What? Why are you looking at me that way, dear? Your face has taken on the expression of a fish gaping at a worm. Oh well, if you must know . . . I've been seeing someone."

Annie's brows shot up. "I thought you didn't have time for such things."

It was true. She had always put her career first. "His name is Mitchell Hargrove. He's very distinguished."

Annie shook her head as if in disbelief. "How long has this been going on?" She almost sounded accusatorial, something Emma never would have expected.

"I met him late last year—around Christmastime. But we didn't start seeing each other until a few months ago. We met through his father. He works in insurance."

"So he's of the working class. Your parents would be appalled." Annie finally smiled, seeming her old self again.

Emma smiled back, relieved. "You are right. Mother would be appalled, though I think Daddy might like him. They are very similar."

"How could your father have anything in common with a man who works?" Annie teased. "You've often complained about your parents' disapproval of the working classes."

"Mitchell comes from wealth, too. But new wealth. Even more horrific! His father owns an insurance company. Mitchell works there." Emma tried to focus on a painting hanging on the wall across the room, but the light was so dim she had to squint. "The interior of this place is rather dreary, don't you think? Quite a departure from the outside." She wrinkled her nose as she ran her finger across the sideboard, creating a clean streak on the dusty surface. A stringent, almost metallic odor wafted through the room. "And what is that vile smell?"

"I don't know," said Annie. "Smelled the same when we were here before. I have to agree, the inside of the house doesn't do justice to the outside of the house. I suppose it's because the doctor is a bachelor."

"Well, he should hire a new housekeeper." Emma circled the dining room table, scowling at the stained lace tablecloth. Try as she might, she just couldn't help but be put off by the atmosphere of the room.

"I think Nettie is the housekeeper. Beth said the girl was upset," Annie reminded her. "Perhaps she's just having a bad week."

"It is simply adorable how you give everyone the benefit of the doubt, Annie," she said. Like Liza's mother. The woman was clearly taking advantage of Annie. She had to agree with Frank there. But Emma knew Annie wouldn't see it that way.

Emma walked over to a painting hung above the dusty sideboard. It was of a European general of some sort astride a gray horse. His face was stern, and he pointed to the distance beyond green hills nestled beneath a stormy sky.

Her musings were interrupted by the sound of someone entering the room. He was tall and blond, with a boyish face and cavernous but charming dimples. He looked to be deep in thought. He was quite handsome.

"Hello," she said, giving him her brightest smile.

He flinched upon seeing her and Annie standing there.

"Oh. Hello." He nodded and abruptly left the room.

Emma placed her hands on her hips. "How rude!"

"He seemed quite preoccupied," Annie said, making an excuse for him. She always made excuses for people's behavior. "He's Dr. Gordon's assistant. He must be busy. I wonder if we should come back another time?"

"Perhaps," said Emma. "But we've come all this way. Let's just wait a few more minutes. Besides, we can't skip out on Beth. She seemed positively delighted to entertain us for lunch."

Just then, Beth and Bobby returned with the firewood, and Bobby set to work lighting the fire. Nettie entered the room and went to the sideboard. She began pulling out dishes, teacups, saucers, and flatware. Seeing a spot on one of the knives, she held it up to her face, breathed a fine mist on it, and then wiped it with her apron.

Dear God. What kind of housekeeper does that?

Emma glanced at Annie who shrugged, obviously nonplussed by the girl's lack of civility.

Beth, having caught Emma's eye and witnessed the whole abhorrent thing, silently picked up the knife and retrieved another one from the sideboard. She helped Nettie finish laying the table.

"Please, everyone, have a seat," she said, pulling out a chair for Emma. "Mrs. Harper will bring the food in directly." She crossed the room to a small table with a whiskey decanter and several glasses, and began pouring. She brought Emma and Annie a glass, and when Annie declined, she placed it in front of Bobby, who thanked her profusely. She poured Annie a glass of water and herself a glass of ale, and returned to the table just as a very spindly and ancient Mrs. Harper emerged into the room struggling with a large array of meats, cheese, and bread. Her bony arms trembled beneath the long black sleeves of her dress.

Cottony gray hair sprouted beneath her white cap, set crookedly on her head.

"Let me help you," Beth said, rising from the table.

"Sit back down, you little chit. I may be old, but I'm not dead," the woman snapped.

Beth sat down again, a tremulous smile on her tightly closed lips. Blotchy patches of red crept up her neck.

Mrs. Harper set the tray down on the table with a bang and then left the room, creating an uncomfortable silence in her wake.

"Lovely," Emma said. "Just lovely."

❧

Annie looked at her watch necklace several times during the meal, concerned about getting to the police station to request help in finding Alison and then back to the Expo in time for her afternoon performance.

"This is such an unusual arrangement with the infirmary and pharmacy lodged in this large house," Emma said, wiping the corner of her mouth with a napkin. "How long have you worked here, Beth?"

"Not long, miss. About three months. I came to Chicago because of the fair and all. It seemed like a good opportunity." Beth popped a grape into her mouth and chewed. There was an air of shrewdness about the girl that Annie admired. She wasn't much older than Annie had been when she had set out on her own. She recognized the same determination, fearlessness, and spunk she had possessed as a girl.

"Your family must miss you very much." Annie's mother nearly fell apart when she'd left, even though it was solely for the purpose of supporting the family. She wondered if Beth had a mother pining at home.

"Yes. It's just my pa now," she said, answering Annie's silent question. "Mama died of the influenza a few years ago. My brothers help my pa with his ranch, and my sister keeps house and cooks for them, but I wanted to live in the big city. When I arrived in Chicago, I found Dr. Gordon's advertisement in the newspaper."

"This is quite a large home," said Emma. "It must take a sizeable staff to keep it running."

"Yes, miss. Dr. Gordon is forever advertising. Said girls and nurses are a fickle lot."

"Fickle? I'm not sure I understand." There was an edge to Emma's voice that often surfaced when she was insulted.

"Most girls only stay on here for about a month or two," Beth explained. "It doesn't help that Deborah just left. I think the doctor is getting downright fed up with having to find replacements all the time."

"And why is that? Is Dr. Gordon a difficult employer?" asked Bobby.

Beth shook her head, her eyes wide. "Oh no. He's ever so kind, but . . ."

"But what?" The gleam of interrogation surfaced in Emma's eyes. She fluttered her fingers, discarding them of the flour that powdered the crusty loaf of bread.

"I really shouldn't say." The girl averted her eyes and then swung her gaze back to Emma. "I think it's on account of many of the girls coming to Chicago to find husbands. They want to work at the hotels, in the restaurants, in large office buildings— you know, to meet people."

"I see," said Emma, disapproval wafting off her like a wave of pungent perfume. Annie knew Emma would never condone taking a job just to meet a husband. She felt women needed to stand on their own two feet.

"And you?" Bobby asked with a tenderness in his voice that touched her. It was sweet to see him so enamored of this girl. "Is that why you came to Chicago?"

"Well, I didn't come out here to find a husband so much as to be on my own. But you never know. I might meet someone," she said, targeting her bright smile at him. His freckles appeared to darken as pink flooded his cheeks.

"Now *that* is an attitude I can get behind!" said Emma. "Good girl."

Annie looked at her watch again. "I'm not sure we can stay much longer. I'd like to go to the police station."

She thought about Liza and how she snuffled in her bed every morning. The child was absolutely miserable without her mother. Annie knew what that felt like when she had been sent to the Darke County Infirmary to learn how to cook, sew, and clean house. Mrs. Edington, or Miss Nancy as she liked to be called, though as kind as could be, had been no substitute for her mother. She remembered missing her mother at night the most. She and Alison would stay up late, talking under the covers. Alison had dreamed up a family and talked about them all night while Annie talked about her mother and her younger siblings, John Henry and Hulda. Liza had no one her own age to commiserate with. Chayton was around the same age, but he had a happy homelife. Annie's heart went out to Liza. She had to find Alison, and the sooner the better.

Annie was just about to get up to go when Dr. Gordon walked into the dining room.

"Ah, Beth," he said, "I see you are keeping our guests comfortable. I am so sorry to have kept you waiting, Miss Oakley. I am delighted to see you again." Dr. Gordon nodded at Bobby. "Hello, young man." Bobby stood up to shake his hand.

"Beth has been so kind to feed us lunch. Though it really wasn't necessary," Annie added.

"On the contrary, Miss Oakley," said Dr. Gordon. He turned to Emma. "I don't believe we've met." His gaze lingered on her high cheekbones and soft, well-formed mouth.

"We haven't." Emma held out her hand, confidence rolling off her in waves. She was fully aware of her ability to attract the attention of the opposite sex. "Emma Wilson, reporter for the *Chicago Herald*. Pleased to meet you."

The doctor took her hand in both of his like a prized possession. "The pleasure is mine." He then turned to Annie. "What
can I do for you today, Miss Oakley?"

"We've come to check on Mr. Barnes, to see how he is feeling." She thought she would stall the inquiry into a possible
interview between the injured man and Emma until she could
get a read on the doctor. He stared at her blankly. "Mr. Barnes.
From the Ferris wheel?" she tried again.

"Yes. Yes," said the doctor. "Forgive me, but Mr. Barnes left
early this morning."

"He did?" Why hadn't Beth said anything about it? Perhaps
she hadn't known. Though, Annie didn't know how it could be
possible for Mr. Barnes to walk out under his own auspices. He'd
been shot only a few days ago. Even though his wound had not
been life threatening, the man had lost a good amount of blood.
When Annie had been shot in the hand several years ago, she
remembered her body going into shock. She hadn't bled as much
as Mr. Barnes, but it took her a few days to feel somewhat
herself again.

Dr. Gordon sucked air through his teeth. "I tried to get him
to stay and rest awhile. Told him I wouldn't charge him for the
room, but he insisted. I can't keep someone here if they don't
wish to stay."

"No. Of course you can't," Annie said. "Well, is Mr. Barnes
going to be all right?" She glanced at Bobby, whose disappointment was written all over his face.

"Oh, sure," said Dr. Gordon. "It just would have done him
better if he'd stayed to rest another day."

"Did he leave a forwarding address?" asked Emma.

"I'm afraid not."

"Dr. Gordon, would you be willing to give a statement about
your assessment of Mr. Barnes's injury—that the injury was not
life-threatening and that his prognosis was good?" Emma asked.
"An unfavorable article has been printed about Bobby, practically
accusing him of shooting Mr. Barnes for no reason. I am hoping

to exonerate him by writing another article claiming Bobby shot Mr. Barnes in defense of Miss Oakley."

Dr. Gordon pressed his lips together. "Well, I . . . I'm not sure I am comfortable with that, on account of the fact that Mr. Barnes left before it was advisable. With the blood loss, I'm not exactly sure how it would have affected him without another day or so of observation."

"Oh, I see," Emma said, regret in her tone. "Are you sure?"

He shook his head. "I'm afraid I can't help you."

"Well, I suppose there is nothing to it, then," Annie said with a sigh, well aware of the time slipping by. "We really must go. Thank you, Dr. Gordon, Beth."

"It was my pleasure," said Beth.

"And mine," said Dr. Gordon. "Again, I'm sorry I couldn't be of more help."

A tall, wisp of a woman in a nurse's uniform entered the room. Her fair, freckled complexion and emerald eyes were in striking contrast to the black fringe of bangs pressed on her forehead underneath her nurse's cap. Her brows shot up at seeing Dr. Gordon with guests.

"Oh, excuse me," she said.

"What is it, Bonnie?" Dr. Gordon asked.

"Nothing, Doctor. It can wait." She turned to go like a frightened filly ready to flee.

"Stay, Nurse," he said. "Our guests were just leaving."

She nodded at them all in turn, her lips twitching in a half-hearted smile.

As they stood up to leave, they heard the clicking of heels on the wooden floor outside the dining room, and then a woman in a deep-blue dress breezed in, out of breath, her cheeks flushed. "Lee, I'm so sorry I'm late—" She faltered when she saw the group of people and made eye contact with Annie.

The woman in the blue dress . . .

Annie finally was able to see her face. Her heart thumped in her chest. "Alison?"

CHAPTER 10

Texas Joe To Perform with Female Sharpshooter
and National Sensation Annie Oakley!
– *Chicago Star Free Press*, Wednesday, June 7, 1893

The recurring dream that had plagued Frank for months flashed in his mind as he watched Frida working with one of her horses in the practice arena. The steady rhythm of the horse's gait and the warmth of the sun radiating through Frank's shirt and leather vest prompted drowsiness, bringing back the vividness of the dream.

He recalled the heavy weight of the water pulling him down, the panic that rose in his chest as he flailed in the murky lake— and the strong arm of his brother coiling around his back, under his arm and securing itself around his chest. In his terror, he'd brought up an elbow, hitting his brother squarely in the temple. The arm released him as his brother let go of his grasp. Frank kicked and thrashed and felt his brother's body sink below him, falling through the water like a weighted stone ...

He blinked, chasing the memory of the dream away. He'd been having it nearly every night, and he couldn't reconcile why.

He turned his attention back to the woman and horse in the arena. When he'd picked her up at the train station, with her little boy in tow, he was immediately struck by her beauty, and then the thick, brusque accent. She reminded him of a lover of long ago, and he wondered why he always had been so attracted to darker complected women with long black hair and ebony eyes. Yet, the woman he'd fallen head over heels in love with, Annie, looked nothing like them with her five-foot tall, curvaceous frame, light brown wavy hair, hazel eyes, and a whisper of light chocolate freckles covering her nose and cheeks. Could it be that the dark beauties reminded him of his mother? Black Irish she was called, with sable hair and olive skin.

As Frank watched Frida work with the tall, powerfully built black stallion, he marveled at her intense and seemingly invisible communication with the horse. The horse, wearing no halter or bridle, followed at her elbow like an eager, oversized puppy. When she stopped in the center of the arena, he stopped behind her. She turned to face him, and then with a gentle upward motion of her raised finger, the horse backed away from her, in a perfectly straight line. When she lowered her hand to her side, the horse stopped, ears pricked, his attention riveted to her. She then raised her arm again and then pointed to her right. The horse leapt into action and began trotting to her right in a perfect circle. She did not turn and watch the horse as he passed behind, her, but stood casually relaxed, her arms at her sides. The beads on her skirt twinkled in the sunlight.

Frida took two steps backward, and the horse moved toward her. She moved two steps forward and he changed direction. When she raised her finger in the new direction, the horse picked up a canter and continued in a circle. He blew out, lowering his head in a relaxed and rounded posture. After the horse circled her four or five times, she tilted her head to one side, and the horse stopped and faced her. She raised her palm to the air and curled her fingers, beckoning him. He trotted toward her and stopped a respectful two feet in front of her. She raised both arms in the air and the horse rose into a rear, dancing on his hind legs. He came down to the ground in a graceful motion, and she went to him, wrapping her arms around his neck.

As if sensing his gaze on her, she turned and looked at Frank.

"Pretty impressive," he said. "What's your secret?"

She walked toward him, the horse following behind.

"What is this word, secret?" she asked.

"How do you get him to do those things with just a flick of your wrist?"

"We have, how do you say—connection? I speak with him in his language."

"I don't follow," Frank shook his head, smiling. She really did have captivating eyes.

"Horses don't speak in words."

"Yes. I know." He laughed.

"They speak with their bodies. A movement, the turning of an ear, the facial expression—it says so much. But first, they must have trust. They must see you as their leader."

Frank thought back to his boyhood on the farm. His family, newly settled from Ireland, had taken to horse breeding. He loved watching the horses move within their herds across the rolling green hills of his family's Kentucky farm. He remembered the roan mare, always herding the others to where she wanted them to be—scolding the rambunctious colts with pinning of her ears, or the bearing of her teeth, or the way she would swing her backside to any of the other mares who came too close to her or her foal, ready to fire off kicking at any moment.

"I'm still not sure I follow," he said. Annie had the best horse handling skills he'd seen up till now. Sure, any one of the cowboys could get their horses to do whatever they wanted— Frank could too— it was the willingness of Buck to so wholeheartedly want to please Annie that had been the magic of their relationship. She had sacrificed her own safety and well-being to save Buck from the hands of that scoundrel McCrimmon, and Buck seemed, on some level, to understand that.

"I must teach you, then." Frida said. "I love explaining the language of horses."

"I think I'd like that."

Thinking of Annie, he pulled his watch out of his waistcoat pocket. She had a performance in a little more than an hour. He looked up to see Ivan running toward them.

"Mama! Kartuli is ill." He reached them out of breath.

"Kartuli?" Frank asked.

"One of the horses," Frida said. "I must go."

"I'll go with you. Perhaps I can be of some help."

"Please," said Frida.

Ivan took him by the hand and pulled him forward. "Thank you, Mr. Frank. We must hurry!"

⚜

Annie and Alison stood staring at one another.

"Annie. What are you doing here?" Alison asked, alarm in her eyes.

"I might ask you the same question." This was the woman Annie had seen at the fair, watching her, watching Liza, but not taking any responsibility for the child. And here she was, dressed in well-made garments and shoes that were fashioned from fine silk and adorned with glittering buckles. The ensemble reminded Annie of something Emma would wear, of the most excellent quality, best cut, probably custom-made. This was not a woman who looked to be struggling in the least. The deep blue of the dress complemented the fairness of her skin and the paleness of her eyes, which now cut through Annie like glass.

"You two know each other?" Dr. Gordon directed his question to Alison.

"Yes. We're old friends. Right, Annie?" Alison's voice was clipped, shaky. She was clearly disturbed to be found out.

Emma stepped forward and introduced herself, then turned to the doctor and Bobby. "Why don't we let these two catch up for a moment? Dr. Gordon, I'm so intrigued by your home and your infirmary. Could I be so bold as to ask for a short tour?"

"I'd be delighted to show you around." Dr. Gordon offered Emma his arm.

Nurse Bonnie's jaw tightened and patches of pink mottled her neck. Annie couldn't be sure if the reaction was due to the appearance of Alison or at the doctor's easy compliance to Emma's request, but she was clearly annoyed. She turned abruptly and left the room.

"Come on, Bobby." Emma gestured at him with a tilt of her head, indicating she knew full well that Annie wanted to speak with Alison alone. Annie was so grateful to have such an intuitive and resourceful friend.

Emma led the men out of the room, babbling on about the interesting décor and giving the doctor tips on how he could improve the ambiance.

Annie turned to Alison. "Do you know that your little girl has cried herself dry over the past few days? How could you do this to your own child?"

"Where is she?" Alison asked. "Is she all right?"

"Yes. She is safe. She is with a dear friend."

"What are you doing here, Annie? Did you follow me? I thought I was so careful." Alison's fingers trembled as she lifted a hand to her throat.

Annie told her about Mr. Barnes and how they came to be at the doctor's house. "What are *you* doing here?" Annie asked.

"I work for Lee— I mean, Dr. Gordon. I'm employed here, as his office assistant."

"But what about Liza, Alison? Why isn't she here with you?" If Alison had regular employment, why on earth did she want to foist her daughter off on someone else?

"We were living in a boarding house, but it was not safe for

Liza. It's not safe for her here, either. It's not safe for us to be together."

Annie pinched her brows together, confused. "I don't understand."

Alison pulled out one of the dining room chairs and sat down. She gestured for Annie to do the same. She sat in silence as if trying to gather her thoughts. All of a sudden, her face crumpled and tears spilled from her eyes.

"Oh, Annie. I am in so much trouble." She took a handkerchief out of her handbag and dabbed at her face.

Annie took in a deep breath and let it out, her sympathetic nature getting the best of her. She reached out and took Alison by the hand. "Tell me."

Alison looked over her shoulder, as if she feared being overheard. "I know you need an explanation, but I can't talk here. Can we meet somewhere else later today?"

Annie didn't want to be put off. How could she know that Alison would be true to her word? What if she vanished again?

"You can't tell me now?"

"No. Please, Annie."

Annie sighed, trying not to sound as irritated as she was. "Very well. I have a performance in an hour or so. Perhaps after that? Where could we meet?"

"At the fair. But not near the Wild West encampment. I don't want Liza to see me. I know this has been hard on her. Seeing me would make it so much more difficult. She's been through quite enough already."

"She doesn't understand why you left her. And neither do I, especially now that I know you are gainfully employed. Where do you live?"

"Here," Alison said. "Please, I don't want to talk here." She turned her attention toward the task of putting her handkerchief back into her handbag.

"Perhaps we can find a quiet place to talk this evening,"

Annie acquiesced. "The Wooded Isle? Or maybe we can secure one of the electric boats on the lagoon. What do you say?"

"That would be lovely." Alison sniffed and met Annie's gaze head-on. "I am truly sorry for troubling you so. You will understand. I promise."

Annie mustered a tight-lipped smile, not sure she would. "Very well." They gazed at each other for a few silent moments. "It's good to see you, Alison."

Alison laid her hand on Annie's arm. "You too, my dear friend. Now, if you will excuse me, I have some work to do for the doctor. Until later?"

They hugged, and Alison left the room. Annie wondered where Emma and the others were. She stepped out of the dining room and headed toward the foyer when she heard voices.

Must be Emma, Bobby, and the doctor finished with their tour.

She arrived at the foyer to find no one there. The voices came from the other side of it—to a part of the house she hadn't seen. She followed the sound down another hallway, hoping to catch them and hurry them along. She stopped when she heard a male voice rise in anger.

"I see how you look at him," the voice boomed. It didn't sound like Dr. Gordon, but it definitely did not sound like Bobby. She couldn't make out what the female voice said, but the tone was soothing, as if she were placating him. Then nothing.

"I'm running out of patience," the male voice hissed.

"You're hurting me," the woman said.

Fearing the woman was in some kind of danger, Annie followed the sound of the voices to an open doorway.

"Stop it!" A distinct sound of a hand slapping flesh followed the woman's demand. Annie entered the room to see David clutching Nurse Bonnie by the arms and her trying to wrench herself free.

"Is everything all right in here?" Annie directed her question to Nurse Bonnie.

David immediately let go of her, and she backed away, rubbing her arms, her face contorted with anguish.

"Yes," she said. "Just an argument."

It looked like more than an argument. She'd been arguing with Frank for weeks, but he would never lay a hand on her.

David, his face bright red, stepped forward. "Yes. I'm sorry you had to see that. And, Bonnie, I'm sorry I lost my temper."

The nurse glared at him and then turned to Annie. "I'm fine."

Annie got the distinct impression she was being dismissed. "Are you sure?" she asked.

"I *said* I'm fine. Mind your business." With that, Nurse Bonnie sailed past her and out of the room. She was left standing there with David and the sheepish look on his face.

Annie looked him directly in the eye. "You need to keep your hands to yourself."

His face still the color of a ripe tomato, David nodded and then also swept past her.

"Well, he was in a hurry." Emma appeared in the doorway. "Ready to go?"

"Yes. But you'll not believe what I just witnessed." She told Emma about the argument.

"Should we mention it to Dr. Gordon?" Emma asked.

"Nurse Bonnie seemed almost offended that I tried to help her, but yes, we should," Annie said with a firm nod of her head.

They walked out to the foyer where Dr. Gordon and Bobby stood waiting for them.

"Found her," Emma said.

"Dr. Gordon, may I have a word?" Annie indicated with a tip of her head to see him away from the others.

"Of course," he said, and they moved into the hallway.

Annie told him what she'd encountered.

"I see." Dr. Gordon rubbed his chin, his blue eyes filled with concern. "Thank you for bringing this to my attention."

Annie smiled, pleased she had let him know. And she had to agree with Alison: this seemed like no place for a child.

❦

Upon leaving Dr. Gordon's house, Emma had opted to take another coach back to the Expo grounds. Fresh out of time before her performance and no longer needing to solicit the help of the police to find Alison, Annie had headed back to the Wild West encampment with Bobby. Emma had considered going to the police station herself to see if she could get anyone to talk with her about the two female murder victims, but given the current over taxation of the force, decided to start with the Exhibition Guard to see if they might have any new information.

When she arrived at the Guard's office, she found only one officer manning the station, and he was busy detaining two men —one an older man who was completely inebriated, and the other a much younger man whose belligerence and language would make a sailor blush.

Once the guard sufficiently wrested the young man behind the bars of a small cell, he noticed her standing there. The young man let out another series of angry expletives.

"Shut your trap!" the guard yelled, then turned to her, wiping the sweat from his temples. "What can I do for you, miss?" He walked over to the drunk, who had slid from his chair and now lay in a heap on the floor. He hauled him to his feet.

"I'm Emma Wilson, reporter for the *Herald*."

The guard opened the door to another small cell, and the drunk man shuffled in. The guard closed the door and locked it. "A lady journalist, huh?"

"Yes. I was hoping you could give me some information." Her eyes darted to the younger man, who leered at her. "But perhaps we could step outside?"

The guard led the way to the door and held it open for her. They stepped out into the sunshine.

"I understand there were two women buried in shallow graves here in Jackson Park. I was actually at the location where one of them was exhumed. Can you tell me anything about them? Who they were? Where they were from?"

"Look, lady. I don't know anything." He pulled the waist of his pants over his bulbous belly.

"Has the Guard launched an investigation? Are they working with the police?"

He chuckled. "I said I don't know anything. And if I did, I wouldn't say anything to a reporter—much less a lady reporter."

Emma bit down, her jaw flexing. She was used to this kind of treatment, but it didn't make her hate it any less. She held his gaze, refusing to be intimidated.

"I got paperwork," he said, tilting his head toward the door. "Good day." He went back inside.

Frustrated, Emma left and made her way to the Wooded Isle, sat down on a bench, and took her pad and pencil from her handbag. She sat under the shade of a Chinese maple tree. The afternoon was still and serene, and the passersby spoke in muted tones, as if afraid to disturb the perfect tranquility in the air. Her thoughts drifted to the visit to Dr. Gordon's infirmary.

How ironic that instead of finding Mr. Barnes, the person they ended up finding was Annie's childhood friend? The poor woman was so surprised she looked as if she'd been completely caught off guard.

A lanky gentleman with a handlebar mustache and a thin-rimmed derby pressing down on his gray head tipped his hat to her in passing. She smiled and nodded to him in greeting, and he passed by, never slowing his brisk walk. Next came a couple holding hands. The woman's free arm was held across her tiny waist, and her fingers curled around the gentleman's bicep. They strolled slowly, their eyes smiling in delight as they gazed into each other's faces. The scene made her smile, and she thought of Mitchell.

She really should be working on the insurance fraud case, but she knew Mitchell was working on it and the murder of the two women seemed more pertinent. After all, a killer was on the loose. And with the Exhibition Guard and the police department stretched so thin, she felt it her civic duty.

Someone walked toward her, his blond head looking familiar. He walked fast, his focus on the ground, his hands resting in his trouser pockets. It was Dr. Gordon's assistant, David. David, who had slighted her and threatened Nurse Bonnie.

"Hello." She stood up. She would not let him get away with rude behavior again, to her or anyone else.

He looked up, a puzzled expression on his face. He stopped, staring at her. He didn't recognize her—something she was not used to, particularly from men.

"I saw you today at Dr. Gordon's house," she prompted.

Recognition finally dawned. "Oh, yes. How do you do?"

"I don't think we were properly introduced. You left quite abruptly." She raised her chin in disapproval. *And quite rudely.* "I'm Emma Wilson."

At her words, a mottled flush bloomed on his cheeks. "Forgive me. I was looking for something when you were there." He took a hand from his pocket and laid it on his chest. "I am working on a, um, well . . . a project for Dr. Gordon. He would have been furious with me had I not found it and finished the task."

She noted grime beneath his fingernails and forbade her face to wince. She found it hard to abide a lack of nail hygiene and any man who threatened women. She indulged him with a half-smile, somewhat pleased with his contriteness. "And did you? Find it?"

"Yes." His eyes flicked away from hers, not meeting her gaze.

"Finished the task?" She kept her face placid, her voice even.

He finally looked at her in earnest. "Yes. Not that it is any of your business." The splotchy flush on his face now made an appearance on his neck.

Emma gritted her teeth. "I don't appreciate your rudeness,"

she said evenly. "And I don't appreciate how you threatened Nurse Bonnie."

His jaw flexed. "I don't appreciate your meddling," he retorted, his neck now an angry red, bordering on purple. "If you will excuse me, I need to get back to the infirmary."

"Don't let me keep you."

The cheek of this man!

He nodded to her. "Good afternoon."

She did not return the sentiment as she watched him leave. She sat back down, trying to calm herself, shocked at his insolence. How could Dr. Gordon employ such a man?

She took in a deep breath and let it out slowly, collecting her thoughts. What had she been thinking about before? Oh, yes. Getting the exclusive on the story of the murdered women . . . She didn't know the new editor of the *Herald*, Mr. Kline, very well, but she got the distinct impression he was less than thrilled at her, a woman, having been previously allowed to cover murder investigations. Little did he know, she'd paid her dues over the years.

It was true, she hadn't worked very long at writing her fashion column all those years ago. She had gotten the job purely by accident. She and her former beau at the time, Carlton, had been enjoying ice cream at a soda fountain when a stately looking gentleman had approached her, complimenting her attire. He said he was the editor of a small local paper and wanted to know if she would be interested in writing a fashion column. Since her parents had been threatening to cut her off if she didn't cut Carlton out of her life, she decided to tie her rebellion up in a neat little bow by taking a job with the paper.

She had worked at the paper until she got wind of a high-profile murder on the south side of Chicago. She covered the story on her own and presented it to the previous editor of the *Herald*, and the rest was history. She only hoped she could impress her investigative skills and writing acumen upon the new editor. Sometimes it was utterly frustrating to be a woman, subjected to men's opinions, their prejudice, and in the case of the two women—and perhaps Nurse Bonnie—their violence.

ఉక్షు

Despite her worries about Alison and Liza, and also about Bobby's situation, Annie performed to her usual flawlessness. She had been scheduled to perform with Bobby today, but because he was banned, she had to work with another one of the cowboys, Texas Joe. Annie liked the young man and thought him a fine horseman, but he suffered from tremendous stage fright and had a habit of taking a drink or two before he performed. Annie had been familiar with the predilection as Lillian Smith, her former rival, had done the same.

Any time Annie had to perform with either one of them, Frank insisted their access to booze be monitored and that she be the first to have a go at the targets. Monitoring the booze intake proved much harder than it seemed. Frank and the Colonel went round and round about it, and finally settled on Texas Joe shooting at targets fashioned from lightweight balsa wood using blanks as ammunition. Joe had to get closer to the targets, allowing the percussion of the blanks to knock them over. Without the benefit of real bullets, Joe's aim often "appeared" to be off and it bruised his dignity, but Frank would not have his wife, or the audience, subject to stray bullets.

Annie and Texas Joe, who by all accounts seemed sober, made their final laps around the arena to rapturous applause and steered their mounts through the stadium gates and out into the paddock. Annie spied Frank talking to Frida and the rest of Cossacks. The young boy, Ivan, stood directly in front of Frank, head bent back to stare up at him, hanging on his every word. It was sweet how the boy seemed to idolize him, but she couldn't help but wonder why it also bothered her so much. Was it because she could never give Frank a son? She bristled, wondering if Frank had even watched her perform. When he wasn't a part of her act, he usually watched from the paddock gates or sat in the box provided by the Colonel, if he wasn't in the arena with her.

"How'd it go?" he asked as she approached. Frida nodded a greeting to her.

"You didn't see it?" She tried to keep the irritation out of her voice.

"One of Frida's horses, Kartuli, is showing signs of colic. I offered to take a look at him."

If Frida was such an expert horsewoman, why did she need Frank to give his assessment? And Mr. Salisbury had hired on the veterinarian who had traveled with them on the European tours to continue his employment with the show. Why hadn't they alerted him?

"Isn't that why the Colonel employs Mr. Everett?" Annie asked.

Frank looked at her with a cool gaze. "Yes. But some of the buffalo are ailing. Mr. Everett thinks they got some bad hay. He's a bit shorthanded at the moment."

Annie sniffed, not wanting to relinquish her irritation at Frank. Did he really need to come to the aid of the fair Frida? Wasn't she surrounded by her completely able-bodied, even handsome, countrymen?

Ivan came up behind Frank and Frida, and he took hold of his mother's hand, looking up at Annie with large dark eyes rimmed with curling, black lashes. He smiled, revealing two missing front teeth, just like Liza. She had to admit, the boy was adorable.

She indulged him with a quick upturning of her lips and turned her attention back to Frank. "May I have a word with you . . . in private?"

Frank nodded, hooking his thumbs in the pockets of his vest.

"We must get back to the horses. Come, Ivan," Frida said, pulling the boy away. Ivan waved at Frank and gave him a gap-toothed smile.

When they were out of earshot, Annie took hold of Frank's sleeve and turned him to face her. "You seem to be spending a lot of time with Frida." She crossed her arms over her chest.

"What do you mean?"

"You heard me."

Frank lifted an indifferent shoulder. "I took a look at one of her horses. Besides being your manager, I do know a few things about our equine friends."

Annie pressed her lips together. It was true. Frank's family had once been in the business of breeding horses. Suddenly, she felt silly for her accusatorial feelings, and she really didn't want to argue.

"Of course. Never mind." She waved her hand as if erasing her words. She decided to focus on something positive. She looped her arm in his, and they continued walking. "I have some good news. I've found Alison."

Frank stopped again, turning to face her, his eyes lit with surprise. "That is good news. How in the world did you manage that?"

Annie told him about visiting Dr. Gordon's house. "We didn't have any luck speaking with Mr. Barnes. He left Dr. Gordon's care, but I'm very pleased to have found Alison. I'm meeting her this evening at the Wooded Isle. She said she would tell me why she left Liza with us."

"Maybe she will take the girl back. It will be nice to reclaim my place in our tent." Frank smiled. Something in the smile bothered her. Was it relief? He'd finally be rid of the little girl?

She fixed him with a cool glare. "You don't seem to mind spending time with Ivan."

Frank's grin faded. "What do you mean?"

"The boy is completely infatuated with you. Surely, you see it."

Or is it his mother?

"Ah, well. He's just lost his father and his brother. The boy is in need of some male companionship." He shrugged, folding his arms over his chest.

"He's surrounded by male companionship with the other Cossacks. Why you, Frank?" She realized how trite her words sounded, shrill even. She wished she could bite them back.

"What is this about, Annie? I can't see why it would bother you that a young boy should look up to me."

"It doesn't bother me," she quipped. But it did. Or maybe it was that he was Frida's child. "I just don't see why you have an objection to Liza. Ivan has his mother. I don't think you understand how difficult it can be to be separated from your family at such a young age. You've never had to endure anything like that. Your family has always had the luxury of money. You didn't have to be separated from your mother to go out and make a living. Your father didn't die, leaving you the responsibility of supporting your family. Not everyone has been as fortunate as you." She spat out the last statement, irritation at him surfacing to the boiling point.

"I don't know what has gotten into you, Annie. We've all had our hardships. You just wear yours like a banner emblazoned across your chest."

The shock of his words struck her like a slap in the face. "How dare you—"

Frank turned and walked away from her.

"Where are you going?" she demanded.

"To get a drink."

"That won't fix things, and you know it," she yelled after him. Frank had never been much of a drinker and would only occasionally imbibe. Usually when he was upset about something.

"Well, it might be worth a try," he shot back over his shoulder and strode away from her, leaving her with nothing but sarcasm in his wake.

CHAPTER 11

THOMAS EDISON AND SUSAN B. ANTHONY
AMONG SPECTATORS AT WILD WEST SHOW!
– *The Chicago Herald*, Wednesday, June 7, 1893

DAMN, THE WOMAN CAN BE INFURIATING, FRANK THOUGHT AS he walked away from her. He whistled for Jep to follow him. He understood that she was tired, and probably did need some time off, but they had agreed to sign on for the fair—together. No one had twisted her arm, namely him. So now they had a responsibility to the Colonel and the other players of the show.

And the business with Ivan? What was that about? It never used to bother her when people idolized him. She had been one of those people herself once. How long ago that seemed.

She wanted him to have more compassion for Liza, and granted, she wasn't wrong—the poor kid had been dumped by her mother—but Annie ought to have more compassion for Frida's boy, too. He'd just lost his father and his brother. Annie had lost her father when she was not much older than Ivan, and then two sisters. Of course, she was not entirely without compassion—she always seemed to be on a mission to help others. But why did he get the sense that she wanted no part of these two newcomers to the show? She was usually so welcoming. Even after all these years, would he ever get her figured out?

Frank made his way back to the stables where Mr. Post, Bobby, and some of the other grooms and cowboys were brushing down the horses that had just performed. When she came out of the arena, Bobby had taken Buck from Annie and worked at the horse's sweat-matted coat with a curry comb while Buck nibbled at a pile of hay. He nodded to Frank as he passed by.

Feeling sorry for the young man, Frank stopped to talk to him. "Hey, Bobby, I'm sorry you've been sidelined. But I know why you shot that man, and I appreciate it."

"Thanks, Mr. Butler."

"I know it's hard, son. But you must understand the Colonel and Salisbury's position."

"Yes, sir." Bobby focused on the task of swirling the curry brush in circular movements across Buck's golden back. The straight dark stripe down the center of the horse's topline wavered with the hair being swirled one way and then the other.

"Care to get a drink?" Frank asked.

Bobby stopped what he was doing and turned to look at Frank. "I'd like that very much."

"Looks like you could use a friend, and I could use the company."

Bobby grinned. "It would be a pleasure, sir. Just let me finish up with Buck here, and then we can saddle up and go."

"I'll give you a hand." Frank sifted through the grooming box and found a stiff-bristled brush and started on Buck's ebony mane. The horse nickered and swung his head around toward Frank, bumping his arm with his nose. "Hey there, my fine fellow," he said, stroking Buck's forehead. "I wish you could tell me what's gotten into that mistress of yours."

"Is Annie doing poorly?" Bobby asked, now stroking Buck's hide with a brush.

"Nah," Frank said. "Just out of sorts."

"I didn't mean to cause any trouble, sir."

Frank immediately regretted bringing up Annie. Bobby had enough to contend with without making him feel even more terrible about shooting Mr. Barnes.

"It's not you, Bobby." Frank tried to allay his guilt.

But it is certainly me.

Once saddled up, the two mounted and then headed out of the Wild West encampment, as the late-afternoon sun hung stubbornly in the sky, beating down on their backs. Frank knew of a saloon and beer garden on the southwest corner of the German Pavilion. He'd been frequenting it since they'd arrived. The whiskey was fine, the beer stout, and the girls serving it pretty and quick to make him laugh. He'd even found a card game or two, though he didn't particularly like gambling. He'd never really been one to drink on a regular basis, either, but the amber liquid warmed his bones and calmed the restlessness of his soul.

They headed out of the encampment on the northeast side and headed down 62nd street toward Stoney Island Avenue. The crowds were thick today and his horse, the trusty palomino named Biscuit, absorbed the energy of the crowd surging through the streets. Excited, chattering women with brightly colored dresses and parasols, and staid gentlemen strolled the tree-lined streets that were bedecked with a profusion of floral bushes.

As the sun started its decline, the air turned cooler as it rolled off Lake Michigan, and Biscuit pranced in a rhythmic cadence, invigorated by the activity. When they reached 60th Street, they turned west onto the Midway Plaisance. They passed the nursery and stopped to watch a juggler who stood in front of the Javanese settlement, tossing a variety of fruits in a circular motion about his head.

Spotting the two horsemen, the juggler approached them, never losing his concentration. The apples, oranges, and plums danced before their eyes. He leaned toward Bobby's horse and, while increasing the speed of his rhythmic hurling of the fruit, managed the feat with only one hand while he stroked the nose of Bobby's horse with the other. The crowd laughed with delight.

"We ought to tell the Colonel about that fellow," Bobby said as they moved away from the group, which was growing in increasing numbers around the juggler. "He might want to add that act to the show."

"He'd fit right in with our circus, that's for sure," agreed Frank. The Wild West Show was becoming more and more like a sideshow attraction in his opinion. When he had been headlining, it had been more about celebrating marksmanship and equestrian skill as opposed to recreating sensational scenes and exaggerated truths just because people had a bloodlust for violence.

They continued past the German settlement, heading for the beer garden, when they noticed another large crowd gathered near the Ferris wheel across from the Egyptian exhibit.

"Have you been on the Ferris wheel yet, Mr. Butler?" Bobby asked.

"Can't say I have."

"You ought to, sir. Being up so high gives a person a true sense of freedom. I was terrified of going up so high at first, but now I come here near every day, in the evenings. I like to fly with the birds. It feels as if I can reach out and touch the clouds. It's a beautiful thing. I just hate it that I had to go and spoil things when Mr. Barnes went after Annie like that."

Bobby's words jolted Frank into the memory of accidentally shooting Annie in the hand once, during one of their performances long ago when he was the star of the show. He'd been too proud to admit his eyesight was failing, and he'd missed the card Annie had been holding up for him and hit her palm. He recalled with horror the look on her face. Utter shock and disbelief before her cheeks had drained of color and she had fallen to the ground in a faint. He could have ruined her career had she not healed properly. It had taken him years to get over his guilt. He hoped Bobby would not be as hard on himself.

"You didn't spoil anything. You reacted the way anyone with your skills would have: you shot where you aimed."

"I couldn't abide anything happening to Annie."

"I know, son, and we're all grateful to you."

The crowd gathered near the Ferris wheel, and it looked like people were craning to see something on the ground.

"What do you suppose is going on over there?" Frank asked, pointing to the group. From the crowd, a woman started screaming. "What in the Sam Hill . . . ?"

Two gentlemen dressed in white coats with red crosses on their sleeves emerged from the crowd carrying a body on a canvas stretcher. A German shepherd dog circled them, whining. Jep was about to run to the other dog, but Frank whistled and Jep sat down.

"Someone take hold of that dog!" one of the medics yelled.

Another man approached the shepherd, knelt down, and beckoned to him. The shepherd, his head down as if in shame or feeling as if he were about to be scolded, obeyed the command and went to the man, clearly agitated. The man stroked the dog's back, trying to soothe him.

Frank and Bobby urged their horses to a trot to join the crowd.

"Jep, heel," Frank commanded. The dog stayed at Biscuit's side.

The man lay on the stretcher, lifeless, his eyes wide open, unblinking, his pallor the color of an icy sky in winter. His clothes were dirt-stained and wrinkled.

"What happened here?" Frank asked the man holding the whining dog.

"Body was partially buried here. This dog must have been wandering by. Dug it up."

"Dear God." Frank tried to steady his horse as he pranced with nervous energy, probably at the smell of death.

"Whoever buried him must have been in a hurry. Didn't do a very good job," the man said.

The medics pushed their way through the curious crowd who all wanted to get a closer look.

"Poor old soul," the man continued. "Wonder if he has any family."

The medics took a sheet out of the back of their horse-drawn ambulance and placed it over the body, covering his head.

"He doesn't have any family," said Bobby, his voice flat. His face had gone as pale as the dead man's.

"You know this man?" Frank asked.

"Yes, sir, I do." Bobby's voice wavered. "It's Mr. Barnes."

❦

Annie secured a coach and told the driver to take her to the Wooded Isle. She watched out the window as the people and carriages glided past her. The clip-clop of the horse's hooves on the hardened dirt path lulled her into a thoughtful reverie. She reminisced about the brief time she had spent with Alison when they were children. Alison had been such a sad and tender-hearted child—much like Liza—and Annie couldn't fathom why in the world she would make Liza suffer as she had.

The carriage made its way down 62nd street and finally reached the boat lodge, where Annie had the driver drop her off at the ticket booth. She sat on a bench under an elm tree, waiting for Alison as the sun sank into clouds resting on the horizon, turning the sky the color of a summer peach.

She thought about Frank and the argument—the most recent argument—they'd had and his declaration of going off to get a drink. It concerned her deeply. Why did he have to turn to alcohol? What did he have to numb himself from? Her? Their life together? Life on the road?

While she'd never been one to imbibe, she could see how life on the road might foster a person to take on foreign behaviors. She couldn't remember a time in the last two years when she hadn't felt exhausted. She never had the desire to drink, but she knew her mental and emotional fatigue sometimes made her act in ways that surprised her and added tension to her life with Frank.

Another coach pulled up, and Alison stepped out with the help of the driver. She handed him some coins and approached Annie.

"I'm glad you came," Annie said.

Alison's eyes betrayed the hurt of Annie's statement. "Did you think I wouldn't?"

Annie hadn't meant to offend but always knew that in times of conflict, honesty usually was the best approach. "I'm not sure what to think, but I am anxious to hear what you have to say, what your life has been like, and to learn more about your little girl."

Alison's face crumpled in anguish, and she pulled out her handkerchief and alternated holding it to her mouth and dabbing at her tears.

The man selling tickets at the ticket booth recognized Annie immediately and wouldn't take her money for the boat ride. She told him she was comforting a friend, and they would like some privacy if possible. Observing the state Alison was in, the man ushered them quickly aboard a gleaming, small, white vessel with bright-blue trim and told the captain of the electric conveyance sitting at the stern to depart from the dock directly, before anyone else could join them. Annie nodded her appreciation to both the ticket master and the captain.

Once she and Alison were comfortably seated, the captain steered the boat away from the dock. Annie handed Alison one of the small paper bags full of pellets that rested on one of the bench seats.

"Food for the ducks," she said, taking up a bag of her own.

Alison kept her face averted while she absently threw food into the water, using her other hand to continue dabbing at her eyes with the handkerchief. Several ducks and a regal black swan began to follow them, their yellow feet paddling in the water. Annie waited for Alison to collect herself. She finally lowered the handkerchief and looked up at her.

"You may or may not have known this, but Mr. and Mrs. Edington left the Darke County Infirmary rather unexpectedly." She blew her nose and then placed her handkerchief back into her handbag.

"Yes, I gathered as much. They'd abandoned me to the McCrimmons. She didn't even notify my mother that they had left. The McCrimmons stopped paying for my services . . ." Annie held back, afraid going into the story would unleash the anger that always simmered below the surface when she thought back to that time. She'd always thought Miss Nancy kind, so why had Annie been forgotten? She had been sure she was doomed to a life of abuse and neglect. Her mother hadn't known where she was or even how to begin to find her. It was a particularly dark time in Annie's life, and she didn't like to think about it.

"One of their sons had acquired a good deal of debt and had gotten involved in illegal activities with some terrible men," Alison went on. "He stole all their savings and fled the country, but the bad men came after the Edingtons. They had to leave Ohio. They took me with them."

Miss Nancy had always had a soft spot for Alison. It didn't surprise Annie that she had never been farmed out to a different family. Miss Nancy wanted Alison for herself.

"That explains a lot. Go on."

Though it still doesn't excuse not letting my mother know where I was.

Alison gulped in a breath and then let it out slowly, steadying herself from her crying jag. "They took a different name, and we moved to New York. All three of us worked very hard to make our living, and we did everything we could to stay together.

Their health did not hold out, however, being older and all. Mr. Edington died a year after we went to New York and Miss Nancy about six months after that." Alison emptied the rest of the food into the water and crumpled the bag in her hand, gripping it so hard her knuckles turned white.

The anguish in her friend's face made Annie feel sorry for her. "And then you were alone."

"Yes. And I couldn't make enough money to keep the place we rented, so I had to live in the streets. I did what I could to survive . . . things I am ashamed of . . ."

Annie felt her chest tighten. How horrible to have felt as if there was no other choice. She couldn't imagine . . . At least when she had finally freed herself and Buck from the McCrimmons, she'd had someone to go home to. Alison hadn't had anyone. Suddenly, she felt sorry for judging the Edingtons so harshly. They had been everything to Alison. "I am so sorry, Alison. You must have been terribly frightened."

Alison nodded, took out her handkerchief again, and held it under her nose, trying to keep her composure. "The madam I worked for was very kind to me. She gave me shelter, food, and would only sell me to the kindest men. Some of the things the other girls had to endure—" She closed her eyes as if willing the memory away.

Annie reached out and took hold of Alison's hands. Life had been hard for Annie, and sometimes she had to fight to avoid letting the memories of that hardship taint her feelings, but she'd never had to endure what Alison had.

Alison finally looked up and met Annie's gaze. "But from it came some happiness. One of my wealthier customers grew very fond of me, and I of him. He was a widower. Howard Emmett. We fell in love, and he asked me to marry him. He is—was—Liza's father."

"What happened to him?"

"He died unexpectedly. I think his business partner—" She looked down at their intertwined hands. "He didn't know that

Howard had changed his will and left everything to Liza and me —including his half of the business."

"That's wonderful, Alison," Annie said, relieved.

"Not exactly. The circumstances of my husband's death are suspicious." Her ice-blue gaze met Annie's.

"What do you mean, suspicious?"

Alison sighed. "I think he may have been murdered. But I can't be sure."

Annie took in a deep breath. "How awful!" Poor Alison. She'd seen such hardship, and when she'd finally found happiness, it had been taken from her.

They sat in silence as the boat rounded a corner, skirting a small island with three Japanese willows sitting upon a mound of grass lined with bright-pink impatiens flowers. A group of pink flamingos stood, each upon one leg, with their necks curled in U-shapes and their beaks tucked under their wings, napping in the cool of the willow's shade.

Alison's hands trembled, but she began again. "The company accountant, Miles Drake, told me that when Winston—that's my husband's business partner, Winston Peale—found out about the changing of the will, he became enraged. Miles told me we had to leave New York. He said he would protect me and Liza, and he did, for a time. We moved to Springfield and married four months later, and I thought my troubles were behind me." Alison paused, tears pooling in her eyes. "Until I saw him try to smother Liza in her sleep . . . He said he was comforting her, that she'd had a nightmare. He tried to convince me that I hadn't seen him put the pillow over her face in the dark, but—" she stopped, her chin quivering. Annie placed a hand on hers for encouragement "—I know what I saw."

"Oh, Alison," Annie said softly, giving her hand a squeeze and trying not to convey the shock and horror she was feeling at Alison's story.

"You see," Alison continued, "in the will, Howard stipulated that whatever wealth Liza and I had would go to charity after our deaths and full ownership of the business would be given to Winston—unless I remarried. In that case, if something happened to me, the money would go into a trust for Liza. I am so worried that if I should die, Miles will find a way to break the trust as my widower and as the guardian of Liza. Miles married me for my wealth, and to obtain half of the business—I know that now."

Annie shook her head in disbelief, her pulse racing with the details of Alison's story. "I am so sorry you and Liza had to endure this."

Alison bit her lip and blinked back tears, then set her jaw. Annie could see the muscles pulsing beneath her friend's reddening skin. "When I saw him doing that to Liza, I lost my mind! I hit him over the head with a lamp. It enabled me to grab Liza and flee the house. I'm sure he was hurt, but the blow didn't kill him. I had some money in my handbag, so we caught the first train to Chicago. I had picked up a Wild West Show flyer in Springfield and I knew you would be performing here in Chicago, and it is a great place to hide within the thousands of people who have come for the fair. I also wired my banks in New York and Springfield and froze the accounts."

"Did you go to the Springfield police? Or go to the police here in Chicago? Surely, if there is a threat to your or your daughter's life—"

"Miles's uncle is the chief of police in Springfield. He also has connections here. I just can't trust anyone, Annie."

"And what about Dr. Gordon? How do you know him?"

At the mention of his name, Alison's cheeks flushed again, but this time they became a pleasing shade of pink. "Lee has been so good to me. I answered his ad in the newspaper, and he hired me on as his office assistant."

"You refer to him as Lee? That's a rather informal way to speak about your employer, isn't it?" Annie would never think of calling the Colonel "Bill" or Mr. Salisbury "Nate"—and they had employed her for a decade.

"It's become a bit more than that, Annie. Lee and I . . . well . . ."

"But you are living with him." The statement came out louder and more judgmental than Annie had intended. She couldn't hold back her astonishment at her friend's immodesty.

"Yes, but there is nothing improper going on." Alison squeezed Annie's hand in assurance. "He is most respectful of me. It's just that we have both developed feelings for each other. Now you can see why it was important for Liza and me to be separated. To get my inheritance, Miles would have to kill both of us."

"So you will marry Dr. Gordon?" Annie hoped she sounded encouraging and not pushy.

"He hasn't asked me yet and I have not yet secured a divorce, but I feel in my heart we will, eventually. He really is a good man, Annie. I am happier than I've ever been."

"And you believe your husband is after you?" Annie could scarcely believe this horrific tale.

"Yes."

"And possibly your late husband's—I mean, *your* business partner?"

"I'm not entirely sure about Winston, but yes, definitely Miles. He's made it clear he wants to kill us. I need to keep Liza safe, and the only person I can truly trust her with is you." She squeezed Annie's hands again. "I live in fear that he will find me —or worse, Liza. He is very cunning. I really should not even be seen with you," Alison said. "I should not have been lurking in your encampment. I don't want to endanger Liza. I just needed to see that she was safe. That she was being taken care of. It breaks my heart to be separated from her." Alison's chin trembled, and she pressed her fingers to her lips.

"And hers to be separated from you." Annie remembered the pain of losing her own child—the one who died in her womb. Would it have been a boy or a girl? She felt the loss as keenly as if she'd known the child for years. And to learn she would never have children brought on a whole different kind of sorrow.

She wondered if that was part of the reason Frank had been so distant lately and maybe why he'd attached himself to Frida and her boy. But they had received the news that Annie couldn't bear children over six years ago. At the time, Frank had said that it didn't matter, that she and her love were enough. But maybe he'd changed his mind, or maybe, because he was growing older, thirteen years older than her, in fact, he felt the opportunity to have children would permanently slip away.

Alison blew her nose into her handkerchief and then tucked it away again. "Do you now understand my predicament?"

Annie nodded. "I understand. We will get this sorted out, Alison. But it would do Liza a world of good to see you once in a while, to know that you have not forgotten about her. Do you suppose we could meet in secret? Somewhere on the Expo grounds?"

"My heart aches to see my little girl. But if we do, let's make sure we meet at a different place every time."

"Good idea," Annie agreed. She motioned to the captain to take them back to the dock.

Not long later, the boat pulled up to where they had first embarked. The ticket master and captain helped both of them out of the boat, and they walked to one of the benches that had been placed among the flowered beds lining the grass.

"Yes," Annie said. "Let's meet tomorrow at the east lagoon, in front of the Woman's Building. I can bring Liza between performances, say, two o'clock in the afternoon?"

Alison's eyes welled with tears again. "I can't thank you enough, Annie. I hope this isn't too much of a burden for you."

Annie wrapped an arm around Alison's shoulder, hoping beyond hope that her marriage and her career would withstand the decision she'd just made to take care of Liza indefinitely.

CHAPTER 12

Buffalo Escapes from Wild West Encampment!
Captured Near Midway Plaisance!
– *The Chicago Evening Post*, Wednesday, June 7, 1893

Annie sat cross-legged, a blanket nestled around her shoulders, at the small campfire she'd built upon her return from the lagoon, waiting for Frank to come back. She and Liza had picked up two bowls of beef stew and some freshly baked biscuits from Hal and ate in silence at the table outside of the tent next to the small fire. The little girl had barely been able to hold her head up as she picked at her stew, so after she'd managed a few spoons full and a bite or two of biscuit, Annie had tucked Liza into the blankets on the cot, and the girl had fallen asleep the moment her head hit the downy pillow.

Now, waiting for Frank, Annie warmed her feet and her hands. She was determined to wait for him even if she had to sit out there all night. She felt awful about how they'd left things and how he'd stalked off to go find a saloon. She tried to quell the horrible thoughts that arose in her mind, thoughts of Frank blind drunk, though she'd never seen him blind drunk, thoughts of Frank spending the evening in the company of Frida, though Frank never gave her any reason to mistrust him, thoughts of Frank deciding he was through with the show and through with her, though she knew he loved her.

She hoped he would return soon so they could make up and these horrible thoughts that plagued her would go away. It was absolute misery to let her imagination run away with her. She needed to focus on something else. She closed her eyes and willed away all thoughts of Frank and tried to open her mind to other thoughts and sensations. The sound of spurs jangling in a steady rhythm caused her eyes to pop open, and she saw the outline of Frank's slender body walking toward her, his gait steady and sure. Annie sighed with relief, flung the blanket off her shoulders, and ran to him, throwing her arms around his neck. She laid her head on his chest.

His arms went around her, and he gently pressed a hand against her hair, resting his chin on top of her head. He didn't say anything, but his tender embrace let her know that underneath all their squabbling, he truly did love her and wanted to mend things, just as she did.

She pulled away from him, took his hand, and led him to the fire. He sat down in the chair, and enfolding the blanket around them both, Annie seated herself on his knee. He wrapped his arms around her.

"How did it go with Alison?" he asked, tucking a stray lock of hair behind her ear.

"She's asked me to keep Liza a while longer." She told him Alison's story.

Frank's eyes softened. "The woman's had some hard luck, I'd say. Must be tough."

"Yes, she has. I don't know what to do, Frank. How could I tell her I wouldn't help?"

Frank shook his head. "You couldn't. I see that now." He went quiet, staring at the fire. Annie knew he was still not happy about the situation, but at least he was being more understanding. She continued. "Alison is assuming that everyone in the police department would take her husband's side, even here in Chicago. Miles' father has many connections in Illinois."

"There are hundreds of officers here. Seems unlikely," Frank said.

"True. I may be able to persuade her to go to them after all, but that still doesn't guarantee Liza's safety. At this point, it is Alison's word against her husband's. And the police would have no cause to do anything about her situation. I have to help my friend, Frank."

He squeezed her in an abbreviated hug. "Well, finding Liza's mother is a good start, my dear. I'm sorry I was so harsh with you."

Annie smiled, comforted that Frank had finally apologized. "Did you find a saloon?" she asked, noting that he did not smell of alcohol, which relieved her, but where had he been all evening?

"Yes. I asked Bobby to come with me, and we had planned to go to the beer garden near the German Pavilion, but we never went in."

"Oh?"

Frank recounted the story of the dog unearthing a dead Mr. Barnes near the Ferris wheel. Annie gasped and put a hand over her mouth.

"Bobby was pretty shaken up about it," Frank said.

"Dear God, I should say so. But . . . I don't understand." Her mind reeled. "According to Dr. Gordon, Mr. Barnes was on the mend. He insisted on leaving the doctor's care. What could have happened? And how? And buried on the Expo grounds? Near the Ferris wheel, you say?"

Frank nodded. "Damnedest thing I'd ever seen—or even heard of. It's downright frightening if you ask me."

"Indeed." A million thoughts ran through Annie's mind, and she remembered Emma telling her that two other people had been buried on the Expo grounds. She told Frank what Emma had said. "This is obviously murder, Frank. But why would someone bury their victims in such a public place?" She wondered if all these burials were somehow connected. Could the murders have been committed by the same person?

Annie wished she could tell Emma about Mr. Barnes before any of the other reporters got wind of it. She knew how fast word traveled, especially when there were so many people who had witnessed Mr. Barnes being carted away. It suddenly dawned on Annie that she had no idea where Emma was staying right now. She wouldn't even know how to reach her.

Frank stroked his chin. "Just for that very reason. Because it is such a public place, it would make tracing it very difficult. We are sitting on over a thousand acres of grounds."

"Yes," Annie said under her breath, her mind spinning with questions.

"I suppose Miss Wilson is angling to cover the story?" There was a warning tone to Frank's question.

"Of course. You know Emma," Annie said absently, still thinking how strange it was that three bodies had been found on the grounds. She wondered what the cause of death could be for all three victims because it was unlikely that Mr. Barnes died of the gunshot wound. He was well enough to walk out of Dr Gordon's infirmary. Maybe if she could find out what happened to the women, it could lead her to what happened to Mr. Barnes. Could the two young women have been buried before the designers of the park had started working? It didn't seem possible. The area had been ripped apart in the building of the mini city, and the bodies weren't that decomposed.

Frank patted her knee. "Not surprising. I'm sure she will find a way to investigate. That woman always finds a way."

What if Mr. Barnes's death was not related to the other two? What if he did die of his gunshot wound? That would make Bobby a murderer in the eyes of the law. Annie swallowed and placed a hand on the bodice of her dress, worry for Bobby flushing through her like water.

"Annie?" Frank asked, concern in his voice.

"What if Mr. Barnes died from loss of blood, Frank? That would implicate Bobby."

Frank sighed. "We might never know what killed Mr. Barnes."

"But if Bobby—"

"Annie." Frank's voice took on a soothing tone. "We don't have all the information yet. Please try not to distress yourself over this. You have more than you can handle right now."

Annie thought about Liza asleep in their tent and Alison, her long-lost friend who had come upon such troubled times. "Yes. Yes, you are right, Frank. I need to see this situation with Liza through." She leaned against him so the sides of their heads were touching.

"Promise me you will try not to worry about Bobby and try to get some rest?"

She was happy they had made up and didn't want to cause any more tension between them. Frank was, of course, right. She always worried too much. She already felt worn out and over-taxed with her performance schedule, and they had several months to go.

She sighed and turned her head to kiss his temple. "Yes, Frank. I promise."

And she meant it.

❦

After her afternoon performance the following day, Annie went to Ska and Ohitekah's tent to retrieve Liza. It was time to tell her that her mother had been found and she wanted to see her. Annie had thought about telling Liza when they had awakened but decided against it. She wanted to tell her without any distractions, and give Liza time to process the information without Annie having to run off to perform.

Given what the child had been through over the past year, it was no wonder she often seemed anxious and overly sensitive. The only time Liza truly seemed happy was when she played with Chayton. The two had become inseparable, and Ska and Ohitekah treated Liza as a member of the family.

"I have a surprise for you today." Annie ran a brush through the girl's auburn hair. Liza, seated at Annie's vanity, dipped a powder puff into a pot of talcum.

"Can I put some of your powder on my face?" Liza asked.

"Yes. Don't you want to know your surprise?"

"Is the nice lady going to take me to get ice cream again?" Liza raised her eyes to Annie's in the mirror and then playfully patted the puff to her face, batting her eyelashes and leaving white, peach-sized round spots on her cheeks.

"Miss Emma? No. She will not be here today, but there is another nice lady who wants to see you . . . Would you like to see your mother?"

Liza looked up at her from beneath downturned brows. "Mama?"

"Yes. I've found her, Liza. She would like to see you."

The girl's expression of puzzlement clouded over with something else, something darker.

Unsure what the look on her face meant, Annie knelt down to her eye level. "Liza?"

The girl crossed her arms over her chest and declared, "Well, I don't want to see her!"

"But why not?" Annie didn't understand. The girl had cried herself to sleep every night because she missed her mother.

"You can't make me!" Liza shouted, her brow pinched low over her eyes.

Before Annie could say anything more, Liza jumped off the stool and ran out of the tent. "Liza!" Annie emerged from the tent to go after her, but the girl had disappeared behind a row of tents and vanished from sight.

A group of people walked down the row, accompanied by the Colonel, who seemed to be showing them around the encampment. The same young woman she'd seen sitting on the Colonel's knee in his tent hung on his arm with an air of possession and familiarity about her that unnerved Annie.

"Well, folks, you are in for a treat," said the Colonel to the group. "Here is our most excellent sharpshooter, Miss Annie Oakley."

Annie nodded, forcing a smile.

"It is such a pleasure to meet you." An older woman with an overly large pink hat approached Annie with an outstretched hand. "You are even tinier than you look on that beautiful horse of yours."

"Oh, she is small, ma'am, but she is mighty," said the Colonel with pride.

"Did you see a young girl run through here?" Annie asked, her anxiety over Liza making the blood pound in her ears. If she lost the girl and something happened to her, she'd never forgive herself.

"Did you lose your charge?" The Colonel's voice was pleasant enough, but the look in his eyes said something different. He was already upset with her for taking Liza in, afraid her commitment to the child would take her focus away from performing.

"She's probably just in the Indian encampment," Annie said, feigning nonchalance. "It's such a pleasure to meet you fine people, but if you'll excuse me . . ." Before the Colonel could protest, Annie left, hoping Liza had indeed gone to see Ska and Chayton.

She reached Ska's tent just as Ska emerged from it. "Are you looking for Liza? She is right inside, playing marbles with Chayton."

Annie let out her breath, relieved. "Oh, thank goodness! I thought she'd run away. Did she seem upset?"

"Not in the least. Why?"

"I've found her mother, who wants to see her, but when I told Liza about it, she got mad and ran off. I don't understand why she doesn't want to see Alison. It doesn't make sense."

"But it makes perfect sense." Ska smiled, her eyes creasing in the corners. She led Annie farther away from the tent. "Liza feels abandoned and rejected by her mother. From what you've told me, the child has been through a tumultuous time. She is only protecting her heart. This is not a bad thing."

"I suppose not. But her mother is expecting to see her. I hate to disappoint her." Annie frowned.

"You must give Liza time, as should her mother. This has been a hard adjustment for her."

Annie sighed, not looking forward to meeting Alison without Liza in tow. But she did understand now. She remembered when she'd been abandoned at the McCrimmons, and she'd felt as if her family had forgotten her, had gone on and lived happily without her. Alison would have to understand.

"Will you watch Liza for me?" she asked.

"Of course I will. Perhaps, she could spend the night with us? You look exhausted."

"I couldn't ask—"

"You didn't," Ska said, laying a hand on Annie's shoulder. "I offered. Just for the night."

"It would be good for Frank and me to have a night alone," Annie said, thinking out loud.

Ska gave her a reassuring nod. "Go. Find Alison, then spend some time with your husband."

A stinging sensation rose in Annie's nose as tears filled her eyes. She didn't know why she felt so emotional at Ska's gesture. She guessed it was because she had been under so much stress lately that the offer gave her more relief than she'd imagined.

"Thank you, Ska." Annie wrapped her arms around the woman's shoulders and left before the tears threatened to surface again.

CHAPTER 13

FLORENZ ZIEGFELD JR. INTRODUCES
THE STRONGEST MAN IN THE WORLD TO FAIRGOERS!
– *Chicago Daily Journal*, Thursday, June 8, 1893

ANNIE LOOKED AT HER WATCH PENDANT AND PICKED UP HER pace as she walked toward the gates of the Wild West encampment, hoping she could make it to the Woman's Building on time. Her performance had run over a bit due to the audience demanding Annie perform another feat with the playing cards. Instead of shooting a card head-on while Frank held it, she turned her back to the target and, using a mirror, aimed and shot with her rifle placed backward on her shoulder. It was a crowd favorite, and Annie often used it as an encore.

She only hoped that today it did not result in making her late to meet Alison. She thought about taking the electric cable car but didn't want to be waylaid by anyone who might recognize her and want to chat. She'd done her best to disguise herself with a severe bun at the back of her head and a large hat, but she feared it wasn't enough. Instead, she secured one of the Colonel's rented coaches that stood at the ready at the Wild West encampment gates.

Annie had heard so much about the Woman's Building since the fair had opened, she wished she had time to see it properly. It was the only building on the 1,055-acre grounds that had been planned by an all-women committee, and it was designed by a female architect named Sophia G. Hayden. Bertha Honoré Palmer, wife of the hotelier Potter Palmer of the Palmer House Hotel and president of the Board of Lady Managers, along with help from other champions of women's rights, including Susan B. Anthony, set forth to erect a fitting monument to the women's cause.

The building, with its model hospital, model kitchen, and a vast collection of art by female artists had been the talk of the fair. Perhaps on one of her days off, she and Emma could tour it properly. Emma had mentioned in one of her letters that she hoped to write a story on the building but had been denied in favor of her male counterparts. It was something Emma could not abide but, nonetheless, had to accept.

The coach dropped Annie off at the east lagoon in front of the Woman's Building. She alighted from the coach, thanked the driver, and then stood facing the building, admiring the beautiful white terraces, porticos, and colonnades. It reminded her of the buildings she'd seen in the Italian countryside, the ones that were built during the Renaissance. She particularly liked the statues of the winged seraphs set upon the rooftop corners of each side of the building. She walked up the steps and sat in one of the comfortable, cushioned, white wicker divans under one of the colonnades to wait for Alison.

In her mind, Annie rehearsed what she would say to Alison about Liza's not wanting to see her and what Ska had told her the girl was probably going through. She hoped Alison would understand and not be too disappointed. As much as Annie herself did not want the added responsibility of a child, she was fond of Liza and particularly enjoyed introducing her to Buck.

Annie recalled what a comfort Buck had been to her in times of trouble. It would be good for Liza to spend time with him. Perhaps Annie could teach her how to ride if the girl was interested. It would be very healing to her injured little soul.

Realizing she'd been sitting there for quite some time, Annie consulted her watch again. Alison was ten minutes late. Annie hoped she hadn't changed her mind, and if she did, Annie was certainly glad she hadn't brought Liza. The girl would no doubt see her mother's not showing up as further rejection. Annie stood up to get a better view of the carriageway leading up to the building. To her relief, she saw Alison walking toward the building wearing that familiar indigo dress. Annie waved to get her attention, and Alison waved back, acknowledging her.

As Alison walked up the steps, she looked unduly fatigued. Annie wondered if Alison had walked all the way from Englewood. As she reached the top step, Alison placed her hand against one of the white marble pillars as if to steady herself and then pushed off it to give herself momentum. Annie met her halfway and noted the dark half-moons beneath Alison's eyes. She looked as if she hadn't slept for days.

"Annie. So good of you to come. Where is Liza?" she asked, out of breath and scanning the area shaded by the colonnade.

Annie reached out and took her by the elbow. "Are you well, Alison? You look exhausted?"

"Yes, yes. I'm fine. Where is Liza? Is she all right?"

"She is. Why don't we sit down?" Annie suggested, fearing the woman would collapse right in front of her. Not letting go of her elbow, Annie led Alison to one of the cushioned divans. They sat down, their knees practically touching. Alison adjusted her hat and looked at Annie with expectation. They sat in silence for a few moments, watching people go in and out of the large courtyard just inside the building.

"Liza was not up to coming with me today," Annie started.

Alarm rose in Alison's eyes, and her cheeks flushed pink, color returning to them. "Why not? Is she ill?"

"No. She is perfectly well. She is playing with an Indian boy she has befriended."

"An Indian boy?" Alison looked even more alarmed.

"I trust his mother implicitly," Annie said to quash any fears Alison might have. She took for granted that not everyone lived with the Indians on a daily basis. Alison, like many people who'd resided in big cities, had likely never actually seen one and only based her opinion of Native people according to what was written about them in dime novels or newspapers.

"But why did she not come? I thought you said she needed to see me. I *need* to see her." Alison's face paled again, and a slight shimmer of perspiration covered her forehead.

"We need to give her some time. This has been a difficult adjustment for her," Annie said. She could see from Alison's demeanor and pallid features that it had been just as difficult for her.

"She is angry with me," Alison said, her chin quivering. "I've lost her."

"No, no, no." Annie put her fingertips to Alison's knee. "You've not lost her. She is just confused right now."

Alison slumped against the divan, resting back against the cushions. She pulled her handkerchief from her small handbag once again and wiped her eyes, removing some of the white powder she'd used in an obvious attempt to conceal her dark circles. Annie wondered how many handkerchiefs her poor friend went through in a day. She cried often, no doubt distraught at her situation. Alison absently rubbed at her arm, something Annie had noticed her do before. Perhaps it was a nervous tic of some sort.

"Is all well at work?" Annie asked, not wanting to ask why her friend looked so dreadful and wondering if she'd had some kind of falling out with the doctor. When she'd seen her before, Alison said she'd been happier than ever. She wondered why Alison looked as if her world had crashed down around her, why she looked positively ill.

Alison blew her nose into her hankie. "Yes, well, aside from having to endure Nurse Bonnie."

"Endure?"

"The woman is wretched, Annie. She has disliked me from the moment she set eyes on me. I don't understand why. I've been nothing but kind to her."

"I'm sorry," Annie said. She'd only been in the presence of Nurse Bonnie for a few moments before the woman had been accosted by David. She seemed quite terse, but under the circumstances, Annie understood. Did Alison realize the stress Nurse Bonnie might be under?

"And Dr. Gordon? How is he? Has he heard the news of Mr. Barnes?" Annie asked.

Alison squinted her eyes in question. "Mr. Barnes?"

"The man we brought to the infirmary," Annie reminded her.

"Oh, yes. We haven't discussed him since he left Lee's care. Why? What has happened?"

Annie told her, and Alison sank deeper into the cushions, her face going pale—or rather, paler. "Heavens. How awful. If Lee does know about it, he hasn't mentioned it to me. Probably doesn't want to worry me further . . ." She pressed her handkerchief to her nose and blinked, as if on the verge of more tears.

"What is it?" Annie asked.

Alison let out a shuddered breath. "There is something I didn't tell you before. I don't know why. I suppose because it is too ghastly."

Annie pressed her lips together, preparing to be shocked. How much worse could Alison's predicament be?

"Before Miles attempted to kill Liza, I found something very disturbing at our home. There was a food cellar off to the side of the house that he always kept locked. He said it was full of vermin and he never used it. One day, I could not find Liza. She had gone into the yard to play, but I found her in the cellar. Miles must have forgotten to lock it. What I found there, on the back wall, I didn't understand at first. There were various newspaper clippings." She stopped, staring at Annie.

Annie waited for a moment, but unable to contain her curiosity, she prodded her friend. "Of what?"

"Stories of murder from across the country—murders involving heirs of estates. I didn't think anything of it at the time. Since Miles was an accountant, I thought he was interested from the trust aspect."

"Oh dear . . ." A thought occurred to Annie that made her stomach seize. Could Miles have committed the murders of the two women? Did they stand to inherit a large sum of money?

Alison folded her crumpled handkerchief and placed it back into her bag.

"Why didn't you leave immediately?" Annie wondered out loud.

"I don't know," she said, shame washing over her features. "I had no proof of anything. I still have no proof of anything. But when Miles went after Liza, I had no choice. That is when I left. And because I didn't want my accounts accessible, I had to seek employment."

"That's understandable," Annie concurred.

"But Lee has done something that makes me very uneasy." Alison's lower lip twitched. "He had a lawyer friend of his send a summons to my husb— to Miles . . . To tell him of my death."

Annie stared at her blankly, not understanding. Then it dawned on her. "The lawyer has informed him that you have died so that puts your fortune in Liza's trust. And Miles could potentially have access to that fortune and part ownership in the company, but he needs Liza alive so the money won't go to charity."

Alison squeezed her eyes shut, shaking her head as if to chase the notion away. As Annie spoke the words out loud, she wondered what kind of lawyer would send such a duplicitous summons to someone. But she knew that not everyone had scruples.

Alison took a deep breath and continued. "When Miles arrives, Lee plans to tell him the truth, and to tell him of what I'd seen in the cellar, to force Miles into a divorce."

"So Dr. Gordon is luring him in to blackmail him." Annie could scarcely believe it. It was all so shocking.

"In a manner of speaking," Alison said, defiance in her voice.

"But if there is no proof—"

"Lee has hired a detective from the Pinkerton Agency to look into the matter. He plans to tell Miles that, too. Lee believes that will be enough to deter Miles from any further action against me. He thinks he will grant the divorce and leave the state of Illinois. At least, those are the terms."

Annie had a sour feeling in her stomach, and her chest twisted with anxiety for her friend. "It sounds rather risky. No wonder you're frightened and have doubts."

"Not in Lee," Alison was quick to respond. "But you are right. I am frightened of what Miles might do." Her eyes welled with tears again. She gripped hold of the side of the divan, and then a ghostly pallor washed over her features and her eyes rolled back into her head. She slumped backward, unconscious, her mouth hanging open.

"Alison?" Annie shook her shoulders. "Alison!"

Annie was just about to call out for help when Alison raised her head, her eyes blinking. "What happened?" she asked.

"You fainted. You are not well, dear. I need to get you home to Dr. Gordon. Stay here a moment." Annie stood and walked out onto the steps, waving at her coach driver, a reedy young man with a hawk-like nosed and a mass of curls sticking out from under his hat. He stood next to the horse, smoking a cigarette. When she caught his attention, he crushed the cigarette under his boot and strode over.

"I need to get my friend home. She is ill. Can you help me get her to the coach?"

The driver nodded and followed Annie over to Alison, who sat with her head propped up on her palm, her elbow resting against the arm of the divan. Some of the color had returned to her face, but she still looked wretched.

"What's this?" Alison asked, alarm skittering across her face.

"This is my driver. He's going to help me get you to the coach." Annie said.

"It's not necessary, I'm fine." Alison stood and then immediately grabbed the arm of the divan as her knees buckled. The driver, quick on his feet, had her by the arm in a breadth of a second and wrapped his other arm around her waist.

"I've got you, miss." His voice was surprisingly deep and resonant, and did not match his wiry, gazelle-thin frame.

"Oh. Very well," said Alison in a whisper, as if too weak to use the full timbre of her voice.

Annie stood on the other side of Alison and wrapped her arm around her waist, too, not that she needed to help the strong young man but out of concern. She wanted physical contact with her friend. She swallowed down the walnut-sized lump that ached in her throat, surprised at her emotions. Alison had been so dear to her as a child, and now, having been reunited, Annie feared losing her all over again.

As they made their way gingerly down the steps, Annie looked up to better navigate them in the direction of the coach and stopped short, her heart in her throat. Peter Farnham, her too ardent and too earnest fan, stood at the base of the steps looking directly at her. He worried his hat between his hands, rotating the brim of it through his fingers. He was an attractive man, tall and robust with a sandy beard and long waves of light-brown hair, but his pleasant countenance was offset by the wild look in his dark eyes that had always set Annie's nerves into spasms. Sickness washed over her at seeing him, and nettles pricked at the back of her hands and over her scalp. How long had he been there watching her? Had he followed her from the encampment?

Grateful she had chosen to take the coach, she dropped her

gaze from his and concentrated on Alison and the driver once again.

"Miss Oakley," Mr. Farnham said, approaching her.

Annie ignored him.

"Miss?" the driver said.

"Please," she said, glaring at the driver, "keep moving. We must get Alison into the coach."

He obeyed, and they hustled Alison down the remainder of the steps and helped her into the coach. Annie climbed in behind her, and icy chills skittered up her spine as she sensed Mr. Farnham's eyes burning a hole in her back. Instinctively, she reached for her pocket, feeling the Derringer nestled there. The driver closed the coach door behind her.

"We need to leave. Now!" she said to him. She refused to look in Mr. Farnham's direction so as not to encourage him in any way and held her breath until she felt the coach lurch forward, the driver whistling the horses into a brisk trot.

CHAPTER 14

MARK TWAIN DELIVERS PAIGE TYPESETTING MACHINE TO
FAIR!
– *Chicago Star Free Press*, Thursday, June 8, 1893

EMMA SAT IN THE RECEPTION AREA OF THE *CHICAGO HERALD'S*
editor's office tapping her pencil against the pad of paper she
held in her lap, silently seething. Earlier that morning, she'd
received a telegram informing her that she'd been pulled from
the insurance fraud story and had been reassigned to the domestics column. This would set her back years. The domestics
column was a step up from the fashion column, but not by much.

She supposed this horrendous slight and insult was the result
of the bias against her as an investigative journalist by the new
editor of the paper, Ernest Kline. In their first—and *only*
meeting thus far—he had made it abundantly clear he did not
approve of women in journalism at all. Granted, she was fortunate be on staff as an investigative journalist, thanks to her
contemporary and idol, Miss Nellie Bly, *the* first female investigative journalist who had paved the way for women in the news-

paper business; however, it was still an anomaly for the fairer sex to work in this predominantly male trade.

At the time of said first meeting, Emma realized there was a chance Mr. Kline might not give her the best stories going forward, but she never considered he'd take her off the story she'd been assigned to by the previous editor and had been working on for weeks. And how would she ask to cover the story of the murdered women now? Well, if he wouldn't listen to her, she'd investigate and write it anyway. Maybe someone else would buy it. It would just be better if she had full access to the police force, which would be a lot easier with the clout of an editor behind her.

She looked at her wristwatch and then stood and walked over to the secretary sitting at the desk situated near Mr. Kline's door.

"I thought you said he'd be back by now," she said, trying to keep the impatience out of her voice. "I've been waiting for over two hours!"

The secretary, Mrs. Milford, a woman of substantial bulk, in height and width—a veritable giantess compared to Emma—with a pinched mouth and small steel-blue eyes, peered at her over half-moon spectacles. "Well, as you can see, he is not." Mrs. Milford's eyebrows arched high into her forehead.

Emma had begun to wonder if Mr. Kline was in his office, after all. Perhaps he just didn't have the courage to face her.

She raised her chin and took in a deep breath, steadying herself for control. She had half a mind to go knock on the door of his office herself but refrained. Annoying him would do nothing to help her cause.

She turned her wrist to look at her watch again and sighed. She was supposed to meet Mitchell for lunch in twenty minutes. If she didn't hail a cab soon, she'd never make it. She'd have to come back to talk to Mr. Kline later.

"Tell Mr. Kline that I will be back to see him. He's not going to get away with not giving me an explanation. I'll sit here all day long if I have to," she said, exasperated. "But not today. I have plans today. If I didn't, I would be here *all day*. You be sure to tell him. I won't leave until I get my answer. He won't be able to come in or go out without seeing me. He'll have to avoid the office altogether, and I know he can't do that." She knew she was rambling, even without viewing the blank yet patronizing expression on Mrs. Milford's matronly face.

"Is that all?" Mrs. Milford asked, monotone.

"Yes, that is all. I'll be back. I promise." Unable to bear the look on Mrs. Milford's face any longer, Emma turned on her heel and walked out.

"The domestics column, I daresay," she muttered under her breath.

Out in the street, she hailed a horse-drawn cab and climbed in. "The Palmer House in the Loop," she said to the driver.

She settled her skirts and then took in a deep breath, trying to calm herself.

If he doesn't give me the story back and support me in the story of the murders. I'll go to the rival paper, the Chicago Star Free Press. Hell, I'll start my own paper!

At the latter thought, she smiled to herself. Why not start a paper? She was almost certain she could persuade her father to finance it, or even partner with her, albeit silently. He'd never admit it to her mother, or perhaps even to himself, but he was darned proud of his girl for using her brains and her talent to make something of herself. Her own paper! Tingles skittered up her spine and down her arms at the thought. She could write whatever she wanted, cover whatever stories she wanted. Ah, the freedom! It would be bliss.

But reality snuck into her enthusiastic planning. She needed time to start a paper, to get the momentum going, to convince her father she needed the funding. In the meantime, she wanted to cover the murders and get the insurance fraud story back—or she'd take her information to the *Star Free Press*. They were always looking for well-written stories and savvy reporters. And she was determined to find a way to investigate the murders, come hell or high water.

The cab stopped in front of the seven-story Palmer House Hotel. Classic in structure with its Corinthian-style columns, the Palmer House was one of the most luxurious hotels of its time and a favorite of Emma's. Her father had maintained rooms there for a decade after it had been remodeled and restructured by its owner, Potter Palmer. Bertha, his wife, had spared no expense with the furnishings including her friend Claude Monet's paintings. Emma had once covered a story of the artwork as Bertha had accumulated the largest Impressionist collection outside of France.

Emma paid the driver after he helped her down from the cab. She entered the hotel, and as she usually did, she stopped for a moment in the lobby and took in its opulence. She looked up at the breathtaking ceiling fresco painted by the French painter Louis Pierre Rigal. Oh, how she loved the finer things in life!

Smoothing her hair with a gloved hand, she made her way to the Lockwood Restaurant and Bar where she was to meet Mitchell.

She breezed into the restaurant to find him sitting at a table, casually smoking a pipe. He rose when she approached him, his smile nearly breaking his face. The adoring expression in his large, hazel eyes tugged at her heart.

My, but he is handsome in his double-breasted frock coat and white winged-collared shirt.

He greeted her with a featherlight kiss on the cheek, and she breathed in his familiar scent of pine trees and spicy pipe tobacco.

"I'm sorry I'm late. Mr. Kline kept me waiting." Emma seated herself in the chair he'd pulled out for her.

"Ah. Did he give you the story back?" he asked as he sat back down.

"No. He wasn't there. Or that's what Mrs. Milford said. I will have to go again. I'll just keep going until he talks to me," she said. "For the life of me, I don't understand what happened. I know he doesn't approve of female journalists, but he seemed impressed with my coverage of the steelworkers story. If he doesn't give the insurance fraud story back, I'll quit. Besides, I have another plan."

"Really? Care to share it?" Mitchell leaned closer to her, his gaze roaming over her face, his scent making her feel flush. The way he looked at her, as if he wanted to ravish her right then and there, made her tingle all the way down to her toes. She wondered if he worried about someone he knew seeing them together. If someone did recognize him, there would be no hiding the fact that they shared something intimate. With this public display of affection, he was playing with fire, risking his reputation, risking his father's disapproval. As much as it concerned her, his boldness also thrilled her.

"Not yet. I need to think on it some more," she said, moving away from him slightly, his nearness making her feel uncomfortably warm.

"I'm disappointed," he said. "Not in the fact that you aren't sharing—I understand a woman has to keep some things to herself—but that you won't be on the story any longer. I was rather enjoying working with you on the insurance fraud investigations."

She smiled at him and resisted the urge to brush away a wisp of hair that had fallen onto his forehead. "I know. But I can still help. I also plan to cover the story of the two mystery bodies at Jackson Park. I just hope Mr. Kline doesn't beat me to it."

"Speaking of which," he added, a more serious tone to his voice, "you might find this of interest. One of the women found on the fairgrounds has been identified—a Millie Turnbill."

"You don't say." Emma's romantic notions were immediately swept aside and replaced with the hunger for information that always seemed insatiable when she wanted a story, even if it wasn't hers. "Did a family member identify her?"

"No. So far, it seems that the poor girl had no family. Apparently, the police found a piece of paper in her handbag with an address on it. It was to a boarding house. According to the couple who runs the place, Miss Turnbill had lived there for just under a month. She had recently moved from a work-for-rent situation in Englewood. Said she and her employer didn't get on. The couple grew concerned when she hadn't returned for several days so opened her room to find that all her belongings were still there, but the place was an absolute mess. Food on the table, tea grown cold in the pot, bed unmade. According to the woman, Miss Turnbill was always neat as a pin. Seemed the girl left in a hurry."

"How did you get wind of this?" Emma asked, her eyes riveted to his face, waiting for more detail.

"The police paid our offices a visit, inquiring into a substantial life insurance policy the woman had taken out on herself. They'd found a copy in a dresser drawer."

"If she had no family, why would she take out a life insurance policy on herself? Who would stand to benefit?" Emma asked, intrigued.

"A man by the name of Gregory L. Harris," Mitchell said.

"Do the police suspect him of the murder?"

"They didn't say. I'm sure they will look into it, though his address is in Adamsville, Tennessee. We've sent him notification of her death."

"That doesn't mean he isn't here in Chicago. There are thousands of visitors for the Exhibition. But did he kill her? Who is he? If he stands to gain by her death, he certainly has motive." Emma tapped her index finger against her cheek, thinking.

Mitchell reached up toward her face and grasped her hand. He took it in both of his and lowered it to the table. His hands were strong and warm, and they completely engulfed hers. "Of course. But sometimes tracking down a beneficiary can take weeks, months, or even years. And just because he stands to benefit doesn't mean he is a murderer. Really, my dear, that mind of yours."

Emma was about to pull her hand away, but he drew it to his lips, setting a light kiss on her fingers. Her stomach flipped at the feel of his soft mouth and at the boldness of his action in such a public place.

"A business lunch, I see." A sharp voice made Emma jump, and she turned to see a woman standing at the table. She was tall, pretty, with delicate features, and her eyes were so pale they looked like ice. She had a wispy-thin body that looked as if it might bend like a willow in the breeze.

Mitchell dropped Emma's hand and shot up from the chair. "Anna!" he croaked. "Darling, what are you doing here?"

Emma's heart plummeted to her stomach.

"I knew it was her," Anna said. "I could tell the way you both ogled each other at the Christmas party last year." Her chin jutted out, and the nostrils of her refined nose flared.

Emma hadn't formally met Mrs. Hargrove at the Christmas party Mitchell's father had held last year here at the hotel, as there had been over one hundred people in attendance. And she and Mitchell hadn't even started seeing each other until the last few months.

Anna turned to Emma. "How's the newspaper business?" Her words came out clipped, with an edge.

Emma swallowed, hoping the heat she felt crawling up her neck and into her face didn't show.

"Anna, this isn't how it looks," Mitchell said, his words coming out in a rush.

Anna ignored him, her attention still focused on Emma.

Emma felt a stab of disappointment at Mitchell's denial of their love. "It's . . . um," She was taken aback by Anna's attempt at what could be polite small talk, but somehow she knew it wasn't.

"Over for you at the *Herald*. I've personally seen to that." Anna's lips widened into a smile, but her eyes still bore the hard coldness of a glacier. "Really, who do you think you are, Miss

Wilson? Working in a man's field . . . You are a disgrace to womanhood."

Emma blinked at the venom in the woman's tone and stifled a gasp. "But how did you—"

"Ernest Kline is a dear friend of my family's," Anna said, triumph in her eyes. "He'd do just about anything for me."

Emma's heart slammed into her ribs and the sensation made her light-headed. So Anna had been responsible for her losing the story—perhaps, soon, her job. Was that why Mr. Kline wouldn't see her? She cleared her throat to prevent herself from gagging, feeling the eyes of the other diners on them. She wanted to run from the room.

"Anna," Mitchell said through clenched teeth, finally finding the strength of his voice. "We will discuss this later."

Anna turned to her husband. "Of course, darling. Anything you say. But for your own sake, and mine, please stop embarrassing yourself by cavorting with this harlot, or I'll do more than get her fired. I will tell your father. I'd hate to think of what an upstanding, good, and righteous Catholic man would think of this devilry. If I can't put a stop to it, he will."

"Will you excuse us, Miss Wilson?" Mitchell asked, his eyes frantic with concern, or embarrassment, or shame—she couldn't be sure which. Either way, the look on his face tied her stomach in knots.

Not able to find words—and even if she could, unable to speak because of the stone lodged in her throat—Emma nodded and watched as Mitchell grasped hold of his wife's elbow and escorted her from the dining room. Emma wanted to crawl under the table and hide within the cover of the white linen cloth until the restaurant closed. Her heart ached with the reality that Mitchell had not defended their relationship, that he had not stood up to his wife and declared his love for her. But then again, why would he?

CHAPTER 15

EGYPTIAN EXHIBIT AT COLUMBIAN WORLD'S FAIR NOT TO BE
MISSED!
— *Chicago Daily Journal*, Thursday, June 8, 1893

WHEN ANNIE HAD GOTTEN ALISON INTO THE HOUSE, SHE
helped Beth get her to her bed. They perched her atop it, each
of them holding on to an arm. Beth nodded and said she would
help Alison undress. Annie left the room and waited outside the
door until Beth re-emerged.

"I'll go fetch Dr. Gordon," Beth said.

Annie went back into the bedroom to find Alison tucked in
bed, wearing a white nightgown with a ruffled lace collar and
sleeves. The lace was shot through with a delicate yellow ribbon.

"I'm so sorry to have caused you any trouble, Annie."

Annie suddenly remembered she had a performance that
afternoon. She looked at her watch necklace, and her stomach
twisted. She should have gone into the arena five minutes ago.
She refrained from letting out an audible groan. She had never
missed a performance before, not even when sick or injured. The

Colonel would be furious, and Frank would be worried. Annie sucked in a breath, chastising herself, but she didn't want to make Alison feel worse than she already seemed to.

"It's no trouble, Alison. That's what friends are for." Annie swallowed, her heart palpitating with anxiety at what would await her when she returned. How could she have forgotten a performance?

"So you're ill?" Annie turned around to see Nurse Bonnie standing in the doorway with an implacable expression on her face.

Alison gave her a faint smile. "I feel a little weak is all. I'll be fine after I rest."

"I'll decide what's best for you," said Nurse Bonnie. "You are overanxious. More laudanum is needed, I should think."

Alison grimaced. "No, please. It makes me feel sick to my stomach."

The nurse pulled a bottle out of her uniform pocket. "You must rest. Dr. Gordon—"

"Did I hear my name?" Dr. Gordon interrupted her when he came into the room. "What's this I hear about you not feeling well, my dear?" he asked, approaching the bed.

Nurse Bonnie thrust the bottle at him and walked out of the room.

"It's nothing. I'm just feeling a bit weak," Alison said, smiling up at him with adoration in her eyes.

"She fainted, Dr. Gordon," Annie said.

"Let's take a look at you." Dr. Gordon lifted Alison's wrist and pulled his watch out of his pocket. He held the watch in front of his face, studying it as he felt for her pulse. It was then Annie noticed his cuff links. They were identical to the golden-faced lion door knockers. How amusing. The lion must have some kind of special meaning to the doctor.

"I like your cuff links," Annie said to him.

"Oh, thank you. Some of my favorites," said the doctor, never taking his eyes from the watch.

"He has about three dozen pairs of cuff links," Alison said weakly. "Quite a collection. He collects cuff links like I collect earrings."

"You are too silly, my dear," he said, smiling at her. "Your heart rate is a bit elevated, but you will be fine." He bent down to kiss Alison's forehead. "The dictation can wait until tomorrow."

Annie's heart was warmed by the caring gesture but concerned by the now even darker circles beneath her friend's eyes. Her cheeks were ashen and sunken, giving her the look of a skeleton. She certainly didn't appear fine. Perhaps Nurse Bonnie was correct and Alison needed something to help her rest. She must be sick with worry over Liza.

But the doctor didn't seem too concerned. In fact, Annie was surprised that taking her pulse was the extent of the examination. But what did she know? She wasn't a doctor.

"I'll just give you your injection and something to help you rest, and you will be right as rain," Dr. Gordon said. He set the laudanum on the dresser next to the bed.

Alison smiled weakly at him, and then he left the room. "He's so good to me," Alison said, her voice a whisper.

"I'm glad you've found someone so caring." Annie squeezed Alison's hand. "I'm sure Liza will be pleased to have a father again."

"Yes, in time. I've told Lee that Liza is with a friend, but he doesn't know it's you."

"What? But why?"

"Because I don't want *anyone* to know where Liza is. It would put her at risk. I want her out of the way until all is settled and Miles is no longer a threat."

"But—" It seemed like an important thing to share with a potential fiancé.

Alison shook her head. "I know him, Annie. He would want her here, and it just isn't safe yet. She's better off with you right now. Please?"

The look of desperation on her friend's face pierced Annie's heart. The poor thing was so overwrought with worry. "Shh." Annie stroked her hand. "I won't say anything."

Dr. Gordon returned to the room with a syringe in one hand and a teaspoon in the other. He set the spoon down on the dresser and approached Alison with the syringe. He deftly pulled up her sleeve with one hand, raising the needle to her shoulder. Purple bruises bloomed on Alison's upper arm, and Annie's stomach clenched at the sight.

"This arm is really sore," Alison said, wincing. "Can we use the other?"

"Not a problem," said Dr. Gordon.

Annie had to step aside to let him cross to the other side of the bed. He pulled up her other sleeve. That arm was also bruised, but the blooms had faded to a sickening shade of greenish yellow. Annie wondered what kind of medicine was in the syringe. Dr. Gordon administered the injection while Alison's face pinched with pain. In a few seconds, it was over, and Dr. Gordon passed by Annie again and went to the dresser. He poured a measure of laudanum into the teaspoon and offered it to Alison.

"Must I?" she asked.

"You must," he said.

Alison nodded and then took it without further issue.

"It will help you to sleep. You need rest, my dear. You've been far too anxious of late. Sleep is the ticket," said Dr. Gordon, winking at Annie.

"I was just leaving," Annie said, suddenly feeling the urgent need to get back to the encampment, reluctant as she was to face the music.

Alison looked at her with pleading eyes. "Wait until I fall asleep? Please, Annie."

Annie looked at Dr. Gordon, and he nodded with a smile. "She'll be off in a few minutes." He gathered up his things and left Annie and Alison alone.

"Your arms look painful." Annie couldn't help herself. The last time she'd seen bruises like that, it was from abuse. Her former assistant Kimi had been repeatedly beaten by Twila Midnight, the Colonel's ex-mistress. Suffering under the abuse by the McCrimmons had made Annie intolerant of that kind of behavior.

"It's from the injections," Alison said, her voice becoming thick.

Annie nodded. Though she didn't like the fact that her friend had the bruises, it gave her some relief to know they weren't from something more sinister.

"I have . . . I, well, I'm not sure how to say this, but I have what is called gonorrhea, from my work as a . . . well, you know. It is a disease that is passed on through . . . relations. Lee is so understanding. Most men would have thrown me out, but he wants to cure me. And if we are to be married—"

"I see." Heat crawled up Annie's face.

"I'm sorry if I embarrassed you," Alison said, sympathy in her eyes. "But it is the truth."

"I'm not embarrassed," Annie lied. "Don't worry about me. And don't worry about Liza. You just concentrate on feeling better."

Alison smiled, closing her eyes as the sedative got the best of her. In seconds, she was asleep.

Tiptoeing out of the room, Annie gently closed the door behind her. She was about to head down the stairs when she heard soft giggling coming from the room next door. She figured it must have been Beth. Annie wanted to find her to say her goodbyes, and she followed the sound. This time, she heard a man's deep chuckle. The door was ajar so she knocked and peeked her head in only to find Dr. Gordon and Nurse Bonnie hastily breaking apart from what might have been an embrace. The room appeared to be his office.

"Excuse me," Annie said meekly, suddenly embarrassed.

Nurse Bonnie straightened her cap, tucking in a loose strand of hair as she squeezed herself between Annie and the door, never making eye contact with her. Dr. Gordon cleared his throat and fixed Annie with a confident, bold grin. "Miss Oakley. Can I help you? Was there something you needed?"

Stunned, Annie searched for words. She couldn't just stand there gaping like a fish. "No, Dr. Gordon. I was looking for Beth . . . to say goodbye . . . Do you know where . . . ?"

The doctor rested his fingertips on the desk, still smiling, still exuding confidence, or was the smile an attempt to cover his embarrassment? Shame? Perhaps she'd been mistaken. Alison spoke so highly of the doctor and reveled in the attention he showered upon her. Still annoyed with the Colonel for his inappropriate behavior with the woman in his tent, Annie presumed she might see infidelity around every corner.

"No idea where she's run off to," he said. "Shall I show you out?"

Annie waved a hand in the air. "No need. I know the way. Do tell I her said goodbye."

"I will."

A shiver tickled her spine as he continued to stare at her with a Cheshire grin. She promptly left the doorway and nearly bounded down the stairs and out the door, feeling as if she'd just been undressed by the doctor's eyes.

⚜

Annie stepped into the sunshine and made her way to the property gates, walking at a fast clip in an attempt to erase the last few minutes from her mind. She was beyond late and didn't need to rush, but the pounding of her heart at letting down the Colonel, her fans, and Frank wouldn't let her slow down. She had to get back to the grounds as quickly as possible. She'd figure out what to say to smooth over the situation on the way there.

As she exited the gates, she turned left onto the street in search of the coach she'd come in. Spotting it, she started to jog over to it, but then she stopped short, her breath catching in her throat. Standing near the door of the coach was Mr. Farnham, smiling like a fool.

"What are you doing here? Where is my driver?" Annie demanded.

Mr. Farnham lazily put his fingers into the pockets of his waistcoat. He looked like the Big Bad Wolf who'd just eaten her driver.

"Call of nature," he said. "Told him I was an old friend of yours and that I'd mind the coach till he got back."

The thumping in Annie's chest made her feel light-headed and weak. She lowered her hand to her dress pocket to feel the reassuring hardness of the Derringer pistol that lay within it. "Step away from the coach, Mr. Farnham." Annie kept her voice steady.

"Look, Miss Oakley, I just want to talk. It's so good to see you again." Mr. Farnham stepped closer. Annie held her ground and reached into her pocket. She knew if she retreated in any way, he would have the upper hand. "What's wrong with your friend? She looked distressed."

"It's none of your business." Annie's hand went around the butt of the pistol. He must have followed them from the Woman's Building. "Please step away from my coach."

Where is that driver?

Mr. Farnham's smile vanished, and it was replaced by a look of dejection. "Did you read my letters?"

Annie's jaw clenched. "My husband intercepts them. I'm not interested in your letters."

Mr. Farnham's face hardened. "Your husband is quite the catch, isn't he? Handsome, strong, a famous marksman. I guess most women think him to be Prince Charming. Women like that gypsy with the horses."

Tingles of adrenaline spread through the back of Annie's hands and up her arms. So Mr. Farnham had been on the show grounds. How had no one noticed? Frank had given everyone explicit instructions to be on the lookout for Mr. Farnham wherever the show traveled. Though, she supposed with all the people swarming through the camp, the public and the players, it would be hard to single him out. He also had a way of blending in with his benign features.

Annie didn't respond. If the driver did not return soon, she would go back in the house.

"That pretty little girl who's been hanging around . . , She a relative? I know you don't have any children." Mr. Farnham smiled again, taking another step closer. Annie's blood froze in her veins at his mention of Liza. "Come to think of it, she looks a bit like your ailing friend but with darker hair. What's the little girl's name?"

"You don't need to know her name," she said to Mr. Farnham, her voice almost a growl.

Just then, the driver came jogging up to the coach. "Sorry, Miss Oakley. Didn't mean to be gone so long." The driver, oblivious to Annie's distress, went to the coach door and opened it for her.

Without a word, Annie pushed past Mr. Farnham. He reached out and grabbed her elbow.

"Don't touch me!" Annie shouted, rage overtaking her.

Mr. Farnham released her elbow and raised his hands in the air as if in surrender. Annie stepped up into the coach, and the driver closed the door.

"Everything okay, Miss Oakley?" he asked.

"Fine. Just get me to the grounds. Fast." She could sense Mr. Farnham's eyes on her profile, and in her periphery, she could see he hadn't moved. She refused to look at him. The coach bounced as the driver took his seat up front. He clucked to the horse, and the coach lurched forward.

When the coach rounded the next corner, Annie finally let out a shaky breath. Tears pricked the back of her eyes, and her mouth trembled. In that moment, she hated everything about her life: the touring, the friction with Frank, the show, Alison and her needs, and the constant demands of her celebrity. In that moment, she wanted to vanish into thin air, never to be found again.

৩৳৺

Annie stepped down from the coach at the Wild West encampment and thanked the driver. She tried to offer him a tip, but he shook his head, declining it.

She thanked him again, and her heart heavy with dread, she walked toward Ska's tent, head down, as fast as she could. She didn't want to have to explain to any of the show's fans why she hadn't performed that afternoon. She would have walked straight to her tent, but she knew Ska and Liza would be worried that she hadn't appeared in the arena.

A pang of guilt pierced her chest at the thought of making Liza anxious. The girl was already distressed at what she'd been through in the past few months, namely almost being killed by her stepfather and then feeling as if she'd been abandoned by her mother.

Annie perceived eyes on her as she walked toward the Indian encampment. Usually, she loved visiting with the fans, signing autographs, encouraging her younger admirers to pursue their dreams as she had. But since the Columbian Exhibition had begun, she'd been gripped with irritation and anxiousness.

I am so tired, she thought, which she rarely was except for when she had been pregnant six years ago. *Could I possibly be pregnant again?*

The doctor had said she couldn't bear children because of her weak cervix, but could he have been wrong? She shook her head in an attempt to chase away the thought. A knife twisted in her stomach at the thought of going through another miscarriage. It had been one of the most devastating events of her life.

Putting those dreary thoughts out of her mind, she turned down the road leading to the Indian encampment. As she approached Ohitekah and Ska's tent, she spotted Liza and Chayton playing marbles several feet away.

When Liza looked up and saw her, she dropped her bag of marbles and ran over to Annie, a look of sheer terror and anguish on her face. The girl flung herself at Annie and wrapped her arms around her waist, squeezing so tightly that Annie could feel the bones of her corset sink painfully into her ribs.

"I was so scared, Annie!" She sobbed into Annie's dress, and Annie stroked the girl's hair.

"What's this, Liza?" she asked. "Why were you scared? Did someone frighten you?"

"I thought you were never coming back. I thought I made you leave," Liza choked out.

Annie gently took hold of her arms and pushed the girl away from her, looking into her blue, tear-filled eyes. "Oh, sweetheart. You didn't make me leave. I went to meet your mother, remember?"

Liza sniffed loudly, a new wave of tears filling her eyes. "But you missed your performance. Ska said you never miss it. I thought you left for good or something bad happened to you." She buried her face into Annie's dress again, sobs racking her little body. Annie held her close, letting her cry.

Ska walked casually out of the tent, a knowing smile on her face. "You look like you've been through the wars."

Annie brushed off the statement with a weak smile. Liza pulled away from her and wiped her cheeks with the back of her hands. "Are you going to stay here now?"

"Yes. I'm not leaving the grounds again today. You go play with Chayton while I talk to Ska."

Chayton, watching them from a distance, came up to Liza, took her by the hand, and led her back to the game of marbles. Within seconds, Liza was giggling again.

"Are you all right, Annie? You look exhausted," Ska said.

"Yes. I'm fine. Just a little concerned. I ran into Mr. Farnham today. Apparently, he's been to the grounds."

Ska's eyes widened in alarm. "How was he not seen?"

Annie shook her head. "Everyone has been told to look for him, but with all of these fairgoers roaming the encampment—"

"You must tell the Colonel. And Frank."

"Yes. I know. I'm not looking forward to it. They probably both want my head right about now." Annie put her fingers up to her temples, envisioning the angry expression on both their faces.

"Why did you not return in time?" Ska asked. "It's not like you to miss a performance."

Annie explained what had happened to Alison. "I had to see her safely back to Dr. Gordon's house. I couldn't leave her. It couldn't be helped." Annie noted the waver of emotion in her own voice. Ska reached out and touched her arm.

"The girl can stay with us, Annie. I will see that she comes to no harm."

Annie bit her lip. She wanted to decline the offer, to say that it was all right, that she had everything in hand, that she could handle it. But she felt her resolve melting at the generousness of the offer and the undeniable truth that she wasn't handling it very well. She wasn't handling anything very well. She could never have asked Ska to take on such a huge responsibility, but now that she was offering . . .

"What about Mr. Farnham?" Annie asked. "He mentioned something about Liza today. Trying to get under my skin, no doubt, but—"

"All the more reason to keep Liza with us. I will keep her away from your tent and your performances."

Annie was about to protest, but she realized that perhaps Liza wasn't as safe with her as she could be with Ska. Ska wasn't performing. She wasn't in the public eye. "I see your point."

"Now that I know he has been lurking around, I will be more vigilant, too," Ska said, raising her chin.

Annie smiled inwardly at the woman's prideful countenance. Ska had been trained by her elder brother as a tracker. She had been an expert at finding horses that had been stolen from her tribe by their enemies, the Pawnee. Annie knew she could trust Ska's skills of observation.

"Maybe just for a few nights." Annie exhaled a sigh of relief. Perhaps Liza would be safer with Ska and Ohitekah.

"As long as you like."

"But how will I explain it to Liza? She was so worried I'd left her. I don't want her to think I don't want her."

"She feels as if she is not needed. If we task her with something that connects her to you, she will feel needed by you. When I was baking bread the other day, she said she wanted to learn how to bake. Maybe if we bake bread for you every day, she will have something that connects her to you and her fears of abandonment may be lessened. And if you come to see her in the evenings, it will reassure her."

"Ska, you are a genius. Thank you."

"Miss Oakley!" the Colonel's voice rang out.

She turned around. He and Frank were walking toward them.

"I will tend to the children," Ska said, offering Annie a sympathetic smile. "We will take good care of your Liza tonight. Perhaps I will take the children to the Midway tomorrow, get them away from the camp."

"I'm glad to see you are well," the Colonel said. "Imagine our surprise when you did not show up in the arena this afternoon."

Annie's eyes darted to Frank, who looked at her expectantly. "It's not like you, Annie. I was worried."

"I'm sorry to have worried you, I—"

The Colonel glowered at her, his cheeks pink with emotion, the whiteness of his beard shining in contrast. "We'll discuss this in my tent." The Colonel stalked off toward his tent, but Frank remained, hands on his slender hips, his shoulders taut with tension.

"Where were you?" he asked, his voice even.

"I had gone to meet Alison. I had every intention of coming back in time for my performance, but she fell ill."

"Alison." Frank shook his head. "Annie, once again, you have taken on too much. It is affecting your performances, it is affecting your job, and—" he turned his head away from her for a brief second, then faced her again "—it is affecting our relationship."

Annie's mouth fell open. "Do you think I wanted to miss the performance? Have I ever missed a performance before, Frank?"

Annie took in a slow, deep breath, trying to calm her anger before she said something she would regret. The problems with their relationship were not solely her fault. Frank had been distant, moody, and dare she even think it, emotionally neglectful, as he spent much of his free time with Frida and her darling boy.

She clenched her fists, trying her hardest not to let her anger get the best of her, but she was losing the battle. "And when you say it's affecting our relationship, do you mean our business relationship or our personal relationship?" She couldn't help herself. She knew her words would sting. Frank was sensitive about Annie constantly aligning the two sides of their relationship, making them one and the same when, as she knew, they were very different.

"Both," he said, his voice raised.

Annie clenched her jaw, annoyed that she hadn't seemed to ruffle him. "We mustn't keep the Colonel waiting," she said, not bothering to hide her sarcasm. "I assume you wish to be there when he gives me a dressing down for neglecting my responsibilities, even though a good friend needs me right now."

"Well, nothing *I* do seems to have any effect," he said, his words clipped.

With a sharp exhale and her fingernails biting into the palms of her hands, Annie walked past him, following the Colonel. Frank's footfalls, clanking with the spurs he wore, echoed behind her. She counted to ten, trying to keep her emotions at bay.

When she stepped into the Colonel's tent, he did not

acknowledge her. He stared at the evening newspaper he held in his hands, his expression grim.

"God Almighty," he said, throwing the paper down.

"Sir?" Frank said as he came in behind her.

"Look at this." The Colonel handed her the paper. Annie read: WILD WEST SHOW STAR BOBBY BRADY SHOOTS FAIR-GOER IN COLD BLOOD. CORONER'S REPORT STATES VICTIM DIED FROM HIS INJURIES.

"Oh no." Annie grimaced. She handed the paper to Frank.

"You best go get him, Frank," said the Colonel. "I'm sure the police will be here any minute. We want to show our full cooperation."

"I don't know how this happened," Annie said. "Bobby didn't kill Mr. Barnes, Colonel. I would bet my life on it. We must stand by Bobby."

The Colonel glared at her. "I want you to stay out of this business with Bobby. I need you focused, which brings me to the point of this meeting. You didn't show up for your performance today, and I must say, Annie, since we've arrived in Chicago, you have been acting quite peculiar. I'm going to give you a chance to explain."

Annie didn't know what to say. Should she tell him that life on the road for the last nine years with very little respite was getting to her? That she couldn't handle the pressures and demands of her job? That she felt like she might crumble at any given moment?

Instead, she told him the more immediate truth about Alison's illness. She couldn't risk being fired from the show. So many people depended on her: her mother, her brother and sister, Alison, Liza, Frank, and now possibly Bobby. "I'm sorry, sir. It won't happen again."

"See that it doesn't." The Colonel picked up the paper again and shook his head. "Now it looks as if Bobby won't be at work for quite a while, maybe for the remainder of the fair. I'm counting on you now more than ever, Annie. I need to be able to depend on you."

"You can, Colonel. I promise. But I need to tell you something else."

"Lord . . ." He rolled his eyes. "What now?"

"I've had an encounter with Peter Farnham. He made it clear to me that he has been in the encampment."

"What's this?" Frank asked, re-entering the tent, this time with Bobby behind him.

The Colonel rapped his knuckles on the top of his desk. "In addition to all this other good news, Annie's number-one fan seems to have made an appearance in camp."

"Farnham? Why didn't you tell me, Annie?" Frank's voice dripped with accusation.

"I've hardly had the chance! I only saw him today." It wasn't fair of Frank to imply that she was keeping something so important from him.

"Settle down, you two." The Colonel sounded like the parent of two squabbling children. "We will just have to be more vigilant. And, Annie, you go nowhere alone. Understand? We don't know if this man is dangerous or just amorous."

Annie's stomach caved in on itself at the thought of being the object of someone's inappropriate infatuation—and that he kept showing up. No good would come from this.

"I'll alert Nate," the Colonel said, jotting down a note. "Frank, would you be so kind as to give him this when you leave?"

Frank took the note.

"Mr. Butler said you wanted to see me, Colonel?" Bobby had taken off his hat and was twisting it in his hands, as he always did when nervous.

"I think you'll need to sit down for this, son. Pull up a chair."

Bobby glanced at Frank, then Annie, his eyes filled with question and concern. He went over to the chair at the corner of the Colonel's desk and sat down, placing his hands with the twisted hat between his knees, his arms rigid.

"You two can go," the Colonel said to Annie and Frank.

"I'd like to stay." Annie wanted to support her friend and provide comfort if needed.

"What's happened?" Bobby croaked.

Annie approached him. "It's going to be all right. We will get through this together."

He nodded, his eyes conveying complete bewilderment. Annie reached out and touched his shoulder. The Colonel glowered at her, but didn't insist that she and Frank leave, much to her relief, even though she knew the Colonel had little patience with her at the moment. He focused his attention on Bobby and showed him the paper.

Bobby sank back into the chair, the color draining from his skin. The newspaper slipped from his hands onto the floor. "But . . . but I didn't. He couldn't have— How did this happen?" He looked over at Annie, and she knelt down next to him, taking his hand. It was cold and clammy.

"I'm sorry, son," the Colonel said. "This is a blow, indeed. I know you would never kill someone intentionally—"

Bobby sat up straight, squeezed Annie's hand. "I aimed for his shoulder, and that is where the bullet hit him! It wasn't a fatal shot. It couldn't be. The doctor even said so. I couldn't take the chance of him shooting Annie!"

"Of course not." The Colonel's voice softened. "But you do understand, we are going to have to cooperate with the police. If we resist, it could make things worse. We will stand by you, son."

"We're here for you, Bobby. We will get to the bottom of this," Annie said.

"Anything you need," Frank assured him.

Bobby slumped in the chair again.

The Colonel sighed. "You two best go," he said to Annie and Frank. "I'll sit with Bobby here for a while." The sadness in the Colonel's voice nearly broke Annie's heart. Bobby had joined the show when he was very young and truly was like a son to the Colonel.

Frank reached out and touched Annie's sleeve. She stood, and they turned to go.

"Oh, I almost forgot," the Colonel said, stopping them. "There is a party at the Palmer House Hotel Saturday night after the performance. I expect you both to be there. Annie, you'll need to pull out one of those fancy dresses. Mrs. Palmer is quite particular, and with this latest scandal, we need to put our best foot forward."

Annie wanted to protest. How could any of them enjoy an elaborate gala with one of their players allegedly accused of murder? Would Bobby be sitting in a jail cell while the rest of them were hobnobbing with American nobility?

"But, Colonel," she protested.

"That is all, Miss Oakley." There was a distinct air of warning in the Colonel's tone.

Annie sighed, not knowing which was worse, attending a party when her friend's reputation and character were at stake— and with Frank when they were barely on speaking terms—or having to make nice with people she barely knew when she felt anything but festive.

CHAPTER 16

MAN'S BODY FOUND ON EXPOSITION GROUNDS!
WILD WEST PERFORMER BOBBY BRADLEY ARRESTED!
– *The Chicago Morning Herald*, Friday, June 9, 1893

THE FOLLOWING MORNING, ANNIE LAY IN BED STARING AT THE tent's ceiling, myriad thoughts swirling in her head. She pondered one thought only for it to be interrupted by another. She wondered how Liza was doing with Ska, Ohitekah, and Chayton. The girl was so happy in their company. She probably liked feeling part of a family.

She flung her forearm over her eyes, closing them and trying to still her mind, but it didn't prove successful. A sleepless night didn't help matters. It had been Frank's and her first night alone since Liza arrived, but both of them had been so exhausted they fell into bed without so much as a conversation, leaving things still strained between them. Frank had even arisen early and headed out before the sun had peeked over the eastern horizon.

Annie sat up just in time to hear a voice outside her tent.

"Miss Oakley, Mr. Butler, I need a word." It was Nate Salisbury.

"Just a minute." Annie grabbed her dressing gown from the

foot of her bed and slipped it over her shoulders. She quickly stood and wrapped it tight at the waist, tying it firmly around her middle as she made her way to the tent flap. She stepped through into the sunlight, her eyes squinting at the brightness.

"Yes?"

Mr. Salisbury took off his hat in greeting and his cool, brown eyes met hers. "Frank in there?"

"No. He . . . He got up early."

"Oh. Well, I have some news," Mr. Salisbury said. "Bobby was arrested a few minutes ago for the murder of Mr. Barnes."

Annie sucked in a breath. She knew it would come to this, but it was still a shock. "Poor Bobby. He isn't responsible, Mr. Salisbury. The wound was not a fatal one. I was there. I witnessed the whole thing. The doctor said—"

"The doctor confirmed that Barnes died of his injuries." Mr. Salisbury put his hat back on, pulling it low on his forehead.

"What? Dr. Gordon?" Annie could scarcely believe it. Doctor Gordon had said Mr. Barnes would be fine, that he just needed rest. "But I don't understand—"

"I'm sorry, Annie. We've hired a criminal defense lawyer, and he assures us that because Bobby has no record of criminal behavior, and the fact that the Colonel is so well respected, we can get him out on bail. He still won't be able to perform, so we are going to add another act for the Cossacks. Well, for Frida actually—to demonstrate her horsemanship skills."

Annie clenched her jaw at the news. More billing for Frida.

"Listen, Mr. Salisbury. Yesterday was an anomaly. I can take up the slack for Bobby. I promise I'll step up. I'll work harder. I thought maybe I could add some trick riding to my mounted shooting routine. Buck is so much more solid than—"

The manager held up a hand. "Our minds are made up, Annie. Frida is new to the show, and she's doing something quite different from the rest of the performers. The Colonel and I feel that she will win the hearts of the Exhibition crowd. We are on a roll, and we don't want to jeopardize that, especially with this news of Bobby."

Annie forced a smile, chiding herself for her jealousy. She knew she had to put it aside for the sake of the show, her own reputation, her marriage, and Bobby. It would do him no good for her to fret over something so petty when he could be facing a possible hanging.

Poor, sweet Bobby.

How could the doctor have said Bobby was responsible? He'd basically accused him! It didn't seem to fit his character. Or perhaps she had completely misjudged him. She remembered what she'd seen between him and Nurse Bonnie in his office.

"There is a lot of money to be made here, and we want to take advantage of that fact," Mr. Salisbury finished, snapping her out of her thoughts of the doctor. He bade her good day and reminded her when she needed to be in the arena for a practice warm-up. He'd never done that before, but she supposed she'd fractured his confidence in her reliability, and her stomach clenched at the thought.

She would perform at her very best from here on out. She'd have to find a way to help Bobby, care for Liza, and repair her marriage in her spare time—not that she had any.

❧❦❧

The sound of the evening dinner bell rang throughout the Wild West encampment as Annie watched Buck finish the last of his hay. Not in the mood for supper, she remained sitting on a bucket in his pen, watching him nose around for stray strands of the rich grass hay Mr. Post insisted upon feeding him.

As people flooded out of their tents, the barn, and various areas of the camp, Annie remained where she was, enjoying the time with her beloved horse.

"You headed to the mess tent?" Mr. Post came up to the fence behind her. She stood up, stretched, righted the bucket, and walked it over to him. He reached out a shaking bony hand and took it from her. His rheumy blue eyes regarded her with a fatherly kindness.

"I'm not very hungry right now. Maybe I'll get something later. I think I might take Buck out for a sunset ride through the park."

The Colonel said he didn't want her to be alone, but she had her Derringer and Buck was lightning-fast should she need to flee. Her urge to be alone outweighed the Colonel's orders. Besides, Ska had said she might take the children to see the Midway and Annie wanted to find them. She inwardly smiled when she realized she actually missed Liza and wanted to see her.

"Suit yourself. You want me to get him ready for you?"

"No. I can manage," she said, noting that her old friend looked particularly tired that evening. His leathered face had lost much of its volume in the past year, and the threadbare gray beard cascading down to the middle of his chest was tangled and knotted.

"You sure? I don't mind."

"I'm certain, Mr. Post."

"Okay, then, missy. I'll go get some grub. I'll be sure to check on your boy here later tonight. Don't you worry."

Annie smiled at his devotion to her and to Buck but wondered with mixed feelings when Mr. Post might take it upon himself to retire. She watched him shuffle away, his bent and rigid body looking as if it might snap with even the tiniest misstep.

She crawled through the rungs of the wooden fence and went to the barn to get Buck's grooming supplies and her tack.

After she got Buck's coat smoothed to gleaming, she saddled and bridled him, and mounted up. They left the barn area and set off down 62nd street headed toward the Midway. She settled into the saddle and exhaled, finally feeling like she was free. Buck's rhythmic cadence lulled her into a pleasant feeling of contentedness. As the sun lowered in the sky, the gray-white clouds blushed to soft pinks and yellows. She casually waved to people and occasionally voiced a "hello" when they stopped to watch her and Buck pass by.

Up ahead of her, several yards away in the middle of the street, she noticed a father bend down to meet the eyes of his little girl. He handed her a large lollipop.

"Is that you, Miss Oakley?" a spindly older woman with gnarled hands and a cane called out to her.

Annie brought Buck to a halt. "Yes, ma'am, it's me."

"Oh my!" She turned to the well-dressed, much younger gentleman next to her. "It's Annie Oakley, Jonathan!" She tottered over to Annie and Buck. "Oh, my dear, I think you are the most wonderful girl in the world. I have seen you perform four times. I do so love to see you shoot. And that handsome husband of yours! Oh, you are such a wonderful pair. Although, I would have loved it if you had married my son, Jonathan." She cackled at her own mirth as Jonathan indulged Annie with an embarrassed upturn of his lips.

"Why, thank you, ma'am. I appreciate your kind words."

"And you, Mr. Buck the Wonder Horse," she said, holding her skeletal hand out to Buck's nose. "You are such a beautiful creature."

Buck lowered his head, allowing the woman to pet his forehead and poll, the area between his ears. The old woman giggled with delight.

"Nice meeting you," Annie said, anxious to get on with her walk. She left the woman excitedly exclaiming to her son that she had "actually met the genuine Annie Oakley."

Her attention was drawn again to the father and his little girl farther down the road, and she thought of Frank and Liza. If they weren't under so much pressure with the show, she knew Frank would have probably been agreeable to the idea of taking the child in. He, too, had been devastated with her miscarriage and the news she would not be able to carry a baby to term. The father handed the girl something else and then turned and left the girl standing alone as he walked away. Why would he just leave her there in the middle of the road? The girl looked after him and then walked toward Annie.

Annie's heart dropped to her stomach when she realized the girl was Liza.

Annie called out to her. Recognizing her, the girl ran toward her, the large lollipop still in her hand.

"Annie!" she beamed. "Look what I got!" Breathless, she held the lollipop up for her to see.

Annie's heart raced, and she felt like it was going to explode in her chest. "Who was that man, Liza? Why aren't you with Chayton?" And why hadn't Ska kept a better eye on her? "Where is Ska?"

Liza shrugged her shoulders. "I don't know who the man was, but he was nice. He gave me this lollipop."

"But where is Ska?" Annie repeated. Her stomach fell in on itself. She never should have let Liza out of her sight. Then another horrible thought had occurred to her. Had something happened to Ska and Chayton?

"We went to see the jipson sibit." Liza sucked on the lollipop.

"The what?" Annie asked, trying to keep the panic out of her voice. She dismounted and took the reins from Buck's neck.

"The jipson sibit with the shiny-dressed ladies with straight black hair and dark circles around their eyes. They're real pretty. They had kitty cats in there and peermids."

Annie shook her head trying to understand. It suddenly dawned on her. "Do you mean the Egyptian exhibit?"

"Yes, the jipson sibit."

"But why are you alone?" Annie couldn't fathom how Ska could lose Liza.

Liza wrinkled her nose. "Chayton fell and hurt his nose. It was bleeding all over."

"There you are!"

Annie turned to see Ska and Chayton rushing toward them.

Chayton held a bloodstained handkerchief to his nose. "Annie, I am so sorry," Ska said. "Chayton fell, and when I turned around, she was gone."

"I wanted to pet the kitty cat, but it ran away from me," Liza said with a pout.

"Liza, you have to be more careful," Annie scolded. "It's not safe for children to be running around here alone."

Liza looked at her with large eyes, flooding with tears. "I'm sorry, Annie. I didn't mean to be bad. I just wanted to pet the kitty."

Annie took in a breath, trying to still the hammering of her heart. Liza opened her mouth, squeezed her eyes shut, and let out a wail.

"Shh," Annie said, pulling the girl close. "It's all right. You are safe now, and that's all that matters."

"It's my fault," Ska said. "I was responsible for her."

Annie shook her head. "Don't worry, Ska. Things like this happen. Everything is in hand now," she said, reassuring her friend, as well.

It was understandable that Ska would have been distracted if her child was hurt. Liza should not have run off like that. Annie would have to have a stern talk with her once they returned to the camp. Though, the girl seemed to have learned her lesson. Liza's sobbing gradually turned to light sniffles and hiccups.

Annie hugged her tight and kissed the top of her head. "How would you and Chayton like to ride Buck back to camp?" she asked.

Liza pulled away from her and looked into her eyes. "Really, Annie?"

Annie nodded. "Really."

"But I'm scared," Liza said, her lower lip quivering.

"There's nothing to be scared of. Buck won't hurt you. And I'll walk right next to you, holding his reins. What do you say?"

Liza nodded, a smile brightening her tear-stained face.

Annie took the lollipop, and she and Ska helped the children to mount, Liza in front and Chayton snugged in behind her.

"All set?" Annie asked them. The kids giggled.

"Oh!" Liza said. "That man said to give you this." She dug her hand into her dress pocket and handed Annie a folded note. She opened it and read:

My dearest Annie,

I've met your little friend. She told me that you are her ma now. She is a sweet little girl and loves you very much, as do I. I know in my heart that someday you will be mine, and we can be a beautiful family—all of us together, forever. I will be patient, Annie, as I know you need time to realize your true destiny.

Forever yours,

P. Farnham

Annie froze. With a sinking feeling in her stomach, she handed the note to Ska. After reading the note, Ska's eyes met Annie's.

"He must be following our every move," Annie whispered.

"Giddy up, Buck!" Liza said, flailing her feet against Buck's sides.

"Be careful, Liza. Ask him gently with a squeeze of your legs. Chayton, you hold on to Liza's waist." They both obeyed, and Buck moved forward at a leisurely walk. Annie and Ska walked ahead of him, Annie holding the reins and leading him, so the children would not hear them talking.

"This makes me nervous, Ska. Perhaps Liza should move back in with me."

Ska shook her head. "You are the real target for Farnham. The girl is but a consequence. You should stay separated, just in case."

Instinctively, Annie reached down into her dress pocket to feel the cool metal of her Derringer.

"He is just trying to get a reaction out of you, trying to get your attention. You must stay the course and not let this man influence how you live your life, Annie."

Annie sighed. "You're right. He seems to be harmless. He's just an annoyance."

Ska reached up and wrapped an arm around Annie's shoulder. "It's going to be all right, my friend."

Annie nodded, listening to Ska's reassurances. She only wished she could believe them.

CHAPTER 17

CHICAGO POLICE FORCE UNDERMANNED.
MAYOR HARRISON INCREASES HIRING EFFORTS.
– *The Chicago Herald*, Saturday, June 10, 1893

FRANK STOOD AT DIABLO'S PEN WATCHING THE SUN RISE OVER the White City to the east of the encampment. Its ascent cast a pink glow on the clouds above and the buildings below. The air was crisp and dewy, and the dusty smell of horse gave him comfort. He had hoped he and Annie could spend some time together last night to talk things out and make up. He'd missed their intimacy—the feel of her skin, the brush of her hair against his chest, the way she snuggled into his neck after lovemaking, their late-night talks and early mornings by the campfire.

He'd gotten in last night, only to find her asleep. It had probably been for the best. Her missing her performance, albeit for a good reason, hung in the air between them, and he certainly did not want to risk another argument. He knew she was dead tired and overwhelmed so he quietly got into bed without waking her.

Not that he got much sleep. And the little sleep he did get had been plagued with dreams of his brother, Kenny.

Frida's Ivan hauntingly reminded Frank of his brother. The carefree way in which he was around Frida's horses. His bright smile and dancing eyes when he spoke of them.

In Frank's dreams since the boy arrived, Kenny and Ivan were often together, or as one, the two interchanging and morphing into each other.

Diablo whinnied, and Frank looked up to see Frida with her prized black stallion, Shiva, heading toward them. Frida's hair was untied, and the mass of black curls hung down to her slim waist. She wore a bright-red blouse tucked into her black, wide-legged Cossack uniform trousers. The stallion pranced next to her, no halter on his head, and no rope to lead him. She carried Shiva's halter and a long, flexible, reed-thin pole in her hand, dragging the end of it on the ground. Shiva danced at her side like a faithful puppy.

"How is Kartuli?" Frank asked.

"Much better. Thank you for your help."

Frank nodded. "It was my pleasure. I hate to see any animal suffer. Especially a horse. We keep those herbs on hand for Buck as he's prone to nervousness, which seems to make him prone to colic."

"Well, I appreciate your kindness. The herbs worked wonders." She stroked Shiva's neck. "I am heading over to the practice arena. Mr. Salisbury has asked me to perform more routines in the show."

"He has?" Frank couldn't keep the surprise out of his voice. He thought they would have given more billing to Annie, as she was the bigger draw. But given her state of exhaustion lately, it was probably the prudent thing to do. "Not that you aren't deserving. You excel at what you do."

"The boy, Bobby, was arrested," Frida said.

"I know," said Frank with a shake of his head. "So you are filling in for him on his solo acts?"

"Yes."

Frank turned his attention back to his horse. Annie should be the one filling in for Bobby, but because she missed her last performance, he supposed the Colonel and Nate didn't feel confident about adding more to Annie's plate. He couldn't blame them, but he also couldn't help feeling disappointed—both with Annie and for her.

"Frank? Did I do something wrong?" Frida's brows pointed downward prettily.

"No, no, you didn't. Congratulations. I'm sure the fans will love to see you dance with your horses."

"Thank you." She gave him a dazzling smile. "Would you like another lesson? We can work on building Diablo's confidence and your communication."

"Well, I'm not sure that is possible with Diablo here, but it's worth a try."

Frank had been trying to practice what she had taught him in his first lesson, but it seemed the minute he and Diablo were alone without her, the communication fell apart. But he refused to allow himself to be discouraged. He could feel, however slight, Diablo's resistance to him lessening. Using Frida's suggestions, the last time he had been in the pen with Diablo, the horse actually approached him for a change. As he'd been instructed, Frank hadn't moved.

It was nice to have something of his own to work on. It gave him a sense of satisfaction and purpose, something missing from his life in recent months.

He took his watch out of his vest pocket. It was still early. He hadn't had breakfast, but he supposed missing a meal couldn't hurt. "Yep, I have some time."

"Wonderful," Frida said, opening the gate to Diablo's pen.

"What are you doing?" Didn't she understand? The horse would bolt.

"I'm opening the gate so we can go to the practice arena."

"But he'll just run off."

Frida smiled again. "He will follow Shiva. You'll see. Come, let's go. Bring the halter."

Frank plucked the halter and lead rope off the fence post. Frida surprised him by taking his arm as they walked to the practice arena, the horses following behind, Shiva at her right shoulder, and Diablo behind the black stallion, as Frida had said.

Frank wasn't quite sure what to make of her hand curled around his bicep, especially since he hadn't offered her his arm. In his travels with the Wild West Show, he knew customs varied in different countries. The women in France seemed to be much less inhibited than English or American women. Perhaps the women of Georgia were less inhibited, as well.

Several of the other players were at the practice arena already. Frank wondered if Annie and Buck would make their way over soon, too. He hoped she hadn't become too upset with the news of Bobby. If she didn't arrive within the next hour, he'd have to go fetch her, which would make her furious. The woman did not like to be told what to do. But she had to make her performances a priority, regardless of what was happening in her personal life.

Frida released his arm as they headed toward the center of the arena to be out of the way of the Indians as they raced their horses around the perimeter. Shiva's focus remained on Frida, despite the electricity of activity around them, while Diablo let out a frantic whinny, distracted by the other horses.

When they reached the center of the arena, Frida turned and faced the horses. "Now, let's try to get the halter on him."

Frank held the halter up and approached Diablo's head. The horse pinned his ears and backed behind Shiva.

"Remember, don't face the horse head-on," Frida said. "Walk with your eyes and your middle facing a little bit away from him. When you get next to his shoulder, wait."

Frank did as he was told. Diablo raised his head but didn't move.

"With your left hand, reach out and gently touch his wither.

This horse is asking that you respect his communication that he does not want his head touched first."

Frank raised his hand and ran it down the top of the horse's neck and laid it on the bony protrusion at the base of the horse's mane. Diablo did not move.

"Now scratch."

"What?"

"Scratch his whither," Frida repeated. "Have you ever noticed horses nuzzling each other's withers? This is their sign of friendship."

Frank scratched.

"Now work your way back from his withers to his neck and then his jowl, but do not turn your body to him. He sees you—a human—as a predator, like the lion waiting to pounce and kill him. You must show him that you can be like a horse."

Frank moved slowly, amazed that Diablo still hadn't fled.

"Good," said Frida. "Turn away from him and turn around so that you are facing the direction he is facing. Lay your right hand at his poll. If he seems comfortable, rub the halter on his neck and then on his jowl. If he seems contented with that, then try putting on the halter."

Frank followed the steps, and within seconds, he had the halter secured around Diablo's head, exhilaration coursing through him. He'd done it!

"That's amazing!" Frank beamed at her.

"It is proper communication," she said, patting him on the shoulder. "I think that is good for Diablo today. You have come to an agreement, which was difficult for him, so we will let him be rewarded with just standing quietly with you." She rested her hand on his shoulder.

"I appreciate you helping me with this horse," he said, turning his head to meet her gaze. "I've needed the challenge."

She smiled up at him. "Challenge? Your job does not keep you busy enough?"

He chuckled. "Oh, I'm busy all right, but I can do the job

with my hands tied behind my back. I manage Annie's career, take care of our finances, help with the show. I'm actually a pretty good horseman, too, but your methods of training are different, innovative. It's nice to learn something new, something challenging. Thank you."

She held his gaze, her smile fading. "It is I who should thank you," she said, her tone turning serious. "Ivan was so unhappy until we joined the show. Your kindness to him has helped with his grief—and mine."

The sound of a horse approaching from behind broke the invisible thread between them. Frank looked over his shoulder to see Annie sitting atop Buck, watching them, a crestfallen expression on her face. When they made eye contact, Annie turned her head, swung Buck into a pivot, and cantered away from them.

✦✦✦

That evening, Annie sat on the corner of a plush, high-backed divan as straight as her back would allow. The stays of her corset, which was pulled tight to accentuate the loveliness of her small waist, dug into her ribs, and she could scarcely breath. For the occasion, she had chosen a pale-rose-and-ivory gown trimmed with pink velvet. She felt as if she could fly away with the two tiers of lace that sat upon her shoulders like wings, but she rather liked the puffed sleeves that gathered at her elbows and then flowed down her forearms. Hulda had made the dress for her when they had been in France nearly four years earlier. She first wore it to a party she had attended in Paris celebrating the newly built Eiffel Tower.

The coach ride to the Palmer House Hotel with Frank had proved tense, with menial small talk of her upcoming appearances and performances. He'd made several attempts to find out what seemed to be bothering her, but she could not bear to tell him it was witnessing him and Frida gazing into each other's eyes. She didn't want to admit to him, or to herself, that she was jealous. Jealousy was a sin of the worst kind, and she had always been taught that it ate at one's soul like a cancer. She should be able to rise above the demeaning emotion, but at the moment, she was finding it difficult. She thought it best to remain silent on the subject.

He approached her now with a couple of drinks in his hands. "Coca-Cola?" He handed her the glass.

"What is it?" She took it from him and peered into the bubbly, dark-brown liquid.

"Looks a little like sarsaparilla." Frank took a sip. "Good. I think you'll like it."

She tried it, and her taste buds came alive with the sugary-sweet taste, and her nose tingled from the carbonation. It was delicious. She gave Frank a tight smile of approval.

Annie's gaze traveled to a corner of the room where she spotted Emma in conversation with a tall, elegant-looking man with well-defined cheekbones accentuated by a handsome mustache. But instead of the vibrant glow that always seemed to envelope her friend when talking to such a fine male specimen, the aura surrounding Emma seemed fraught with friction. Emma quickly wiped at her cheek, and stormed off, slipping through a doorway.

"Oh dear," Annie said, standing up. "Emma looks upset. I'm going to go to her." She handed Frank her Coca-Cola and left before he could protest. She was indeed concerned for her friend, but she also needed some space from Frank in order to rein in her emotions. She could not let her envious feelings run away with her. There had been too much strain on their relationship already.

She made her way through the crowd of finely dressed men and women, and followed Emma through the doorway. To her immediate right, she saw a door labeled LADIES POWDER ROOM and entered it. She found Emma in front of the mirror, holding a handkerchief to her nose, her cheeks pink with emotion.

At seeing Annie, Emma quickly lowered the handkerchief,

sniffed, and attempted a bright smile. "Oh, Annie. There you are. How are you, darling?" She wiped away some moisture left on her chin.

"I'm well, but how are you? You look upset."

"Oh, it is nothing, dear. Mitchell and I had a little argument is all. You know how that goes." She smiled prettily at Annie.

"Yes. All too well," Annie had to admit. "Would you like to talk about it?"

Emma shook her head, but her eyes welled with tears.

Annie took hold of her friend's elbow. "Please, tell me what is troubling you."

Emma waved her handkerchief in the air. "I thought I meant more to him than that. He told me he would speak to his wife about a divorce, but I just found out tonight, he hasn't."

Annie stepped back, Emma's words like a punch to the stomach. "His wife? Divorce? He's married?" She couldn't be sure she'd heard correctly. Could Emma really be involved with a married man? How could she?

Emma took in a deep breath, still not looking directly at Annie. "Yes. He's married. Unhappily, but also unwilling to divorce."

Annie felt the declaration like a blow. She thought she knew her friend, thought she shared the same moral code, the same values. "That doesn't give him, or you, the right to—"

"Please, Annie," Emma cut in. "I don't need a lecture. Not every man is as happily married as Frank." She finally looked at Annie, irritation shining through her emerald gaze. Annie swallowed, her friend's words hitting home that Frank hadn't seemed very happy at all in the last few months.

"But don't worry," Emma continued. "His wife has taken her revenge. She's seen to it that I be fired from the paper. So that is that. I have no job, no beau. Mitchell has made his choice. He didn't stand up for me. Everything he told me was a lie." Her voice cracked, and fresh tears sprung to her eyes. She pressed the handkerchief to her mouth.

Instinctively, Annie reached out and pulled Emma into an embrace. It pained her to see her friend, who was so strong, so sure of herself, so unbreakable, crumble before her.

"I'm so sorry." Annie held her tight while Emma sobbed onto the lace epaulets of her dress. "Maybe he felt he had no choice."

Emma pulled away from her and blew her nose into her handkerchief, the crying jag over. "Everyone has a choice, Annie. It's just that not everyone has the courage to make a choice. He could choose to be happy, but he won't."

Annie didn't know what to say. She didn't want to further upset Emma. Mitchell had chosen his wife, something Annie couldn't disagree with. Though, how could Mitchell have made the kind of promises he wasn't free to make? The whole idea was more than unsettling.

"You deserve better," Annie finally said, meaning it.

"I'm sorry. I should stop blubbering like a baby. After all, I love my independence. I don't need to be tied down by a relationship." She smiled with the declaration of her resolve, but Annie could see the uncertainty in Emma's eyes.

"Besides," she continued, her tone lifting, sounding like the confident, pragmatic woman Annie knew her to be. "We need to help Bobby. I saw the story in the paper. How's the kid holding up?"

"The police have arrested him. He's devastated, as you can imagine. To be accused of murder! You and I know that Mr. Barnes couldn't have died from his injury. He walked out of Dr. Gordon's under his own power. Why would Dr. Gordon say that Mr. Barnes died from the gunshot wound?"

"He may have feared he would be accused of medical malpractice," Emma stated matter-of-factly.

"What is that?" Annie had never heard of such a thing.

"It started in Ancient Rome. Written laws concerning the concept of *delicts*, *iniuria*, and *damnum iniuria datum*. That's Latin for wrongful conduct that involves legal penalties. It isn't very common in today's society, but if Dr. Gordon were accused of wrongful conduct in the care of Mr. Barnes, he could face severe financial penalties or be accused of murder himself."

"Oh. That makes sense, I guess." Annie was always amazed at Emma's knowledge.

"Interesting that Mr. Barnes's body was found on the Expo grounds, though, much like the two women. I think we may have a connection. If we can find out how those women died, it might give us a clue as to how Mr. Barnes died."

"That's what I thought. We may have a way to clear Bobby's name." Annie smiled, her spirits rising at the notion.

"Maybe. It's worth a try." Emma narrowed her eyes, thinking.

"But without your job—" Annie wondered how Emma would have access to any information about the women.

"I don't need the paper to investigate what really happened to Mr. Barnes, or those poor girls, or the insurance fraud story, in fact. I have my wits, my experience, and my skills. I have friends in the police department. I can write the stories and then sell them to Bill Havers, the editor of the *Chicago Star Free Press*, Mr. Kline's fiercest competitor. And I know just where to start."

CHAPTER 18

BERTHA PALMER ENTERTAINS ELITE SOCIETY OF
CHICAGO AT HUSBAND'S FAMED HOTEL
– *The Chicago Morning Herald*, Monday, June 12, 1893

AFTER BUCK SLID TO A DRAMATIC STOP, ANNIE SITTING
astride, sank her pistols into her holsters and tapped Buck's
shoulders with her toes. His forelegs rose up into the air in a
dramatic rear and the crowd cheered with thundering enthusiasm. When Buck's front feet touched down, she tapped the left
side of his neck and he sank into a bow, his left leg underneath
him as Annie waved to the crowd, a smile plastered on her face.
Buck righted himself again, and they took a final two laps around
the arena at a gentle lope, allowing Annie to make eye contact
with her adoring public as she waved herself out of the arena.

Frida stood just outside the gates with her team of black
horses, waiting to go on next. "That will be a hard act to follow,
as usual," Frida yelled to her.

Annie gave her a tentative wave. The woman had been
nothing but pleasant to her, which almost made things worse for

Annie. How could she feel so negatively about someone who seemed so kind? And she'd had no real reason to dislike the woman.

"You looked fantastic out there, honey," Frank said, walking up to her, a grin spreading across his handsome and tanned face. "One of your best performances yet." He gave Buck a few stout pats on the neck. It warmed her heart to see her husband beam at her. It seemed such a long time since she'd seen that face.

"It felt really good." Since she had missed the performance last week, she'd made a concerted effort to try harder, despite her lack of enthusiasm. Frank, the Colonel, and Mr. Salisbury seemed all the happier for it, and that eased Annie's conscience and made life at the encampment much more tolerable.

Liza had continued on with Ska and Chayton. Annie visited her every morning to receive the gift of bread, every night to tuck her into bed, and sometimes midday if she wasn't practicing. Ivan also spent much time at Ska's tent, and the three children had become inseparable. Much to Annie's relief, the Colonel had instructed everyone to keep an eye out for Mr. Farnham, and he had not been seen in the last few days, which made her feel less troubled about not caring for Liza herself, as Alison had wanted. Annie had been so busy with late-night and early-morning practices through the weekend that she could not give her full attention to Liza. With a heavy practice and performance schedule, having Ska care for Liza seemed the best thing.

Annie's pride was a bit wounded at the reality that Liza was much happier with Ska, but since Liza had moved out of their tent, Annie and Frank could coexist more peacefully, though their relationship was still fraught with tension.

Frank's interactions with Ivan lessened, as he was busy organizing Annie's schedule and working on his own horsemanship, which also eased her mind. Perhaps Frank truly was at peace with the fact that they would never have children. He had just been kind to the boy, and there certainly wasn't any harm in that.

Frank had told her he was taking lessons with Frida. At first, Annie was not at all happy about the declaration, but when Frank asked Annie to come along to watch the lessons, she realized her fears had been silly. She had attended one or two and admired the way Frida handled her horses, but she grew restless with wanting to spend the time working on her own skills in her own way. And it appeared that Frank's interest in Frida was solely based on her talent with the training of horses. Annie hoped it was true.

She curled her reins loosely around the saddle horn and dismounted, and she and Frank made their way back to the barn, Buck following.

"Any news about Bobby?" Annie asked.

"Yes. They're keeping him at the jail."

Annie stopped. "What? But why? Mr. Salisbury said they got him a good attorney, that he would probably be let out on bail. What happened?"

"Judge said he didn't want it to look like favoritism because of Bobby's and the Colonel's celebrity."

"We have to do something, Frank." Annie imagined Bobby stewing in a filthy jail cell, scared, hungry, and feeling all alone.

"We? Annie, you need to let law enforcement and Bobby's lawyer handle the case."

"Yes, I know, but—" She couldn't stand by and not help Bobby, who had been such a good friend to her. She would help him but decided to change tack in her delivery.

"Emma has taken on the cause with fervor. She got fired from the *Herald* and is more motivated than ever to have her voice heard. I'm sure she can help us—I mean, Bobby."

"Fired?" Frank stopped walking. "Whatever for?"

They continued walking, and Annie explained what had happened.

"Messy business," Frank said.

"Yes. I must say I'm a bit disappointed in her for entering into an intimate relationship with a married man—much as I don't understand the Colonel's periodic dalliances. Marriage is sacred."

"It is. But not everyone is happy in their marriage. People stray. It isn't right, but they do."

Annie stopped, but Frank kept walking. When he realized she was no longer at his side, he stopped and tuned to her.

"Are you happy, Frank?" she asked.

Silently, he placed his thumbs in his vest pockets. Annie's heart sank at his hesitation.

"Of course," he said. "Are you?" His words said yes, but why couldn't she feel it? Would he stray? How had they gotten to this place?

She sighed. "Of course." But she wasn't, and she couldn't pinpoint why.

They stood staring at each other for another moment, and then he took her hand and they continued walking toward the barn.

⊗✠⊗

Sitting at a table in the tearoom of Marshall Field's department store, Emma pulled a small hand mirror out of her handbag to check her face. She pinched her cheeks to make them rosy and bit her lips to deepen their color. She noticed a sadness in her emerald eyes that she tried to alter but to no avail. Her breakup with Mitchell was still fresh. As much as she wanted to admit she didn't *need* him, she couldn't deny she *wanted* him in her life. But the situation was impossible.

She put her mirror away and fingered the long-stemmed red rose that lay on the tablecloth at the top of her plate. All place settings were graced with a beautiful rose—a touch Emma found very satisfying. She picked it up and pressed the soft petals to her nose and inhaled the sweet floral scent, the aroma giving her an immediate sense of ease and comfort.

It had been years since she'd seen Carlton Chisolm, and she

was surprised he'd agreed to see her after all the time that had passed. She had broken his heart—something she could now readily identify with—but when she'd sent him a letter requesting a meeting, he'd responded immediately. She'd arrived a few minutes early to settle her mind and organize her thoughts. Inhaling the scent of the rose helped.

She glanced around the room. The patrons were mostly ladies out for a day of shopping, but a few of them were accompanied by gentlemen, no doubt here for the famous chicken pot pie or corned beef hash. She quite preferred the chicken salad accompanied by orange punch served in a delicately cut shell of orange rind.

"Emma?"

She turned to see Carlton standing behind her. He looked like the same lanky, carefree boy with sun-kissed hair, but now he had a smattering of gray at his temples. His long limbs and languid movements were still reminiscent of a graceful giraffe.

"Beautiful as ever," he said, taking her hand and kissing the top of her knuckles.

"Carlton! So lovely to see you. Won't you sit down?" She indicated the chair next to hers.

He folded his long body into the chair, and they sat, staring at each other in uncomfortable silence.

"I'm sorry," she said. "This is a bit awkward, isn't it? It's just been so long."

A waiter appeared at the table. Emma ordered tea, Carlton coffee.

"It has. How have you been?" he asked her when the waiter left. "I see your byline occasionally in the *Herald*."

"Oh, yes, well . . ." She felt heat creep up her neck. "I'm no longer with the *Herald*. I've . . . I've gone on my own. Independent. You know, it allows me more freedom. I can cover the stories I want to cover."

A grin split his face, increasing the shallow of his dimples that anchored his full lips. "I see. You've always had an independent spirit." She'd never quite appreciated his good looks before. Perhaps age and time had changed that.

"Yes. How are things in the police department?" she asked, wanting to take the attention off herself.

"Going well. I've just been promoted to detective."

"Oh, Carlton, that is wonderful news. Congratulations. And are you married? Do you have a family?"

His grin slowly evaporated. "I was. My wife died two years ago. We didn't have any children."

"Oh dear. That's terrible. I'm so sorry." She reached out and laid her hand on top of his. He offered a polite smile, but when his eyes reached hers, she pulled her hand away.

The waiter returned with their tea and coffee. Emma poured cream into her tea, acutely aware that Carlton's eyes remained fixed on her face. She dropped two sugar cubes into the teacup and stirred.

"Did you ever marry?" he asked, breaking the silence. He sipped his coffee.

"Me? Oh, no. I don't think marriage is for me—still. I love my work. I love my causes. I love my freedom." As she spoke the words, her sadness threatened to break through the veneer of her resolve. "Yes. My work is actually why I wrote to ask if you would see me. I wonder if you could give me some information."

Carlton shrugged his shoulders. "If it doesn't involve a case I am working on, possibly."

Satisfied, she continued. "I'm sure you know about this business with Bobby Bradley of Buffalo Bill's Wild West Show." Emma raised her teacup to her lips.

He nodded. "I do."

"Well—" Emma set her teacup down, ready to launch in "—I think the story has been blown entirely out of proportion. Yes, Bobby did shoot Mr. Barnes, but he did so in defense of Miss Oakley. Mr. Barnes had a gun pointed at her face. Bobby aimed for Mr. Barnes's shoulder, knowing it would not be a fatal shot. I personally know Bobby, and he really is the sweetest boy. I have also met the doctor who treated Mr. Barnes, and it was his opinion that Mr. Barnes couldn't have died from the gunshot wound." She stopped to take a breath and waited for Carlton's response.

Carlton leaned back in his chair and crossed his lanky legs. "Perhaps initially, but I believe we received a statement from him to the contrary."

"I know. But did the coroner actually do an autopsy?"

Carlton shrugged. "He did not. Based upon the evidence of the gunshot wound and

Dr. . . ."

"Dr. Gordon," she answered for him.

"Right. Based upon Dr. Gordon's statement, there was no need."

Emma leaned forward, lowering her voice. "But you see, the judge seems determined to make an example out of Bobby. He doesn't want to show any kind of favoritism toward him because he is a famous person, which I suppose I understand, but this is just not right. And I believe it might be political. The Expo officials refused to grant the Colonel participation in the fair, and there is no question his success is making those officials look bad." Emma took a sip of her tea.

"What would you like me to do?" Carlton asked, a hint of impatience in his voice.

"Have someone else examine the body. Like the coroner." It seemed so simple to her.

Carlton shook his head and indulged her with a sympathetic smile. "But it's not my case, Emma. I can't make a request like that. Besides, I'm sure the body has already been laid to rest."

"I see." She tapped the table with her index finger. Annie had said Mr. Barnes had no family so the body would be unclaimed. That would mean the body would be buried at the pauper's cemetery. She wondered what it would take to have the body exhumed. When they'd had Kimi's body exhumed, Annie had found convincing evidence for the request. She wondered if they could do the same in Mr. Barnes's case.

"Since I have you here, Carlton, may I ask you another question?" She gave him her most dazzling smile.

"That depends," he said, his sunny demeanor reappearing. "Say you'll join me for dinner tomorrow night? It's so wonderful to see you again."

Her heart leaped. "Oh. Well, I don't know, I—"

"Please. Let me treat you to a nice meal. We can talk about old times. We did have some fun, didn't we? Do you remember the bicycle ride along the shore that summer?"

Emma laughed. "My mother would not allow me to wear bloomers, so I got my skirts caught in the spokes and went head over heels."

"And that's when I fell head over heels." Carlton's voice lowered a register.

Emma felt heat rise to her face again. She and Carton did have many good times together. She'd initially agreed to let him court her just to spite her parents, but she did grow quite fond of him. It had made it especially hard to reject his proposal of marriage, but she had been young, full of rebellion, full of ambition—still was, really. Marriage would only have gotten in her way. But she did have to admit, she was enjoying his company. It was a balm to her hurt feelings over Mitchell.

"If I say yes, will you answer my other question?" Emma asked.

"Same case?"

"No."

"Oh my," he said, grinning. "What am I getting myself into?"

"Then yes, I will join you for dinner tomorrow night."

Carlton clapped his hands together in delighted approval. "Ask away, my dear."

Emma grinned. "The two women found at the fair . . . Do you think their deaths could be related to Mr. Barnes'? After all, he was found buried there, too. Did they die of gunshot wounds?"

Carlton shifted in his chair and cleared his throat. "You don't miss much, do you?"

"Not much," she said with a flirtatious upturn of her lips.

Carlton reacted to her smile with a deepening of his gaze. "Again, not my case, but no, they did not."

"Then what?"

"As of yet, undetermined."

"I see. Interesting. Will there be an investigation?"

Carlton shook his head. "I almost hate to admit it, but the department has been kept very busy. We don't have the manpower for an investigation right now. Could be awhile."

"Have there been that many crimes at the fair?"

"No, strangely enough. Just the girls and now Mr. Barnes, but we don't know if a fairgoer committed those crimes or not. Could have been anyone—a visitor or a local from the city. It's elsewhere in the city that our officers have been overly tasked."

It was not a great time for the Chicago Police Department to be inundated with thousands of visitors and a potential killer on the loose. And it didn't bode well for Bobby getting out of jail anytime soon. The courts were probably behind schedule on their cases, too.

Emma had a suspicion, one that was becoming more and more persistent, that the three bodies found on the grounds were the victims of the same killer. If she could find the link, she could vindicate Bobby. But how in the world was she going to do that?

❦

That afternoon, there was no performance as the Colonel and Mr. Salisbury felt the performers and animals needed some rest. Annie had taken the opportunity to visit Bobby at the Cook County Jail. To her delight, Beth had also shown up. Annie didn't stay as long as she had planned in order to give Bobby and Beth some private time together. She hoped that spending time with Beth would cheer her friend who—no surprise—was down-hearted and feeling hopeless.

After Annie returned to the encampment, feeling a bit down-hearted herself, she decided to spend some time with Buck. Basking in the warmth of the sun, Annie leaned against Buck's side as she watched him munch on a large pile of grass hay that Mr. Post had just tossed into his pen.

Buck raised his head, his attention caught by some passersby, and then he let out a relaxed, full-bodied sigh. He, too, seemed grateful for the break.

"Miss Oakley."

Annie turned to see Beth standing at the fence railing.

"Why, Beth!" Annie left Buck's side and joined her at the fence. "How was your visit with Bobby? Did you cheer him up?"

She smiled, shaking her head. "No. He was sweet to me, but I could tell he was sad."

"I know," Annie groaned. "It must be so terrible for him. How kind of you to give him some comfort." She reached out and laid her fingers on Beth's sleeve, touched by the girl's compassion. "We were all surprised that Dr. Gordon told the police he felt Mr. Barnes died of his gunshot wound when he had assured us Mr. Barnes would be fine."

"I was surprised, as well," said Beth. "I asked Dr. Gordon about it, and he said he couldn't be absolutely sure that Mr. Barnes would have been all right because Mr. Barnes had up and left. But when the police came to the house on Saturday, they were there for a different reason, not Mr. Barnes."

"What were they there for?" Annie hoped it had nothing to do with Alison.

Beth cast her gaze toward the ground. "It was Nettie."

"The maid?"

"Yes. Remember how I told you her sister had to leave Dr.

Gordon's employ abruptly because their mother was ill and Deborah had to go home and tend to her?"

Annie nodded, encouraging Beth to go on.

"Well, Nettie just cried and cried about it so I told her she should just go on home to Ames. You know, for a visit. So she wrote to her mother and told her she was coming home for a few weeks, but apparently she never arrived. Her mother sent a telegram to Dr. Gordon's house—addressed to Deborah. I thought it strange that her mother would send a letter to Deborah when Deborah should have been at home with her, so I opened it. She explained that Nettie had never arrived and she was worried. I wired her mother back and told her that neither Nettie nor Deborah was here any longer. She must have contacted the Chicago police. That's why they came to visit Dr. Gordon. They thought he might have some information on why the two girls might have run off."

"And did he?"

"No. He told the police he had David take them to the train station. Dr. Gordon believes that family comes first, and it was important for them to take care of their mother. He had told both the girls they had a position at his infirmary if they ever decided to return."

"That was kind of him."

"Yes. It's just like Dr. Gordon to be so helpful. He's been very upset since we've heard the news, says he feels somehow responsible. I told him it wasn't his fault."

Annie knew all too well what it was like to feel responsible for those who worked for you. When Kimi was murdered, Annie had been devastated. She felt as if she should have been able to prevent such a heinous act, as if she had been somehow negligent in providing the proper protection for Kimi.

"David . . . What's your assessment of him? I saw him threaten Nurse Bonnie the other day."

Beth rolled her eyes. "They argue all the time. I heard him threaten her just this afternoon. I don't see what Dr. Gordon sees in him. Well, I suppose he does need him to tend to the plants in the greenhouse. Dr. Gordon makes many of his own medicines. David helps him, but he's terribly arrogant—and not very kind to any of us who work for Dr. Gordon."

"How did he threaten her this morning?" Annie asked.

Beth lowered her voice. "Said if she didn't stop meddling in Dr. Gordon's affairs, he'd nix her. She got so mad, she left."

Nix her?

So David made a habit of threatening Nurse Bonnie.

"Left? For good?" Annie asked.

Beth shrugged. "I don't know. She hasn't been back for a few days."

"*Did* she meddle in Dr. Gordon's affairs?" Was there some kind of inappropriate relationship there? She hoped upon hope Dr. Gordon was true to Alison. She deserved some happiness in her life.

"She's his right hand. I don't know what he'll do without Nurse Bonnie. She can be a bit curt, but she knows her doctoring, that's for sure."

"I see." Annie rationalized that, of course, a doctor and his nurse would be close, but how close? Perhaps Dr. Gordon had been consoling her in some way. There could have been a variety of different reasons they might have been in an embrace, if indeed they had been. Annie wanted to get back to the topic at hand. "How did the subject of Mr. Barnes come up? With the police?" she asked.

"Dr. Gordon asked the police about him, said he treated Mr. Barnes for the gunshot wound. Then the police asked Dr. Gordon if he knew who shot Mr. Barnes, and he told him . . . told him it was Bobby."

"Well, I suppose Dr. Gordon had to tell the truth." Annie conceded that he'd been concerned about his patient, especially since Mr. Barnes had not heeded his instructions and had left the infirmary before he was well enough. He probably felt responsible for the fate of Mr. Barnes, too.

"Oh, I nearly forgot." Beth pulled a folded piece of paper from her dress pocket. "I meant to give this to you when I saw you at the jail, but you left in such a hurry. It's from Miss Alison."

Annie took the note. "Thank you. Is she feeling better?"

"I believe so. The color has come back to her cheeks, and she seems to have more of an appetite, but she is still rather anxious. She can't seem to sit still."

"Well, she probably has a lot on her mind." Annie knew all too well the truth of her words. The separation from Liza must prove to be quite a strain. Not to mention that someone was likely out to kill her. She wondered if Miles had answered the summons from the attorney.

"Well, I need to get back," Beth said. "Miss Annie, I'd like to help Bobby. Please let me know if there is anything I can do."

"Perhaps you can implore Dr. Gordon to speak with the police again on behalf of Bobby? Perhaps even request or encourage an autopsy? Your friendship with Bobby means a lot to him, and your continued support and visits will give him solace."

"I will speak with Dr. Gordon," Beth said with a shrug of her shoulders.

"Have faith, Beth."

"Yes, Miss Annie. Thank you. I must go now. Dr. Gordon will be worried that I've run off, too!"

"Then you best get back."

Beth hugged her and then walked away. As soon as she had, Annie opened the letter from Alison:

Dearest Annie,

I hope this letter finds you well and that you and your colleagues continue to be a rousing success at the fair.

I am writing to give you some news. Remember how I told you Lee had a plan to lure Miles to Chicago at the news of my death? Well, Miles answered the summons, and Lee and his friend from the Pinkerton Agency arranged to meet with him. As I had feared, when Miles learned I was indeed alive and that I wanted a divorce, he was furious at having been duped. Lee and the detective let him know they knew of his sordid collection of newspaper articles and that he was a person of interest in the murder of two women here in Chicago. Did you know there were two women buried on the Expo grounds? That and Lee's offer of a very generous sum of money was enough to persuade him to divorce me. The Pinkerton man has informed the police about Miles and plans to keep an eye on him and his whereabouts until the police learn more about the deaths of the two women.

Lee is working with the lawyer, and we are to meet with him in the next couple of days. My heart feels jubilant, but my body, alas, does not. I am still in bed but feeling a little better every day. Lee is researching an alternative to the injections to treat my condition, as the current treatment is making me feel so low. He's such a brilliant doctor, I know he will come up with a cure soon.

As soon as the divorce is final, Liza will come to live with us, and Lee is ecstatic at the prospect of being a father. Once we are married, and I am cured of this dreadful disease, we plan to try for another baby. Finally, dearest Annie, for the first time in my life, I will have a family. A real, honest-to-goodness family of my own. My heart soars as I write this.

How is my sweet Liza? Is she ready to see me yet? I don't want to rush her, but I would so love for Lee to meet her. He wanted me to thank you for him, for taking such good care of his future daughter.

Please write back to me as soon as possible with news of Liza. I miss her so!

All my love and gratitude,
Alison

Annie folded the letter and placed it in her pocket, relieved and elated that Alison and Liza would soon be taken care of and together once again. She thought about the lawyer's part in the ruse and wrinkled her nose. Would a lawyer really send notification of someone's death if they hadn't died? She'd didn't know much about the practice of law but felt certain that lying about such a matter was unethical. She shrugged. It really wasn't any of her business as long as Alison and Liza were safe, and Alison had mentioned the Pinkerton man keeping an eye on Miles and his whereabouts. And how much money had Lee given Miles as the bribe? Could it have been more than Alison and Liza were worth?

She felt certain she was not getting the entire story, but again, was it really her business? She had agreed to keep Liza safe until she could be returned to her mother, and that was what she intended to do.

Now, she just had to persuade Liza to see her mother. Given how Liza felt about her mother at the present time, it would be best if they had short visits, as she and Alison had originally planned, before the girl moved into Dr. Gordon's house. Small steps would be the ticket.

Annie would certainly miss the girl, more than she had imagined, but life would be easier for her and Frank if Annie did not feel under so much pressure. She could focus on Frank and on her performances, and give Emma any assistance she might need in investigating the murder of Mr. Barnes to clear Bobby's name.

Yes, things were finally looking up.

CHAPTER 19

ANNIE OAKLEY, FRANK BUTLER, AND JEP THE DOG
DAZZLE CROWDS AT WILD WEST SHOW!
– *Chicago Record*, Tuesday, June 13, 1893

ANNIE LAY ON HER SIDE, WATCHING FRANK SLEEP IN THE
warm glow of the tent as the sun began to light the world once
again. He slept on his back, his chest rising and falling in a slow,
steady rhythm. Her gaze lingered on his face, so still and
peaceful but for the movement of his eyelids.

He'd come in late the night before, and though Annie had
been awake when he crawled into bed, she had feigned sleep,
deciding that in the morning she would tell him the good news
about Alison's pending divorce and that Liza would soon be
joining her mother.

Jep, sleeping on the floor on Frank's side of the bed,
groaned a yawn, waking to the morning light. Annie heard him
pad across the wooden floor of their tent and slip through the
tent flap. Frank rolled his head back and forth on the pillow,
and his brow pulled down over his nose. His lips parted, and his

Adam's apple bobbed up and down as he muttered, "No," over and over.

Annie reached out and touched his shoulder. He woke with a start. "You're having a nightmare," she whispered.

He rolled his head to look over at her and then exhaled, his breath releasing like a floodgate opening. "I was. Same one again."

"About Kenny?"

Frank nodded and turned his head to stare up at the ceiling. He blinked slowly, obviously lost in the tragic memory once again.

Annie knew Frank struggled with the guilt of what happened with his brother. Though, it really hadn't been his fault Kenny had drowned.

She herself strove to overcome her responsibility in the death of another human being—even though it had been in self-defense or in defense of another. If she had not taken that action, loved ones would have died. If she had not taken that action, she could have died, and where would that have left her family? But still, she'd been raised to believe that to take another's life is a sin, and it was. At some point, she would pay a penance, but she reckoned the price of her own soul was worth saving and helping others.

A melancholy weight settled on her heart as she looked at Frank, who seemed so far away in his thoughts at the moment. She longed for a time when the two of them could be together, away from the show, away from their responsibilities, away from the distractions. Perhaps at the end of the Columbian Exhibition they could take some time off. Go home to New Jersey with Jep and Buck. Frank could sit in his rocker on the porch reading the newspaper while she worked in the flower garden, tilling the soil and listening to the bees drone on in her flowering bushes. They could sit in the chair swing Frank had hung from the large oak in the side yard, sipping lemonade, hearing birdsongs and watching butterflies.

"Mr. Butler, Miss Oakley?" a woman's voice broke Annie's train of thought.

Frank sat up and then pulled on his pants.

Who is it? Annie mouthed to him. He shrugged.

"Mr. Butler?" the voice called again.

"Frida," he whispered.

Annie rolled her eyes. "So early?" How incredibly rude of her to wake them at—she rolled over to look at Frank's pocket watch, which lay on the table beside her—6:00 a.m.?

"Just a minute," Frank yelled out to Frida.

What on earth would prompt her to disturb them at this hour?

Frank stepped outside the tent, and Annie listened.

"He's gone! I can't find him anywhere!" Fear laced Frida's words. "I thought he might be with you, at breakfast or something."

Annie got up and pulled on a dressing gown.

"I'm sure he isn't far," Frank said, his voice even and soothing as he tried to comfort Frida, just as he had comforted Annie so many times. "We'll find him."

Annie stepped outside the tent to find Frank facing Frida, his hands wrapped reassuringly around her arms.

"Oh, Miss Oakley," Frida said. She reached out and took Annie's hand. "I am so sorry to disturb you and your husband, but I cannot find my boy."

"Oh dear," Annie said. The look of fear in the woman's eyes suddenly made her feel bad for being annoyed with her. "Did you check Ska's tent? He's been playing with Liza and Chayton," Annie said. "Perhaps he rose early and went to see them."

Frida sucked in a breath, her eyes lighting with the shine of hope. "Of course! That must be where he is. I don't know why I didn't think of it." She ran a hand through the mass of tangles in her hair, obviously embarrassed.

"Come. Let's go," Annie said, squeezing her hand to assure her she needn't be embarrassed. "I'm sure he's with them. Liza has become fond of making bread in the mornings. She probably invited Ivan to help her and Chayton."

The three of them set off toward the Indian encampment, and as they rounded the corner of one of the tent rows, they saw Ska running toward them, a panicked expression on her face.

"Are Chayton and Liza with you?" she asked, wrapping a wool sweater around herself to shield her bare arms from the morning chill.

"We thought they were with you," Annie said, feeling the blood drain from her face.

Ska shook her head. "When Ohitekah and I woke, their bed mats were empty. I thought they had gone out to play marbles or had gone to see you."

"Let's check the stables," Frank said, his voice calm, rational.

As they all walked toward the stables, the Wild West encampment slowly came to life. Whenever they passed someone stepping outside of their tent or warming themselves with coffee and a fire in the gray light of the early morning, they asked about the children, but no one had any information to give them. Finally, they reached Buck's pen, situated in front of the wooden barn. Mr. Post was there, scooping up Buck's nighttime leavings.

Frank asked if he'd seen the children.

"Haven't seen a one of them," Post said, spitting some chaw onto the dirt.

"Where could they be?" Frida asked, her voice almost a wail.

A bloom of chills swept over Annie's arms and legs. "They have to be here somewhere," she said, refusing to give into her own fear. "Let's split up and cover the grounds. I'll get on Buck. Frank and Frida, you get your horses, and Ska can track on foot."

"The encampment is fifteen acres, Annie," Frank said. "They could be anywhere—or, they could have gone over to Jackson Park which is even bigger. I think we need to go to the police."

"Not yet," she said. "We can ask the Colonel to call a search party. He did it for Buck, remember?" When Buck had gone missing during Annie's first tour with the show, the Colonel had stopped at nothing to help find him. After the performances, he'd had all the cowboys mount up and search for hours, even overnight.

"With the current show schedule, we won't have the manpower," Frank said. "We have over forty thousand people coming to the performances today. He won't spare anyone."

"But Liza aside, what about Ivan and Chayton?" she asked. "They are the sons of his esteemed performers. Surely he would want to help Frida and Ohitekah, " Annie added, a bit hurt at the notion that Frank would think the Colonel would refuse to help her. "Going to the police right now will take too long. The children could be close by."

"We should at least contact the Exhibition Guard," Frank pressed.

"Yes," said Annie. "Good idea. Tell them about Mr. Farnham, too—that he has been seen on the grounds and knows about Liza. He gave her this." She pulled the note from her pocket and handed it to him.

He read it, his jaw flexing. He looked at Annie, his eyes as hard as granite. "When did he give this to her?"

"The day Ska took her and Chayton to the Egyptian exhibit."

Frank crumpled the note in his fist. "Something needs to be done about that man," he said. "If I ever get my hands on him—"

Ska came up to them, panic in her eyes. "We need to go!"

"Agreed," Annie said. "If we don't find them soon, I will have to alert Alison. There is a chance her husband may have taken the children. Dr. Gordon has been in contact with him and may know where we can find him." Annie thought back to the letter she had read from Alison, stating that her husband had agreed to the divorce and to leave Liza and her alone. But, as she had feared, perhaps he'd changed his mind.

Annie led Buck out of his pen, her heart racing. All three children were missing. They had to be somewhere on the fairgrounds. Annie remembered that Liza had taken off to chase after a cat while at the Egyptian exhibit. Once the girl got it in her mind to do something, she was off. Liza reminded her a bit of herself in that way.

She hoped upon hope that the children were just off on an adventure at the fair, and it wasn't Miles or Mr. Farnham who had taken them. How would Miles have found Liza, though? How could he have known that Alison had left Liza with Annie? And that Annie had left her with Ska? Alison wouldn't have asked Annie to take Liza if Miles had known about Annie and Alison's relationship.

Mr. Farnham was another story. He knew Liza was staying in the encampment, and he had spoken to her when he gave her the lollipop and the note. There was nothing threatening in the note, but still, it had been unsettling. Perhaps Mr. Farnham knew she would come looking for the girl. It might be a ploy to get her to come to him, instead of him finding her, and perhaps Frank or the Colonel.

She and Buck headed for the barn where Frank was saddling Biscuit the palomino. Frida had run to the Cossacks barn to get Shiva, and Ska had set off on foot already. She would cover the Wild West encampment. Ohitekah, a less experienced tracker, decided to go on horseback to cover the North Pond. Frank would cover the Midway, Annie the Wooded Isle, and Frida the area surrounding the South Pond. They would meet back at Ska and Ohitekah's tent in two hours, just before Annie had to perform.

She jogged over to the row of saddles, Buck trotting behind her. She grabbed her saddle blanket and tossed it on Buck's back. Searching the fairgrounds would have to suffice as the warm-up for their act. She dreaded the thought of the Colonel or Mr. Salisbury finding out that she would not be in the warm-up arena, but as long as she made it back in time to perform, they might forgive her. And her performance would have to be flaw-less. The pressure of a perfect performance was nothing compared to the angst in her gut at the thought of any harm coming to Liza. Besides the fact she would have failed her dear friend, she had come to care for the little girl immensely. A lump formed in her throat thinking about Liza scared, hurt, or worse.

She had to find those kids. "Sorry, pal, I'm going to have to saddle up without grooming you this time."

Mr. Post emerged from one of the stalls in the barn carrying two feeding buckets, his gait shuffling and his beard strewn with bits of hay. "What's this, little missy?"

"We have to look for the children, Mr. Post." Annie straight-ened the blanket and got her saddle.

Mr. Post put the buckets down and rushed over to her. "You let me do that now, Miss Annie."

"Mr. Post, I don't have time."

Mr. Post did an impeccable job of grooming and saddling, but he was slow. She swung the saddle up onto Buck's back, her shoulders aching with the weight of the heavily tooled leather. "We are spreading out to cover the grounds. If you see the chil-dren, keep them with you until we get back."

"Will do, Annie." He handed her Buck's bridle.

Annie organized the reins, and Buck lowered his head for her to place the bit in his mouth. She did so and then adjusted the headstall over his poll. She gathered the reins and lifted her calf for Mr. Post to give her a boost. Once settled, she picked up the reins, and with her seat, she urged Buck forward.

"Hold on a minute," Mr. Post said, rushing back to the barn. He emerged seconds later with a gun belt holstering two pistols. "You take this, little missy. Just in case."

Annie had her Derringer in her dress pocket but realized it would be harder to reach when riding. Grateful, she thanked Mr. Post and secured the gun belt around her waist. It was a little big and rested on her hips, but she didn't care. She cued Buck to a canter and headed out of the encampment and onto 62nd street where she brought the horse to a walk, her eyes scanning each side of the street, her heart still pounding.

Once she passed under the elevated railway, she scoured the area around the Horticulture Building before entering the Wooded Isle. The once peaceful setting now seemed a veritable maze where the children could easily be hidden. She decided to circle the island, heading south toward the boat lodge. Once there, she trotted over to the ticket master.

She brought Buck to a halt. "Have you seen three children come through here?"

"Seen lots of children." He frowned. "Could you be more specific?"

"An Indian boy, a little girl with auburn hair, and a smaller boy—all about six or seven years old?" Buck pranced, feeling Annie's anxiety, eager to keep his feet moving.

"Doesn't ring a bell," said the ticket master with a shake of his head.

Annie let Buck have his head, and they moved on. They passed the Australian squatter's hut to the southeast, passed the Fire and Guard Station, and finally passed the Japanese Bazaar and off the island to the Fisheries Building.

Nothing.

She trotted out to the edge of the White City toward Lake Michigan, hoping and praying the children had not gotten it in their heads to go for a swim on this hot and muggy day. After trotting back and forth along the shore twice, stopping to ask people if they'd seen the children at the various lakeside kiosks and booths, she turned to walk down the southeast side of the Manufactures and Liberal Arts Building and brought Buck to a stop at the edge of the North Canal, her spirits flagging. Where could they be? If Mr. Farnham or Miles had taken them and harmed even one hair on their heads, she would kill them, morality, guilt, and religion be damned.

Disheartened, Annie went back to the Wild West encampment to prepare for her performance. She wished she could implore the Colonel to cancel her act, but each and every performance had been sold out. She knew he would never agree.

She was the last of the searchers to arrive, and the others were all standing at the barn talking. "Anything?" Annie asked. Silently, they shook their heads. It was clear Ska and Frida had been crying. "Did you alert the Guard?" she asked Frank.

He came up to Buck and held the reins while Annie dismounted. "I did. Unfortunately, they didn't seem very concerned but said they would keep a lookout. I told them what the kids looked like."

"Then we will have to keep searching," Annie said with conviction.

"We will," Frank said. "But you'd best get your costume on. You go on in fifteen minutes. I ran into the Colonel on my way back, and he was none too pleased that you were nowhere to be seen."

Annie set her fists on her hips, annoyed. "Did you tell him why I was gone?"

"I did." Frank hurriedly checked Buck's girth, then pulled a handkerchief from his back pocket and ran it over Buck's face. They wouldn't have time for Mr. Post to groom him.

"And?" She took off Mr. Post's gun belt in preparation for changing her clothes. She hoped the Colonel would understand the direness of the situation.

"I asked if he could spare a few of the crew to search while you and Frida perform, and he agreed." Frank smiled at her.

"Oh, thank you, Frank." She stood on her tiptoes to kiss his cheek. She was relieved to have more help, but her heart was still heavy with the monumental task of finding those little needles in such an enormous haystack.

Frank tucked a stray lock of hair behind her ear. "You'd best get ready. I assured him you'd be back in time to go on."

She was about to leave and go to her tent to change when she looked over at Frida, who had tears running down her face and her fist clenched over her mouth. Her anguish rolled off her in waves.

Her eyes met Annie's, and in that moment, Annie felt the woman's terror sink into her bones. She mustered as much resolve as she could. "We *will* find the children, Frida."

Frida nodded through her tears. "My boy is everything to me. Everything. If I lose him, it will be like losing his father and brother all over again. I don't think I could bear it."

Annie fought the sting of tears behind her eyes. Witnessing Frida's fear at never seeing her boy again brought back the feelings she'd experienced when she'd lost her own child. She'd never got the chance to meet the baby, but she knew what the child would look like, how he or she would smell, what it would feel like to hold the small bundle in her arms. But she couldn't have those feelings right now. She had to get out there and perform, and then put her all into finding those children. She didn't have time to grieve. In that moment, she realized she'd *never* had time to grieve . . .

She forced herself to smile at the distraught woman. She motioned for Ska to come over to them and took them both into an embrace.

"I know you are terrified right now, and so am I. But we mustn't give up hope. They have not been gone very long, and there is so much ground to cover here, we could very easily have missed them. Ska, you and Ohitekah should keep looking. Frida and I will join you after our performances.

Annie released the women and turned to Frank. "After the performance, I'm going to have to go tell Alison. She needs to know, and *we* need to know if anything new happened with Miles." She stood frozen where she stood, almost unable to move at the thought, but she girded herself against the guilt and sorrow and walked to her tent to get ready.

෯෬ඁ෯

Annie and Buck performed to their usual aplomb, but the standing ovation they received held little joy. She should have never let Liza out of her sight. The child had been her responsibility, and she had been too preoccupied with her own emotional struggles to properly care for her and help her oldest friend. Annie had not been prepared for such a huge responsibility, and anger burned around the edges of her guilt and anxiety. She tried to tell herself she would have handled things differently had she been in Alison's shoes, but given the circumstances of Miles's previous attempt on Liza's life, Annie surmised she, too, would have tried to find a place for Liza. But Annie had failed her. The reality twisted her stomach into a knot.

As she left the arena, Frida was standing by, encircled by her horses, waiting to go on. Her expression was strained, her face pale.

Annie gave her a reassuring smile. "Have faith, Frida," she said. "We'll find your boy." Annie wished she could be more convincing, but her own doubts proved too overwhelming. If Mr. Farnham had the kids, he probably took them to get to Annie so she presumed he would eventually contact her. If Alison's husband had them, the situation could be dire. Liza was worth more to him dead than alive, and no doubt he'd plan to kill Alison next.

She walked Buck back to the barn, where Mr. Post was waiting for her. She dismounted and asked if he'd seen the children yet. He replied with a slow shake of his head, taking the reins from her. Silently, Annie walked back to her tent to change her clothes. Her disguise would have to be more complete, with maybe a veil, because she didn't want to speak to any of the fairgoers. She wondered if there was a hat with a veil in one of her trunks.

When she arrived at her tent, she saw Frank emerge from it. "There you are. How did it go?" he asked.

"Perfectly." But she felt anything but perfect. "This is all my fault, Frank. I never should have agreed to let Ska take Liza. I should have kept her with me."

"This isn't your fault, Annie. You couldn't have kept her with you every single minute. It was impossible."

Annie put her hand over her trembling mouth. "The obligation was mine, and I couldn't handle it. I failed."

"What am I going to do with you?" Frank said, his voice tender with sympathy. He reached out and pulled her to him, wrapped his arms around her, and she melted in his warm embrace. He smelled of earth and leather and fresh air. He'd always been her refuge.

"I need to go tell Alison," she said into his shirt, dreading it.

He stroked her hair. "We'll keep looking for them. I just checked the mess tent and combed the encampment again. Ska and Ohitekah have gone out to Jackson Park on horseback to save time—they can cover more ground that way. We'll find the kids, my dear."

She closed her eyes and wrapped her arms around his waist, squeezing him tighter, not wanting to let go, not wanting to face Alison, not wanting to leave this moment when they were melded together as one. The way they used to be. The way she wanted to be.

"We'll find them," he said again.

She wished with all her heart that she could believe him.

"Miss Oakley?" A young boy came up to them. "This is for you." The boy handed her the note. She took it from him and read:

If you want the children back, I'll need $2,000 in cash. I'll write again to give further instruction.

She looked up at the boy, who stared at her, grinning. "Who gave you this?" she asked, her heartbeat pounding in her ears. She handed Frank the note.

"Some man. Gave me two pennies. It sure is nice to meet you, Miss Oakley. My sister says she's going to grow up to be just like you."

"Who gave you this note? What did he look like?" Annie pressed again, her mind racing almost as fast as her pulse.

The boy shrugged. "He looked reg'lar, you know. Not too tall, not too wide. Whiskers."

"That's all you remember? It's very important," she said, trying her hardest not to scream at this boy.

"That's all. Bye, Miss Oakley. I gotta run. My mama will give me the switch if I'm gone too long." He turned and ran off.

She stood there, dumbfounded, numb, and disbelieving.

"A ransom note," Frank said. "We need to tell the others. We also need to take this note to the Exhibition Guard. Maybe now they will take this a little more seriously."

"And it's time to notify the police now, too," Annie said. "Emma has friends in the police department. I think we should go through her. Given how busy they are, she might be able to get some attention on the matter quicker that we would. Can you send word to her? She is living at the Palmer House Hotel."

"Of course," Frank said, his tone gentle. She almost cried with relief at his willingness to help. She put a trembling hand to her temple, her head suddenly pounding. "Oh, Frank! How could this have happened?" Her voice rose in an emotional squeak.

Frank pulled her to him again. "It's best not to think about what might have been, Annie. We need to move forward and not wallow in blame, or guilt, or regrets. It won't help the children, will it?"

Annie shook her head and buried her face in his shirt. She knew he was right. They had to take action, even if it meant that the children— She couldn't even bear to think it. The blood in her veins turned to ice.

CHAPTER 20

PICKPOCKETS ABOUND AT COLUMBIAN EXHIBITION!
— *Chicago Daily Journal*, Tuesday, June 13, 1893

ANNIE WALKED UP TO DR. GORDON'S FRONT DOOR WITH HER heart in her throat and the note clutched in her hand. Taking a deep breath, she reached for the golden lion head door knocker and rapped several times.

In moments, Beth answered. "Oh, Miss Annie. Please come in. I was just getting ready to go to visit Bobby and then come to the grounds to see you."

"May I speak with Alison?" Annie asked, her voice weak. Feeling light-headed, she walked to a chair in the foyer and sat down.

"Miss Annie?"

"I'm afraid I need to tell her of some disturbing news. I just need a moment to collect myself."

Beth placed a hand on Annie's shoulder. "Oh dear. Is there anything I can do to help?"

"Not at the moment, thank you. I need to do this myself. It's a complicated situation." How could she break this news to Alison? She was already ill. Would it completely devastate her? Would it kill her?

Annie closed her eyes, wanting to will away her horrible thoughts, but they kept coming. How could she tell her that she had failed miserably? She'd put the child in danger. If it was Mr. Farnham who had taken the children, she prayed he would be satisfied with the money. She would take every penny she had out of savings, she'd get a loan. But if it was Miles, the situation would be much worse. Mr. Farnham would have nothing to gain by the child's death, but Miles had everything to gain—and he would be out for Alison next. And who knew what he'd be willing to do to poor Ivan and Chayton . . .

Annie got to her feet. "Would you take me to her, Beth?"

"Yes, ma'am."

They climbed the stairs to the second floor and turned left down the hallway, past Dr. Gordon's office. They entered Alison's room to find her sitting in bed chatting with Dr. Gordon, who sat next to her. Beth closed the door behind Annie and left. Annie was relieved the girl had the decency to leave them alone while she imparted this horrible news.

When Annie saw Alison, her eyes widened in astonishment. Her friend looked so fragile, so weak. Annie wanted nothing more than to turn around, run out of the room, and never come back.

"Annie, my dear, how are you? How is Liza? Is she ready to see me yet? I so want Lee to meet her." She took Lee's hand and squeezed it, looking adoringly into his eyes. He returned the gesture of affection.

"I, um, I . . . have some unsettling news." She tried to keep the tone of her voice even, calm.

"Oh no. What is the matter? Is it Liza? Is she unwell?" Alison asked, looking from Annie to Dr. Gordon and then back to Annie.

"Liza has— She and two other children have—" She hesitated, took a deep breath. "They've gone missing."

"Missing? What do you mean, missing?" Her eyes widened in fear.

Annie swallowed, her mouth going dry as dust. "She was with two other children, and they've gone missing," she repeated, tried to keep her voice steady. Alison's fingers wrapped around the bedsheets, pulling them into her fists, her face going as white as the sheets. "We've scoured the grounds, both the Wild West encampment and the fair. We've contacted the Exhibition Guard, and they are nowhere—"

"How could you have let this happen, Annie?" she asked, voice raised. "I trusted you! You were the only person I could trust! And now she's gone! She's gone . . ." Alison's voice trailed off into a high-pitched wail.

Dr. Gordon fixed his gaze on Annie, his mouth turned down in a frown, his eyes like that of a wounded animal. "This is unthinkable," he said. "The poor girl."

Alison wailed again. He released her hand, his movements hurried. "I must fetch her a sedative. It isn't good for her to be so distraught," he said, walking past her.

"Wait," Annie said, stopping him. "There's more. I received this just less than an hour ago." She handed the note to Dr. Gordon, who read it out loud.

Annie's chest caved in on itself, and her face burned with heat. She slowly approached Alison's bed. "I'm . . . I'm so sorry, Alison," she whispered.

"Noooo!" Alison yelled. "He's got her! He's got her! He is going to kill her!" She ripped the covers off and got out of bed unsteadily. Still, she lunged at Annie. "Why?! Why, Annie? Why did you let her out of your sight? How could you have done this to me? To her? You were supposed to protect her!"

Annie caught Alison's arms as they flailed in her face. Dr. Gordon grabbed Alison around the waist and dragged her away from Annie.

"You must not upset yourself so, dear! Sit down!" he commanded her. Alison sat perched on the edge of the bed, her arms and legs shaking, her face blotched and red, her eyes like that of a wild woman. "Get back into bed and stay there until I return."

Alison vehemently shook her head, her mouth screwed up in rage.

"Don't make me get the restraints," he said.

Annie flinched at his words. Restraints? Had he used them on her before?

Alison looked up into the doctor's face, and her features softened ever so slightly. She let him lift her legs into bed and get her settled under the covers. She stared straight ahead at the wall.

"I'll be right back," Dr. Gordon said to Annie. "If she tries to get out of bed again, leave the room and lock the door."

Under most circumstances, Annie would be alarmed at Dr. Gordon's drastic measures for instilling calm, but this wasn't like most circumstances. She nodded silently, and he left the room, closing the door behind him. She stood, facing her friend, her heart shattered into a million pieces. Alison sat immobile, refusing to look at her.

"Alison, we are going to find her. *I* am going to find her." She knew her words meant nothing.

"Have you alerted the police? He's going to kill her." Her words came out measured, even. "And it will be your fault, all your fault." Her voice and her body crumpled, and she buried her face in her hands.

Annie approached her and pulled Alison's hands down to her lap. Alison tried to resist but was too weak. "We are getting word to the police, yes. But it may not have been your husband, Alison."

Alison looked at her bleary-eyed. "What do you mean not Miles? What do you mean?"

"Is there any way your husband could have known that you would bring Liza to me? *Any* way at all? Think, Alison."

"No," she said. No!"

"Then how likely would it be that he found her?" Annie spoke softly, trying her best to soothe her friend. "There is a man who's been following me for quite some time now. A fan. He seems to show up wherever I am performing. He even followed us to Europe the last time we went. I think *he* may have taken Liza and the two other children from the encampment in an attempt to get my attention. He followed us that day you became ill at the Woman's Building. I saw him when I left here. He knows she is staying with me."

For the moment, Annie decided to leave out the part that she had left Liza in Ska's care and that Mr. Farnham had spoken to the girl when she had escaped Ska's watchful eye.

Alison stared at her, her face blank.

"Do you hear what I am telling you, Alison? It very likely is not Miles, and Liza is very likely not in harm's way, not truly. You must have faith."

Alison snapped out of her trance. "You knew this man was following you, and you never told me? How could you have done that when I had placed my daughter in your care?" She raised her voice again. "If it was this man who took her, then how do you know he won't harm her? What makes you so certain?"

"I don't believe this man is violent." Annie shook her head. "Just a little . . . lost and obsessed."

"I don't believe you. How can I believe you?" Alison's eyes were wild again. "You lied to me, Annie."

Annie shuddered. In not telling her about Mr. Farnham, in withholding that information, Annie had as good as lied to her friend. Her heart thudded with heaviness as it folded in on itself.

"I want you to leave," Alison said, her swollen, bloodshot, and wild eyes piercing Annie with their venomous gaze.

"Alison, I'll make this right. We will find her."

"I said, get out."

Annie's heart wrenched in two. "Alison, please . . . I want—"

"Get out!" Alison shrieked.

"What's going on here?" Dr. Gordon showed up at the door, syringe in hand. He quickly came to Alison's side.

"Get her out! I want her out!" Alison collapsed against the pillows sobbing, her mouth opened in a rictus of anguish, her face red and mottled.

Annie shrank away from them, her insides caving in, her spirits dashed, and a feeling of disconnectedness from her body took hold of her. She felt as if she were in a dream—a nightmare —watching the scene from afar. She backed out of the room, closed the door, and fell into a heap at the foot of it.

"Miss Annie, are you all right?" Beth had just come up the stairs.

"I feel so terrible," Annie said, shaking her head. "I just feel so terrible."

"What's happened?" Beth asked, and Annie told her everything.

She took hold of Annie's arm. "Come on. Let's get you to your feet."

Beth helped her to stand. Just as she smoothed her dress, Dr. Gordon came out of Alison's room and quietly closed the door behind him.

"She will rest now. Hopefully for a few hours," he said. "This news has put her out of her head."

"Dr. Gordon, Alison told me that you and your friend from the Pinkerton Agency had met with her husband to ask him to start divorce proceedings. She said that he had agreed. What happened during that meeting? What exactly transpired?"

The doctor gestured with a tilt of his head for Annie to follow him into his office. "Let's speak in here. Just to make sure we don't disturb Alison. Beth, please fetch Miss Oakley some tea. Or would you prefer something stronger?" he asked.

"No. Tea is fine."

Beth left them, and the doctor motioned for Annie to sit in the chair opposite his at the desk. She gratefully took it, her knees still shaking from Alison's outburst.

"We did meet with Mr. Drake." The doctor settled himself in his chair. "We told him in no uncertain terms that we had enough information to bury him."

"But did Alison tell you that Miles' father is head of the police department in Springfield? That he has connections with the police department here, too? Wouldn't they help him in some way?"

"Yes, yes, she did." He stroked his mustache, silent for a moment. "I took the liberty of wiring his father. He wrote me back, and he mentioned that the two were estranged. He knew his son was a good for nothing lout and he wanted to wash his hands of him, so he would be of no help to his son."

"Oh, I see. That must have given Alison some relief." Annie wondered why Alison hadn't mentioned this bit of information.

Beth arrived with a tray and set it on Dr. Gordon's desk. She poured tea for both of them. Dr. Gordon took his with cream and two large helpings of sugar, and Annie took hers without. She sipped at the tea. Chamomile. The aroma and the warmth instantly made her feel more at ease. Beth left, and Annie and the doctor sat in silence for a few moments.

"But he did agree to take the money?" Annie asked, finally ready to talk again.

"Yes." The doctor put his teacup down on the saucer with a *clink*. "I was supposed to meet him tonight. He was to have secured the papers for Alison to sign, and I would take them to the attorney's office on her behalf. But now the game has changed, hasn't it?" he said with a smile.

Annie blinked at his words. She hadn't really thought of this as a "game," and she certainly found no reason to smile at the circumstances. She leaned back against the rungs of the chair, feeling as if she couldn't support her own weight, even while sitting down.

"There is something else I should tell you," Annie said. "I had just told Alison when you came in . . . It may not be her husband who took the children." She recounted the story about

Mr. Farnham. "I have a friend who also has connections with the police department here in Chicago. I am going to ask her to intervene on our behalf and help us find whomever took the children. If it is Miles, he will want the money, and if it is Mr. Farnham, he will want . . . well, me."

Dr. Gordon nodded, and then he took in a deep breath. "I am worried about Alison. This news has clearly upset her, and her health is quite fragile as it is."

"Is her condition life-threatening, Dr. Gordon? She looks worse every time I see her."

"Her affliction is quite advanced. If not treated right away, the disease can spread to the blood and the joints—and yes, it can be life-threatening. I hope I have caught it in time, but the recovery is slow. I fear she may have another condition, as well." The doctor pressed his lips together, and his eyes clouded with concern.

Annie set her teacup down. "Oh?"

"She might be in the late stages of syphilis—another venereal disease."

Heat flooded Annie's face. Poor Alison—to be so riddled with such horrible diseases, and to have contracted them just trying to stay alive. It was admirable that Dr. Gordon had taken Alison on and wanted to marry her. But there was still the question of his relationship with his nurse, and the fact that he had pinned Mr. Barnes' death on poor Bobby. She couldn't make him out.

"Is there something more to be done for Alison?" Annie asked.

"I'm doing all that I can, Miss Oakley. I love Alison, and I want her to be my wife. I'll do anything to make her healthy again. This situation with her daughter is not at all good for Alison's health. I hope we can get her back."

Annie swallowed down the pang of guilt that strangled her throat. She lifted her chin, refusing to accept defeat. "We will, Dr. Gordon. We have to."

CHAPTER 21

Who is the Exposition Killer?
Investigation of Bodies Found on
Exhibition Grounds Commences.
– *Chicago Star Free Press*, Tuesday, June 13, 1893

Emma sat perched on the edge of a bench near the Columbian Fountain in the Court of Honor. She tapped her foot in a staccato rhythm and resisted the temptation to look at her watch—again.

Mitchell had sent a note to her room at the Palmer House this morning, requesting to meet her here in front of the fountain. He'd claimed it was urgent, of the utmost importance. He'd probably chosen the spot because it would be flooded with people and there was less chance of him running into someone he knew—or his wife.

Initially, she planned to decline the invitation, insulted at the clandestine way he wanted to meet with her. If he truly loved her, he would meet with her at the hotel, in the restaurant, wife and others be damned. Why should she make any effort to see him when he had been willing to abandon her the moment his wife made the accusation? But the urgency with which he wanted to meet had her curious.

She sighed and stood up. Just sitting there made her stomach tangle into knots. She paced back and forth in front of the bench, worrying her gloved hands around each other. She vowed that if he didn't arrive in the next few minutes, she would leave. How dare he request to meet her and then show up late, or god forbid, not show up at all?

Just as she was about to look at her watch, she saw him walking toward her, his gait smooth, his posture elegant. Damn, but he was good-looking. But she mustn't be distracted by such shallow thoughts. He'd hurt her to the core. He didn't deserve her adulation.

She stopped pacing and waited for him. He approached and went to give her a kiss on the cheek. She backed away from him. "What is it, Mitchell?" she asked, her voice clipped. Seeing him flooded her with emotions—anger, sadness, regret, and desire. Her stomach felt as if it would come up at any moment. She steeled herself against the rising tide of conflicting feelings.

"I had to see you. I'm so sorry for what happened the other day. I panicked—" His eyes implored her with sincere regret.

She diverted her gaze. "I don't have much time," she lied. "What did you want to see me about?"

"Oh, well . . . Shall we walk?" he asked.

"No. You can tell me right here."

Go for a leisurely stroll? Was he joking?

"Um, okay. Can we at least sit?" He indicated the bench with an outstretched hand.

Emma sighed and fought the urge to roll her eyes.

"I know you wanted to keep abreast of the insurance investigations, and I know you are also interested in the story of the two girls' bodies found in the park so you can write a story for the *Chicago Star Free Press*."

Her interest was suddenly piqued. "Yes." She didn't want to seem overly eager.

"The second woman has been identified. Her name was Deborah Granger."

Emma swung her head to look at him full in the face. "A positive identification?"

"Yes. And a life insurance policy. The benefactor is someone by the name of Grant Harvey."

"You don't say," she said, wondering. Two women buried near each other, both with life insurance policies, and both with male beneficiaries. "Were either one of these women married?"

"No."

"Who identified Miss Granger?" she asked.

"Apparently, her mother. Her sister has also gone missing. Poor woman dragged herself across state lines to make the identification. She looked as if she had just been on her own deathbed. Ill, with one daughter dead, and one missing . . . I shudder to think . . ."

Emma's heart began to race. Didn't the housekeeper, Nettie, at Dr. Gordon's house have a sister named Deborah who went to take care of their ill mother? And hadn't Annie told her that Nettie had gone missing recently, as well? She would have to confer with Annie to make certain, but it sounded like too much of a coincidence.

"Do you know the sister's name?" Emma asked.

"I don't."

"Did Mrs. Granger know her daughter's beneficiary?"

Mitchell pressed his lips together. "She didn't."

She worried her lip, then asked, "Where does this beneficiary live? Where is his residence?"

"Atlanta, Missouri."

"So not the same beneficiary. Millie Turnbill's beneficiary was a Mr. Gregory L. Harris from Adamsville, Tennessee," Emma recalled aloud.

Mitchell pulled his chin back, a look of surprise on his face. "I can't believe you remembered that."

"You'd be surprised what I can remember," Emma said absently. "How strange. Isn't it unusual for a woman to have a life insurance policy?"

He nodded. "Yes. Not unusual for men, as they are the breadwinners."

She wanted to quip back that men were not always the breadwinners. What about the single women who slaved in the factories to feed their families? Or the widow who took in other people's dirty laundry to survive? Or the countless women who had to turn to prostitution because they had no other choice? She decided it wasn't worth her breath.

"Is that all?" she asked.

"No. We also discovered another policy . . . One for a Mr. Donald Barnes."

Emma's eyes shot open. "Mr. Barnes! That's the man that Bobby is accused of killing! Who benefits from Mr. Barnes's death?"

"That's where it gets interesting. A Helen Leigh Grant from Alexandria, Kentucky."

"A woman? That *is* interesting."

"Yes, but it's more likely that he would have a life insurance policy."

"But Annie said he was widowed."

Mitchell shrugged. "Could be a sweetheart. Or a relative by marriage. We have no way of knowing."

"Unless we paid her a visit." Emma pulled her pad of paper out of her handbag and wrote her name down.

Mitchell quickly grabbed her hand. "Emma, I am so sorry about what happened at the restaurant." She pulled her hand away, but he grabbed it again, squeezing harder. "I told Anna I wanted a divorce."

She turned to look him in the eye.

"It's going to take some time. I haven't spoken to my family yet. I'm not sure what my father will do—if he will let me stay on at the company or not—as he is a most devout Catholic and very vocal about it in the community. But I can start over. We can move somewhere else. Somewhere new. We can start a life together." His eyes pleaded with hers.

She gently pulled her hand away, confused by her own thoughts and emotions. She hadn't expected him to tell his wife he wanted a divorce—not so soon.

"What do you say?" he asked.

"I . . . I'm not sure. I have to think about it, Mitchell." She had no desire to be tied down by marriage. She wanted to be her own breadwinner, thank you very much, but she did so enjoy what they had together. She shook off her sentiment and placed her notepad back in her bag. "I really must go. Thank you for the information, Mitchell." She stood up.

Mitchell got to his feet, too. "You'll think about it, darling? Promise me?"

She gave him a quick nod and walked down the pathway in front of the Columbian Fountain. Her mind a jumble of emotions and her hands shaking from the encounter, she decided to take some time to think and go to the Midway Plaisance. She'd wanted to view the Egyptian exhibit over on Cairo Street. She headed west, deciding she'd take the electric cable car to the Midway.

After being packed into the car like a sardine, Emma was never so happy to set her feet on the ground again. Whining children, leering men, and pinched-faced ladies had occupied the car. It was getting late in the day, and she surmised that these fairgoers had had quite enough fun and frivolity. When the car stopped at the Midway, she couldn't get out fast enough. She headed west again, toward the Ferris wheel looming in the distance.

Her shoulders began to relax as she casually strolled past the Libbey Glass Company, the Irish Village, and the Javanese settlement. She breathed in the fragrance of the lilies that lined the path. Thoughts of Mitchell kept creeping into the corners of her mind, no matter how hard she tried to bar their entrance. He'd told her he'd asked his wife for a divorce. He was willing to risk his job, his family, everything for her. Would she be willing to do the same for him? She didn't think so. She couldn't even bring herself to say if she truly loved Mitchell.

She had never been in love. Not really. At least, not like Annie was in love with Frank. The sun rose and set in Annie's eyes where Frank was concerned. Although Emma had been very fond of a few of her beaus, she'd never felt as if they'd hung the moon. Her feelings for Carlton Chisolm had come close, and Mitchell closer, but to her, the moon held no such rapture.

A chilling, primordial scream sent her heart into spasms. Over near the Egyptian exhibit, a woman sank to her knees in front of a hedge. Her hands, clasped over her mouth, did nothing to silence the blood-curdling screech that continued to rake itself down her spine.

A crowd quickly started to gather, and Emma ran to see what had caused such a commotion. Elbowing past two gentlemen, she pushed her way toward the hedge. Her breath caught in her throat when she saw the offending sight. The body of a woman had been shoved under the hedge.

"Stand back," one of the gentlemen said, his hand on her shoulder.

"Let go of me," Emma said. "She might be alive." Though, another glimpse of the mottled skin on the woman's arm told her differently.

She shrugged the man's hand off her shoulder and crouched down to get a look at the face, and she felt the blood drain from her head. The woman's face was battered, unrecognizable. Her hair was caked with blood and dirt, and she'd been tossed under the shrubs like a piece of unwanted rubbish. Next to her hand lay a gold piece of metal. Perhaps a pendant? Emma reached for it, and when she grasped it in her palm, her hand brushed up against the woman's ice-cold skin. Emma's gaze traveled up to the marred, pulpy flesh of the woman's face. It wavered in her vision. Emma stood up too quickly, and as her knees started to buckle, she felt someone's arms going around her.

৩১৩

Frank, Frida, Ska, and Ohitekah stood facing the Colonel, who sat slack-jawed at his desk.

"A ransom note you say?" The Colonel's gaze traveled from Frank to the others. "Aye, God. How much does this person want?"

"Two thousand dollars," said Frank.

The Colonel shook his head. "Of all the— And you think it might be this Farnham fellow who took the children?"

"Possibly," Frank said. "I've taken the ransom note to the Guard. They said they couldn't help because the Wild West Show is not on the Expo grounds at Jackson Park."

"Hmph. Sounds political to me. The Exhibition officials wouldn't accept our proposal, and now they are fit to be tied because we are doing such a bang-up business over here. Have you all contacted the police?"

Frank nodded. "We've heard they are pretty stretched with all the crime throughout the city. We've sent word to Miss Wilson. She has some connections with the police. We hope she can persuade them to make this a priority."

"Good. If I know Miss Wilson, she won't take no for an answer. So how can I help?" The Colonel leaned forward and rested his elbows on his desk.

"We were hoping you could spare some more of the crew to help search," Ohitekah said.

The Colonel sighed, stroking his beard, thinking. "All right. But the public is expecting the show to go on, come hell or high water, and I'll not disappoint them. We've already lost Bobby for the time being. Ska, Ohitekah, Frida, I am sorry that your boys are missing, and I'll spare as many of the crew as I can—I'll send some of the boys out right now—but I need you to continue to make your performances. And Frank—"

Frank raised his hand. "I'll make sure Annie is committed to the show." He said the words with more conviction than he felt. The Colonel was at his wits end with her. Top headliner or not, if she wasn't dependable, he'd have to fire her.

"You're dismissed," the Colonel said with an impatient wave of his hand.

Once outside the tent, Ska and Ohitekah said they were going to continue their search.

"With all due respect," Frank said, "you two need to rest. Let the Colonel send out some of the boys. We know that whoever took the kids will reach out again to give instructions. He'll likely not harm them for fear of not getting his money. We need to sit tight."

"I feel so helpless doing nothing," Frida said.

"I know, but we need to be patient. Wait him out. He wants his money. In the meantime, we still have people searching."

"Perhaps you are right," Ohitekah said. He turned to Ska. "Come, let's rest for a while.

Ska reluctantly agreed to follow him back to their tent.

Frank turned to Frida. "You could stand to do with some rest, too."

She shook her head. "I don't think I can."

He took hold of her elbow. "You need to try. C'mon. I'll walk you to your tent."

Frida silently agreed, and they walked to the Cossacks small encampment. When they arrived, the others were gone. Probably practicing or getting ready for the afternoon performance. Frida was scheduled to go on last for her solo trick-riding act. He knew it would be difficult for her to concentrate, but she would just have to do her best.

When they reached her tent, she turned to him. "Would you like to come in? I can make some tea."

"Oh, naw, but thanks," he said. "I need to get back to our

tents. If that reprobate sends another note, I want to be there to
intercept it."

"Yes," she said, her voice cracking. She put her hands to her
face and began sobbing.

"Oh, hey," he said, lowering his voice. "I know this must be
terrible for you."

She nodded, wiping her eyes. "Ivan is my world," she said,
attempting to smile. "I don't want to be alone right now. Won't
you stay? For just a few minutes?"

Frank bit his lip. He really didn't want to. He wanted to be
there when Annie returned from seeing Alison, and if the
kidnapper returned or sent another messenger. Annie would
probably be a mess. But Frida looked so forlorn and lost. Her
anguish pulled at his heartstrings.

"Perhaps just a few minutes."

They stepped inside her tent, and she went directly to the
small woodburning stove with a neat metal pipe fitted through a
hole in the canvas to let out the smoke. "Please, have a seat."
After lighting the stove, she set the teakettle on the burner.

Frank sat in a sleek wooden chair with a blue cushion. The
tent was sparsely furnished with said chair, a matching small
table, two small beds, and a leather trunk. There were large,
brightly colored cushions set upon the thin carpet, as well. She
didn't have much, but what she did have was of the finest quality.
Frida settled herself on one of the pillows on the floor while they
waited for the water to boil.

"You know, your Ivan reminds me of someone." Frank
crossed his legs, getting more comfortable.

"Really? Who?"

"My brother, when we were kids. When I saw Ivan riding
that horse the first day you all arrived, tearing around the arena
bareback—so young, with such confidence with that animal—it
reminded me of Kenny. When he wasn't riding, he was shy, quiet
—I was the boisterous one, gave my mother fits—but when
Kenny was on horseback, he sort of came alive like your boy."

Frida fingered the beads on her skirt. "Ivan misses his father, who was a great horseman. The horses give him solace. I think he feels like his father is with him when he rides."

The teakettle rang out, and Frida got up to take it off the fire. She gathered up two metal cups and prepared the tea. She handed Frank a cup and then settled herself on the floor again. Frank blew on the steaming liquid, its spicy aroma filling his nostrils. He sipped it and was pleased with the woodsy flavor.

"Perhaps you and Annie will have a boy like Ivan," Frida said. She held her teacup with both hands as if warming them.

"We won't," Frank said flatly. "Annie cannot bear children."

"Oh." She sounded surprised. "I'm sorry."

Frank didn't respond. He realized he'd never said the words out loud before. Or realized how much they hurt. They sat in silence, sipping their tea, both caught up in the world of their thoughts. The tea was good and strong. Not as good as coffee, but he could feel the effects of it fortifying his blood already. He stared into the last remnants of the liquid, watching the bits of leaves swirl in the bottom of the cup. It was time for him to go.

"Well, I really should be going." He stood up and waited while Frida got up from the cushions on the floor. He handed her his cup, and she took it, wrapping her fingers around the back of his hand. Startled, he looked into rich, brown eyes rimmed with tears.

"I'm so frightened," she whispered.

"I know. We'll get your boy back." He hoped his words gave her some comfort.

Still, she did not release his hand. The tears came in earnest now, and he could feel her hand trembling. "What if he . . . ?"

"Now, now," Frank said and pulled her to him in a friendly embrace. "Don't think such things."

She lifted her face and suddenly pressed her lips to his. The fragrance of lavender from her hair and the spicy taste of the tea on her breath enveloped him. Shocked, he pulled away from her.

"Whoa. Hang on, there," he said, taking a step back.

"I . . . I've come to have feelings for you, Frank," she said, her eyes searching his.

"Look," he said, shaking his head. "You haven't. You are just upset and looking for a little comfort."

"But I—"

"Understand me, Frida. I love my wife." He did his best to ignore the crestfallen look on her face. She had mistaken her fear for her boy and the sadness of the loss of her husband for affection for him. Of course, she would be lonely, and she probably wanted a man in her son's life, and as much as he liked young Ivan, that man would not be him.

CHAPTER 22

ANNIE OAKLEY FAIRGOER FAVORITE!
– *Chicago Daily Journal*, Tuesday, June 13, 1893

ANNIE GOT BACK FROM DR. GORDON'S HOUSE IN PLENTY OF time for her afternoon performance, her heart heavy with guilt and despair. But after she'd made a few laps with Buck around the practice arena, her head cleared and she was focused.

When the announcer called out her name, she and Buck charged into the stadium at full speed, and the crowd was on their feet. She sped past the banners and signs emblazoned with her name, and she and Buck ran through their course with precision and deftness. After the mounted-shooting portion, Annie handed Buck off to Mr. Post. Twenty live pigeons were released from a crate in the arena, and she proceeded to shoot all of them within fifteen seconds.

Texas Joe showed up sober once again, much to Annie's relief. After she'd accomplished her feat with the live birds, Texas Joe came in with Jep and set him on the stool against the wall at the far end of the stadium. Joe put an apple on Jep's head and told him to stay. Annie took her aim and shattered the apple into a pulpy mess while the crowd roared with delight.

Jep jumped off the stool and ran to her. He raised himself up on his haunches, put his front paws on her shoulders, and joyously licked her face.

Next, Annie and Joe took turns performing the mirror trick. Standing with their backs to their targets, they settled their rifles on their shoulders and held up a hand mirror to view the targets at their backs. Annie hit all of her targets, and Joe hit all but one.

For their finale, Annie pulled one of her pistols from her holster and shot a burning cigarette out of Joe's mouth. Next, Joe performed the card trick. Annie held up the ace of diamonds, and Joe's bullet pierced a hole right in the middle of the center diamond.

The two then held hands and made several bows to the audience, who shouted her name so loudly she could feel the vibration down to her bones. As she skipped out of the arena waving to the crowd, she noticed Frank waiting for her at the gates. Once she had exited and the gates were closed, she walked over to him, breathless.

"Outstanding, my dear. I know you have much on your mind." He wrapped his arm around her waist and pulled her to him, planting a passionate kiss on her lips.

Her heart leaped, and her knees went weak. "Oh my," she said unsteadily when they had unlocked from their embrace. "I'll perform that well every time if that is my reward." She smiled up at him, and he ran his hand over the back of her head and through her hair.

"I love you, Annie." He looked into her eyes, his voice soft with emotion. "I want you to know that."

"I do know that, Frank. Are you okay?" She was surprised at this sudden declaration.

"Yes, I'm fine. I know I've not been myself lately, and I apologize."

Annie hugged him tighter. "Same, my darling. Let's put our quarreling aside."

"Agreed," he said and kissed her again.

From the corner of her eye, Annie saw someone approach them. She released Frank. "Emma, I'm so glad to see you. How did you get here so quickly? Did you get my message?"

"No. But I wanted to see you. I have some terrible news." Emma put a hand to her temple, looking as if she might buckle. She lowered her hand to her stomach. "Another body was found on the Midway Plaisance. Another woman," she said.

Annie fixed her eyes on Emma's mouth, unable to believe the words that had come out of it. Another body? Clearly, there was a madman on the loose. No one was safe. And with the children missing?

Annie's chest felt as if it was going to cave in on itself. She met Emma's gaze.

"Did you hear what I said?" Emma asked, her eyes darting from Annie to Frank.

"This is horrible. Oh god, Frank. The children." Annie pulled at his sleeve.

"The children?" Emma's face clouded in confusion.

"Now, hold on here, you two. Let's just stay calm." Frank said. "Let's head on over to the tent where we can talk in private."

Annie nodded and wrapped her arm around Emma's trembling shoulders. She must be in shock. They walked silently back toward the array of tents. If people tried to approach her for some conversation or an autograph, Frank intervened and told them she was comforting a friend and couldn't stop to chat. One look at Emma's face and anyone would have understood. Annie tried to quiet the hammering of her heart, her fear for the children growing with each beat.

When they reached their tent, they all ducked inside. Annie got Emma to the rocking chair and pulled a stool up beside her. Frank put the kettle on the stove to boil.

"Do they know who she is, Emma?" Frank asked.

Emma shook her head. "I don't know what happened. I fainted. I can't believe I fainted. I never faint! Anyway, the next thing I knew, I was sitting on a bench between an older man and his wife. They told me that I collapsed. When I finally had my wits about me, the medics were hauling off the body."

"You saw the body? Oh my goodness, no wonder you fainted." Annie put a comforting hand on Emma's knee. It was then she noticed one of Emma's hands clenched tightly into a fist. So tight the skin on her knuckles stretched taut, as if it would break the bones beneath.

"Emma, what's wrong with your hand?" Annie asked, worried about her friend's detached behavior.

"I can't open it," she said, looking up at Annie, her eyes wide with alarm. She held her fist up to Annie's face. Annie lowered her hand and, with gentle fingers, pried open Emma's rigid hand. Inside her palm lay a small, diamond-shaped piece of metal, about one inch in length and a half an inch in height. It was gold with a deep indigo-blue design.

"What is it?" Annie asked.

"I don't know." Emma's voice still carried that otherworldly quality that made Annie increasingly nervous. It was not like Emma to sound so unsure—about anything. "I remember seeing it next to the body. I guess I picked it up."

Annie was vaguely aware of the tinkling of teacups and the tinny sound of the teakettle as the water began to heat up. She took the object from Emma's hand and saw that it was a pin, the decorative kind one would wear on a dress or perhaps the lapel of a man's jacket. She held it up to her face. The blue design looked like an insect of some sort. Perhaps a beetle?

Frank handed each one of them a cup of steaming tea and then sat himself down at the foot of the bed. Calmly, he lit a cigar.

"Tell us what you remember, Emma," he said.

"Can we go outside?" she asked, pulling at the lace collar of her dress as if it were strangling her.

"Of course," said Frank.

Holding their teacups, Annie and Emma stepped outside and sat in the chairs by the firepit that was positioned between their two tents. Frank sat down on a large log.

Once settled, Emma sipped at her tea, her hands still trembling.

After a few seconds, she began. "Mitchell wanted to meet me to talk. He told me he was getting a divorce, that he wanted me back."

Annie inwardly cringed. She felt that any man who would step out on his wife lacked character, but she knew Emma did not believe this to be true. She only hoped Emma would think about the proposition seriously and not throw caution to the wind.

"But that's neither here nor there," Emma said, waving her hand in the air. "He also had some information about the two women who were previously found on the grounds . . . and Mr. Barnes."

"What is it?" Frank asked.

Emma proceeded to tell them what Mitchell had told her about the life insurance policies, including the ones for Mr. Barnes and Deborah Granger.

"Deborah Granger?" Annie sat forward so fast she nearly dropped her teacup. "Could she be Nettie's sister?"

Emma nodded. "I think it's very possible. Deborah's mother identified her body, and also told the police her other daughter had gone missing, although Mitchell did not know the name of the other daughter."

"Oh my!" Annie said, placing her hand on her rapidly beating heart. "It has to be Nettie, don't you think?" Annie felt sick to her stomach at the thought of what Mrs. Granger must be going through.

"We can't be entirely positive." Emma shook her head.

"This is turning out to be quite a mystery," Frank said.

"I'll say," said Annie. They all sat quietly a few moments and then a dreadful thought came into Annie's head.

"This woman you saw under the hedge." Annie finally broke the silence. "Could it have been Nettie?"

Emma shook her head again. "The face was terribly disfigured, but I would have recognized Nettie's blond hair. This woman's hair was darker."

Annie sat back in the chair, relieved that the body wasn't Nettie's. "But, the woman must be a victim of the same killer. Wouldn't you think?"

"More than likely." Frank exhaled a mouthful of cigar smoke. "But what about the pin?"

Emma reached for it, and Annie handed it to her. "This symbol is intriguing," Emma said. "I'll have to research it. It might give us a clue as to who this woman was or who the murderer is. What do you think of my taking the train to Kentucky to visit this Miss Helen Leigh Grant, Mr. Barnes' beneficiary?"

Annie still couldn't shake the thought of the children out there with a cold-blooded murderer on the loose, and her anxiety over it was reaching a fever pitch. "It will have to wait, Emma. We have a more pressing problem, a more personal problem, and I need your help."

Emma frowned. "I don't like the sound of that. What is it?"

Annie told her about the children, Alison's husband, Mr. Farnham, and the ransom note.

"Dear God," Emma said. "Have you contacted the police?"

"We were hoping you could help us with that," Frank said. "We've alerted the Guard. They said they would keep a lookout for the children, but beyond that, they won't be of much help. And, the police are so inundated right now, we thought with your connections you might be able to urge them to make this a priority."

"I'll certainly do what I can." She took hold of Annie's hand.

Just as Annie was about to thank her, she spotted someone in the distance over Emma's shoulder, watching them.

Mr. Farnham.

Annie's breath caught in her throat, and she stood up and pushed past Emma.

"Hey, where are you going?" Emma said.

"Annie!" Frank called after her.

She marched directly toward Mr. Farnham. "You!" she shouted.

Mr. Farnham smiled, clearly pleased to see her. He took off his hat and held it against his chest. She clenched her fists so hard, her fingernails bit into her palms.

"Where are they?" She strode up to him and placed a hand on the butt of the pistol sitting snugly in its holster at her waist.

"Hello, Miss Oakley. You look lovely today." Mr. Farnham's eyes glittered with adoration. "You and old Buck did extremely well in there."

"Stop it, Mr. Farnham." She gripped her pistol harder. "Where have you taken them? If you've hurt one hair on—"

"Annie, what are you doing?" Frank was at her side. "Let me handle this."

"What have you done with them?" she asked again, ignoring Frank.

"I . . . I don't know what you are talking about," Mr. Farnham said, raising his hands in the air. He looked at her and then at Frank. His face blanched.

"Come on, Annie," Frank said, grabbing on to her elbow.

She shook him off. "Tell me where they are," she said, stepping closer to Mr. Farnham.

"Who?" he asked, his brows pinching together.

Annie's blood boiled. What kind of sick game was he playing? Anger flooded through her, hot and furious. She lunged at him, flailing her fists against his chest. "You animal! What have you done with them?"

She felt Frank's arm go around her waist. "Annie! Get ahold of yourself."

She struggled against his grasp, never taking her eyes off Mr. Farnham, who backed away from her, shock, disappointment, and bewilderment registering on his face.

"Frank!" Annie said, pulling at his arm, which was still wrapped tightly around her. "Let me go. Let me go!"

Mr. Farnham turned and ran. Frank let go of her and ran after Mr. Farnham. Luckily, Frank was faster and grasped the man's collar and jerked him to a stop. Mr. Farnham's feet slipped out from under him, and he fell to the ground on his back. He gasped for breath, the air obviously knocked from his lungs.

"He's got him!" Emma said, grabbing hold of Annie's hand.

Frank stood over him, straddling him, and then took hold of his lapels and hauled him to his feet. Mr. Farnham's eyes bulged as he continued to gasp for air. Frank slipped around him, taking one of his arms and wrenching it behind his back.

"We're going for a walk," Frank said through clenched teeth. He turned to Annie. "Your pistol?"

Annie pulled it out of her holster and handed it to Frank. He pressed the muzzle to Mr. Farnham's side. "I'm going to release you, and we are going to walk back to my tent where we're going to have a little chat. You make one false move, and I'll shoot, hear?"

His breathing coming back to normal, Mr. Farnham nodded.

The three of them escorted him back to Annie and Frank's tents. They slipped inside the tent they used for storage.

Frank shoved Mr. Farnham toward one of the wooden trunks. "Sit down," he commanded.

Mr. Farnham, still looking confused and bewildered, obeyed.

"What have you done with the children?" Annie asked, trying to remain calm. Emma put a steadying hand on her shoulder.

"The children? I honestly don't know what you mean," he said.

"I saw you talking to Liza, the girl who is—was—staying with me."

Mr. Farnham looked over at Frank and then back to Annie. "I only wanted her to deliver my note. You did read it, didn't you?"

The nerve of this man!

Annie took in a deep breath. "Yes, I read it, and no, we will *never* be together. Did you take Liza hoping it would change my mind? What kind of depraved person are you?"

"I didn't take the little girl!"

Annie shook off Emma's hand and drew her other pistol. She walked up to him and pressed the muzzle of it against his temple.

"Annie," Frank warned.

"Aren't you tired of him following me around, Frank?" she asked. "Why don't we get rid of him here and now?" She looked directly into Mr. Farnham's dark eyes, seeing deep into his disturbed soul, and a chill raised the hair on her arms.

Emma stepped up next to her. "This really isn't the way we should handle this," she said under her breath.

"I haven't heard you come up with any ideas," she replied, still holding her gaze on Mr. Farnham.

"Why have you done this?" Emma asked him. "What do you want?"

"I haven't *done* anything. And I think I've made it clear. I want Miss Oakley," he said, as if the request were simple enough.

Annie could feel Frank tense behind her. She gritted her teeth. "If I go with you, will you release the children?"

"I don't have the children."

"You better not be lying." Annie pressed the gun into his temple harder and cocked it.

He flinched at the sound of the metallic click, horror passing over his features. Was he afraid she would actually pull the trigger, or was he dismayed at her wholehearted disgust toward him?

"Miss Oakley?" a young voice rang out from outside.

"Find out who that is, would you, Emma?" Annie asked. She turned her attention back to Mr. Farnham. "You didn't answer my question."

"I told you—"

"Annie," Emma said, rushing back into the tent, "I think he's telling the truth." She handed something to Frank.

Annie continued to hold the pistol, cocked, to Mr. Farnham's temple. He'd begun to sweat, tiny dots of moisture popping up on his forehead.

"Annie, let him go," Frank said. "It's another note."

Annie heard Frank's words but couldn't pull herself away from her rage at Mr. Farnham. She stared hard into his watering eyes. She was tired of him dogging her everywhere she went. How could he even think he could in any way, shape, or form hold a candle to Frank Butler? How dare he continue to show his face, time after time, place after place!

"C'mon, sweetheart," Frank said. She felt his hand on her shoulder. "I'll take care of Farnham."

She knew she should listen to Frank, should let him go, but her guilt over the missing children and anger at having been put in the situation of taking Liza in, not to mention the consistently mounting pressures she'd been under for the past couple of years, culminated in her complete and utter revulsion for this man. She wanted nothing more than to pull the trigger and be done with it all.

Mr. Farnham let out a choked sob, and Annie could feel him trembling through the metal of her gun. She blinked. As if coming out of a dream, she stared at the end of the gun pressed to his head and her hand holding it there. His face was now covered in sweat, and his body shook as tears seeped from the corners of his eyes. She was suddenly engulfed with indifference.

She removed the gun from his temple and backed away from him.

"You go on outside with Emma," Frank said to her.

Annie holstered her pistol but leaned in close to Mr. Farnham's face, so close their noses almost touched. "I don't ever want to see your miserable face again, do you hear me?"

Mr. Farnham's lower lip quivered slightly, but holding her gaze, he nodded. It was almost imperceptible, but Annie knew he understood. She turned away from him and followed Emma out of the tent.

❧

Emma took hold of Annie's elbow as she came out from under the tent flap. Annie made her way to one of the wooden rockers placed in front of the firepit and sat down. She leaned her head against the back of the chair and closed her eyes.

Emma had never seen Annie in such a state. She really had thought her friend might pull the trigger and couldn't even begin to reconcile her relief that she hadn't. Annie's life would have changed forever, killing a man in cold blood. She had killed before but only in self-defense, and Emma knew that Annie still struggled with the hard reality that she had taken a life at all. She would never have forgiven herself if she'd lost control and pulled the trigger on Mr. Farnham.

Frank emerged from the tent with Mr. Farnham in tow, the man's hands behind his back. "I'll be back soon," Frank said. "Annie, you need to rest. You've been through quite an ordeal."

Annie didn't move, didn't even open her eyes. Frank took Mr. Farnham by the arm, and the two of them walked away. Emma sat down in the other rocker and remained quiet. She would wait for Annie to collect herself.

Emma took in the vibrant tones of the landscape as the sun began to set. The rows of white tents blazed brightly against the contrast of the lavender and blood-orange sky. The crowds touring the Wild West encampment were thinner today, much to her relief. She knew it would be difficult for Annie to interact with fans after what had just happened.

Finally, Annie opened her eyes.

"Hey," Emma said.

"Hey."

"Are you all right?"

"Yes. May I see the note?" Annie held out her hand and Emma gave it to her.

"It has to be from Miles," Annie said. "His first note demanded ransom. Now, he wants Alison in exchange for the children. He says to meet him at the warehouses at the far south end of the park tomorrow at two o'clock in the afternoon. Alone. No police. Well, that's not going to happen."

"My sentiments exactly. We should definitely go to the police with this," Emma said.

"Absolutely not," said Annie, the fire returning to her eyes. "He specifically says no police. If he so much as whiffs the scent of the police, he won't return the children . . . or worse."

"You're thinking of meeting his demands? Exchanging your friend for the children?" Emma was surprised that Annie would even entertain such a notion.

"No. Not Alison. Me, dressed as Alison. If I can keep him fooled long enough, we can get the children to safety, and then I'll handle Miles."

Emma snorted. "Annie, that's absurd! Handle Miles? Like you almost handled Mr. Farnham? You aren't speaking rationally, my dear."

"Liza was my responsibility."

"You need to think about this. You aren't making any sense."

Annie started to rise from the chair. "I need to go tell Alison about this note. She needs to know."

Emma reached out and took her hand, stopping her. "Nothing can be done until tomorrow. You need some rest. And don't you have a performance in the morning?" Emma knew it would be difficult to dissuade her. She hoped that if she could get Annie to at least get some sleep, she might be more reasonable in the morning.

Annie sighed. "I suppose you are right. No sense in disturbing Dr. Gordon and Alison tonight."

"That's more like it," Emma said. "You look exhausted, dear, and I am quite done in. What a day! If it's all the same to you, I'd like another cup of tea, and then I'm going to head back to the hotel and turn in myself. We will need our wits about us tomorrow."

Annie set her elbow on the arm of the chair and then rested her forehead on her fingertips. Emma let out her breath, relieved that Annie was willing to listen to her. She then made her way with the kettle to a nearby water tank and filled it up. Soon, it was rumbling on the grate above the fire.

They sat quietly as the sun sank lower in the sky and the muted colors of dusk filled the encampment. After about an hour, in the distance, Emma could see Frank walking toward them. Thank goodness. She'd been stalling for time, hoping he would return soon. With him here, she knew for sure that Annie wouldn't leave the encampment tonight.

When he reached the little campfire, he squatted down next to Annie's chair and took her hand. "Well, he won't be bothering us again."

"What did you do?" Annie asked, alarm in her voice.

"I bought him a one-way ticket to Biloxi, Mississippi, made sure he got on the train, and then waited until the train pulled out."

"Why Biloxi?" Emma asked.

"That's where the next train was headed." Frank smiled.

But he might come back," Emma said.

Frank shook his head. "He might, but I doubt it. Whatever fantasy he had about Annie and him being together someday was shattered. I think he pissed himself when you had that gun held to his head. Smelled something awful."

Emma nearly spit out her mouthful of tea, laughing. She looked over at Annie, and when they made eye contact, Annie let out a burst of laughter. Frank, too, joined in. Tears streamed down Emma's face while Annie's turned red as she clutched her middle.

As their laughter died, Emma looked at her wristwatch and took her handkerchief out of her clutch. "Oh my, it's getting late. I need to get back to the hotel." She dabbed at her cheeks with her handkerchief, still chuckling at the image of Farnham peeing his pants.

They all three stood, and Frank wrapped an arm around Annie's shoulders. "Thanks for staying with Annie," he said.

"Are you sure you are all right, Emma?" Annie asked. "You've been through an ordeal, too."

"Oh." Emma swatted the air. "I'm fine."

"Can I walk you to a coach?" Frank offered.

"No, you two get some sleep now. We'll reconvene in the morning and figure out how we are going to handle this kidnapping situation," she said, pointing at the ransom note.

"Good night," Frank said.

"Good night!" she called back as she walked away from them. She picked up her pace, hoping to catch a coach as soon as possible.

She thought about Annie's idea to stand in as a decoy for Alison and bit her lip, entirely uncomfortable with the whole idea. She hoped it wasn't too late to make a visit to Detective Carlton Chisolm.

⁂

Emma rested her elbows on the wooden counter of the police station, her fingers tapping a staccato beat as she waited to hear if Carlton was in. It had grown dark, and she knew the chances of him actually being at the station were slim. He'd either be working a case—possibly one involving the woman at the fairgrounds—or off duty, which would mean he would be at home. The problem was, she didn't know where he lived.

A rotund officer with round spectacles came through the doorway opposite her.

"Detective Chisolm is not in, madam. He's gone home for the evening."

"Oh, I see," she said, mustering her most charming smile. She also knew the chances of this officer telling her where Carlton lived were slim. "I don't know what I'm going to do."

The officer blinked at her.

"I've just arrived in Chicago by train, and I spent my last few cents hiring a coach to get here. I'm Carlton's cousin. I simply must see him, and I don't know where he lives."

The officer looked her up and down, probably questioning how a woman dressed so fine would have spent her last cent.

"You see, I left my bag on the train." She smiled, then worked her face to make her lower lip quiver. "I have nothing. I have come to bring Carlton news of our grandmother. News that is—" She let out a whimper and pressed her fist to her mouth. "Well, not good news, I'm afraid." She thought about how Mitchell had disappointed her, hurt her, and the sting of tears welled in her eyes. "I don't know where I will stay." She sniffed loudly.

The officer reached into his pocket and pulled out a handkerchief. "Very well," he said, resignation in his voice. "I'll put you in a cab and give you the address of his residence. This is highly unprecedented and I could lose my job, but seeing as this is a family matter, I suppose I can help."

Emma reached out to place her hand on his arm and looked into his small eyes, set deep in his pudgy face. "Oh, I can't tell you how much I appreciate this." She used the handkerchief to wipe away a tear and then handed it back to him. "You are so kind."

Not long later, the horse-drawn cab dropped her off at Carlton's door. Smoothing her hair, she walked up the steps and rapped on the wood. She could hear movement inside and then the click of the knob turning.

Carlton, chewing on something, opened the door. When he saw her, he could not hide his surprise. "Emma! What are you doing here?" He craned his neck to look behind her and swiveled his head to look down the street to the left and the right.

"I need to speak with you. May I come in?"

"Yes, yes, of course. Please." He opened the door wide and gestured for her to enter his domicile.

She walked into the narrow entry. His home seemed small but cozy. A fire burned in the room to her right, a parlor, and the smell of something delicious came from the room to her left.

Carlton ushered her into the parlor and indicated for her to take a chair next to the fire. "Can I get you something? I've, unfortunately, just finished my supper. My landlady prepares it for me and brings it over."

"Do you have some wine?" Emma asked, wanting something to smooth the frayed edges of her thoughts and emotions.

"No, I'm afraid. Whiskey?"

"Yes. That will do."

Carlton went over to a small table, picked up the bottle and two glasses, and sat himself in the chair opposite her. He poured and then handed her a glass. She sipped at the amber liquid, its warm sting on her tongue a welcome sensation. She swallowed, feeling its heat go all the way down to her stomach.

"What can I help you with?" Carlton asked. He placed the bottle on the floor and leaned his elbows on his knees, his glass between his hands. She could smell the sweet scent of pipe tobacco wafting from him.

"I wanted to alert you to something my friend, Miss Oakley, plans to do. Something that makes me nervous." Emma said. She told him of Annie's distress at the missing children and her plan.

"Does she realize the danger she's placing herself in posing as her friend?" he asked.

"She does," Emma said and then sipped again. The muscles in her shoulders began to release. "Annie fears nothing. Except letting down people who are close to her. I believe she is capable of pulling this off, but I am concerned for her safety."

"Your testimony is good enough for me. I'd like to be there, though. For her protection—physically as well as legally."

Emma sighed with relief. Her body had molded itself to the chair. The warm fire, the whiskey, and the presence of an old, dear friend had lulled her into a sense of comfort she hadn't felt for quite some time, not even with Mitchell.

"And there is something else." She told him what Mitchell had told her about the two women, and the beneficiaries of Deborah Granger and Mr. Barnes' life insurance policies. She also told him about the dead woman she'd seen earlier at the Midway. It seemed he hadn't heard about the third woman as he had been buried in paperwork all day.

"I found this next to the body." She handed over the pin. Carlton took it and rolled the edges between his thumb and forefinger. "I don't know what the beetle symbolizes. I'm going to do some research," she said.

"You took evidence from a crime scene?" he said, condemnation in his voice.

"I just wanted to look at it. I must have grabbed it before I passed out. Does the symbol look familiar to you?"

Carlton shook his head. "No, but I will need to take that from you."

Emma sighed. She doubted he would let her hold on to it, but she wouldn't forget what the pin looked like. Its image was burned in her brain forever. She'd have no problem conjuring it up for her research.

"You look exhausted," Carlton said, his voice soothing, caring.

"I am."

"Shall I get you a cab?"

She didn't answer, letting the silence fill the room. Their eyes locked and held. She could see the longing in his, the renewed affection. Perhaps he'd never lost his affection for her.

He reached over and took her hand. "Or you can stay." He said the words without emotion, without pressure, and with complete sincerity.

She placed her other hand over his, their gazes drawing an invisible but palpable connection between them. "I'd like that."

CHAPTER 23

BOBBY BRADLEY AWAITING DATE FOR TRIAL
– *The Chicago Herald*, Wednesday, June 14, 1893

ANNIE, CLAD IN ONE OF ALISON'S DRESSES AND WITH A HAT
pulled low on her head, stood between Warehouse C and Warehouse D, just where Miles had instructed. It was no wonder he
wanted to do the exchange here. It was quite deserted and far
from the activity of the Exhibition.

She wiped a trickle of perspiration from her temple and read-
justed the floppy-brimmed hat that partially covered her face
but was a bit small in comparison with the dress that was a little
large.

Frank, Detective Chisolm, Dr. Gordon, and a very weak
Alison waited nearby, hiding behind Warehouse B. Annie had
pleaded with Alison to stay in bed, but she would not hear of it.
She had wanted to make the sacrifice of herself in exchange for
the children, but Dr. Gordon and Detective Chisolm had
dissuaded her. She had agreed on the condition that she be
allowed to come with them. She wanted to be there for Liza.

Annie had not at all been pleased with Emma when she showed up at the grounds before Annie's performance with the police detective in tow. But she quickly changed her mind when he agreed that her plan to stand in as a decoy was a good one—but only if he was present, armed and at the ready while she enacted the plan. Detective Chisolm had instructed Annie as to what to do, as well as encouraged Ska, Ohitekah, and Frida to stay behind, as it would be far too risky to have so many people there.

The June day was particularly warm. Annie had to stand in full sunlight to prove she wasn't hiding anything, though she did have her Derringer nestled deeply in her dress pocket. Between the sun beating down on her and the anxiety welling up inside her, perspiration dampened her armpits and trickled down the backs of her legs.

She startled when she saw Liza peek out from behind Warehouse D, a man's hand firmly on her shoulder and the muzzle of a pistol pointed at her head. He did not show his face. They were far away, but Annie could see Liza's eyes wide with fear—or recognition, she couldn't be sure.

"You there?" Miles shouted.

"Yes." Annie tried her best to imitate Alison's lilting voice.

Miles came out from behind the building, but he didn't come forward. She grasped her Derringer and wanted to shoot him, just to incapacitate him, but he was out of range for the small pistol. She couldn't risk hitting Liza.

He held on to the girl and kept the gun at her head. He was a short man, much shorter than Alison, with a stocky build. He wore his hat low on his brow, which only served to accentuate a large, bulbous nose.

"You didn't think I'd ever find you, did ya?" he yelled. "You probably thought you'd left me for dead."

Annie didn't move. She thought the statement strange since he had met with Dr. Gordon. The doctor had found Miles, not the other way around.

"When you skedaddled out of the house so fast, you left some things behind. Like the brochure for the Wild West Show." He grinned, clearly pleased with himself. "I did some snooping around and found some newspapers you'd saved with articles about Miss Annie Oakley. I figured she just might be a friend of yours. You sure are pretty, but you're not very smart, my dear. We could have had a wonderful life together, but you changed all that when you hit me over the head with that damn lamp."

Tired of the diatribe and roasting in the sun, Annie wanted to get on with it. "Where are the other children?" she hollered back, trying to keep her voice flat, disguised.

"They're safe behind this building here. Don't you worry none. I'm not interested in them. They can't get me that cool fortune like you can. You just come on over here, and I'll let those other two go."

"What about Liza?" she asked. "You said you'd let her go, too."

His grin faded. "You just come on over here," he yelled. "You don't want anything to happen to those fine boys, do you?"

Annie shook her head.

"Come on, then. Real slow."

Annie started to walk toward him, counting her steps. She lowered her head to further hide her face. She stopped at twenty steps. From behind the straw mesh of the hat, she could see the pistol pointed directly at her.

"Release the boys," she said, holding up her hands. "Please. You'll have me. You can have all my money and my share of the company. I'll sign it all over to you if you release the boys and let me and Liza live. We'll go directly from here to the bank. I don't want the money or the company. I just want Liza."

Miles kept the pistol trained on her, hesitating, thinking. Probably imagining what he would do with Alison's fortune. Annie's jaw clenched.

"Boys," Miles finally said, "you can come on out, now. You

run back to your mamas and don't you stop or I'll shoot you dead."

Both Chayton and Ivan came out from behind the building and ran toward Annie. When Chayton registered recognition of her, she shook her head slightly, hoping he wouldn't say a word. Luckily, they ran past her and out of the area. She inwardly breathed a sigh of relief.

"Okay, then," he said, pointing the gun to Liza's head again. "No funny stuff. Come on over here."

The sun beat down, causing a tightness at her temples and at the base of her neck. She continued to walk toward him slowly. Suddenly, the expression on Miles's face changed. He looked puzzled, confused. Annie was closer now and could see the girl's eyes widen when she realized that the woman standing before her was not her mother.

"Stop!" Miles commanded. "You look different."

Annie froze.

He studied her some more, and then his face hardened. "Just how stupid do you think I am?" he yelled. "I'm going to kill her, I swear. And then I'll come for Alison. It will be one less person between me and that fortune."

"Miles!" Alison's voice rang out. Annie cringed. "Here I am."

She turned to see Alison come out from behind the warehouse, staggering a bit, unsteady on her feet. Dr. Gordon came out after her and took hold of her elbow for support. Annie held her breath.

"I told you to come alone," he yelled. "What kind of a fool do you take me for?"

Liza flinched and silently started to cry as if he'd tightened his grip on her arm. Annie clenched her fists, furious with the ogre. She wanted to rush to Liza but held her ground.

"No!" Alison said, coming forward. She shook Dr. Gordon off her. "I'm here. Let her go. I'll go with you, Miles. You don't want to run the risk of going to prison and not getting the money. There are witnesses here. If you kill us, you'll hang for sure. I'll turn it all over to you. Just give me back my daughter." Alison, somehow finding the strength, boldly walked toward them, holding her arms out to Liza. The girl began to cry in earnest. Miles trained the gun on Alison.

"You," he said to Annie. "Back away. I'll kill her and the girl, sure as I'm standing here if you don't."

Annie obeyed and backed several yards away from them. He let go of the girl, and she ran to Alison, flinging her arms around her middle. Alison held on to her tightly. The two held each other so close it was as if they'd morphed into one.

"Let her go," he said to Alison.

Alison pried herself away from Liza. "Go to Miss Annie, Liza."

"No!" Liza clung to Alison's waist again. Annie's breath caught in her throat, her heart breaking for the little girl. Finally reunited with her mother only to be wrenched away again.

"I mean it, woman!" Miles shouted.

Alison wrested Liza away from her once more but kept her hands firmly on her shoulders. "You must be a good girl and go with Miss Annie. I'll be back soon. We will have a new life, my little love bug. We will be so happy. Just do as your told, and you will see." She kissed the top of the girl's head and released her. Liza ran to Annie, sobbing.

Alison made her way slowly to Miles, her body swaying. She faltered and then folded over and fell to the ground.

"Alison!" Annie started to run for her but stopped when Frank emerged from behind Building D, behind Miles.

Quickly, Frank tackled him to the ground. Detective Chisolm rushed toward the two men as they wrestled in the dirt. Frank had Miles by his shooting arm, struggling to keep the gun away from himself. He slammed Miles's arm down against the ground in an effort to dislodge the pistol. Reaching the two men, Detective Chisolm kicked the pistol out of Miles hand, and Frank scrambled to his feet.

Detective Chisolm pulled out his weapon and trained it at Miles's head. "Police! Don't move."

Miles flopped his head to the ground, his chest heaving. From behind her, Annie heard Dr. Gordon let out a guttural howl. He passed her and headed toward Miles at a dead run. Distracted by the commotion, Detective Chisolm lowered his gun a fraction, and Miles kicked the detective's feet out from under him. He landed with a thud. Scrambling to his feet, Miles lunged toward the gun.

"Frank!" Annie yelled, still holding on to Liza.

Miles picked up the gun, and as he was about to turn around, Dr. Gordon and Frank shoved him to the ground again. Annie couldn't see what was happening as the three men rolled around in a scuffle, arms and legs flailing in the dirt, and then her breath froze. Somehow Miles had knocked Frank out cold and had pinned Dr. Gordon, straddling his middle and pointing the gun at his face.

Annie reached into her pocket, pulled out her Derringer, and didn't hesitate to squeeze the trigger. Miles sat stunned, a perfect circle of red blooming on his forehead. His shoulders sagged, and then he toppled over to his side. Dr. Gordon wriggled his way out from beneath him.

Annie ran over to Frank. By the time she reached him, his eyes were open and blinking. A trickle of blood seeped down his forehead from within his hairline. She leaned over him, her heart clanging like a fire alarm. "Darling, are you all right?"

Frank blinked again and then attempted to sit up. Annie took hold of his arm and helped him. He shook his head as if trying to clear it and then winced, placing his fingertips to his wound. He pulled his hand away to look at the blood. "I think so. Just got my bell rung. I think he coldcocked me with that pistol."

Annie ripped off a piece of fabric from her hemline and pressed it to his wound. He flinched. "You were wonderful, Frank," she said.

"Not as wonderful as you, darlin,'" he said, grimacing in pain.

Just then, she remembered that Alison had collapsed to the ground. She turned to see Dr. Gordon and Liza kneeling down beside her.

"I'm okay, Annie," Frank said. "You go to your friend." She helped Frank get to his feet. "I'm going to see if Detective Chisolm needs any assistance," he said.

When she felt confident that he was steady, she hurried over to Alison, Liza, and Dr. Gordon.

Alison blinked up at them. "What happened? Where is Liza?"

"She's right here," said Annie. A sobbing Liza knelt down and pressed her head against Alison's chest. Alison wrapped her arms around the child, tears of joy streaming down her face. Annie swallowed the lump rising in her throat.

"And Miles?" Alison asked Annie.

She took Alison's hand. "He won't be bothering you anymore."

"Your friend here made certain of that." Dr. Gordon smiled at Annie, his blue eyes twinkling. He took Alison's other hand. "Let's see if you can sit up, eh?"

Annie guided Liza away from Alison, and Dr. Gordon helped her to sit up. "I think I fainted," she said.

"You are still weak from the treatment. Let's get you back to the house. Doctor's orders." Dr. Gordon helped her to her feet, and then, placing an arm around her shoulders and the other arm under her knees, he picked her up. Annie was touched at his tenderness toward her friend, and she was elated that Alison would hopefully, finally, have happiness in her life.

Alison held her hand out to Liza. "You come with Dr. Gordon and me. We won't ever be separated again. I promise."

Liza took her mother's hand and then looked over at Annie, her cherubic little face beaming.

CHAPTER 24

WILD WEST SHOW PERFORMANCE COMEDY OF ERRORS!
– *Chicago Star Free Press*, Tuesday, June 20, 1893

ONE WEEK LATER

Annie knocked at the door of Emma's suite at the Palmer House Hotel. Not hearing any movement from within, she knocked again.

She was surprised when a tall, pinched-faced man with an eye monocle opened the door. He wore a gray tailed suit and white gloves. He looked at her expectantly.

"I'm here to see Emma Wilson. Is this her suite?" Annie asked, peering in.

The man stepped back and opened the door wider for her to enter. He held out both arms bent at the elbows. Annie was confused. Pulling off her gloves and taking off her hat, she smiled at him. He raised an eyebrow, and his gaze traveled to the accessories in her hands.

"Oh," she said, embarrassed, and handed him her hat and her gloves. He indicated with a wave of his arm for her to enter the suite.

It was beautifully appointed with dark-mahogany furnishings, claret-colored silk wallpaper with a design of velvet burnout Fleur de Lis in rows. A sparkling crystal chandelier caught the rays of sunlight streaming through the tall windows and cast colorful rainbows on the white ceiling. Emma stood over her desk, leaning her hands on the wood as she studied something. She clearly hadn't heard Annie enter.

"Emma?" Annie said.

Her friend whirled around. "Oh, Annie dear! I'm sorry. I'm quite ensconced in this map of the Expo grounds. Do come in and sit. Chauncy!" she called out.

The dour-faced man entered the room. "Be a love and do ring the restaurant and have tea service delivered. Plenty of milk and sugar."

He gave an almost imperceptible nod, turned on his heel, and left.

"The hotel provides you with a butler?" Annie asked, not at all surprised that Emma would engage the services of one. She was used to a certain standard of living. Yet, she wasn't above living in a tent with the Wild West Show as she had done so many times before. It was one of the things Annie liked best about Emma. She was a refined and pampered woman who wasn't afraid of getting her hands dirty.

"The hotel? No." Emma waved a hand in the air. "I've employed his services on my own. I don't think he's very happy with the arrangement, though. He hardly says two words."

Annie laughed. "So I noticed."

"I'm surprised you were able to come so early." Emma indicated for Annie to sit on the settee while she took an armchair. "I would have assumed you had a performance this afternoon."

"The Colonel has been pushing all of us pretty hard." Annie sank deep into the generous cushion. "Truth be told, he is making money hand over fist here in Chicago, and it's almost as if he's afraid it will all go away if we slow down. However, many of the performers are so exhausted, myself included, that mistakes are being made. Yesterday, one of the crew forgot to load blanks into Texas Joe's gun, and he nicked one of the horses with a bullet!"

"Heavens!" Emma exclaimed, her tawny brows pressing down over her emerald green eyes.

"The horse was fine, just startled as you can imagine. Then Frida nearly toppled off the back of one of her horses when he spooked at a child waving a banner. One of the Mexican vaqueros lost hold of his *reata*, and the bull he'd roped ran halfway around the arena before he and his horse could pull it to a stop. I myself only hit nineteen of the twenty pigeons released at my last performance." She shook her head, still disgusted with herself.

"Nineteen out of twenty? I'm surprised you weren't fired," Emma teased.

Annie gave her a wry grin. "You know what I mean. What I am telling you is that the Colonel realized if we all didn't get some rest, that money sure as shootin' would dry up if people were disappointed. So he's given us a couple of days off. Now that Liza is settled with her mother, I can focus on Bobby's case. Have you learned anything new? Anything that might help him?"

Just then, another knock came on the door. "Oh, that must be our tea. I am just famished," Emma said. "You?"

"I could eat."

Chauncy brought in the tea service while one of the hotel staff brought in the tiered trays of cucumber-and-butter finger sandwiches and cake. Emma's eyes glittered as she perused the delicacies.

"Brilliant." She helped herself to a bite of cake while Chauncy poured both of them some tea.

After he'd left, Annie placed two finger sandwiches on a tiny, gold-rimmed porcelain plate. Emma dusted cake crumbs from her fingers. "I hate to admit it, Annie, but I am stumped. I can't seem to make a connection between the four deaths. The most recent one, the body I saw, clearly had been beaten. Either she was killed by someone else or the murderer had a different motive and method for killing her. Carlton told me the other bodies showed no evidence of violence, except of course in the case of Mr. Barnes with the gunshot wound."

Annie sighed. "There has to be something we can do. I went with the Colonel to see Bobby this morning. Poor kid is so downhearted. The lawyer was there and said they were preparing to appeal for bail again."

Emma raised a finger. "I do think we are onto something with these life insurance policies, however."

"Yes, well, that's something," Annie said, hopeful. It wasn't much, but it was a connection between the first three.

"Yes, but I can't seem to find anything concrete." Emma told her about her meeting with Detective Chisolm and how she asked about having an autopsy done on one or all of the bodies, without any luck.

"That would have been helpful," Annie said.

"But—" Emma brightened "—I did find information on the pin."

Annie squinted in confusion. "The pin?"

"The blue pin with the beetle on it?"

"Oh, yes, what does it mean?"

"It's a nurse's pin from the State Lunatic Hospital at Danvers in Massachusetts. They opened a training program for nurses there in 1889."

"So the woman must have been a nurse," Annie said, thinking of Nurse Bonnie. Didn't Beth say she hadn't been around for a couple of days? She also mentioned something about the nurse being threatened by Mr. Morton. She wondered if Nurse Bonnie had returned to Dr. Gordon's.

Yet, there was no evidence indicating the woman Emma saw was a nurse, though, and until she was positively identified, she could be anyone from anywhere. There were so many travelers to the state of Illinois for the fair.

Holding her teacup and saucer, Annie got up and walked to the desk. It was strewn with newspapers, notes, and folders, some of them haphazardly thrown on top of Emma's beloved and much used Remington typewriter. Her friend was a brilliant writer and one of the smartest women Annie had ever known, but how she could work with the chaos on her desk was a complete mystery.

"Tell me about the beneficiaries again." Annie set the teacup and saucer down on a corner of the desk. Emma repeated what she had told her, including the beneficiaries names and where they were from.

"Do you have a map of the United States?" Annie asked.

Emma stood up. "Perhaps in one of my trunks. It might take a minute to find." She went into one of the adjoining rooms of the suite. Annie walked to the window and watched the people and coaches bustling down below. How could her friend concentrate with all that noise?

After a few minutes, Emma reappeared with a large, rolled-up piece of parchment. "Here we are," she said, going over to the desk. She shoved some papers aside and unrolled the map. Annie took the liberty of using her teacup and saucer to hold down one corner, while Emma used a paperweight and her pencil box to hold down the two corners nearest her.

Annie ran her hand over the map. "Here is Illinois," she said, circling the state with her index finger. "Where are the beneficiaries from?"

Emma consulted her notes. "Atlanta, Missouri; Adamsville, Tennessee; and Alexandria, Kentucky. Oh my! They all begin with the letter *A*."

Annie bit her lip. "Strange coincidence." She circled the three cities on the map and then drew lines connecting them in a triangle. Emma leaned over her shoulder. "And maybe a little silly, actually." She traced her finger from city to city. "According to this map, they all seem to be equidistant from each other, too."

Yes. But there is something else . . .

Annie turned to Emma. "May I see your notes?"

"Help yourself." Emma handed the notebook to her.

Annie scanned the page. "Harvey G. Langston from Atlanta, Missouri . . . Gregory L. Harris from Adamsville, Tennessee . . . Helen Leigh Grant from Alexandria, Kentucky." She gasped. "The names! The letters! Gregory L. Harris, Harvey G. Langston, Helen Leigh Grant—*L, G,* and *H!*"

Emma's eyes widened as Annie continued. "All three names have variations of the letters, and all three cities start with the letter *A,* and all three states are in close proximity to Illinois! Now that is just too many commonalities to be coincidence, don't you think?"

Emma took hold of Annie's hand and squeezed it. "Indeed, I do, Sherlock. *You,* my friend, are amazing!"

⚜️

Frank leaned against the railing of the sixty-foot round pen he had the crew make for him. He figured he'd have better luck with Diablo if they had a smaller space in which to get better acquainted if he was going to succeed in creating a bond with him.

Diablo paced on the opposite curve of the pen, occasionally calling out to the other horses, his attention focused on anything but Frank.

Frank thought about trying to approach the horse but knew that he would more than likely take off at a run and career around the pen in a panic. He looked down at Jep, who stood at his side.

"You stay here," he said to the dog. With a pathetic whine, Jep lay down and rested his chin on his paws. Frank took a wooden bucket sitting outside the pen, walked to the center of the circle, flipped it over with a hollow *thunk*, and sat on it. He'd seen Annie do this many times with Buck.

Diablo swung his head around to look at him.

"Well, that's a start, old boy," he muttered under his breath. He was determined to sit there until the horse became curious enough to approach *him*. The horse's reward would be the three carrots Frank had stuffed in his back pocket. He pulled out the rolled-up newspaper from his other back pocket and unfurled it. He then took his spectacles out of the breast pocket of his shirt and put them on. Leaning his elbows on his knees, he settled in to read the paper.

There was nothing of much interest so he perused the articles and ads. Soon, his mind drifted to thoughts of Ivan and Frida. Since he had rebuffed her, she'd kept her distance. He missed having his lessons, but he supposed it was for the best. He hoped that he hadn't led Frida to believe he would entertain thoughts of betraying Annie.

Years ago, Annie had thought he had been unfaithful to her with his old flame, Twila Midnight, who had later become the Colonel's mistress. The whole thing had been a giant misunderstanding, but it had nearly broken his heart to see his beloved so shattered. He never wanted to bring that kind of pain to Annie ever again, and no matter how stubborn, strong-willed, and sometimes infuriating she could be, he had no desire to be with anyone else. His love for her was the purest thing in his life, and he would never do anything to tarnish it.

He was relieved the children had been returned for both their mothers' sakes but also for Annie's. She had worked so hard to make everything right for Alison and Liza. He hadn't been too keen on his wife's involvement in it all, especially when it came to Annie acting as a decoy, but it was in her nature to help others, and he really couldn't fault her for that. In the end, it had all turned out fine and everyone was safe and in their proper place once again. Except Bobby. Annie was determined to help him still, and Frank didn't protest. Bobby was a member of their

Wild West family, and he told Annie he'd help in any way he could.

He glanced over his spectacles to look at Diablo. The horse was still focused on him, but he'd stopped whinnying to the other horses. He stood quietly, his head lowered, both eyes fixed on Frank.

Frank directed his gaze to the paper again.

Thinking of Ivan brought the image of Frank's brother into his mind. He'd dreamed about Kenny again last night, but this time the dream was different. Instead of a replay of the frantic thrashing in the water and the feel of his elbow squarely hitting the side of Kenny's face, his brother floated peacefully below the surface of the water. Shafts of bright sunlight penetrated the murkiness and shone on Kenny's eyes, which were closed as if in sleep. Frank stood at the edge of the pond, searching, the rope swing moving like a pendulum as it hung from the branch of the tree. Then he'd woken up. The dream had been disturbing but not filled with its usual heart-pounding angst.

Diablo huffed out a breath, distracting Frank from his reverie. The horse had turned his entire body to face him. Acting as if he hadn't noticed, Frank flipped the page of the paper, holding it in front of his face.

"Now, we're getting somewhere," he said to the newsprint.

He shifted his weight to get more comfortable on the bucket and continued to slowly turn the pages, scanning the words but not taking them in. Then his eye was drawn to a headline: WILD WEST STAR BOBBY BRADLEY SCHEDULED FOR TRIAL AUGUST 31. He shook his head. That was nearly two and a half months away. He and the Colonel had hoped the lawyer could get the judge to reconsider keeping the boy in jail for that long, but so far, it didn't look promising.

The horse huffed again, and Frank lowered the paper just below his line of vision. Diablo had moved closer, but instead of being directly in front of him, he'd moved to Frank's left side. Something bumped his shoulder, and a jolt of adrenaline shot through him. Warm puffs of air passed over his neck. Diablo had made contact.

Frank could feel his muzzle pass over his shoulder and then felt a tug at his back pocket as Diablo yanked out a carrot. Frank chuckled. He took the chance and looked over his shoulder at the horse, who looked back at him, big brown eyes blinking, mouth chewing. Slowly, Frank reached into his back pocket and pulled out the two remaining carrots.

Diablo pushed on his shoulder with his nose and made his way around to face him. Frank lifted a carrot, and Diablo took it out of his hand, pulling it into his mouth. It was gone in seconds, and Frank gave him the last carrot. As Diablo chewed, Frank presented the back of his hand under Diablo's nose, and the horse stopped chewing to sniff. When he started munching again, Frank cautiously laid his palm on the flat area between Diablo's eyes.

The horse exhaled a rush of air again, and Frank's heart leaped with joy.

CHAPTER 25

INDIANS PERFORM BUFFALO DANCE AT WILD WEST SHOW!
– *The Chicago Herald*, Friday, June 23, 1893

ANNIE WAVED TO THE ENTHUSIASTIC CROWD AS SHE AND BUCK ran their final laps around the ring. They came to a sliding stop in the center of the arena, and Annie tapped Buck's shoulders with her toes. He raised himself up in a rear, his front hoofs pawing at the air. Annie rode the upward momentum, smiling and waving. She loved the feeling of their two bodies moving as one. When she was this connected with Buck, she felt she could ask him to do anything.

When she left the arena, Mr. Post was waiting for her. She threw her leg over the saddle horn and then jumped down.

"Attagirl." Mr. Post took Buck's reins. "You did not disappoint the fans, as usual, little missy,"

"Thanks, Mr. Post," Annie said with pride. "I've got to run, though. Can you take care of Buck?"

"Don't I always?" he asked, a look of injury crossing his features.

She smiled. "Yes, sir, it's just polite to ask."

"Indeed, it is." He stroked Buck's neck.

"See you tomorrow, Mr. Post." With that, Annie took off running, fearing that if she didn't hurry to her tent and change clothes, she'd be late for her meeting with Emma, Detective Chisolm, and Mr. Ellis, Bobby's lawyer.

After they had made the connection between the matching initials of the beneficiaries, and also the *A* cities of the surrounding states in which they resided, Annie and Emma had requested a meeting with Mr. Ellis via the Colonel, to tell him what they had discovered. Mr. Ellis was impressed with this new information and said he would take it to the judge. He had sent Annie a note with the happy news that the judge had agreed to have Millie Turnbill's body exhumed and examined to shed light on the true cause of death. Now Mr. Ellis was calling a meeting to disclose the findings.

An hour later and breathless, Annie breezed into the restaurant and spotted Emma and Detective Chisolm seated together, their heads close together. She thought they looked quite cozy. A becoming blush graced Emma's perfectly alabaster cheek. Her feelings for Detective Chisolm must have been rekindled— something Annie took great delight in. Detective Chisolm was widowed, *not* married, and from what little she knew of him, he seemed to be the kind of man who would let Emma be Emma.

The two of them stood when Annie approached the table. She shook hands with the detective, and then she and Emma greeted each other with a kiss to each cheek. Just as they were about to sit, Mr. Ellis entered the restaurant. An unusually tall man, his legs were so long he gave the appearance of walking on stilts. He had a pleasing face with angular features and large, deep-set eyes that had a hardness to them, as if they shielded something tender inside. After exchanging niceties, they all sat down. Detective Chisolm called over a waiter and the gentlemen ordered beer, Emma champagne, and Annie a sarsaparilla.

"What news, Mr. Ellis?" Emma asked. "Was it determined how Miss Turnbill died?"

"Not exactly. The only thing of note the coroner found was a damaged liver, which is unusual in one so young."

"Could have been a drinker," the detective said.

"Possibly. Or it could have been the result of illness," said Mr. Ellis.

"That's it, Mr. Ellis? Nothing else?" Annie asked, disappointed. She had so hoped they would find something more concrete.

"Well, then what about the other woman, Deborah Granger?" Emma chimed in. "Can a postmortem be done on her body?"

Mr. Ellis clucked and shook his head. "The family would need to give their consent. It was easier with Miss Turnbill because she had no family."

"Miss Granger has a mother living in Missouri." Detective Chisolm said Missouri with an *ah* at the end. "That's who identified her, and I'm sure that is where the body was sent. We have also since found out that her daughter, Nettie, has gone missing, although there has been no trace of her."

"I had a feeling it was the same Deborah Granger," Annie said with a frown.

We would have to contact Mrs. Granger and the authorities there to get permission for a postmortem."

"It might be prudent," Annie said. "Although from what we've heard, Mrs. Granger is quite ill. I don't know what state of mind she might be in, or even if she would consent. Poor Mrs. Granger—one daughter dead, another missing."

"Could Nettie have turned up at Dr. Gordon's again?" Emma asked Annie. "Have you asked Beth?"

Annie shook her head. "I haven't been by to visit Alison lately. I wanted to give her and Liza some time alone to get reacquainted."

"What are we talking about?" Mr. Ellis asked, impatience in his voice. It must have sounded like they'd gone off topic.

"We are familiar with Deborah and Nettie's employer, Dr. Gordon. But back to why you are here, Mr. Ellis," said Emma. "What about Mr. Barnes' body? Could we have him exhumed? The coroner's report stated that he died of the gunshot wound, but no postmortem was performed."

Mr. Ellis took in a lungful of air and then let it out. "I'll have to approach the judge again. It would certainly help my case with Mr. Bradley if we could find some other evidence of foul play besides the gunshot wound."

"Excellent," said Emma, clapping her hands together. "Things are certainly starting to get interesting."

Annie smiled at her friend wondering if "interesting" would be enough to save Bobby from hanging.

۞

Annie sat in the visitors' room of the Cook County Jail waiting to see Bobby. She sat at the far end of a table with built-in wooden dividers that allowed visitors and prisoners to speak with their loved ones, friends, or legal representation with some modicum of privacy. She could hear the woman next to her crying as she spoke to her husband. She tried not to listen, but it sounded as if the prisoner was going to be sent to the state penitentiary to await execution. Annie took a deep breath and said a prayer that she could help her friend avoid the same fate.

She looked up to see Bobby walk through a door at the back of the room, dressed in the customary black-and-white-striped uniform of inmates. His hands and feet were also shackled together. Even from a distance, Annie could tell from his bent posture that Bobby's spirits were low—much lower than they had been at her previous visits.

The guard held Bobby by the arm and escorted him to the

seat across the table from Annie. Releasing him, the guard then went to stand against the wall, not ten feet from them.

Annie studied Bobby's face. He had yet to make eye contact with her. "Hello, Bobby. I'm sorry I haven't been to see you in the past week. The Colonel has had us hopping busy."

He raised his gaze to her, and Annie's heart nearly shattered. His eyes carried the haunted look of someone who'd lost all hope.

"It's okay," he said and stared at the metal cuffs on his wrists.

"Has Beth been to visit you?" Annie asked, hoping to inspire a smile.

"Yes," he said, his voice animated but his eyes still vacant and sad. "Should be here sometime today, though I don't know why she continues to come. I don't have anything to offer her—especially from a jail cell."

"She cares about you, Bobby. As do we all." She wished she could reach out and give him a hug, but it would probably not go over well with the guard, whose eyes kept shifting to her.

"Emma and I have made a little progress in our investigation. We believe we may have found a connection between Mr. Barnes' death and the deaths of two women also found buried on the Expo grounds," Annie said, trying to sound cheerful. She told him about the insurance policies and the matching initials of the beneficiaries.

"Does Mr. Ellis know of this?" Bobby asked, a hint of enthusiasm in his voice.

"Yes. He has been instrumental in getting a postmortem performed on one of the women. He is now inquiring to get Mr. Barnes' body exhumed and examined. If we can find anything that links the two bodies, we might have a leg to stand on. I don't want to give you false hope, but all is not lost, Bobby."

"Yes. I thank you, Annie."

"Anything for you, Bobby. We'll get to the bottom of this. I promise."

Bobby sat a little straighter in his chair and looked directly into Annie's eyes. "Tell me about the show. How's it going?"

Annie told him about all her performances, the numbers of spectators, and the business of the camp. She also told him about Alison and Liza, and how the children had been kidnapped and of their rescue. Just as she was about to tell him of Frank and Diablo, his attention was diverted, and he looked to the door behind her. Annie turned around to see Beth carrying a wicker picnic basket and walking toward them.

Her face lit up at seeing Annie there. "Miss Oakley! So good to see you."

Annie stood to greet her. The crying woman next to Annie had left, so Annie pulled the woman's vacant chair over for her.

"How are you, Bobby?" Beth asked.

"I'm well. As well as can be expected anyhow."

"You look thinner every time I come to see you. I've brought you some soup." She held up a crock with a cork top. "It almost didn't make it past the guards down the hall. They have to inspect anything you bring in," she told Annie.

"Thank you, Beth," Bobby said, smiling for the first time.

Beth handed over the crock and a spoon.

"How is Alison? And Liza? Is she settling in?" Annie asked her.

"Miss Alison is awfully excited about the wedding. She has me sit at her bedside taking notes. Dr. Gordon told her to spare no expense. They are going to have a small wedding, but it will be lavish, I daresay. Oh, I do hope Miss Alison gets to feeling better soon. She seems to be getting weaker with each passing day. Dr. Gordon says it will take some time to build back her strength." Beth frowned slightly. "But Liza is doing well. She spends most of her time at the foot of her mother's bed. Alison is helping her with her letters and is teaching her to read. The girl is quiet and shy, but she is slowly opening up to me. She is a little wary of Dr. Gordon, but I suppose that is understandable given what her stepfather did to her and then seeing him shot dead."

"Yes," Annie agreed. "It is a lot for a child to take in. Well—" she stood up from the chair "—I will let you two visit. Oh, I almost forgot. Has Nurse Bonnie returned? You mentioned that she'd been gone a few days."

"She hasn't. It's put the doctor in quite a mood, too."

"I see." Annie pressed her lips together. "Did you know much about her?'

Beth shrugged. "Not really. She wasn't the friendliest of women, which is a shame because she is a nurse and all."

"And you indicated that she left because of Mr. Morton?"

"Well, I just assumed," Beth said with a shrug. "She left that same day I heard him get after her. But then Miss Alison told me that Nurse Bonnie and the doctor had also quarreled. Like I said, she wasn't the friendliest of women."

"Right. Well, thank you, Beth. And has there be any word of Nettie?"

Beth shook her head sadly. "Nothing. I do feel right sorry for her mother. I hope Nettie turns up soon."

"Yes," Annie said, plastering a smile on her face. She, too, hoped Nettie turned up soon, and prayed that when she did, she didn't turn up dead.

CHAPTER 26

Bobby Bradley's Trial Set for August 31!
The Chicago Evening Post Monday, June 26, 1893

A few days later, after Annie's afternoon performance, Emma was waiting at the gate for her. Her face was flushed, and her eyes sparkled a deeper green than usual, enhanced by her emerald dress and hat adorned with peacock feathers. She looked as if she were about to jump out of her skin from excitement.

Annie rode Buck over to her. "Hello, Emma. You look as if you are about to burst."

"My dear, I am! Get down here."

Annie dismounted. "What is it?"

"Carlton, dear man, just came to me with the news. Mr. Ellis was able to persuade the judge to order Mr. Barnes' body exhumed and examined, and guess what they found?"

"Don't make me guess, Emma," Annie said, exasperated. "Tell me!"

"Mr. Barnes, too, had a damaged liver."

Annie sucked in her breath. "You don't say! This looks good for Bobby, doesn't it?"

"Well, it is good news, but it isn't entirely good. The coroner said that it was not conclusive that the damage to his liver caused his death. He felt it was still more likely that Mr. Barnes died of the loss of blood from the gunshot wound."

Annie's spirits sank. "Oh no. So, we haven't helped Bobby."

"Not yet. But, Annie dear, we are getting closer. If we can persuade Mrs. Granger to have Deborah's body exhumed and examined there in Missouri, and she presents with liver damage, then we can establish further connection between the three bodies. These things take time, Annie. Don't lose hope."

"And what about the fourth body? Do they know who she was yet?"

"I'm afraid not," said Emma.

"Was an autopsy performed on her?"

Emma gave a shake of her head. "Carlton says because she was beaten, they concluded she died from her injuries. But we are making progress, my friend."

Annie took in a deep breath, strengthening her resolve. They were getting a little closer.

"I will speak with Beth. Perhaps she can write to Mrs. Granger.

I need to visit Alison anyway. I want to see for myself how Liza is getting along.

❦

The following morning, Annie rose early. She dressed quietly so as to not disturb Frank, who lay in bed snoring peacefully, his mouth flopped open.

She headed over to the mess tent to grab a quick bite, and on her way there, she ran into Frida and Ivan, who had taken their horses for a morning stroll. Frida walked alongside Shiva, and

Ivan rode his horse bareback without a halter or bridle. Upon seeing Annie, the boy grinned wide, showing off pink gums.

"Good morning," she said to them both.

"Hello," said Frida. "You are up early."

"Yes. I have an errand to run." Annie stroked Shiva's forehead.

"I never got the chance to properly thank you, for helping to release Ivan from that man," said Frida. "I can't tell you what it felt like to see my boy and Chayton come running back to Ska's tent. I was in agony waiting for him, but I understand why you needed Ska and me to stay behind. You are a very wise woman, Miss Oakley." Her eyes flicked up to meet Annie's but then refocused on her horse.

Annie shook her head. "I'm really not, Frida. And please, call me Annie. If we are to be touring together, I think we should become friends, don't you?"

Frida wrapped her hand under Shiva's chin and around his nose. "I would like that very much, but Ivan and I will be returning to Georgia after the fair."

Annie was startled by the news. Frida had been such a popular performer. The crowds loved her. Almost as much as they loved Annie herself. "I am sorry to hear that," she said and meant it.

"Yes," she said, meeting Annie's gaze again briefly. Annie thought it strange that she wouldn't look at her straight on. "We are sorry to go, but Ivan needs the stability of family. My mother and sisters are still in Georgia, and my sisters have many children. I think it would be better for Ivan to be there with them, and I don't want to be separated from him ever again. Perhaps when he is older, we can return to the Wild West Show."

"Yes." Annie smiled. "But we still have a few months together here. We can make the most of it."

Frida finally looked Annie in the eye and held her gaze. "I would like that, Miss—Annie."

Annie took a couple of biscuits from the large basket Hal had set on the table and wrapped them in a cloth napkin. She didn't want to take the time to sit down and eat, reasoning she would eat them in the coach on the way to Dr. Gordon's house. As she left the mess tent, she spotted Ska, Ohitekah, and Chayton all enjoying breakfast together at a campfire in front of their tepee. It made her heart sing to know that all three children had been returned safely to their parents and that no real harm had been done.

When the coach pulled up to Dr. Gordon's house, Annie brushed the biscuit crumbs off her dress and let the driver help her down. She entered through the gates and banged the lion head door knocker on the front door.

As she had hoped, Beth answered, and she ushered Annie into the house.

"Can I get you something to drink, Miss Annie? Lemonade perhaps?" Beth offered.

"No thank you," Annie said, smiling. "But, I wonder if there is something you could do for me? Well, actually for Bobby."

"Of course. Anything."

"Could you write to Mrs. Granger and ask her if she would consider allowing a postmortem to be done on her daughter Deborah's body? Bobby's lawyer will be contacting her, but we thought a more personal entreaty might help. We are following a lead that may connect the murders, but we need to know exactly how Deborah died."

"Certainly. I'll do it this very day." She took Annie's hat and handbag.

"Thank you. May I go see Alison, now?"

"Yes. She'll be pleased to see you, as will Liza. And, I'll get started on that letter."

"Excellent, Beth. Fingers crossed that this is successful."

Annie climbed the stairs and made her way to Alison's room.

She gently knocked on the door. To her delight, Liza answered. Seeing Annie, the little girl's eyes widened, but she pressed the side of her index finger to her lips.

"Shh. Mother is sleeping," she whispered. "But you can come in."

Annie stepped into the room, and Liza closed the door behind them.

"I see you are taking good care of your mother."

"Annie?" Alison said from the bed. "It's so good to see you." Her voice was heavy from sleep. She pushed herself to a seated position, and Liza quickly went around the other side of the bed to fluff the pillows.

"You have a good little helper," Annie said.

"Yes, I do." Alison reached out and touched Liza's cheek.

"How do you like your new home, Liza?" Annie asked her.

"It's very big," she said, holding her arms out wide. "But I like it. Dr. Gordon is nice, too. He says he's happy to have me here with Mother. I'm happy here, too."

"Darling girl, why don't you go see if you can help Beth downstairs?" Alison suggested.

"Goodbye, Miss Annie." Liza flounced out of the room and closed the door behind her. Annie was glad to see the girl so happy.

She turned to her friend. "How are you feeling, Alison?"

She didn't look much better than she had a couple of weeks ago. She still had purple moons under her eyes, and her skin was as white as a sheet. Though her spirits seemed higher, probably because she had Liza back.

"I'm coming along, Annie dear. I must apologize for my behavior when I learned that the children had gone missing. I didn't mean to lash out at you so. It's just—"

Annie settled herself at the foot of the bed and raised a hand in protest. "There is no apology necessary. I completely understand. The children are safe now. That is all that matters."

"Yes. I'm so happy to have Liza with me. Now I am free to

marry. We've set the date for July twentieth. I've been ever so busy making arrangements. I can only do so much before I am exhausted." She grimaced. "I'm parched. Would you please get me a glass of water? There is a pitcher there on the dresser."

Annie got up and went to the crystal pitcher. She poured the water into the glass sitting next to it. Her gaze settled on a vial of medicine on the other side of the dresser. The label read ACONITE. This must be the medicine used to treat Alison's affliction. She took the glass over to Alison and then settled herself on the bed once again.

"Are you planning a large wedding?" Annie asked, wondering how in the world her friend would be recovered in less than a month.

"No. Not large. Quite small, actually. Of course, I'd love for you and your husband to attend. And perhaps the families of Chayton and Ivan. Liza has talked about those two boys nonstop. Lee has an aunt in Tennessee, I believe. And of course, all of the staff here. They have been so dear to me."

Annie was surprised to hear her say so. "I thought you said Nurse Bonnie wasn't kind to you."

"She had her moments of grumpiness, but she was a good nurse. I know now that David was putting pressure on her, and I suppose that is why she was so contrary. I'm sorry she left."

Annie nodded. "Yes, Beth told me she'd gone. Do you think there is any chance she might come back?"

"I don't think so," Alison said, shaking her head. "Not as long as Mr. Morton is here. They were engaged to be married, you know. They had a bit of a falling out." Alison lowered her voice to a whisper. "I think Mr. Morton has a temper."

Annie raised her eyebrows.

A temper, indeed.

"I had no idea they were engaged," she said.

"Yes. They arrived to work for Dr. Gordon together. The hospital in Massachusetts where they were previously employed would not allow the staff to marry. Well, they wouldn't allow the *nurses* to marry, so Mr. Morton and Nurse Bonnie answered Dr. Gordon's advertisement and came here."

"Massachusetts?" A niggling feeling crept into Annie's mind, and she thought about the pin Emma had found near the body of the beaten woman. "Do you know which hospital?"

Alison shook her head. Her lips had turned an unbecoming shade of ash. Annie feared she was taxing her friend.

"Wait," Alison said, just as Annie was going to take her leave. "I think it was an asylum. You know, for the insane."

A heavy feeling wrenched Annie's insides. Could Nurse Bonnie have fallen victim to the killer of the other three women? It didn't seem possible, but how many nurses from the State Lunatic Hospital at Danvers could be wandering around Chicago? If the woman Emma found was indeed a nurse—and Bonnie—how would they find proof with the woman's face rendered unrecognizable?

"Mrs. Harper said that Mr. Morton accused Nurse Bonnie of seeking Dr. Gordon's affections, which was, of course, absurd. Mrs. Harper is a bit of a gossip, if you ask me, and Nurse Bonnie was professional in every way. Besides, Lee is devoted to me." Alison managed a weak smile.

"I should leave you to rest." Annie patted her hand. "You look quite done in."

As Annie stood to go, the door opened, and Dr. Gordon entered. "Miss Oakley! Liza mentioned you were here. How lovely to see you." He closed the door behind him. "What have you two birds been talking about?" He cast a smile at Alison, who looked at him adoringly.

"Why, the wedding, of course," Annie said. "It sounds divine."

"I am so looking forward to making this wonderful woman my wife," he said and walked over to Alison. He kissed her forehead and then picked up her hand, placing his fingers at her wrist.

"You are tired, aren't you, darling?" he asked. Alison nodded.

"Time for your injection." He picked up the vial of aconite and pulling open one of the dresser drawers, took out a leather pouch and produced a syringe.

"I must go," Annie said. "Alison needs her rest, and I need to get ready for my mid-morning performance."

"Thank you for coming by," Dr. Gordon said. "It means so much to my girl."

"Oh, I almost forgot to tell you," Annie said. "My friend Emma, the journalist, has been investigating the death of Mr. Barnes—to help exonerate poor, dear Bobby. She has been successful in having one of the female bodies exhumed and examined by the coroner, and also, Mr. Barnes himself. It's quite extraordinary, really."

Dr. Gordon cocked his head, and the corner of his mouth twitched. "I should say so." He set the bottle back down on the dresser, his attention riveted to Annie. "And what have they found?"

"Well, not much. But both the women and Mr. Barnes suffered liver damage. What do you think could have caused that, Dr. Gordon?" Annie looked over at Alison, who had apparently fallen asleep.

"Oh, a number of things, I imagine—namely drink."

"Yes," Annie said. "That's what we have surmised. But is there anything else that could have caused it?"

He shrugged. "Illness? A defect at birth?"

"I see." Annie squinted her eyes, thinking. "I suppose we will have to wait to see if poor Deborah's mother will allow her daughter's body to be exhumed and examined, as well. If she, too, had liver damage, we might have something to go on."

Dr. Gordon stared at her in silence. He suddenly seemed to be completely preoccupied. Probably with concern for his fiancée. Annie had outstayed her welcome.

"Well, I really must go," she said. "I will check back in a few days." She peered over Dr. Gordon's shoulder. Alison was still fast asleep.

"Of course," said Dr. Gordon, showing her out. "And, Miss Oakley, do keep me informed on Mr. Bradley's case. I feel awful about his arrest. He hasn't been released, then?"

"No," Annie said flatly. Hadn't he read the papers? The reporters were as good as hanging the boy themselves.

"I see." Dr. Gordon continued to stare at Annie, making her the slightest bit uncomfortable.

"I'll let myself out," she said.

He watched her leave without uttering another word.

CHAPTER 27

Buffalo Bill Dime Novels for Sale on Midway
Plaisance!
Get Your Copy Before They Sell Out!
– *The Chicago Evening Post*, Wednesday, June 28, 1893

The following day, after both her performances,
Annie, Frank, and Emma sat at the little campfire between
Annie and Frank's tents sipping coffee. It had been two days
since Annie had gone to see Emma directly after she'd left Dr.
Gordon's to tell her about Nurse Bonnie and Mr. Morton. Emma
had said she would wire a colleague in Boston to look into the
asylum's records to corroborate what Alison had said about Mr.
Morton and Nurse Bonnie's previous employment.

Meanwhile, Annie wanted to get caught up on what was
happening with Bobby's case.

Holding her pinkie delicately aloft as she sipped her coffee,
Emma lowered her cup and cradled it in her lap. "Deborah's
mother has agreed to the postmortem."

"That's wonderful," said Annie. "Beth's letter must have helped, then."

"Well, the Colonel was not messing around when he hired Mr. Ellis. The man is a bulldog. He is running with your theory of the initials and cities, and now the liver damage of the two victims. I feel we are close to getting a resolution."

"This is great news," Annie said. "Things are finally coming together."

"It's been a tough row to hoe here at the fair," said Frank. "I sure do hope we can put this business to rest soon and get Bobby out of jail."

"He was so despondent when I was there the other day," Annie said. "Beth cheers him though. I'm grateful he has a sweetheart."

"How is Alison faring?" asked Emma. "Are she and the handsome doctor married yet?"

"No. But she is making plans for a small ceremony," said Annie.

"Am I invited? I could run a story and sell it to one of the local papers."

"I believe she would like us to attend. Though, I am concerned about her health. She looks positively horrible."

"Isn't the doctor giving her some kind of treatment?" Frank asked.

"Yes, but I don't think it is working. She should have been better by now. I saw a bottle of medicine on her dresser labeled 'aconite.'"

"Oh," Emma said, the register of her voice deepening. "That comes from a plant in the wolfsbane family. It is commonly used to treat the clap. I know because it came up in one of my investigations. Does Alison . . . ?"

Annie nodded, pressing her lips together, feeling a little awkward at revealing the true nature of Alison's condition. She revealed how Alison had contracted the disease.

"Poor dear," Emma said, her brows pinching with concern.

"Well, God bless Dr. Gordon then—both for treating her and looking past her affliction to marry her."

"He seems to adore Alison, and now Liza," Annie said. "It's so nice to see them settled."

Frank reached out and took Annie's hand. "And you more rested." Annie met his eyes, and he smiled at her. He turned to Emma. "How are your career endeavors coming along?"

"I've had absolutely no luck with Ernest Kline—odious man. So I don't think I can talk my way back into my position at the *Herald*. If I can crack this murder case open, though, I'll be able to write my own ticket."

"And clear Bobby's name," Frank added.

Emma nodded. "Indeed."

"I'm so sorry, Emma." As much as Annie did not approve of her friend having a relationship with a married man, Annie felt it was terribly unfair to fire her for it. How one conducted one's life is certainly none of Mr. Kline's business. As long as Emma did her job well, it shouldn't matter who she is intimate with.

Emma handed Annie her empty cup. "Thank you, Annie. I am hopeful for a bright future—on all fronts."

Annie smiled at her friend's joyful spirit. She was a hard woman to keep down, and Annie admired her for it.

"Well, my dear friends, I must be off," Emma said. "Work to do, you know. How are you two going to spend this fine evening?"

"I'd like to take a walk along the Midway," said Frank. "What do you think?" He reached over and squeezed Annie's knee.

"I think that would be lovely," she said. "We haven't spent enough time enjoying the fair. Perhaps a Ferris wheel ride?"

"I'm game," said Frank.

As the three stood up to part ways, a boy dressed in a crisp navy-blue uniform with two rows of brass buttons down the front and a white collar approached their camp. His face was red as a pickled beet, and perspiration trickled down from his hairline to his temples. He looked as if he'd run a country mile. "Miss Wilson?"

"Ah, Charlie. Do you have something for me?"

He handed her a folded piece of paper. "It's a wire, ma'am."

"Emma?" Annie asked, wondering where the boy had come from and how he had found her.

Emma unfolded the paper. "I told the hotel that if I received a wire from Massachusetts, to deliver it directly. I've been keeping them informed about my whereabouts all day." She laughed. "I haven't had to be accountable to anyone for my outings since I was a girl. Quite irritating, really. But I didn't want to wait to receive any news. Here you go, Charlie." She reached into her bag and handed him a few coins. "And here's an extra penny for some lemonade."

The boy gave her a toothy grin and set off.

"Well?" Annie pressed, anxious to hear what the wire said.

Emma held the note out in front of her and silently read. "Fascinating!"

"What?" Frank and Annie said in unison.

"Nurse Bonnie and Mr. Morton did indeed hail from the asylum in Danvers. Nurse Bonnie Francis received training there and was later employed by the hospital, but not Mr. Morton."

"I don't understand," Annie said, confused. "Alison said—"

Emma handed her the paper, and Annie hastily read the handwritten scrawl. Her stomach twisted. Staring at the words, she relayed the information aloud. "He was a patient! Diagnosed with violent mania . . . Classified as criminally insane . . . According to this, the two had begun a relationship, but when the administrators found out, Nurse Bonnie was fired and—"

"Mr. Morton escaped!" Emma finished for her.

Annie's brow furrowed. "You don't think . . . the bodies . . . ?"

Emma placed her hands on her hips. "It's entirely possible. You know, I saw him coming from the horticulture building one day, and I was struck by the untidy state of his hands. His fingernails were caked with dirt . . . And that was shortly before Frank and Bobby happened upon the body of Mr. Barnes." Her eyes widened. "I need to find Carlton."

"Now, wait a minute," Frank said. "Don't you two think you are jumping to conclusions? Dirty fingernails are plausible, given the man's greenhouse responsibilities."

Emma was quick to respond. "If the woman's body I saw was Nurse Bonnie, then Mr. Morton would be a possible suspect, given the two were in a relationship and his history of mental instability, not to mention his temper. I need to give the police this information. It would be negligent not to."

"You are right, Emma," Annie said. "This information could be important in the case."

"Well, toodle-oo, you two." Emma bustled away from them, no doubt ready to start working all through the night.

⚜

Trying to put her thoughts of the murders and Bobby's fate aside, Annie quickly pinned her hair into a neat bun. She wanted to forget about everything for just a few hours and enjoy some unencumbered time with her husband. She searched her trunks for the hat with the netting to help conceal her identity.

She sat down at her vanity to secure the hat on her head and rummaged through the drawers looking for an extra hat pin. She spotted a small pot of rouge. It must have been left in the vanity by her former roommate and rival shot, Lillian Smith. She lightly tapped her cheeks with the small smidgeon of color and then worked it in. She smiled at the effect. It wasn't something she was prepared to do every day, but for an evening out with her husband, why not?

Satisfied with her appearance, she stepped out to meet Frank.

"Don't you look the sophisticated lady?" he asked with a teasing smile.

"Is it too much?" She adjusted her hat. "I don't want to be

recognized. I want all my attention focused on you this evening."
She smiled up at him and threaded her arm through his.

"Well, I can't argue with that. But what if someone recognizes me? They will think I am stepping out on my wife."

She laughed. "That is just the risk we will have to take."

Frank whistled, and Jep scampered over to him, his tail wagging so furiously that his hips swayed back and forth. The dog smiled up at her as Frank secured one of his horse's lead ropes around Jep's neck so the dog wouldn't run off.

They strolled casually out of the encampment and headed toward the Midway. The sun was making its descent, turning the clouds a lovely shade of lavender. They walked down Hope Avenue, then turned left at 62nd Street and walked under the elevated railway. The clacking cars whooshing past made the trellis shake and rumble. Annie covered her ears as they passed beneath it. Once on Madison Avenue, they perused the shops along the street, occasionally stopping to look in the display windows.

"If Emma were with us, we'd never make it to the Midway," she said. "She'd want to stop at every dress store along the way." Annie admired a pair of shoes prominently displayed in one of the windows.

Finally, they turned left onto the Midway Plaisance. The crowds were thick that evening, with families out enjoying the sights. Frank stopped at a popcorn cart and bought them a bag to share as the streetlights began to glow.

They continued their walk until they reached the far corner of the German Pavilion.

Frank pointed toward the Ferris wheel. "That's where the medics dug up your Mr. Barnes."

"Oh, how awful." Annie shuddered at the thought of seeing a body being unearthed, especially by a dog. She looked down at Jep, grateful he hadn't been the one who'd dug up Mr. Barnes.

They continued until they reached the bench where Mr.

Davis, the car operator, had set the fainting woman that fateful day. They sat down and finished their popcorn.

"Where exactly did they find him?" she asked Frank.

"I'll show you."

They got up and walked over to the grassy area where the scar of the turned-up earth remained. New shoots of grass spiked upward, trying to fill the area. Annie walked over to it and knelt down.

"Poor Mr. Barnes," she muttered and ran her hand over the dirt. Her finger hit on something hard. Something gold shined through the loamy earth. She picked it up.

"What's that?" Frank asked, standing over her.

"I'm not sure. It looks like a piece of jewelry." She rubbed it on her dress and instantly regretted it as the earth made a smudge on the silk. She held it close to her face and peered closer at the item. It was a round oval with something finely carved into it. She thought about the beetle pin Emma had found, but this looked nothing like it.

"Can you see what that is?" She stood up and showed it to Frank.

He rubbed his finger over the top of it. "You mean what is carved into the metal?"

"Yes."

"It looks like letters. Either a *N* or an *H*, wrapped up in a *C* or a *G*," he said. "A monogram. It's quite worn."

"Do you think it was a pendant of some kind?" Annie asked. "Or the remains of a pin, like the nurse's pin?"

"Maybe," Frank said. "But anyone could have dropped it. This area is heavily traveled with the Ferris wheel being such a popular attraction." He wrapped his arm around her shoulders. "How about that Ferris wheel ride?"

Annie looked up into his eyes. "And then we could get ice cream?"

"Sounds good," Frank said, smiling down at her.

She tucked the piece of metal into her dress pocket and took

Frank's arm again. Jep slid into his usual position on Frank's other side, tail wagging and grinning ear to floppy ear. Annie wished the night would never end.

◈

Annie lay in bed the next morning, reveling in the luxury of the soft, downy mattress and the weight of the blankets heaped on top of her. Frank had gotten up earlier and had promised to bring her breakfast in bed.

Their night out had done wonders for both of them. Annie could almost forget they were Annie Oakley and Frank Butler, famed performers of the Wild West Show. On their way back to the encampment, they had perused the booths and exhibits, and shared a triple-scoop ice cream cone. Frank had even bought one for Jep.

Annie reached down to her dress that was lying on the floor. She had haphazardly stepped out of it when they had gone to bed. It had been so long since they'd made love that they couldn't get out of their clothes fast enough. Annie smiled at the delicious memory. She picked up her dress and rummaged through the pockets, searching for the gold trinket she'd found the night before. She took it out of her pocket and lay back down on the bed, holding it in front of her. She wiped away the remaining dirt smudges and studied it. She again wondered if it had been some kind of locket or pendant. Her finger rubbed across something hard on the back.

She turned it over. A jagged peg stood out from the back of it as if it had broken off from somewhere. She ran her finger along the rough edges and then flipped it back over.

Her pleasant thoughts faded and were replaced with thoughts of what Emma had discovered about David Morton and Nurse Bonnie, and it set her insides churning. Could he truly have killed the nurse? Could he have killed the other women? And what about Mr. Barnes? Had the first woman,

Mille Turnbill, been a patient of Dr. Gordon? She wished she had looked through the doctor's register she'd seen on Beth's desk.

The register. The letters. The initials!

Her heart racing, she sat bolt upright in bed just as Frank entered with a tray laden with food.

"You must be hungry. I've never seen you get out of bed so fast." Frank set the tray down on the end of the bed.

"We have to go to Alison, Frank. Right now." Annie picked up her dress and started to put it on. "I think I've figured it out." She fumbled with the tiny buttons that went from the waist to the neck.

He tilted his head in confusion. "What are you going on about, darling?"

"Please, Frank. You will need to come with me."

"Annie—"

"Now, Frank! I'll explain on the way. I'll finish getting dressed, and you secure a coach. We'll meet under the banner at the entrance of the encampment."

Frank slapped his thigh in frustration. "Annie, just tell me—"

"Please don't argue. It could be a matter of life or death," Annie said. Still working with the buttons, she went over to her vanity and opened one of the drawers. She picked up her Derringer and shoved it into her dress pocket. "Now hurry. And Frank—"

He stared at her, alarmed at her declaration. "What?"

"Bring your gun."

CHAPTER 28

INDIAN WAR BATTLE REENACTMENT!
WILL BUFFALO BILL'S SOLDIERS SAVE THE DAY?
– *Chicago Daily Journal*, Thursday, June 29, 1893

ANNIE REACHED UP TO THE LION HEAD DOOR KNOCKER AND pounded it against the metal plate on the door. They waited a few minutes, and Annie pounded again.

"Keep your cool, Annie," Frank said. "We have to play this just right."

"Why don't they answer?" she asked, knocking for a third time.

The door whooshed open, and they stood staring at Mrs. Harper, the cook, who had a scowl on her face. Her hair had come loose from her white cap and hung down in greasy strings. Her apron was stained with what looked like day-old food. "What is the meaning of this?" she asked with indignation. "I thought you were going to tear the door down."

"I need to see Alison," Annie said, trying to keep her voice calm. "And Liza. Are they here?"

"Of course they're here." She scolded Annie with her eyes. "The fancy miss has me waiting on her day in and day out, and her brat is a surly one. Woman hasn't been out of bed for days now. Weak as a kitten."

Annie took a deep breath. Alison was still here, still alive. "May I see her?" She changed her tone and smiled sweetly.

The old woman rolled her eyes. "Well, come on in, then. You know the way to her room."

"Oh, is Dr. Gordon here, too? We have some important information for him."

Mrs. Harper harrumphed. "No. He and that little chit Beth went to run some errands for the fancy miss. I thought I would have a moment of peace until you arrived. I suppose you'll be wanting some refreshment."

"No, that isn't necessary, Mrs. Harper. We'll just go up to see Alison."

Mrs. Harper opened the door for them to enter and then walked away.

"She's a pleasant sort," Frank said.

"Indeed," Annie said, shaking her head. She led him up the stairs and to the closed door of Alison's room. Quietly, she knocked.

Liza opened it. "Miss Annie!" She flung her arms around Annie's waist. Annie hugged her back, peeking into the room to see Alison watching them from the bed. Her face was gaunt and pale, and her lips an unbecoming shade of lavender.

Annie looked up at Frank. "You'd better not come in. Can you stand here at the door in case Dr. Gordon comes back?"

Frank nodded. Annie entered the room and closed the door behind her.

"What brings you here today? I thought you would be performing," Alison said, her voice barely above a whisper.

"I have the day off." Annie tried to sound cheerful. "Alison, I need to speak with you about something."

Alison tried to sit up, but her arms were too weak to lift herself.

"You don't need to sit up," Annie said, resting a hand on her shoulder. She turned to Liza. "Sweetheart, do you think you could keep Mr. Frank company? I would hate for him to get lonely."

Liza nodded eagerly and then slipped out the door.

Alison's face paled to an even more ashy shade of beige. Her brow furrowed over bloodshot eyes. "What is it, Annie? What do you have to say to me that you don't want Liza to hear?"

Annie settled herself on the bed and took hold of Alison's hand. "I am afraid you are in danger, Alison."

Alison shook her head, her eyes clouded with confusion. "Danger? From whom? Miles is dead."

"It's not Miles. It's—"

"Winston? My late husband's business partner? Oh no. He doesn't know where I am, does he?"

Annie squeezed her hand. "No, it's not him, Alison. I'm afraid it's Dr. Gordon."

Alison's mouth dropped open. "What? What are you talking about?"

Annie pulled the piece of metal from her pocket. "Do you recognize this?" She held it up to Alison's face.

"No, what is it?" Her eyes grew wide in alarm.

"I think it's part of a cufflink. You said Dr. Gordon has dozens of them."

"Well, yes, but I don't know if that is his. He has many pairs." Her voice, a raspy whisper, took on a defensive tone.

"Are you sure?" Annie implored.

"Yes, I'm sure. Where did you find it?"

Annie took in a deep breath. "I found it where Mr. Barnes' body was buried on the grounds."

Alison somehow found the strength to bring herself to a seated position. "Annie, you are scaring me. I don't know what you are talking about."

Annie didn't think it was possible, but it seemed that Alison's lips had grown even more blue.

"The initials . . . H.G. or G.H." She went on to explain about the life insurance policies of the three identified victims and the initials *G*, *H*, and *L* of the beneficiaries.

"But I don't understand—" Alison shook her head, confusion in her eyes.

Annie considered the register she'd seen downstairs and its golden lettering reading, *H. Lee Gordon.* "Alison, what is Dr. Gordon's first name?"

Alison tucked her chin to her neck as if trying to back away from Annie. "Well, it's Halston, but he goes by Lee."

Annie grabbed Alison's hands, her heart beating a staccato rhythm in her chest. "Don't you see? H.L.G."

Alison's eyes lit with anger. "No, I don't see! And I am insulted that you would come here and tell me something so despicable. Lee would never hurt me. He's given me so much. He wants to make me his wife. This piece of metal proves nothing. You can't even be sure it is a cufflink, and if it is, I've never seen it before."

Annie took in another deep breath. She wasn't getting anywhere with this line of reasoning. Alison would never believe her based on this evidence. If only she could find something more concrete . . .

"I'm sorry to have upset you, Alison. You are right, I have no proof." She wanted to keep her friend calm. She didn't at all like the way the blood had completely drained from Alison's face. Her hands and arms trembled—with fatigue or anger, Annie couldn't be sure.

"I think you should leave," Alison said, tears pooling in her eyes. She turned her face away.

"Alison, I—"

"Leave. Please, Annie."

Annie got up from the bed and opened the door. She turned

back to say something more to Alison, but she had turned over in bed, her back to the door.

Annie slipped outside and closed the door quietly. Frank, who was sitting on the floor playing jacks with Liza, looked up.

"Well?" he asked.

Annie lifted a finger. "One more second."

"Annie," he rasped.

She raised her hand to quiet him and tiptoed down the hallway to Dr. Gordon's office. The door was open so she went in. She walked over to his desk and sat in the large chair behind it. She spread her hands over the top of it, thinking. Quietly, she pulled open the large drawer to the right. She found a bottle of whiskey, a glass, various baubles, and a leather-bound case. She opened it to find a variety of papers but nothing interesting. Setting it back in the drawer, she then opened the drawer to her left. Files were neatly tucked into slotted compartments. She pulled one of them out and opened it.

Her eyes opened wide when she read *Northwestern Mutual* across the top of a piece of paper. She scrolled the document. As she had guessed, it was a life insurance policy. The holder was a Mary Watson. Under the title of beneficiary was the name Henry L. Galveston with an address in Tennessee. The amount listed was $10,000.

"H.L.G." Her voice was barely a whisper.

She dug through more of the files and found another one under *Metropolitan Life* for a Sadie Dennison. Her blood ran cold when she read the name of the beneficiary, Leigh H. Goodman. She dug some more and finally found what she was looking for: a policy for Donald Barnes with Helen Leigh Grant as the beneficiary. She stared at the paper, unable to believe her eyes.

She had proof!

Holding the document in her hand, Annie got up from the desk and hurried to the doorway.

"Frank!" she whispered. When he looked up from the game of jacks she signaled for him to come into Dr. Gordon's office.

"I'll be right back, Liza," he said. She happily continued bouncing the ball and swiping up jacks.

When he stepped into the office, she held the document out to him. "Look, Frank. This is proof." She showed him Mr. Barnes' policy. "Dr. Gordon is the murderer. He's taken life insurance policies out on several people."

"Good God," Frank said, studying the paper.

"I wonder if I can find policies on Millie Turnbill and Deborah Granger," Annie said, returning to the desk. She sat down and started going through the files again. She stopped when she came upon one that made her heart stop.

"Alison Drake." She looked up at Frank, who had come to stand next to the desk. "He's taken a policy out on Alison. For $20,000. So her fortune wasn't enough," she said with disgust. "Oh, Frank, this is horrible! How am I going to tell her? We need to get her and Liza out of here! She is so—"

She stopped midsentence.

"What?" he asked.

"She's so sick . . . Frank, I think he is poisoning her somehow. Maybe it's the aconite. Emma said it's from the wolfsbane family, which can be toxic in high doses. Maybe he's dosing her with too much. Maybe Mr. Morton is helping him to kill people. She's getting weaker and weaker."

Liza's voice sounded from the hallway. In seconds, she was at the door, standing there with Dr. Gordon. He had a vial of medicine in one hand and a syringe in the other. He'd probably just dosed Alison again. Annie froze, holding her breath.

"What are you two doing in here?" he asked, his eyes wide with alarm.

"Dr. Gordon, we've figured out your little secret." She looked at him in disgust.

"My secret?" Dr. Gordon looked confused, but then his eyes traveled to the papers in Annie's hands.

"Liza," Annie said. "Would you go check on your mother?"

Dr. Gordon's face hardened and he reached out and took Liza by the arm. "No. Stay right here, Liza. Your mother is resting. Now what is this about a secret?"

Annie swallowed. "You've killed all those people found on the fairgrounds: Millie Turnbill, Deborah Granger, Donald Barnes . . . and more it seems. And where is Nettie? And Nurse Bonnie? Did you kill her, too?"

Dr. Gordon's jaw flexed. "Get out of my office," he said, his voice unnervingly calm.

"Look, sir," Frank said, resting his hand on his pistol in its holster. "We don't want trouble. It's over. Just come with us to the police station."

"I'm not going anywhere with you," He pulled Liza closer to him and she let out a yelp. He bent down and placed his forearm over her windpipe. He then held the needle up to Liza's neck.

She screamed.

"Shut up!" He jerked her tighter in his grip. He looked up at Annie and Frank. "You're right. I've killed many, and I won't hesitate to kill a child."

Panic froze in Annie's lungs. "You need her. And you need Alison. You won't have access to her money until you two are married."

He stretched his face into a grin, the look in his eyes diabolical. "Who says we aren't married?"

Annie's mouth went dry. What was he talking about? Alison had never mentioned . . .

"Aw." The sneer morphed into a pathetic downturn of his mouth. "She didn't tell you? I bet you thought she'd told you everything, didn't you?"

Anger clenched Annie's jaw shut. She could feel the pulse of her heartbeat in her ears. But she had to keep him talking, had to give her and Frank time to think of how to get themselves out of the situation and save Liza and Alison.

"Was Nurse Bonnie causing trouble between you and Alison, or rather your and Alison's fortune? Is that why you killed her?" Annie forced out.

"You are very astute, Miss Oakley. The woman was a hell of a nurse and extremely well versed in other things, as well, if you know what I mean." He winked at Frank, and Annie could feel the anger roll off her husband in waves. "I was sorry to lose her. But I couldn't have her upset my dear Alison."

Annie's hands went clammy, and her insides trembled. The man was diabolical. "Why? Why did you kill the others?"

He shrugged. "Money. The thrill. But they've also helped with my medical research."

"You are using them to test your medications?" Frank asked.

"I don't need to justify myself to you, you dried-up old cowboy," Dr. Gordon said. He picked up Liza with one arm, still holding the needle to her neck, and left the office.

Annie and Frank chased him down the stairs and through the hallway into the parlor.

Dr. Gordon ran over to a bureau and stopped in front of it, facing Annie and Frank. "Liza," he said, "be a good girl and open that drawer."

Liza, shaking, squeezed her eyes shut and shook her head.

"Do it!" Dr. Gordon yelled, showing her the needle. She let out a squeal of anguish. He released his grip around her neck but held on to her arm. She yelped and obeyed. She opened the drawer.

"See what's inside," he said calmly, as if presenting her with a surprise. "Pick it up. Slowly."

Her back was to them now, so Annie couldn't see what she was doing.

"Please, Dr. Gordon," Annie said, scarcely able to hear herself from the sound of blood pulsing through her ears. "There's a better way than this."

"Now, turn around," he said to Liza, ignoring Annie, "and point the gun at them."

Holding the pistol with both hands, she held the gun out in front of her, pointing it toward the ground.

"Point it at that big cowboy. Mr. Butl— Pardon me, I mean, Mr. *Oakley.*" Dr. Gordon grinned.

Annie gasped, clenching her fists. "You are using a child to do your dirty work? You are despicable.

"Lee? Liza?" A weak voice penetrated the tension in the room.

Annie turned around. Somehow, Alison had gotten out of bed.

"What's going on here? Liza!" Alison stumbled over to her child, but before she got there, Dr. Gordon had grabbed the gun out of Liza's hands, pointed it at Alison, and then pulled the trigger.

As she slumped to the floor, he trained the gun on Liza and another shot rang out. Dr. Gordon's eyes grew wide, and a blood-stain appeared on his shirt. Annie looked over at Frank, who held his gun pointed at the doctor. Dr. Gordon released Liza, confusion clouding his bright- blue eyes before they rolled back into his head and he sank to the ground.

"Mommy! Mommy! Mommy!" Liza screamed over and over. The little girl flung herself on top of Alison's inert body.

Annie ran over to her and pulled her off. Blood seeped through the sleeve of Alison's nightgown. "He only got her arm, thank God. But she's losing a lot of blood. She so weak already . . ."

Frank went to Dr. Gordon and checked the pulse in his neck. He looked over at Annie and shook his head. "He's dead." He holstered his pistol and came over to them. He swept Alison into his arms. "Let's get her to the hospital, fast," he said.

"What's all this noise about?" Mrs. Harper appeared at the door holding a wooden spoon. When she saw the doctor on the ground and Frank carrying Alison, she screamed and then rushed at Frank, beating him on the shoulders with the spoon.

"Mrs. Harper! Stop!" Annie said. "We need to get Alison to the hospital. Dr. Gordon was trying to kill her. You are going to have to believe me. I'll explain later." She took Liza's hand and followed Frank out the door and then out of the house.

They climbed into the coach, and Annie told the driver to take them to the nearest hospital as quickly as he could.

She prayed her friend would have the strength to hold on.

CHAPTER 29

WILD WEST PERFORMER BOBBY BRADLEY FREED FROM JAIL!
EXPOSITION KILLER DR. H.L. GORDON DEAD!
– *The Chicago Herald*, Tuesday, July 29, 1893

ANNIE OAKLEY SOLVES MURDERS!
 by Emma Wilson
 Chicago Star Free Press, July 30, 1893

Wild West Show star Bobby Bradley, who has been held at Cook County Jail under suspicion of the murder of Mr. Donald Barnes, was freed yesterday afternoon. No trial is to take place in regard to his case.

Dr. H.L. Gordon of Englewood confessed to two witnesses that he was the murderer of at least four victims found on the Exposition grounds at Jackson Park, including Mr. Barnes. Famous sharpshooter Annie Oakley and her husband, Frank Butler, confronted Dr. Gordon when they found conclusive evidence of his identity as the Exposition Killer by way of life insurance policies taken out on the deceased. At the confrontation, Dr. Gordon confessed. A skirmish ensued, leading to Mr. Butler shooting the doctor in defense of the young daughter of Dr. Gordon's fiancée, steel heiress Alison Drake.

Victims Millie Turnbill, Deborah Granger, and Bonnie Francis were all employees of Dr. Gordon. Another victim, Mr. David Morton, who served as an assistant to Dr. Gordon, was found dead at Dr. Gordon's residence yesterday and is believed to be the doctor's fifth victim. Mary Watson, Dr. Gordon's former secretary, has been missing since early May, and Nettie Granger, his former housekeeper, has been missing since June 11. Authorities continue to search for them.

A life insurance policy taken out on Dr. Gordon's fiancée, without her consent, leads authorities to believe that she may have been the doctor's next victim. His modus operandi was to slowly poison his victims with various toxic medications while he set the life insurance policies in place. Dr. Gordon had several aliases and would use the aliases and addresses across state lines.

During an encounter with Dr. Gordon, Mrs. Drake was shot. The injury did not prove fatal, and Mrs. Drake recovered at Mercy Hospital and has been released.

Thanks to the observance and intelligence of Miss Oakley, and the quick draw of Mr. Butler, fairgoers and visitors to the White City can enjoy its marvelous splendor in peace and safety once again.

Early that morning, Annie and Frank sat in the tent that served as the Colonel and Mr. Salisbury's office. She and Frank sat opposite the Colonel's desk, where he had his feet propped on the corner on the other side. Mr. Salisbury had pulled up a chair next to the Colonel. They all sipped the strong coffee that the manager had brewed on the grate outside the tent.

"We have a matter we'd like to discuss with you," Annie said.

"I gathered as much," said the Colonel. His face was placid, his gaze steady on her face. Even when he was in the best of moods, the Colonel could be intimidating with his larger-than-life presence, his piercing blue eyes, and his snowy white beard.

She took hold of Frank's hand. "We'd like to leave the show for a while."

The Colonel tapped his fingers on the desk and looked at Mr. Salisbury but didn't say anything.

"I am grateful to you, and to you—" she nodded to Mr. Salisbury "—but I feel it is necessary for me to do something else for a while."

"Don't do this, Annie," the Colonel said. "We need you. Your presence in the show has helped to make it the success that it is. Besides your shooting talent, and your rapport with the public, you helped clear Bobby's name, and I am eternally grateful. I can't emphasize it enough. We need you.

"Is it money?" Mr. Salisbury asked. "We can increase your salary."

Annie looked over at Frank and then back at the two men. "You have been so generous to me. Both of you. No, it's not the money, but I appreciate the gesture. Our reasons are more of a personal nature. We feel it is best for our well-being, and our marriage, if we take some time off after the fair. I hope you understand."

The Colonel raised his legs and took them down from the corner of the desk.

"Frank, can you persuade her to stay?"

"I'm afraid not, sir. Annie is the performer, and she calls the shots." He looked over at her, smiled, and squeezed her hand. Her heart warmed at his wholehearted support.

"Well, I can't say I'm happy about it, but I will respect your decision." The Colonel's words were tinged with resignation. Annie hated to disappoint him, but she had to take care of herself—for the first time in her life.

"Promise us you'll come back in the future?" Mr. Salisbury said.

"I promise to think about it," she said, smiling at him.

"It won't be the same without you." The Colonel said, his voice wavering with emotion.

While he had his faults, he'd almost been like a father to her these past many years. She knew he was sincere in his declaration. "I'll miss you, too." Afraid she might get emotional, she rose from her chair.

The Colonel, Mr. Salisbury, and Frank all followed suit.

"Well, we have a couple of weeks left, I daresay," said the Colonel. "We'll make the most of them."

"That we will," said Annie.

๑๕๛

Later, Annie sat on the fence watching Frank work with Diablo. Jep followed along, sticking close to Frank's side. The horse eagerly walked up to him and nuzzled at Frank's hip. He reached into his pocket, pulled out a carrot, and fed it to the horse, then stroked Diablo's neck. Jep barked, and Frank reached into his other pocket and handed the dog a small biscuit.

The roar of a crowd of young voices came from the show arena's grandstands, filling the air with joy. Annie hoped Alison and Liza were enjoying the show.

In Liza's honor, the colonel had decreed the day, "Waif's Day at the Wild West Show." Though he'd initially been annoyed at Annie for taking Liza in, he'd become enchanted with the girl, and she had become his muse for the idea of Waif's Day. The

Colonel and Mr. Salisbury had sent out flyers and put advertisements in the papers. They offered a full day of free performances to all the orphans in Chicago and the surrounding areas. The children would also have their fill of free ice cream, Cracker Jacks, cotton candy, and the like. Approximately fifteen thousand orphaned children had arrived to share in the fun.

Annie and Bobby had performed two acts earlier in the day. Bobby was thrilled to be in the arena again after Mr. Ellis had been successful in obtaining autopsies on all three of the bodies and it had been conclusive that all victims had succumbed to liver poisoning.

While Annie was grateful to the Colonel for his generosity to the orphaned children and thoroughly enjoyed performing for them, she was glad to have the late afternoon to relax with Frank. The show would close in two weeks' time, and Annie and Frank were anxious to get back to their life in New Jersey.

Frank took the halter from around Diablo's head and slung it over his shoulder. He and Jep moved away from the horse, and Diablo followed right after him, walking calmly at Frank's shoulder. Frank turned to the left, and Diablo followed. He turned to the right, and Diablo stayed right in step. After a few twists and turns, Frank broke into a jog, and the horse trotted next to him, Jep barking with delight. They did a few more circles and turns, and then Frank jogged over to the fence and came up to Annie.

"Impressive," she said. "You've really built his trust in you."

"He's come a long way, that's for sure." Frank stroked the horse's head. "Okay, Diablo, don't make a liar out of me." He guided the horse to stand parallel to the fence, and then he climbed up onto the second rung of the railing. Gently, he draped his upper body over the horse's back and stroked his neck and belly. Diablo stood quietly and bent his neck back, seeking a treat. Frank handed him another piece of carrot and then flung a leg over, now sitting on the horse's back.

"Frank, I am amazed," Annie said, bursting with pride. "This horse was completely wild a few months ago."

Frank nodded, smiling at her. "Frida knows her horseman-ship, that's for sure."

"You're more skilled than you give yourself credit for, Frank Butler." Annie smiled at him, happy that he had found a purpose outside of her and her career. He finally had something of his own since he'd retired from sharpshooting.

Frank clucked to the horse, and Diablo started walking. They made a large circle at a walk, and then Frank kissed at the air, nudging the horse into a rolling canter. Frank took hold of Diablo's thick brown mane, and the two circled the arena.

Annie's heart leaped with joy to see Frank so engaged, so present in the moment. He and the horse moved together in unison, as if they were one being. She knew well the feeling of exhilaration Frank must be experiencing.

Through the gate at the other end of the arena, Ivan, on one of Frida's magnificent black stallions, rode in at a canter. They caught up with Frank and Diablo, and matched their stride. The two pairs rode in perfect unison as they circled, then turned, making flying lead changes and working a figure eight.

Annie's arms tingled at the sight, and tears pricked behind her eyes at the beauty of the synchronicity.

"Well, will you look at that!" Emma said as she walked up and stopped next to Annie. She was wearing an odd ensemble of puffy taffeta pants that gathered at the knee and then were tucked into tall leather boots. The sleeves of her white blouse were equally puffy, and a dark-yellow waistcoat nipped in her slender waist. She wore no hat for once, and her flaxen hair was free around her shoulders.

"Beautiful, isn't it?" Annie said.

"It is. So how is Alison doing?" Emma asked. "I can't believe that snake was trying to kill her and killed all those others . . . Vile man. Frank did the world a favor."

"Yes." Annie nodded. "Dr. Gordon was slowly killing his victims to give himself time to set up the life insurance policies and the beneficiaries, which of course were all aliases for himself.

Nurse Bonnie and Mr. Morton seemed to have just gotten in the way. As for Alison, she's much better." Annie grinned. Saying the words warmed her heart. "She and Liza are enjoying the show right now. She still needs time to recover, and the doctors can't determine if she experienced any damage from the aconite or not. It is one of the side effects of using the drug in excess. They said she most likely suffered some liver damage, but there is no real way to know for sure. I only wish I could have helped Nettie" She took air into her lungs to try to relieve the ache in her chest. "Poor Mrs. Granger. To lose both daughters. She must be completely heartbroken. I wish I had realized sooner . . ."

"Now, Annie. You mustn't blame yourself. You solved the mystery. You stopped that abhorrent man from killing more people. And you were able to save your friend and sweet Liza."

"Yes, by the grace of God. But you really didn't need to mention me and Frank by name in your article." Annie didn't know why she felt uncomfortable about taking credit for solving the crime. She supposed it was because she was sickened by the loss of such promising young lives.

"You are much too modest, my friend," Emma said. "And what about Alison's fortune?"

Annie smiled, heartened by the question. "It's intact. She's a wealthy woman. She won't ever have to worry about money again."

"What about her share in the business?"

Annie turned again to the marvelous spectacle of Ivan and Frank. "You aren't interviewing me for a story or anything, are you, Miss Wilson? I'm not sure Alison wants her life story in the papers—more than it is already."

"Of course not! I've got my story—charming doctor turned diabolical murderer. The *Chicago Star Free Press* paid a pretty penny for the story and then offered me a job. You are looking at the new assistant editor."

Annie turned to her friend. "Emma! That's fantastic. Congratulations."

"Thank you," she said with a nod of her head. "But you haven't answered my question about Alison's interests in the steel business."

"She has been in touch with her late husband's business partner. Apparently, Miles made up the story of Mr. Peale being out to kill her for her half of the business. Mr. Peale and his wife are delighted to have Alison as their new partner. She will make an excellent businesswoman with a little training."

"Another two women paving the way to independence," Emma said with a happy sigh. "I love it."

"And setting a good example for Liza. I think it's marvelous." Annie smiled. "Speaking of women's independence, are you a free woman or have you gone back to your married man?" Annie wasn't sure how she would react to her answer, but she wanted to know.

"He has started divorce proceedings," Emma said, focusing on Frank and Ivan once again.

Annie's heart fell. "Oh, I see."

"But I've broken it off with him. For good."

"And Detective Chisolm?" Annie asked with a knowing smile, much relieved for her friend.

"We're seeing each other," Emma said. "But it's very casual."

"I'm happy for you."

"And you and Frank?"

"Things are improving. Frank has been plagued with guilt over the death of his brother, even though it was years ago. And we both have not properly grieved the loss of our child. We've been on the road and working ever since I miscarried. We've decided to take a break, take some time for ourselves."

"You mean, you're leaving the show?" Emma's voice rose in alarm.

"For a while. We need to get reacquainted. Not as performer and manager, but as husband and wife. We'll go back to New Jersey, to our home, to our garden. Frank wants to buy more horses."

Emma cocked her head, her eyes squinting in dubious question. "Have you spoken to the Colonel about this?"

Annie nodded. "Yes. He wasn't happy about it, but he understands."

"Well, I am happy for *you*, dear friend. And then after you've been in New Jersey for a while? What then?"

Annie laughed. Emma never could ask just one question. Every conversation turned into an interview. She was singularly the most inquisitive person Annie had ever met.

"Well, Emma, you never know what adventure life will bring next."

DID YOU ENJOY THIS BOOK?

I hope this book has brought you some entertainment and enjoyment! I am so grateful and honored that you have chosen to spend some time with me.

If you are so inclined, I would appreciate your spending just one more moment and writing a review on Amazon. It doesn't need to be long, just a few honest words about your reading experience.

I'd also love to connect with with you on a more personal level. Sign up for my mailing list via my website to participate in special giveaways, receive news and information about my events and upcoming releases at https://www.KariBovee.com.

PRAISE FOR THE ANNIE OAKLEY MYSTERY SERIES

Bovée' . . . brings readers solidly into the heyday of the Wild West shows, providing wonderful details about the elaborate costumes and the characters' remarkable marksmanship . . . There are enough entertaining elements to keep readers guessing, including romance, rivalries, jealousy, and at least one evil character from Annie's past. The prose has a charming simplicity, which keeps attention focused on the action and the well-developed protagonist. A quick, fun read with engaging rodeo scenes."

— *KIRKUS REVIEWS*

"A fast-paced plot keeps the pages turning. Readers interested in strong American women will welcome this new series . . ."

— *PUBLISHERS WEEKLY*

Absorbing, heartfelt, and thrilling, *Girl with a Gun* shows off young Annie Oakley's skills as a sharpshooter and as a loyal detective. From the period details to the Wild West setting, I was completely immersed in the story and in the larger-than-life characters. Like Annie herself, Bovée's prose sparkles with precision and skill."

— MARTHA CONWAY, AUTHOR OF
UNDERGROUND RIVER, NEW YORK TIMES
BOOK REVIEW EDITOR'S CHOICE

ABOUT THE AUTHOR

Empowered women in history, horses, unconventional characters, and real-life historical events fill the pages of Kari Bovée's
articles and historical mystery musings and manuscripts.

An award-winning author, Bovée was honored as a finalist in the
Historical Fiction category of the 2019 Next Generation Indie
Awards for her novel *Girl with a Gun*. The book also received
First Place in the 2019 New Mexico/Arizona Book Awards in the
Mystery/Crime category, and received the 2019 Hillerman Award
for Southwest Fiction. She was also a finalist in the 2019 Best
Book Awards Historical Fiction category for her novel *Peccadillo
at the Palace*. Her novel *Grace in the Wings* finaled in the unpub-
lished Romantic Suspense category of the 2012 LERA Rebecca
contest, the 2014 NTRWA Great Expectations contest, and the
RWA 2016 Daphne du Maurier contest. The novel was released
in September of 2019.

Bovée has worked as a technical writer for a Fortune 500
Company, has written non-fiction for magazines and newsletters,
and has worked in the education field as a teacher and educa-
tional consultant. She is the author of the Annie Oakley Mystery
Series and the Grace Michelle Mystery Series.

She and her husband, Kevin, spend their time between their
horse property in the beautiful Land of Enchantment, New

Mexico, and their condo on the sunny shores of Kailua-Kona, Hawaii.

ALSO BY KARI BOVEE

Shoot like a Girl - A Prequel Novella

Girl with a Gun - An Annie Oakley Mystery

Peccadillo at the Palace - An Annie Oakley Mystery

Grace in the Wings - A Grace Michelle Mystery